The Battle of Puffendorf

A NOVEL BY VERNE HULL

Pictorial Histories Publishing Company, Inc.
Missoula, Montana

Copyright © 2004 by Verne Hull
Library of Congress Control Number 2004115915
ISBN 1-57510-115-7

All right reserved.

PRINTED IN THE UNITED STATES OF AMERICA

TYPOGRAPHY & BOOK DESIGN
Arrow Graphics, Missoula, Montana

BACK COVER PHOTO
Jerry Smith, Yankton, South Dakota

Pictorial Histories Publishing Company, Inc.
713 South Third Street West, Missoula, MT 59801
PHONE (406) 549-8488, FAX (406) 728-9280
EMAIL phpc@montana.com
WEBSITE pictorialhistoriespublishing.com

INTRODUCTION

The Battle of Puffendorf is a fictional account of a tank battle fought during World War II. The story is of intrigue and romance on both sides while at the same time focusing on the confrontation of two charismatic tank leaders, the American, Captain Tom Appleby and the German, Major Hans Otto Dietrich. The protagonist of the story is Whip Johnson, a young soldier replacement from South Dakota. Many of the novel's dramatic events take place at and in the vicinity of the Secondary Technical School at Heerlen, Holland. It is September 17, 1944, and the city and the school are just being liberated by the Americans. Philip Vossmaar, a young intellectual and resistance fighter, aids the Americans. Later he will become a close friend of Whip Johnson and introduce Whip to other young Dutch intellectuals of the Gorgo, Philip's debating club, and also introduce Whip to Whip's lifelong love—Lucie Heerkens. In combat Whip Johnson's life is saved by a book: Will Durant's *The Story of Philosophy*, which Whip had tucked under his army sweater. Mainly, though, the philosophical episodes are there to depict the character of Whip Johnson and the young Dutch intellectuals.

The central part of the story is, of course, based on the 2nd Armored Division's famous tank battle fought at Puffendorf, Germany, in World War II. It was at this battle that the author was wounded. His legendary company commander, Captain Robert E. Lee, is the model for Captain Tom Appleby. The other characters are imaginative. Two generals stand opposed at Puffendorf:

Major General Brighton D. Clay, the American, and Brigadier General Gerd Von Bartholomaus, a Prussian German. In fighting the battle both generals are compromised by others. Clay must deal with the rivalry of Appleby and Major Richard C. Burk for the affections of the Red Cross "doughnut dolly," Susan Lavet Montgomery, and Bartholomaus must deal with the take over of the German army by Himmler's SS and Hitler's interference during the Battle of Puffendorf.

A tense development is the confrontation of the two colorful tank leaders, Captain Appleby and Major Dietrich. Both know of the fame of the other, and, during the battle, Dietrich attempts to waylay the Americans.

Two children, also, play major roles in the story. Please-Joe is a twelve-year-old Belgian runaway who becomes a mascot of the Americans. (The author saw such children.) Arnd Hauptmann is a fourteen-year-old "Hitler Youth" commando. Both boys confront one another. The redemption of Arnd Hauptmann is achieved by the friendship that develops between Arnd and Colonel Harold Quinn.

Another subplot involves the "double agent" Hans Spoor (alias The Great Samson). Samson is the uncle of Arnd Hauptmann, and Samson's mistress is being held by the Gestapo as a hostage so that Samson will lure the notorious Resistance leader, Bep Rieksen, into a trap.

A compelling relationship evolves between SS General Fritz Kraus and his prisoner, the beautiful Nicoline Lindemann, the girl friend of the feared Resistance leader Bep Rieksen. Though General Kraus is able to rescue Nicoline from the Gestapo, he has premonitions of his own death. He then prevails upon Nicoline to promise to protect his children, 11-year-old Felicia and 10-year-old Max, in the dangerous days near the end of war. The climax of the book occurs when rogue American soldiers, Second Lieutenant Joe Nicholson and Private Michael "Morbid" Morris, attempt to pillage the hunting lodge of General Kraus and threaten his children.

Animals have a significant part in the story, too. SNOW WHITE is a homing pigeon that sometimes mystically appears, usually as a harbinger of a rescue attempt. HEKTOR is a German Shorthaired Pointer who bravely protects his young master, Max Kraus. BISMARCK is a great stag, symbolic of General Kraus.

A small subplot involves the German spy, CORPORAL "WES" WILLOW and a Jewish immigrant, PRIVATE MILTON "PEEWEE" SILVERMAN. The resolution of their conflict is prophetic of Hitler's "final solution."

Basically, the story is about a citizen soldier's, Whip Johnson's, reaction to the military, war and combat.

For the Gorgo

CHAPTER 1

FROM HIS UPSTAIRS bedroom window, twenty-year-old Philip Vossmaar observed the German soldiers digging trenches in the square in front of the Secondary Technical School. Only moments before a man on a bicycle had shouted that the Americans would soon shell the German positions and everyone should seek shelter. After having accompanied his elderly parents to the cellar, Philip had returned to his bedroom determined to watch and maybe cooperate with the Americans. The calendar showed September 17, 1944.

To the people of Heerlen, Holland, the coming of the Americans had seemed awfully slow. Ever since the Allied victories in Normandy in July the Dutch population had expectantly awaited their liberation from German occupation. Even now, though, Philip guessed, the German rearguard must be putting up a stout defense. Soon he heard a few artillery shells and then noticed sudden movement among the German soldiers in the square. They were abandoning their entrenchments!

Astonishingly, one German soldier even ran around to the back of his house. Then abruptly American soldiers appeared in the street before his eyes, their rubber-soled boots muffling their foot strikes, unlike the clank of the hobnailed jack boots of the German soldiers. He thought, "The Americans walk with cat's feet."

Poking his head out the window Philip yelled, "Hey, Joe. There's a German soldier in my garden."

A dirty face beneath the window challenged, "Come down and open your door, and stand by it!"

Quickly Philip did as he was told.

Peering intently past Philip down the hallway, the GI pointed a short-snout Tommy gun at him and said, "Okay, where's the Kraut?"

"Come on," Philip beckoned and led the way down the hall into the kitchen and a door leading to a backyard. Taking a hurried glance out the window Philip saw his neighbor and best friend, Karel Konijn, holding a pistol on a German soldier whose arms reached skyward. At that moment gunfire erupted from the street.

The GI whirled and dashed back to the open door.

Following closely at his heels, Philip saw the soldier stop and point his weapon toward the square. Dropping to the floor Philip heard the cough of the Tommy gun. Soon a rough voice called, "You got the bastards, Sarg."

Turning to Philip, who had regained his feet, the sergeant pointed at the school and asked, "What's that?"

"It was a school, but the Germans have been using it for their headquarters."

To another GI the sergeant said, "Let's take it, Charlie." With an arm and hand signal the sergeant motioned to his men who were dispersed and crouched on both sides of the street. Again turning to Philip he said, "You'd better find cover, young-fellow, there's apt to be more shooting. . . . By the way, have you got a sister? I just might come back later."

"Sorry, Sergeant, but I do have booze, please come anyway."

When the Americans had gone he shut and locked the door and went to a hiding place for his liquor. Because of his work in the Dutch underground, Philip had always considered the possibility of his early demise. Maybe he still wouldn't survive the war, but at least he'd lived to see "Liberation-Day."

However, before Philip could finish his drink a knock sounded at the door. Parting the curtains, Philip saw a man in brown clerical dress pounding frantically. Promptly he unlocked and opened the door. A red faced monk shouted, "May I use your phone? There are two wounded German soldiers in the square."

"The phones aren't working. Look for a Red Cross sign with the Americans. Their medics will care for the German soldiers."

After the departure of the monk, Philip thought, "Well, maybe the Americans can use me as an interpreter. That would be something to see about."

WITHOUT ASKING, Whip Johnson knew this place was the end of the line, the depot where combat units came to replenish their wasted manpower, and Whip could not repress his morose thoughts. With weekend passes to Louisville, Whip had once thought he might fight World War II stateside at Fort Knox where he'd been a cadre at the Armored Replacement Training Center. Then some lucky tanker with recent combat experience, one who had survived Kasserine Pass in North Africa, had returned to the states to take his place as an instructor. As a result, Whip had become a replacement himself. Now someplace in Belgium, sitting on his steel helmet, trying to keep his butt dry as he ate chunky mush from his mess kit, Whip was not at all consoled by some GIs from Special Services who were crooning "Blue Skies." Last night for the first time he'd seen flashes and heard the rumble of distant artillery. Combat appeared inevitable.

Listening to the optimistic lyrics of the song, Whip could imagine the group performing in Carnegie Hall rather than on a grimy hill in Belgium. They were all real good. But maybe they knew they'd get their butts shipped to combat if they didn't play and sing like hell. Crap, he'd gladly trade places with any of them; but no doubt, while he'd shot hoops and played baseball as a kid, they'd religiously practiced their music. Now came their reward.

Overhead flying in vast V-formations like migrating Canada geese soaring above his South Dakota prairies countless Fortresses and Liberators droned ominously toward Germany. Clouds churned by the bombers bore witness to their exceptional height even as fighter planes traced arcs on the blue sky, apparently ready to pounce upon any enemy aircraft which might dare appear. The spectacle awed Whip. He'd never seen airplanes fly so high they formed vapor trails. Nevertheless, he was at least glad that "D" Day, Normandy and the St. Lo breakthrough were history and the Allies had air superiority.

The "crack" of an M1 rifle interrupted his reverie. Soon he saw MPs and medics rush down the hillside toward the bivouac area. They appeared to lift someone on to a stretcher, which they promptly toted toward a dispensary tent. As the litter bearers struggled up the hill past him, Whip saw the face of the victim: sloping forehead, thick neck and nose, black bushy eyebrows and dark, needlepoint eyes. Remembering the face, Whip momentarily stopped breathing. Back at Fort Knox that man had shouted profane threats at Whip after his chair had exploded. In every class, Whip would booby trap a chair with a firecracker as an "attention-getter." Even now Whip could see the man thrashing and squealing as his platoon buddies laughed. The man had snarled, "You're dead, asshole." Later the drill sergeant had said, "Don't lose any sleep, Corporal. They'll 'Section 8' Morbid Morris out of this man's army sooner or later."

"I wonder how the word gets around?" asked a high-pitched voice.

Looking up Whip saw the skinny private-first-class who'd dished out his cold mush moments before.

"What?" Whip replied, finishing off his coffee as he stood up.

"We get one or two a day," said the gaunt looking pfc. "They're cowards who 'accidentally' shoot themselves in the foot. They prefer a hospital bed to combat. But a firing squad shot the last coward."

"Oh, you know that for a fact," said Whip. "I thought we made room for conscientious objectors and those kinds of people?"

"Sorry, Corporal. Not at the front."

Scrutinizing the pfc, Whip asked, "Are you on the firing squad?"

The hint of a smile creased the pfc's face. "You think I'm kidding?"

"Yeah. But if you're so brave why don't you get a transfer to a line outfit?"

"Maybe I'll do that, Corporal. Remember to keep your ass down when you go into combat." Then with a faint smile the sickly appearing pfc limped back to his serving table.

The pfc's tongue had scored a direct hit on Whip Johnson. Survival! To "live" for his country. One day to have a wife and kids, a good paying job and loyal friends.

Whip felt he had the makings of a good citizen. As long as he could remember, he had been made to understand that both his dad and granddad had served the country with distinction. At Knox he'd viewed most of the "Why We Fight" films. He believed in democracy, his country's leaders and never doubted the need to destroy Hitler and the Nazis. Yet on this fall day on a hill somewhere in Belgium, listening to the entertainers harmonize, ". . . It's only a shanty in old shanty town . . . ," he couldn't help thinking, "But why me?"

Later before returning to his wet, pup tent, he wondered where his buddies from Fort Knox might be? Dale Jenks, "the lover" and John C. Smith, "the philosopher." They'd both shipped out several weeks earlier.

THE FOLLOWING MORNING an orderly called Whip Johnson's name. Soon he and other replacements boarded a 6×6 army truck. The vehicle crawled interminably into heavy military traffic along narrow cobblestone roads. After what seemed an eternity of inhaling exhaust fumes, Whip and the other replacements emerged from the truck before a large, grey stone building.

To Whip's eyes the structure resembled a medieval castle. A grassy square of several acres fronted the building, and it was surrounded by a wrought iron fence at least six foot high with spiked posts. Paved streets ran diagonally from the building like the spokes from the hub of a wagon wheel, while on both sides of the streets, conjoint two and three storied brick houses stretched into the distance. But unlike most of the houses he'd seen from army trucks and troop trains, these houses appeared new, neat and clean with some having latticed picture windows.

Other than apprehensions about his own immediate future, Whip's most compelling feeling was evoked by the sight of swarms of children milling about the soldiers in front of the building. To his amazement some of the children spoke English.

"Hey, kid," one GI asked, "where are we?"

A boy with freckles laughed, "You're in Holland. Can't you see our wooden shoes?"

The other kids snickered.

Whip saw they all wore leather shoes. Then a sergeant ordered the replacements to form up and march through a gate into the courtyard. Before Whip could hoist his duffle bag to his shoulder, he was nudged by a fair haired kid. The boy asked, "Joe, have you any cigarettes for my nice sister?" Then he winked suggestively. Shaking his head, Whip wondered, "Is that kid a pimp?"

In response to a question about the building, the sergeant said it was a technical school before the war.

"Where are the Krauts?"

"Not far, soldier. Not far," said the sergeant wistfully.

THE RECORDS ON ARND, if ever there had been any, were lost. Herr Strassmann had searched the files diligently after being appointed administrator of the orphanage. Everyone called the blond-haired, blue-eyed, fourteen-year-old boy, just Arnd.

"How is it possible that a file has never been made for the knabe?" asked Herr Strassmann.

Expressing no surprise, the staff shrugged their collective shoulders and glanced knowingly at one another as if they were part of a conspiracy they could not share with him.

The folders were fat with information about the other children. Even when Herr Strassmann questioned Arnd, the boy smiled good naturedly and likewise shrugged his shoulders. When Herr Strassmann seemed to be getting angry with the lad, the cook had the nerve to say, "Be patient, Herr Strassmann. Someone will soon come who will tell you all about Arnd."

The cook was correct. The next day an army officer wearing a swastika arm band appeared at the front door of the orphanage and asked for Arnd. When Herr Strassmann objected and wanted to know what was going on, the officer curtly informed him that Arnd along with a few other orphaned youngsters was receiving special training in American English and other things for possible espionage and sabotage work. He reminded Herr Strassmann that the children so chosen served the Fatherland in the name of the Führer—and no greater honor could come to the orphans.

(Soon after the Allies entered Germany SHAEF dispatched a special order and report forbidding fraternization with the enemy. The report read in part: "Innocent looking youngsters, Himmler's werewolves, have dropped grenades into the turrets of Sherman tanks while panhandling for chewing gum and candy!")

ARND GLANCED FIRST at the grey Secondary Technical School and then at the broad sidewalk in front of the building filling with American soldiers. They were unloading from a dozen or so American transport trucks. Arnd himself had recently crossed the German border into Holland with a German spy known as Samson. A local Dutch family now gave him shelter. Before the war Arnd had spent summers in Holland with relatives and could speak enough Dutch to get by on the streets—but he knew he had to be careful because of his German accent. His host, a Mr. Lintens, worked in the local coal mine and was a loyal Nazi; nevertheless, Mr. Lintens was fearful that Arnd might draw too much attention to his family. "Anti-German feeling is running strong now that the Americans are here, and we all have to be doubly careful," he had warned Arnd.

More than just serving the Fatherland and the Führer as a "Hitler Jungend," Arnd wanted revenge against the Americans for having killed his family in an air raid. And already he had killed Americans. But what had surprised Arnd the most was that the killings had been as easy as reading "Life" magazine or talking about Joe Dimaggio; because, as one of his instructors had put it, "American soldiers are quite softhearted when it comes to kids."

Before he left the house, Arnd checked his Hitler Youth dagger in his pocket. Then he focused his eyes on the school. Yesterday Samson had given him an order with urgent priority. With that order in mind, Arnd approached the American soldiers smoking in the street.

JUST AS THE GERMANS before him had done, Brigadier General Brighton D. Clay had established his headquarters in the Secondary Technical School. Presently, the general was listening to his operations officer, Major John Collins, conclude their briefing of Major Richard C. Burk III. The focus of Jack Collins' remarks had to do with the role of Burk's "Combat Command 'B'" in the upcoming "Operation Queen," the code name for the Division's capture of Puffendorf and drive to the Roer River. But the traffic outside had become almost too noisy for Major Collins to be heard, as trucks from Belgium were bringing replacements for the casualties incurred during the Division's breaching of the Siegfried Line—Germany's "West Wall."

"Remember, Dick," said Collins, almost yelling to surmount the din, "the crucial part of 'Queen' is your taking and holding all the objectives given your Combat Command 'B' on the first day." And he pointed to various locations on a wall map.

AFTER BEING DISMISSED by General Clay, Major Burk had his driver head his jeep back to his command post at Ubach, Germany, about a half hour drive. Ubach was located just across the border from southern Holland and was about two miles from the most forward positions of his 1st Battalion.

Hurrying from his jeep Burk assumed an air of nonchalance. As he entered his command post in a red brick farm house, he found his executive officer, First Lieutenant "Junior" Krebs, at a writing desk doing paper work.

"Krebs, I'm to head Combat Command 'B' in 'Queen.' Get the air officer on the phone right away and arrange an L5 flight for me this afternoon."

"Won't that be sort of risky, Major?" Lieutenant Krebs questioned.

"Gotta chance it. Gotta see that terrain with my own eyes. . . . Call Division and ask that the sandbox be rearranged based on those latest aerial photos. Then inform all officers in Combat Command 'B' to be at Division for a briefing at 1300 hours Thursday. . . . They said high brass from SHAEF would likely be observing my briefing."

"Who might that be, Major?"

"I don't know? General Clay didn't say. But wouldn't it be something if it were . . ." Major Burk stopped short of saying who he had in mind. "Shows you the importance attached to this whole operation, Krebs. That's why I have to have that L5 flight." Get on it—right away."

"Yes, sir, Major."

Major Burk was single and approaching thirty years of age. Scholarly appearing in his wire-rimmed glasses, he had been an athlete in college having been good enough to warm the bench and experience occasional action with the varsity basketball team. His R.O.T.C. training had assured him a place in the officer corps at the beginning of the war, and his climb in rank had been steady. Just before "D" Day he'd been given command of a tank company as a captain. After his battalion commander was killed at St. Lo, the command had gone to Captain Burk who was then promoted to major.

Having the afternoon flight in the L5 in mind, he turned to his orderly, and said, "Sergeant Collins, have they repaired the line to Lieutenant Appleby's CP?"

"Yes, sir."

"Then get him."

"Yes, sir."

Moments later, Sergeant Collins said, "Major Burk, sir. Corporal Willow says the Lieutenant is out."

"Tell him to have the Lieutenant call me when he returns."

Lieutenant Appleby's Company "D" was the key to Burk's battle plan, and he wanted to make sure Appleby understood this.

"There's been an air raid up there, sir. Jerry was after the L5s."

That statement reminded Burk of his own imminent flight over the lines. But like most soldiers he was a fatalist. So be it. He had to take the risk. Perhaps it was just as well the Luftwaffe had put in their one-a-day allotment before he took off on his mission.

"On second thought, tell Corporal Willow to find Lieutenant Appleby on the double. Tell him it's an order!"

"Yes, sir," replied Sergeant Collins.

FIRST LIEUTENANT TOM APPLEBY huddled with a group of soldiers playing touch football. After reaching the border of Germany and piercing the Siegfried Line, the Division had set up defensive positions and entered upon a period of rest and rehabilitation. Sergeant Travis, one of Lieutenant Appleby's tank commanders, called the signals: "Why don't you put Witkowski on his butt, Lieutenant? I'll fake a hand-off to Pagano and keep the ball for a sweep around Witkowski. That damn Polack deliberately kneed me on the last play."

Lieutenant Appleby smiled and nodded. The ball was snapped and Appleby charged toward Sergeant Witkowski, another of his tank commanders. Sergeant Witkowski, a big man, was joined by his tank driver, T/5 Nathan Talbot, to stop the end run. Like ten pins Lieutenant Appleby leveled both Witkowski and Talbot.

Returning to help the fallen to their feet, Tom Appleby said, "Sorry, Polack, I didn't mean to hit so hard."

"Jeesus, Lieutenant," cracked Brian Witkowski, stumbling to his feet and brushing himself, "take it easy on us mortals. You'se might need us at Puffendorf."

Hearing the approach of a truck, Appleby knew it was bringing his replacements. His eyes followed the lurching vehicle. Again he apologized, "Sorry, Polack, . . . I have to go. Here come the replacements."

"Don't give me another jerk," pleaded Witkowski. "That last one nearly got us killed."

The object of Witkowski's scorn was a New Yorker of immigrant Jewish parents, Private Milton Silverman, who stood barely five foot tall. In his first combat Silverman froze when Sergeant Witkowski instructed him to load an armor piercing shell into the tank's 75 millimeter cannon. The result was a German Panther tank scored a crippling hit with its long-barreled 75. Fortunately, fire from Lieutenant Appleby's command tank knocked out the Panther with a side shot, rendering it a flaming wreck. The medics later evacuated Private Silverman as a casualty.

"You never know, Polack. The medics said 'Peewee' was only scratched. He could be on that truck," taunted Sergeant Travis, designating Milton Silverman by the nickname Wikowski had bestowed upon the little man.

Either by accident or design Silverman had been assigned to Witkowski's tank by the company's previous commander, Captain Burk. Tom thought, "If Milton is on the truck, I'll reassign him." That and other speculations passed through his mind as he hustled toward his command post in a former German municipal building.

When the muddy, olive drab truck finally braked to a rolling stop, its canvas top concealing its occupants, Tom stood waiting, ready to appraise what the manpower pipeline had to offer. He had been none too happy with recent contributions. On a pass to London he'd seen the athletic types the noncombat services seemed to have. Evidently the cream of American manhood were finagling their way into the rear echelons. Determined, nonetheless, to get the most out of what he got, he uttered his signature expletive, "Judas Priest." Then shaking his head said, "I wish Red was back from Paris. I'll need him to shape up these new men."

Second Lieutenant John "Red" Jordening, Lieutenant Appleby's executive officer, had devised an orientation program for replacements involving the veterans. It was quite effective, and Tom knew it was urgent to get the job done now—before the Division attempted to take Puffendorf and advance to the Roer river.

As the five replacements for Company "D" jumped off the truck, Lieutenant Appleby viewed them with a shake of his head. Perhaps the redheaded one had possibilities. . . . "Judas Priest," he mumbled, "Private Milton Silverman has come home."

"Hi, Lieutenant," said Silverman, clicking his heels and saluting. "They said I'd only been scratched. . . . So here I am." Private Silverman smiled wanly.

"Remember, Milton, at the 'front' you don't salute. We'd rather not be targets for snipers. But I'm glad you're okay."

Having followed Appleby from the touch football game, Sergeant Witkowski strutted up to the newcomers and moaned, "Heaven help us, Peewee, you'se made it back."

"Hi, Sergeant," Silverman said meekly. "I'll do better next time."

Before Witkowski could reply, Appleby interjected, "Knock it off, Polack. I'm glad Milton's back." Facing Silverman, Lieutenant Appleby said warmly, "From now on, Milton, I want you to help Corporal Willow at company headquarters." Staring at Whip Johnson, whose apprehensions had only grown by the tone of the conversation, Appleby said, "Take this redheaded corporal for your loader, Brian, and clear out of here. I've got to assign these other men." After a brief pause and with a grim expression, he apologized, "Sorry, Corporal, to put you in the dozer, but one of you guys has got to go there."

Taking one last glance at Private Silverman, Sergeant Witkowski turned resignedly to Whip and said, "Let's go, Corporal. I'll show you'se your home away from home. We'll try you'se out in the tank tomorrow."

Slowly they walked down a paved street, as if to a funeral, Whip again toting his duffle bag on his back while Sergeant Witkowski whistled something that sounded like a funeral march. Abruptly Witkowski stopped before the rubble of a stone house. Looming like an iron beetle was a Sherman tank But not exactly the kind of tank Whip had trained in at Fort Knox. This one was equipped with a large blade in front of it—a bulldozer tank!

At their approach, three tankers filed from the house. "Polack, why in the hell do you always whistle that dirge when you bring in a replacement? Are you trying to test his nerves or something?" asked T/5 Nathon Talbot, the tank driver.

"My God! It's Whip Johnson, himself, Polack," beamed Private Hank Henry, the bow gunner. "When I was in basic at Knox, Whip was the 'hot-shot' instructor at General Subjects."

Unimpressed, Sergeant Witkowski asked, "What did he teach?"

Wrinkling his forehead and peering intently at Whip, Private Henry said hesitantly, "I believe it was 'Mines and Booby Traps,' Polack. Ain't that right, Corporal Johnson?"

Whip knew his records did not reveal his knowledge of mines and booby traps. Understanding the danger of the devices, Whip wanted no part in clearing mine fields. What bad luck to confront a soldier he'd taught at Knox. But Whip could see the private wasn't none too sure of himself. "No, Sergeant," said Whip with a straight face. "I taught mostly tank tactics."

Hank Henry interjected, "Corporal, you must be forgetting. I can prove you taught mines and booby traps. Don't you remember Morbid Morris getting mad at you when you booby trapped his chair? He joined us yesterday. He's in Lieutenant Nicholson's tank. He'll remember." Hank burst out laughing.

"So what?" said Nate Talbot. "That bullshit's for the sappers anyway. We need a loader. Let's see if the corporal can handle shells better than Peewee. From the looks of him, I believe he can."

For the moment, it seemed to Whip Johnson that this slight endorsement might be the only good thing going for him. And after what had recently occurred at the replacement depot, Whip considered it highly unlikely that Private Michael "Morbid" Morris could possibly be here; after all, it was Whip's understanding that Morbid had shot himself in his foot—unless he really hadn't?

Then the third tanker, who had been standing in the shadows, stepped forward offering his hand. "Hi, 'VD,'" said Corporal Dale Jenks, the tank gunner. "We've been expecting you. John Smith and I talked about you yesterday."

Whip was flabbergasted. No one in the General Subjects cadre stood above Dale Jenks and John Smith as Whip's closest army buddies. Both had shipped out a couple weeks before Whip. Even the pejorative "VD," which someone had tagged on Whip when Whip had expressed fear of getting venereal disease on a pass to Louisville, sounded like beautiful music. So as if reaching for a lifeline, Whip grabbed Jenks' hand. "Damn, I'm glad to see you, Dale."

"What the hell have we got here?" asked Sergeant Witkowski. "Old home week?" Spitting a wad of tobacco juice, he wiped his lips with his sleeve and said, "I don't give a damn what Nate said. Are you'se or are you'se not a 'mines-and-booby-trap' man?"

"Not really, Sergeant," butted in Corporal Jenks. "Corporal Johnson gave the book talk. We had demolition experts who set up the demonstrations."

"How disappointing? But it's still comforting to know both youse guys understand the subject if some predicament like that should ever pop up." Scrutinizing the corporals, he continued, "Jenks, you'se been here a while. I'll leave it to you'se to show Johnson around. Red will test both you'se guys when he gets back from Paris and we have our 'rehearsal,' . . . ha, ha, ha." After splattering an empty "C" ration can with tobacco juice, Witkowski turned and walked back down the empty street toward the company command post.

"Wait up, Polack," said Talbot. "Hank and I have got to go to supply and get some 'K' rations for the dozer."

Nodding at Whip, Jenks said, "Grab your bag, VD, and follow me. I'll show you where we bunk."

Down into a deep basement of a three-storied stone and mortar house, which served as a kind of fortress, Whip trailed his former buddy from the Armored Replacement Training Center. Aided by light flooding in through several ground level windows, they reached the bottom of the stairs; at once Whip spotted five mattresses scattered about on a dirt floor. No doubt, he guessed, the result of scavenging by the tank's crew.

Jenks said, "Drop your bag by that mattress under the window, VD. The others are taken. . . . Damn, I'm glad to see you, too. I'll tell you this, VD, in one way we're both lucky. This Sergeant Witkowski has a charmed life. He's fought in every battle of the Division since Normandy."

"Then how come the big company commander seemed reluctant to assign me to this crew?"

A shadow passed over Jenks' face. "Yeah. . . . Well, the battalion commander, Major Burk, went over Appleby's head and ordered Witkowski to take over the bulldozer tank. I heard he doesn't like Witkowski. I suppose that was the reason. . . . I'm told the Krauts shoot first at the dozer because the dozer buries the Krauts alive in their foxholes. . . . Whatever, we'll soon find out. They tell me this R & R is about over and the big push is about to begin. . . . Company 'D' under Appleby always spearheads the attack, they say."

"Why?" asked Whip.

Affecting a somber tone, Jenks said, "They tell me Appleby is a legend, a sort of god around here. The guy's a born leader, with no army bullshit. He just expects you to do your job. For him everybody does. So will you!"

Whip found little solace in learning that his new company commander was number one on the war hero list. That made getting himself wounded or killed even more likely. "God, my luck has run out," he moaned.

"Hey, VD. We gotta go look up Smith. He's in Lieutenant Nicholson's second platoon. He'll croak when he sees you."

Whip recalled his discussions with John Smith the past summer at Fort Knox. The bespectacled, dried-up, pimple-faced cynic talked like a know-it-all college professor. Backed by his bookworm's knowledge, he usually squashed Whip's arguments in their frequent debates. On the other hand, dark eyed and black haired Dale Jenks, the heart throb of the girls at the USO, won any disagreements on sports. But Whip could never understand why Dale, a ladies man and jitterbug expert, enjoyed tagging along and listening to Smith and himself argue about everything imaginable. That is, when Dale wasn't on pass chasing after broads.

"GET YOUR FUCKING HANDS off me, you mother fucker!" scorched the ears of Staff Sergeant Hap Hardesty, head cook of the 1st Battalion. The supply truck had just returned from the railhead in Charleroi, Belgium, and Hap was leisurely unloading it when he detected motion behind some cardboard boxes. This was the combat zone and anything was possible. Then he observed a breathing object much smaller than himself and close enough to grab by the hair on its head. Hence the painful eruption.

And the coarse army language, though uttered with a nasal French accent, explained a lot to Sergeant Hardesty. The screeching monkey he had hold of was no doubt some kind of street urchin who had previously latched on to some GIs. He'd seen them throughout France and Belgium, homeless, drifting kids dislocated by the war. Some whose parents had been killed. He knew it was against army regulations, but many of the rear outfits adopted and made mascots of these derelict strays, and got a kick out of attempting to Americanize and mature them beyond their years. They even had replicas of GI clothing made for the ragamuffins, as was this brat so dressed whose hair he now released.

Calming down, the kid looked pensively at Hap. "Gees, Sergeant, do you know how much it hurts to have your hair pulled?"

Gruffly Hap said, "How did you get on this truck?"

"Gees, Sergeant, don't get your tit in a wringer. I just hitched a ride. I'm trying to locate my outfit. They moved out on me when I was on pass."

The combativeness in the kid touched Hap Hardesty. His own boy at home was now twelve and maybe about this kid's age. He felt sorry for the kid. Gently he asked, "What's your name, boy?"

"Please-Joe."

Smiling, Hap said, "I'll bet that ain't your real name."

"Sergeant Sullivan put it on me when he found me. I used to beg the soldiers for gum and candy."

"Do you have another name?"

"No!" Please-Joe answered defiantly. "I have to find Sergeant Sullivan. He's going to take me to the states after the war."

Hap knew the matter of "Please-Joe," the stowaway, must be brought to the attention of the battalion commander. On second thought, he believed the major would probably have the kid dumped back on the street. Lieutenant Appleby would more likely try to understand the situation and help the kid. "Come on Joe-Please, or whatever the hell you call yourself. Let's go find Lieutenant Appleby and see if he has any bright solutions for your problem. . . . Say, Joe, do you realize you've just ended up in a combat zone and could just get your butt burned."

"No shit," said Please-Joe.

BEP RIEKSEN, the Resistance leader, knew definitely why it was Nicoline's neck that aroused his passion. Slender and elongated, it reminded him of a picture he'd seen in an encyclopedia of Queen Nefertiti of Egypt, the most beautiful woman of all time. The wood carving of Nefertiti's bust, painted in flesh colors with eyes of rock crystal had entranced him as a boy. His "first love," as it were. Ever after, this beauty of ancient Egypt, far off in time and place, remained his ideal woman. Of course, he never mentioned this to Nicoline. The vanity of beautiful women cannot tolerate an equal.

For the moment, Bep believed most of his needs had been satiated. A night of love making followed by deep, peaceful sleep and then a late morning hour of food, intelligent talk and now music nourished his whole being. Bep was a master of the piano. Friends were always saying that after the war he should become a concert pianist. Other than sex, classical music was his passion. In fact, he thought, the two rather complemented one another. From somewhere he'd heard, "The higher the brow the lower the groin."

To be sure, after he'd moved in with Nicoline his first act was transporting his baby-grand piano to her house; and whenever he had moments to spare from his work in the Resistance, he would go to Nicoline's home and nearly always play Mozart, his favorite composer.

From the kitchen Nicoline called, "Bep, that is not Mozart you are playing. What is it?"

Bep laughed. "No, my pet, it's an American popular song. It's about Queenie of the Burlesque Show. I was surprised to hear a boy whistling it near the Secondary Technical School yesterday. Perhaps he learned it from an American soldier." Bep played and sang: "There's a burlesque theater where the boys love to go. . . . To see Queenie, the cutey of the burlesque show. . . . And the thrill of the evening is when out Queenie steps. . . . And the band plays the polka while she strips. . . ."

CHAPTER 2

Removing a monocle from his one good eye Brigadier General Gerd von Bartholomaus, commander of the "Hammer" Panzer Division, found it impossible to concentrate on his war maps because of reflections that intruded in a stream of consciousness: The war was probably lost. . . . A pity Stauffenberg's group had failed in the attempted assassination of Hitler in July. . . . The stupidity of the Allies by demanding unconditional surrender. Could they not realize the love of Germans for their Fatherland? Surely since Arnhem, the Allies must know the Reich could still fight victoriously! . . . What about Hitler's secret wonder weapons? Might victory yet be wrested from defeat as they continually promised at the Wolfsschanze? But probably it was the usual too little too late.

Nor was General Bartholomaus surprised at how well his outnumbered forces fought. Even the young boys and old men of the Volksstrumm served his purposes well. He placed them up front with a sprinkling of experienced officers. Once he knew the objectives of the Americans and their tanks were out in the open, he successfully repelled them with his few panzers. As a consequence, the Americans had not gone far into the Fatherland in his sector.

Though his remaining Mark IVs and Mark Vs were pitifully few, they easily devoured the Americans' Sherman tanks. True, the Shermans were as countless as locusts. As soon as one flamed, five would take its place. But now if the Americans attacked, they were in for a wonderful surprise. SS Major Hans Otto Dietrich's famous "kampfgruppe" (battle group), which included heavy Mark VI "Tiger" tanks with their 88mm guns, had just arrived from the East to reinforce his "Hammer" Panzer Division.

LOOKING AT THE CUCKOO CLOCK on the wall, Gerd Bartholomaus realized that Hans Dietrich was late for their appointment. As the general was about to call to an orderly, the legendary panzer leader hobbled unannounced into the operations room. "Heil Hitler," the thirty-six-year-old, peg-legged, scar-faced major vigorously saluted the general.

Major Hans Otto Dietrich who by his success as a tank commander had won the personal attention of Hitler was a contradictory man famed both for his ruthlessness and softheartedness and, as with many forceful leaders, possessed a gift for the theatrical. A Nazi prototype of the Nordic man, blond and blue-eyed, Dietrich was of medium build and height. Both his lost leg and scarred face were compliments of the Russians, though his facial disfigurement was slight and added to an unrelenting appearance. His men, highly trained and fanatical, adored him and would follow him to hell and back. Thus with the tide of war turning against Germany in 1944, Dietrich had become the leader of Hitler's battlefield "fire brigade." His "battle group," of about regimental strength, consisted entirely of Tiger and Panther tanks supported by motorized infantry with the necessary logistical support.

On the other hand, Gerd Bartholomaus was an aristocratic Prussian who believed "noblesse oblige" was an injunction of birth. "Duty," more than Hitler, inspired Gerd's actions. Perfunctorily he answered Dietrich with a lackadaisical, "Heil Hitler."

In the days of blitzkrieg and recently on the Russian front, no one in the German army had personally destroyed more enemy tanks than Hans Dietrich. He possessed iron nerves, excellent vision and the hunter's instinct for the kill.

Of course, Hans Dietrich's amazing success as a tank commander had not gone unrewarded. He wore the Knight's Cross with added decorations and, indeed, had been given the command of this special battle group. But many in the officer corps loathed Dietrich. Often quarrelsome and uncooperative, his peers considered him a prima donna.

Touching his lips with his right index finger and bowing slightly in a deferential manner, Hans Dietrich said, "It's good to see you again, mein Herr General. General Rheinhardt sends his greetings and knows you will have success in protecting the Fatherland at Puffendorf."

Gerd Bartholomaus doubted the sincerity of any good will from SS Lieutenant General Rheinhardt. Had it not been for intervention by the SS, he, not Rheinhardt, would likely be the commander of the Third Panzer Corps and probably a lieutenant general. As a matter of fact, even though he needed the reinforcements of Dietrich's battle group, it had troubled him that Rheinhardt had assigned Dietrich to the "Hammer" Panzer Division rather than to the SS "Lightning" Panzer Division. After all, the SS "Lightning" Panzer Division was also at the ready for the anticipated American armored thrust at Puffendorf, and it was commanded by SS Brigadier General Fritz Kraus, a Rheinhardt favorite. Perhaps, Gerd Bartholamaus speculated, the SS had sent Dietrich to keep him under surveillance.

"You must know, Major Dietrich," intoned Gerd, "how fortunate our Fatherland is in these dark hours to have one of your caliber still alive to lead our panzers. But do you think we can work together? Our personalities are so different."

Major Dietrich was on his guard. General Rheinhardt had said Bartholomaus remained under suspicion for complicity in the Hitler assassination plot and that Dietrich was to be his own man, though nominally under Bartholomaus.

Along another line, Rheinhardt had emphasized that contrary to what the defeatist thought, all was not lost, and Hitler would still win the war for Germany. In conclusion, on direct orders from Hitler, General Rheinhardt had ordered Major Dietrich to stay out of his Tiger tank. He was too valuable at this time to risk in combat.

"Ja, Herr General," Hans Dietrich replied to Gerd Bartholomaus, his right forefinger again touching his lips as he bent his head, "we can work together, though I do have special orders from General Rheinhardt and others concerning my status under your command." From his blouse pocket Major Dietrich produced an envelope with the official checkerboard insignia of a group commander of the Wehrmacht.

Gerd's monocle plopped from his eye socket. "This is not from General Rheinhardt. This is from Field Marshal Stein!"

Satisfied, Hans Dietrich repeated, "Ja, Herr General."

When he had finished reading the orders Gerd shook his head. From his perspective the orders gave Dietrich virtual command of the "Hammer" Division. Without second thought, he decided to submit his resignation to Field Marshal Stein. Such a relationship between himself and a mere major as described by these orders was intolerable.

"I think, Major Dietrich, there must be changes in these orders. I need speak with the Field Marshal in person." Slowly Gerd moved away from his map table and then paused.... "Oh, by the way, a reconnaissance patrol picked up a Dutchman who claims he's a German spy. It is beyond me how he would know you were coming, but he said to repeat to you, 'It's at the Secondary Technical School in Heerlen, Holland.' He calls himself 'The Great Samson.' Perhaps he's some kind of egomaniac." Immediately Gerd strode from the room, but he halted at the door. Turning to face Major Dietrich, he again saluted perfunctorily, "Heil Hitler."

CORPORALS DALE JENKS and Whip Johnson found their buddy, John Smith, swabbing a 75 millimeter tank canon. Looking up as they approached, Smith twisted his pimply face into a grin. "I'll be darned if it isn't ole VD himself—the athlete and would-be philosopher. I didn't think I'd ever see you again, VD, but Dale said he wouldn't be surprised if you showed up." Turning to Jenks, he said, "Dale, you must be clairvoyant."

"John, there's one thing I must tell you right off," interjected Whip. "Before I shipped out I was on pass in New York and saw this book in a store window. It's about philosophy with all those guys in it you were always quoting, like Plato and Kant. I bought it and I carry it everywhere." Out from beneath his knitted army sweater, Whip produced Will Durant's *The Story of Philosophy*. "I have a long way to go, John, but already the book has helped me understand some of the stuff you said back at Knox."

"What's up, Smith?" asked a gruff voice from inside the house next to the tank.

"It's two new guys, Lieutenant," said Smith, hesitantly.

Stalking from the house and stopping a few feet from Whip, Second Lieutenant Joe Nicholson looked long and hard at the three corporals. "Well, I see the new replacements are now coming in with rank. What did you men do to earn your stripes?"

"Just like me, Lieutenant. They got their stripes by being on the cadre at Knox," said Smith.

Looking nearly as skeptical as Witkowski, Lieutenant Nicholson said, "That book crap there doesn't mean shit here. Your chances in combat would be nil if you weren't in an outfit with veterans. Let's hope you don't screw it up for the rest of us." With that doleful encouragement Nicholson disappeared back inside the house.

PRIVATE MICHAEL "MORBID" MORRIS had always felt he'd been chosen by fate. But chosen for what? He guessed he would not know until that epochal moment arrived. Meanwhile, he followed the path of least resistance. Other than having a good feeling about his obsession, that he was somehow, someway, a man of destiny, he never felt much good about himself. No doubt his unbecoming features had contributed to his being tagged "Morbid" at the orphanage. Nevertheless, by running away and living on the streets he had managed to get along only to be snared by Selective Service when the war began. In spite of his efforts to get out of the army, the army had perversely kept him in.

Following basic training at Fort Knox, Morbid had been shipped to the ETO (European Theater of Operations). At first the prospect of his dying in combat shook his faith about being born for some earth-shaking purpose. However, he now rationalized that maybe this was it—that this was the time and place where he would at last fulfill his destiny. So be it, he was ready for that moment.

When he'd heard voices in the street and saw Lieutenant Nicholson go outside, he wondered if it was this "Red" everyone was talking about who was to rehearse them for the big battle. After the Lieutenant returned and gave him a disgusted glance without any comment, Morbid figured he might as well go out and have a look for himself. When he saw Whip Johnson speaking with John Smith, his nostrils flared and he growled, "Well, what do we have here? The asshole of the ARTC (Armored Replacement Training Center) is at the front."

At first speechless by the sudden appearance of Morbid Morris, Whip said acidly, "Morbid, I thought they were going to 'Section 8' you out of the army back at Knox. But when I last saw you, you had shot yourself in the foot. There they told me you'd be court-martialed and shot. Yet here you are!"

"Too bad for your sake, asshole."

Corporal Jenks stepped between the two. "Why don't you save your hates for the Nazis, Morbid. They'll be trying to kill all of us soon enough."

Lieutenant Nicholson again emerged from the house and casually sat on the curb. He looked at both Whip and Morbid with an animated, expectant expression. The new replacements backed down.

As if disappointed, Lieutenant Nicholson pointed north and said, "Jerry's over there, men. Maybe I'm glad you two decided to save your fighting for him. He'll give you both all the action you want and soon enough."

Jenks said, "Let's get back to the dozer, VD." Without another word, corporals Jenks and Johnson strolled back up the asphalt street.

THE NEXT DAY the Company "D" tankers assembled at their Command Post for a briefing. Whip could hardly believe the eager anticipation showing on the faces of the soldiers. They behaved like small children awaiting the coming of Santa Claus. They whispered and joked in hushed, confident voices—not like Whip expected from bruised and battered veterans on the eve of a major battle. Whip recalled a movie where the Roman gladiators greeted Caesar: "We who are about to die salute you." Whip couldn't help thinking, "Madness rules the world."

When Appleby and his platoon commanders, along with a pink-faced intelligence officer, entered the room, all the old tankers, beaming with admiration, rose to their feet. Whip shook his head and muttered under his breath, "What am I doing here? Oh, God, please don't forsake me."

With a touch of a smile upon his tanned visage, the big man glanced around the mostly bare room, save for a small table and some rickety chairs salvaged from the debris. His friendly brown eyes rested briefly upon his men. Then with a wave of his hand, Appleby had everyone sit on the floor, including the new replacements, who were only now beginning to sense the esprit de corps of his command. Shaking his head in disbelief, Whip mumbled, "This guy's another Alexander The Great."

"Red, come here," joked Appleby. "You saved us, buddy, by cutting short your pass and leaving your beautiful mademoiselle in Paris."

A second lieutenant then rose from the floor next to Lieutenant Appleby. His hair was bright red. He had freckles—polka dot freckles. He wore a combat jacket, spotless boots and olive-green fatigues. Clean shaven, he was parade-ground spotless. By contrast, everyone else in the room looked grubby.

Appleby said, "Don't worry, Red, there'll always be another."

John Smith had found a place on the stone floor next to Whip. He whispered, "This guy is Appleby's executive officer. His name is "Red" Jordening. He also happens to be your 1st Platoon leader."

Medium in stature, Second Lieutenant Jordening's azure eyes squinted and his freckled face creased with determination. Both lieutenants had a .45 pistol in a leather holster at their right hips and a bandolier with a German P-38 in a holster slung around their shoulders, the latter, spoils of the enemy. Standing next to the large man, Lieutenant Jordening appeared insignificant. But after Appleby sat down and Jordening began to speak, Jordening suddenly seemed nearly as impressive as Appleby. He spoke with the authority of combat experience and one blessed with high intelligence.

Whip wondered if what his senses were telling him was not a dream. How could it be that he, Whip Johnson, was irreversibly committed to killing other human beings or being killed by them. "What's wrong with this son-of-a-bitching world?" he lamented to himself. So overwhelmed by his misfortune was he, that only fragments of Jordening's briefing registered in his consciousness: Something about assembling in an apple orchard for a rehearsal of an operation's order . . . a reconnaissance by fire of the enemy hedgerows . . . the bulldozer tank following to the rear of the other tanks . . . the tanks going full throttle and firing all their weapons simultaneously . . . then cutting short the attack and everyone returning to the CP (Command Post) for a critique . . . and the veterans teaching the new men their jobs.

When Jordening stopped speaking, a voice probed, "Aren't we getting pretty close to Jerry to risk turning our backs on him."

"There will be artillery and air strikes before, during and after our operation, Hank. It's all been prearranged by Major Burk," said Jordening.

Another voice questioned, "I know that you know about SNAFU (Situation Normal All Fucked Up), Lieutenant."

Red Jordening laughed and said, "I sure do, Nate; but this is what the battalion commander wants. To keep Jerry guessing when we're really coming after him. And as I said before; it's as good a way as any to get these new guys shaped up."

After Jordening finished speaking, it was the intelligence officer's turn. A young, clear-eyed second lieutenant quickly described a new supped-up German 88mm gun. The veteran tankers all laughed.

"Why the laughs?" asked Whip.

One veteran said, "The projectile of the old 88 could go in one side of our tank and out the other. So what's the difference?"

Without an explanation the intelligence officer began reading in a monotone from a paper he held in his hands:

> Heinrich Himmler, the butcher-bandit, who is more and more assuming Hitler's powers, has ordered the creation of the "Werewolves." This is to be an organization of completely lawless and ruthless guerrillas behind the Allies' lines. They are instructed to kill and destroy with abandon, to show no quarter and observe no rules except those of destruction and treachery. Many are young Hitler Youth.

Folding the paper and placing it in his pocket, his voice abruptly sounded ominous. "Also, men, there have been unconfirmed reports that SS Major Dietrich's battle group has been sighted in the vicinity of Puffendorf. S2 is making every effort to confirm or reject these reports."

A pall of somberness suddenly settled on the men of "D" Company.

"I don't need tell you veterans that if Dietrich is really here, the taking of Puffendorf will not be easy. But it would give the Division the opportunity to settle an old score with that son-of-a-bitch."

John whispered in Whip's ear: "Dietrich's battle group wrecked havoc with the Division in Normandy. Some say Dietrich has his own Tiger tank painted a dull bluish color that refracts the light and creates a mirage.

Whip immediately saw that the mention of Dietrich's name quickly spoiled the festive mood of the briefing; accordingly, when the subdued group of tankers departed the Company "D" Command Post, they did so believing they would soon be fighting the battle of their lives.

IN NOVEMBER OF 1944 damp and overcast weather usually enveloped the western front in Germany. On such a day, the tanks of Company "D" assembled at a "point-of-departure" in an apple orchard. Air strikes by P-47 aircraft on the enemy lines punctuated the occasion. After the tanks were in place some crews dismounted and engaged in casual conversation as they awaited 1300 hours. Reverberations of the bombs and antiaircraft fire did not appear to bother them.

For his part, Whip Johnson stood alone in the commander's hatch of the dozer wondering if the infamous Major Hans Otto Dietrich was just over the horizon in his blue Tiger tank. He plucked a red apple from an overhanging branch, and nervously bit into the apple's firm rind. Sweet juices tricked down his throat. This, however, did not alleviate his anxiety.

Whip did not discount his need for orientation. He hadn't been in a tank since basic training. He barely remembered how to shove a shell into the breach of a 75mm cannon. Now his life and that of his crew-mates probably depended on how well he executed that simple action.

He took out *The Story of Philosophy* and attempted to read a little from Plato. Soon he stuffed the book back under his sweater. While riding in the tank to the apple orchard his view of the outside world had been limited by a small periscope. It reminded him of Plato's "Allegory of the Cave." What is *reality*? Whip smiled. Plato should have experienced the *reality* of being cramped inside the turret of a Sherman tank. He should have experienced its deafening roar and suffocating fumes, stabbing lurches and quaking jolts. True, the tankers had padded helmets and earphones as part of an intercommunication system. They had goggles to protect their eyes. Yet Whip could only wonder why he never got claustrophobia. So far, he never had. At least in a tank with a decorated commander like Sergeant Witkowski, Whip believed he would not have to worry about being a coward. He thought of the boy who ran away from his first battle in Stephen Crane's book, *The Red Badge of Courage*. In his case, Whip figured he needn't worry. He had no recourse but to go wherever Sergeant Witkowski took the tank.

"Hey, VD," said Jenks climbing on to the turret. "You better get in your place; this shindig is about to begin."

"What is this VD stuff with Johnson?" asked Sergeant Witkowski.

"It's a joke on him from back at Knox," answered Jenks over the intercom. Nathan Talbot continued to rev the tank engine.

"Good luck, VD," said Hank Henry on the intercom thus continuing Whip's embarrassment with that name-tag.

Over the radio, Lieutenant Appleby's resonant voice said, "Let's go." With that command the seventeen tanks of Company "D" left the concealment of the apple orchard and fanned out into open terrain with all guns soon blazing toward enemy positions. Jenks operated the motorized turret, aimed the 75mm cannon with its coaxially mounted 30 caliber machine gun, and periodically stepped on the firing button.

Whip responded to Sergeant Witkowski's commands for a variety of shells: AP (armor piercing), HE (high explosive), or Smoke. Hank Henry fired a thirty-caliber machine gun from his position in the bow gunner's hatch. Witkowski triggered a 50 caliber machine gun mounted on the turret.

Whip became a machine. Rhythmically selecting a shell, he shoved each into the breach of the cannon. Smells of gun powder, engine exhaust, and the feel of the turret swivelling and the tank lurching were omnipresent with the sounds of the engine and cannon roaring, and hot brass casings clanking about on the turret's metal floor. Whip's complete involvement acted like novocaine, desensitizing him—making it possible to momentarily forget his fears. The dim sight of shell racks, an open breach, and the taste of tasteless saliva further benumbed Whip. Nevertheless, Whip was doing his job satisfactorily when grimly the casing of a defective 75mm shell crumpled, spilling cordite onto the breach with its projectile lodged in the barrel. Whip immediately informed the tank commander of the malfunction and jammed round.

Witkowski snapped, "Is it HE or AP?"

"I can't remember for sure, but I think it's AP," said Whip.

Witkowski ordered Talbot to stop the tank. The sergeant quickly dismounted and shoved the ramrod into the tube of the 75. An AP warhead rolled out of the breach on to Whip's lap.

With a gloved right hand Whip cleaned the breach of cordite and armed the 75 with another AP shell. At that moment Appleby ended the exercise.

Abruptly, Lieutenant Nicholson's voice sounded on the radio. "Jerry at twelve." The cough of a 50-caliber followed.

Whip saw daylight out the commander's hatch and caught a glimpse of the dozer's 50-caliber tracers sent skyward.

Over the intercom Witkowski said, "I think he's hit. He's trailing smoke."

The radio crackled and Appleby's confident voice said, "Jerry's just wondering what we're up to and came over to take our picture. See you all back at the CP."

As SUSAN MONTGOMERY kneaded the doughnut dough, she thought about her reputation. Wild, impetuous, irresponsible were just a few of the words some members of her own family had used to chastise her. Now observing doughnuts beginning to rise and brown in the cooking oil, she recalled her volunteering for the Red Cross. In her case the war had changed an aimless life into one with significance. Of course, she got a kick out of being dubbed a "doughnut dolly" by the combat soldiers.

To boost the morale of the fighting men, she'd been told, the Red Cross picked their best "lookers" for the front line troops. Though there was more danger in being so close to the fighting, she did not fear death. Like the guys, she just prayed if it were her "time," it would come quickly and completely. Nor did she dislike the attentions of the young officers. She knew she cut a smart figure in her Red Cross outfit. Under her breath she whispered, "Who knows? I might find what I'm looking for if I live through this damn war."

Corporal Josh Higgins had parked the "clubmobile" in the middle of the street. Sally Brown, her cohostess, was already pouring hot coffee and handing out doughnuts to crews from the parked Sherman tanks. Heavy shelling and house to house fighting had gutted the sturdy houses of the German village. Now with a lull in the action, the tankers could have warm meals and visits from the "doughnut dollies."

Though it was mostly a time of rest and rehabilitation, harassment of the enemy had not ended. With their dug-in 105 millimeter pieces, the division artillery continued to lob occasional shells at selected targets on the enemy side as several L5 aircraft flew spotting assignments searching for targets of opportunity. So far the enemy had not retaliated.

Susan gasped when she first looked into his face. The soldier smiled and held out his hand to receive the paper cup of coffee she had poured, but she missed his out reached hand completely and tipped the coffee onto his uniform. He jumped back in mild surprise, the smile never leaving his face. It only deepened. She saw he was a first lieutenant and a very large man. In comparison, other soldiers awaiting their turn appeared as midgets. He wore a stocking helmet liner perched precariously on the back of his head. Wavy auburn hair speckled with dried grass and leaves gleamed in the sunlight, much as her brother Donald's hair used to look after he'd been wrestling with kids on the lawn back home. Brown eyes and a tanned, smooth-skinned face with a sexy dimple reminded her of a guy she'd once dated.

Just at that precious moment the chatter of machine guns and the roar of a low flying plane caused the soldiers to leap for the side of the street or to drop to the pavement. As Susan frantically jumped from the clubmobile she found herself held and protected by the arms and body of the officer. Clutching her tight he remained standing upright on the cobblestone street. An aircraft with black cross markings passed directly overhead, barely above roof top height, fire spewing from its nose and wings.

The huge lieutenant said soothingly, "Don't worry, lady. He's shooting at the L5s."

Hardly before she could catch her breath another voice sounded, "Lieutenant, the Major wants you on the phone."

Suddenly her rescuer disappeared among the men rising from the street. Believing she'd felt more than just a friendly hug, she swore, "Damn!" He was gone before she could collect her senses.

Then she relaxed; she'd have no trouble obtaining the identity of such a striking officer.

BURLY, HAIRY, APPROPRIATELY GRUMPY for an army cook, Staff Sergeant Hap Hardesty faced a dilemma. He didn't want trouble with Major Burk, but he hoped to help this Belgium kid, Please-Joe, if he could. In fact, Hap often displayed a rough exterior to the world. In reality, he was a softhearted sentimentalist; and this little, belligerent, sassy brat had already found a warm spot in his heart. But he couldn't stand the kid's moniker, "Please-Joe." The kid would just have to be satisfied with being called "Joe."

As the battalion head cook, Hap was not without influence. He believed that a soldier's will to fight was determined by the well-being of his stomach. And many times the battalion kitchen had performed miracles during combat by providing the fast moving, fighting tankers with good warm meals. Nor did the men of the 1st Battalion ever bitch about the cooking. The tankers often said Hardesty could prepare gourmet fare out of crap.

When Hap, with Joe in tow, drove up to Lieutenant Appleby's CP, the critique of the "rehearsal" had concluded. The tankers of the company had departed, including the company headquarters staff. Tom was alone and sat at a table writing to the parents of one of his soldiers who had been killed in action.

Looking up, Tom seemed startled for a moment. Then with his eyes glued on Joe, he smiled and asked, "Well, Hap, did you catch a Nazi spy in one of your potato sacks?"

Undaunted, Joe said, "Lieutenant, I'm not dressed as a German soldier, I'm not a spy. I'm a mascot of a supply outfit. They moved out on me when I was on pass. I just want to find Sergeant Sullivan, who I help at Supply."

For all of his knowledge about Americans, Joe was surprisingly ignorant of the outfit which had supposedly adopted him. That thought had run through Sergeant Hardesty's mind while driving up to Lieutenant Appleby's CP; and the spy thing wasn't entirely out of the question, knowing the fanaticism of the Nazis, especially now that the fighting was on German soil. Possibly the Hitler Youth were the most fanatical of all; or at least, that is what Hap had been told.

Tom noted that Joe did not have the angular features of most pubescent French boys. Though he was dark of hair and eyes, his face was round, almost like a ball. His eyes sparkled and his demeanor was open; but if challenged, his attitude was defiant. And that was what Hap claimed as he related Joe's story to Tom.

When Hap finished talking, Tom asked, "What state did this Sergeant Sullivan live in, Joe?"

"Darned if I know, Lieutenant. Maybe it was South Dakota?"

"Why do you want to go to the United States?" continued Tom.

"Everything's kaput for me here. I don't have nobody. No family. I wanna go to the states. Sergeant Sullivan said he would take me there."

"What would you like us to do for you?" quizzed Tom.

"Oh, I suppose drop me off someplace. You don't have to worry none about me, Lieutenant. I'll find my outfit all right."

Hap could see Lieutenant Appleby was as intrigued with his catch as he was. After a few more questions about this Sullivan and his outfit, Tom motioned Hap aside and whispered, "Could you hold on to this boy for a while? Keep a close eye on him. Maybe he could help you around the kitchen?"

That would be just fine with me, Lieutenant. The little stinker reminds me of my own kid at home."

Turning to Joe, Tom said, "Joe, I just can't have you 'dropped off someplace' now that you've been up front. Sergeant Hardesty said you could work for him in the kitchen for the time being. You would have to be on the ball—no mess ups."

"What do you think? I'm a goldbrick or something? Trust me, I can do a good job for you. . . . Thanks, Lieutenant."

In short order Hap and Joe returned to the battalion kitchen, and Joe was soon doing "pots and pans."

IT HAD NOT TAKEN Susan Lavet Montgomery long to identify her rescuer and protector. Confiding to Sally Brown back at their lodgings in

Heerlen, Holland, Susan said, "Damn it, Sally. I know he's the guy. All my goose bumps tingle every time I think about him."

Sally Brown inhaled deeply on a Lucky Strike and pursed her lips blowing smoke in the air. Then she said, "Suppose the guy's married and deeply in love with his wife." Tapping the ashes from her cigarette on to the floor, Sally smiled demurely. "Besides, from what you say, he's already some big, hero warrior. You know he'll probably be killed or maimed before this things over." And viewing Susan squarely in the eyes, she asked, "How you ever going to meet the guy, let alone seduce him?"

Coyly Susan said, "He's not married, Sally. And even if he was, it wouldn't bother me none. I'll meet him. You wait and see."

"I bet you think he'll be at General Clay's party," said Sally, her expression indicating she'd just thought of that. "God, how can they hold a party in the middle of the war? What if the Germans find out and attack?"

Fussing with her hair while looking into a cracked mirror, Susan said, "In answer to your first question, Sally, I can let you in on a little secret. General Clay assured me he'd see to it Lieutenant Appleby was present and accounted for—at the party, I mean."

Susan turned toward Sally blowing Sally's cigarette smoke back in her emerald eyes. "But if it's necessary, Lieutenant Appleby will be ordered there by his regimental commander. . . . And the General said he himself would take care of the proper introductions.

"As to your second question, it's called morale building. For every American officer present, General Clay is seeing to it that there will be a Dutch gal on hand to match each American officer.

"And about your last question. Maybe it's an American trap to lure the Germans into attacking."

"Ha," rebutted Sally. "If there's a trap being set, I think I know who it's set for. . . . I can hardly wait to meet your heartthrob."

IN THE ABSENCE OF General Bartholomaus, Major Dietrich assumed full command of the "Hammer" Panzer Division. The general's staff were eager to obey the famous major. Now seated at Bartholomaus' desk in the operations room, Dietrich asked that the spy Samson be brought to him.

As his name suggested, Samson was a man of physical strength. At six-foot-plus with black hair and a pox marked face, he looked like he'd just awakened from a deep sleep.

Samson had been recruited by the Resistance as a saboteur, and he had been successful, having once, single-handedly blown up a German ammunition dump. The Resistance, on the other hand, never fully trusted him. A loudmouth, he was forever boasting that he was "The Great Samson." Possessing an insatiable appetite for women, he once blabbed about his Resistance work to a Gestapo Mata Hari. Immediately he was arrested—but not shot, because the Gestapo still had uses for "The Great Samson." By holding members of his family and his mistress hostage, the Gestapo had hoped to penetrate the Dutch underground.

MAJOR DIETRICH HAD STUDIED the file on Samson. Apparently the Gestapo was now ready to put the Dutchman down, believing the Reich wasn't getting its money's worth from the double agent. Escorted by two armed guards wearing steel helmets, Samson's dark eyes glanced nonchalantly about the room before settling on the scar-faced major who was seated behind a scuffed, mahogany table.

Major Dietrich, ignoring the pain caused by an ill-fitting wooden leg, pointed to a chair for Samson and signalled the guards to leave the room. Speaking English he said in an even tone, "I am Major Dietrich. How did you know I would be here, Samson?"

Without hesitation Samson said in a sonorous monotone, "A German boy, a Hitler Youth, in Heerlen, Holland, said Hitler had ordered you from the Eastern Front to lead a counterattack that would defeat the Americans. Then you would lead the final attack that would destroy the Russians. I place myself at your disposal."

Dietrich knew of SS Colonel Otto Skorzeny's special forces created to defend the Reich. He considered it possible that a boy-spy, a Hitler Youth, could be involved; and he knew Hitler never revealed all of his ideas, even to a confidant such as himself.

"What makes you so sure, Samson, that this boy is a Hitler Youth?"

Answering in the same monotone, Samson said, "His name is Arnd. Some weeks past the Gestapo had me take him through the lines to Heerlen. Since I've been gone, the instructions for me to contact you were given to Arnd." Smiling for the first time, Samson said, "It must be accurate, Major, for here before me sits the famous Hans Otto Dietrich."

Dietrich did not appreciate patronization, especially from a dubious spy. He sensed that Samson, must be reminded of his own precarious existence.

"I hope, Samson," said Dietrich, his right index finger touching his lips, "you have not forgotten your family or Janeane Mitterand? Their lives depend on your success. You know the Gestapo."

Samson felt devoted and obligated to his sister and her husband. He was also madly in love with his mistress, Janeane Mitterand. With downcast eyes he replied, "I understand, Major Dietrich."

Pleased that Samson appeared contrite, Dietrich said, "Samson, the Gestapo knows of your contacts in the Dutch Resistance. One man in particular, a Herr Rieksen.... I believe he is an acquaintance of yours. Well, it turns out he is also one of the masterminds in the Resistance. This information should have come from you—but didn't!... So I'm told this is your last chance, Samson.... First, the Gestapo wants this man alive. I repeat.... The Gestapo wants Herr Rieksen. And, as I understand, to help you succeed, Samson, the Gestapo now holds Herr Rieksen's girl friend as a hostage!"

Major Dietrich allowed his words to sink in. He smiled indulgently.

To Samson, Dietrich's eyes looked like blinking stars on a cold winter night.

"I believe you know Nicoline Lindemann." After another pause, Major Dietrich continued, "Secondly, I personally want the American battle plan for the attack on Puffendorf.... It's life or death for all of us, Samson, and I pledge by the word of the Führer that we will keep our promise with you—one way or the other."

Shaken by what he'd just heard, Samson hesitantly replied, "I believe, Major Dietrich, that I asked for you to be informed that it was at the Secondary Technical School in Heerlen."

"Yes, I understand. That school is where General Clay has made his headquarters. So it's up to you, Samson, to get General Clay's battle plan."

"I have already learned," said Samson, "that its code name is 'Operation Queen.'"

Painfully rising from his chair Major Dietrich said, "Good. I'll pass that on. You may go. Others are waiting who have more questions for you. But before you return to Heerlen have my aides help you get whatever you need." With a curt wave of his hand Major Dietrich again turned his attention to the map table as Samson left the room.

COINCIDENTALLY AS SAMSON was leaving the operations room of the "Hammer" Panzer Division, a few miles away General Brighton D. Clay and his operation's officer, Major Jack Collins, were relaxing with cigarettes and coffee at the Secondary Technical School. A pitch black night had recently replaced twilight. Overhead they heard the drone of British bombers. The two men were alone. "Grab your coffee, Jack, and let's go to my office," said General Clay.

"Okay, General," answered Major Collins, "but first I want to make sure the blackout curtains are in place."

General Clay was a West Pointer. Lean and leathery, he stood over six feet tall. His dark-tinted grey hair and resolute eyes bestowed upon him the appearance of a frontline general. Displaying a self-assured manner, he acted like a frontline general. Major Collins, also a West Pointer, was short and stocky with the physique of a halfback. Looking like one who could handle himself in a brawl, his even-paced, low-keyed voice masked an incendiary nature.

When Major Collins returned to Clay's office, he found the general talking with a skinny six footer with rusty blond hair. The man's face had two distinguishing features: a beak-like nose and a high conspicuous forehead. Philip Vossmaar was the newly acquired Dutch liaison officer and interpreter.

Withdrawing a Camel cigarette from his lips, General Clay said, "Your Dutch bureaucracy is nearly as bad as ours, Lieutenant. I had a hell of a time convincing your government to induct you into your Dutch army with a commissioned officer's rank. But it was the least I could do for you after what Sergeant Jones said about your help in the capture of this building."

Momentarily forgetting his usual distrust of motives, Philip answered gravely, "Thank you very much, General Clay. I hope my experience in the Resistance can be of some service to you."

"Yes, Lieutenant, Mr. Rieksen has spoken most highly of you. We know you transported downed airmen back to England. I also understand you are a multi-linguist, which I happen to have need of with all of these refugees coming out of the woodwork." Drawing on his cigarette and winking at Major Collins, General Clay persisted, "But at the moment, Lieutenant, I have a most delicate and important assignment for you." General Clay delayed stating the assignment while he blew a couple smoke rings. "You need not know why we consider this so important to the war effort, Lieutenant, but take my word; it is!" Now he stopped for another drag and a swallow of coffee, again looking at Major Collins.

"We are going to have a big party, Lieutenant; I mean a really 'big' party for some of the officers in the Division. In the neighborhood of a hundred to be exact. . . . Isn't that about right, Major Collins?"

Major Collins nodded in the affirmative.

The general put his face squarely in front of Philip's face. He cracked a smile and slapped his thigh with his hand. "Voss, can you come up with the women and the place for this extravaganza? Major Collins and I figured it's your home town and you might be able to pull it off. For our part we'll provide the men, the booze, unlimited quantities of food and, of course, the Division dance band." The general leaned back in his chair, the American officers intently scanning Lieutenant Philip Vossmaar's face for a reaction.

When General Clay had first begun to speak, Philip had thought some secret and perhaps dangerous mission lay in store for himself. The request for women and a place to hold a large party surprised him. Nervously fingering his recently fitted American uniform, he briefly considered the solicitation. He knew he could get the girls. He was certain they'd jump at the chance to meet and party with American officers; not only out of obligation to their American liberators, but also because they'd heard American soldiers were crazy fun-lovers.

Nodding his head, his eyes opening wide in wonderment, Philip said, "Sure, I can do it, General. No sweat."

Major Collins said, "To satisfy my curiosity, Lieutenant. Where did you pick up your American slang?"

Without hesitation Philip said, "From the American pilots I hid."

"Lieutenant," said General Clay, "come here tomorrow morning and you can have my jeep and driver to line up the girls and the place. We'll talk more about it then." The general's voice and expression indicated he was through for now with Lieutenant Vossmaar.

Promptly, Philip saluted and said, "Yes, sir." Not being a trained soldier, Philip did a sloppy about-face and left the room.

AFTER THE DUTCHMAN HAD GONE General Clay changed the subject. "What do you think about Dietrich being in the vicinity of Puffendorf, Jack?"

"I know we'll now have hell to pay," said Major Collins.

General Clay replied, "I'll match 'Daredevil-Six' (Lieutenant Appleby's radio number) against that one-legged, scar-faced bastard any day."

"Speaking of Appleby," said Major Collins, "did you get Quinn to order his presence at the dance. That Red Cross broad has the hots for his pants. You know its my understanding Tom doesn't go for this social crap."

General Clay said, "Damn it, Jack, I forgot. You have Quinn

issue the order. I don't want Major Burk mixed up with this. That's just the broad for Tom. An American girl from a rich family. . . . What about his formal promotion to captain? Couldn't we do it up big at the dance? Maybe get her dear brother from SHAFF (Supreme Headquarters Allied Expeditionary Force) to pin Appleby's bars on. That'd probably give her an orgasm." The general doubled over laughing.

"Sounds good to me. I agree with you we'd better not get eager-beaver Burk in on this. He's also a bachelor and would probably pull rank on Lieutenant Appleby and . . ."

General Clay interrupted, "Captain Appleby."

"Yeah, That's right. Well, I don't think we want 'Captain' Appleby's battalion commander to screw up a relationship made in heaven."

"That's good of you, Jack, to say that."

The two officers considered this idea humorous and guffawed over it. Then a worn expression returned to General Clay's face. "Do you think our little ploy has an outside chance of influencing the Herr Kampfgrüppe Führer, Jack?"

"I would guess it depends on how much of a loose cannon ball Dietrich really is. Rieksen says Dietrich, being SS, is virtually his own man and at odds with General Bartholomaus. But really I don't see how we have anything to lose from it. 'Operation Queen' goes forward regardless of what Dietrich does in this situation. If he reacts, he's dead, and 'Operation Queen' just get's a head start. Rieksen's idea sounds wild, but a lot of wild ideas have taken wing before."

After more silence and smoke rings, General Clay said, "You spoke earlier about Colonel Quinn ordering Tom to the dance. Do you believe I'm on solid ground in giving Major Burk command of Combat Command 'B' in Queen, rather than Colonel Quinn?

"No doubt about it, General. It's only natural. Burk is the most ambitious, intelligent lower-grade officer I know of in this man's army. . . . And there's something different about Colonel Quinn. In fact, some of his men whisper 'Queer Quinn' behind his back. Perhaps it's just the alliteration with his name. But then maybe there's more. . . ."

General Clay held up his hand. "Easy, Jack, your getting on thin ice. General Bradly, himself, gave Colonel Quinn command of the 67th Regiment back in the states. Under me, Quinn has served well. I have no criticism whatsoever of Harold Quinn's army service."

"May I say one thing more about Colonel Quinn, sir?" asked Major Collins assuming a respectful tone following General Clay's mild rebuke.

General Clay nodded.

"Yesterday after dark I went for a walk and saw an officer who appeared to be Colonel Quinn escorting a young boy. Before I could cross the street and catch up to them, they'd disappeared into one of the houses on the block."

Quickly General Clay said, "Well, I can assure you, Jack, it wasn't Quinn. He was with me most of the evening. . . . It was probably some kid pimping for his sister. Hell, Jack, everybody needs a piece of ass now and then just to keep functioning. Crap, most of these girls feel it's their patriotic duty to their nice American liberators."

CHAPTER 3

As he hurried from his meeting with General Clay, Philip Vossmaar reflected on his good fortune, "This is better than I could have hoped. Almost with the snap of General Clay's fingers I'm made a lieutenant in my own Dutch army and I'm given an interesting job with the Americans." Then his thoughts turned to General Clay's request. He'd assured the general it'd be "no sweat" to lineup girls for the general's party.

Philip rose early the next morning in order to again meet with General Clay and be introduced to the general's jeep driver. As Philip left his house, he saw his best friend, Karel Konijn, talking with an American soldier. Nearing the two, Philip recognized Sergeant Beck Jones whose infantry company now guarded the 15th Armored Division's headquarters.. "Hello," he called.

"Nice uniform," said Sergeant Jones. "I told you General Clay could fix you up, Lieutenant." . . . With exaggerated motions, Jones clicked his heels and gave Philip a highball salute.

Smiling, Philip replied, "I know I'm a phony in this uniform, but the general insisted."

Karel Konijn said in English, "I received your message about General Clay's request when I got home, Philip." Breaking into a wide grin and nodding his head, he assured, "You should have no trouble getting the girls with the help of the Gorgo (Philip's debating club), and the Casino would be a good place for the dance." Briefly displaying a small handgun from his coat pocket, he continued, "I'd help with the arrangements but my services are demanded elsewhere." Karel nodded at a man standing by a vintage roadster parked near the school. Dressed in a trench coat, from the distance the man looked like a journalist. In a whisper Karel said, "Rieksen."

In London, the Dutch government in exile had recognized Bep Rieksen as a leader in the Resistance. In his middle thirties and slight of build, what Bep lacked in brawn, he made up for by skill in judo and a ruthlessness matching the Gestapo's. For relaxation he read the classics and practiced at his piano.

As Philip peered down the street at the slight figure of Bep Rieksen, who had just concluded a meeting with General Clay, Philip was struck by the fact that he'd only once met the underground leader, that being when Rieksen had personally escorted a Jewish couple to his home for temporary shelter and hiding.

AFTER KAREL HAD JOINED RIEKSEN and the two had driven away, Philip said to Sergeant Jones, "I'm supposed to meet with General Clay's jeep driver so he can drive me around the city. I have to make arrangements for a big dance. What do you think of that, Sergeant?"

Jones didn't hesitate. "Bullshit! . . . I think it's crap. The general's gotta be off his rocker on this one. But I'd be on my guard if I were you, Voss. Jimmy Malloti, his driver, is from a New York gangster family. I guess Malloti is supposed to be some kind of bodyguard for the general, but he'd just as soon put a knife in your back as look at you."

Philip replied, "So what? I'm no threat to General Clay."

PHILIP VOSSMAAR'S MEETING with General Clay further underscored the general's enthusiasm for the dance. And Philip's introduction to Private Malloti confirmed Jones' assessment of the man. Malloti's pointed features, slicked-back black hair, dark eyes and throaty, threatening voice personified Hollywood's representation of a gangster.

As Malloti drove away from the school building with Philip seated beside him. He looked at Philip and asked, "Why do all you foreigners look so funny?"

Looking straight ahead Philip replied, "Probably because we haven't eaten very well in a long time."

"Yeah," said Malloti, "I see your people going through our garbage. . . . I suppose you're like the rest; you expect Uncle Sammy to take care of you from now on."

In Malloti Philip recognized the stereotypical American, boastful and narrow-minded. "Not if we can help it," said Philip.

For the first time in days the sun showed itself and the American air force was again pounding Germany. Amid the drone of the bombers, Jimmy Malloti and Philip Vossmaar drove around Heerlen weaving in and out of military traffic. The Casino manager jumped at the chance to host the party and dance, and Philip's friends said they'd find the girls and report back to Philip.

As Jimmy and Philip were returning to the school, Philip saw several German prisoners lined up on a side street. He recognized one of them as being the young soldier who'd run into his garden at the approach of Sergeant Jones' platoon and who had surrendered to Karel. The German POWs were surrounded by a group of Dutchmen, one of whom lived across the street from Philip and whose last name was Lintens. Philip saw Lintens suddenly strike the young prisoner to the ground and kick him as he lay prostrate. Impulsively Philip jumped from the slow-moving jeep and grabbed Linten's arm. In Dutch he said, "My how you are so brave, Mr. Lintens. I happen to know you were the first to comply with any German request. Remember how you went around collecting metal and distributing National Socialist propaganda leaflets. Do you think beating this young prisoner will clear your name, Mr. Lintens?"

Lintens, a scraggly looking man, cowed before Philip's verbal onslaught.

A second lieutenant with a white MP arm band quickly approached Philip and demanded, "What the hell's going on here?"

"Do American officers allow their prisoners to be abused by collaborators, Lieutenant?" replied Philip sarcastically.

Putting his .45 to Philip's stomach the lieutenant said, "Don't give me any shit, fellow. This is war and that prisoner is a fucking Nazi. I might just decide to plug you."

The .45 abruptly clattered to the pavement as Malloti laughed in the face of the grimacing lieutenant. "Hey, Lieutenant, sir," said Malloti, releasing his grip on the lieutenant's arm, then giving him a salute, "this guy's a high ranking Dutch officer. Can't youse see that lion on his uniform? Look at the general's star on that jeep. Do youse want trouble with General Clay?" Smiling, Jimmy purred, "Back off, Lieutenant!"

By now the place was swarming with MPs. The lieutenant, however, had listened and looked. He turned to a sergeant and said, "Let's get these goddamn prisoners out of here."

The prisoner assaulted by Lintens had regained his position in the POW lineup. He turned to Philip and said, "Danke."

When the POWs were being marched away, Philip furtively slipped a few cigarettes into the young man's pocket.

Observing Philip's actions, Malloti said, "Christ youse a softhearted Dutchman. I thought youse people hated these Nazi bastards."

"Just the Nazis. . . . Just the Nazis," said Philip, pensively observing the POWs disappear around a curve in the street.

DRESSED LIKE A COAL MINER and wearing a short-visored cap, Samson entered Heerlen's popular Beer-Garden. Other than being a big man, two other physical features identified Samson: rough facial skin and two sledgehammer fists. With roving eyes he edged his way past tables of noisy miners and a few American soldiers. Then in the back he spotted Bep Rieksen and Karel Konijn seated at a small table next to a stucco wall.

"Ah, Samson. We've been waiting for you at least an hour," said Bep, checking his watch. "Did you have trouble coming through the lines?"

First focusing his eyes on Bep's egg-shaped head and then gazing glumly at the two resistance fighters, Samson finally maneuvered his hulk into a vacant chair at the table. "No, Bep."

Irritated by the indifference in Samson's voice, Bep adjusted a bright red necktie and casually asked, "Then why are you late?"

Starring at empty glasses of beer on the table, Samson grumbled, "I heard the BBC (British Broadcasting Corporation) mention your name on the radio, Bep. Like you're a big hero in the Resistance. Congratulations . . . I always do your dirty work while you get the credit. . . . You probably know why I'm late!"

Samson's defiance surprised Karel Konijn. Until now Samson had always been contrite in the presence of Bep.

Lighting a cigarette, Bep indicated no annoyance with Samson's surliness. "Yes, I can guess why you're late. I suppose you were with Janeane Mitterand?"

Samson seemed to fold into his chair. He whispered, "She's a hostage of the Gestapo."

"How do you know?" asked Bep, displaying some concern.

"I was given proof at Puffendorf."

Thoughtfully, Bep unbuttoned his tweed blouse and again adjusted his red necktie. After a time he asked bluntly, "What do they want?"

"They want the plans for 'Operation Queen.'"

"All right . . . I can get them."

"And they want something else."

"Yes?"

"They want you!"

"Really. . . . How do you propose to deliver me to the Gestapo? Dead!"

"Don't get cute, Bep. I know this place is packed with your men. But before you do anything rash, you'd better check on Nicoline. When it comes to women, Bep, we're two peas in a pod. They've got Nicoline too."

For some days Bep had not called Nicoline. The war he believed was nearing its climax; and with the final battles being planned, he had had to deny his private life. But he did not doubt Samson's words, and blood drained from his face. "Damn, he should have shielded Nicoline. . . . Now he recognized the source of Samson's challenge. But how had Nicoline come into the hands of the Gestapo? . . . Samson?"

No longer was Samson languid in his chair. His whole being riveted on Bep, and he immediately divined the Resistance leader's thoughts.

"No, Bep, it was not I who had a hand in Nicoline's abduction. They know of us and they know of your command in the Resistance. They even threatened me with death for never having revealed my connection with you."

Bep said coldly, "But they let you go."

"Of course. How else can they get 'Operation Queen' or the wanted Bep Rieksen?"

Bep inhaled deeply and asked, "Did you see Nicoline or do you know where she is being held?"

"The answer is 'no' to both. Any further acts of terror by you against the Reich will cause her execution. . . . A part from that, I'm supposed to lure you into a trap if ever I'm to see Janeane alive. . . . Some shit! . . . What can we do?"

After some moments, Bep asked, "Do you know of any of the Gestapo's informants in Heerlen?"

Thinking of Lintens and the Hitler Youth, Arnd, Samson attempted to mask a lie with a firm: "No!"

But Bep caught the lie.

Samson hurriedly changed the subject. "Most of my 'briefings' at Puffendorf were with SS Major Hans Otto Dietrich." Samson raised his eyebrows and slowly repeated, "Hans Dietrich!" Closely looking for a reaction from Bep, he went on, "He's the one who wants 'Operation Queen.'"

Abruptly Bep relaxed and resumed smoking his cigarette. Color returned to his face, and he turned to Karel and said, "Pour 'The Great' Samson a beer, Karel. I'm sorry, Samson, you haven't received your due. I'll see this omission is rectified in my next report to London." Bep looked hard at the man. "At this point, Samson, it seems we must overlook any differences." Bep put out his smoke and deliberately poured himself a beer.

Suddenly, leaning over the table and grabbing Samson by his black sweater, Bep tugged until their faces were eyeball to eyeball. Samson's huge hands resting on the table doubled. Smiling, Bep said in a whisper, "Listen, Samson, we'll give the Herr Kampfgrüppe Führer 'Operation Queen' and we'll do what we have to do for the Gestapo's hostages. But why in the hell is the famous panzer commander not in the East opposing the Red Army's advance? Let's discover the real reason Dietrich's in the West!"

GENERAL BARTHOLOMAUS HAD RETURNED to Puffendorf following a two-day stay at Field Marshal Stein's Army Group "C" headquarters. He had not resigned his command of the "Hammer" Panzer Division as he had intended. To his surprise, he had learned that Stein's order giving Dietrich free-reign within the "Hammer" Division had come from above. The Field Marshal had even pleaded for him to put up with Dietrich and possibly discover what was going on. Obviously, these SS leaders were all taking their cues from Himmler, the SS chief, and Stein felt something injurious and sinister both for the German army and the German people was in the offing.

At first the Field Marshal had been careful not to openly criticize Hitler, and he had tended to speak in innuendo. However, before General Bartholomous' departure, Field Marshal Stein had assured the general that the attempt on Hitler's life in July had not originated within the "old guard," but had had its origin with some Nazi officers, including Rommel. They had failed and had paid with their lives; then the Field Marshal had surprised General Bartholomaus by asserting that the next move against Hitler's life would not fail.

THUS ENCOURAGED by Field Marshal Stein, Bartholomous' first meeting with Dietrich, following his return from group headquarters, was brief. Without the normal "Heil Hitler" greeting, General Bartholomous entered the Hammer Division's operations room unannounced. Surprised, the Major looked up smiling. "Herr General, you have returned!"

"Yes, Major Dietrich. And with amended orders."

With difficulty, because of his artificial leg, Dietrich rose from a hardback chair and faced General Bartholomaus, the only non-SS general in the III Panzer Corps. Of course, Dietrich had not expected Bartholomaus' return. Rheinhardt had assured Dietrich that he'd be given the command of the "Hammer" Division following Bartholomaus' expected resignation. Obviously Field Marshal Stein, another non-SS officer, had turned the tables on SS Lieutenant General Rheinhardt.

From Dietrich's perspective, the main reason the war was not going well was due to the failure of the old Prussian Generals to execute Hitler's orders. That was not the case with Hitler's SS officers. Now, what with the big surprise being planned by Hitler, in Dietrich's view, only SS officers should remain in high command. The time had come to get rid of Field Marshal Stein and General Bartholomaus one way or another.

Dietrich's right index finger went to his lips and he slightly bowed. "Mein Herr General, I hope your 'amended orders' do not compromise my freedom of action; in which case, I would be forced to go all the way to the Führer for clarification."

"Don't be troubled, Major Dietrich. I will not issue you direct orders. You are instructed by Field Marshal Stein, though, to keep me informed of your intentions and actions with respect to your kampfgrüppe—but I am to remain in command of the 'Hammer' Division!

"Furthermore, I must remind you, Major, that SS Lieutenant General Rheinhardt and the III Panzer Corps, of which we all are a part, is still under the direct command of Army Group 'C' and Field Marshal Stein."

As Dietrich's cold eyes beamed at General Bartholomaus' monocle, his pale facial scar quickly looked like an island surrounded by a sea of red. Clenching his right hand, Dietrich snarled, "Don't lecture me on the table of command, Herr General. I'll do what's required to bring victory to the Reich." Gesturing at the operations room, he said, "You can have your headquarters, General. I'll be in the field with my units where I belong—Heil Hitler!" Dietrich then limped from the room kicking the wooden door open with his factitious foot.

THE CHANGE IN ORDERS did not set well with Lieutenant Appleby. He had thought "Operation Queen" was signed, sealed and delivered—only the timing, based on the weather, had not been decided upon. Now apparently "Operation Queen" was off. At 1800 hours his forward units were to begin their withdrawal. The entire 1st Battalion, the opening "strike force" of Combat Command "B" in "Operation Queen," was being repositioned to the outskirts of Heerlen, Holland. Appleby sensed something ominous in this move, and he knew he could expect a lot of grumbling among the men.

"Judas Priest, Wes, haven't you got your communications stuff loaded on the personnel carrier yet?" Appleby complained.

Corporal Wesley "Wes" Willow, a scurrilous and myopic man, replied, "Sorry, Lieutenant, I wasn't expecting such an order at this time. What's up? Has Jerry broken through somewhere on the line?"

Before Appleby could respond, "Red" Jordening hurried into the Company "D" Command Post. "God, I've never seen such confusion and anger as at the Battalion CP. Clay refuses to talk on the phone with Burk; and Collins told Burk to get his ass in gear and get the 1st Battalion moved back to Heerlen. Burk thinks it's the end of 'Operation Queen,' but nobody will tell him why. He's as much in the dark as we are. I hope 'Jerry' doesn't find out."

"It does seem incredible after all the bloodshed getting here we'd just pull up stakes and invite Jerry to take everything back," said Appleby.

Lieutenant Jordening allowed himself a chuckle and said, "I believe Burk is mad because he thought if we took Puffendorf, he was hoping to make colonel and probably take over the regiment from Quinn."

Appleby laughed. He knew all about Major Burk's appetite for fame and glory. Nodding in the direction of Corporal Willow, Appleby put a finger to his lips and said, "Careful where you air your views, Red."

After Corporal Willow left the room lugging some of his radio equipment to the three-quarter-ton, Lieutenant Jordening said, "Burk hinted he thought big shots from SHAEF would be present for his sandtable briefing. I suppose this pullback will cancel that?"

"You know as much as I do, Red. I don't know. We'll just have to play it by ear." Glancing at his watch, Tom continued, "At least in this fog, it's almost pitch dark. . . . I can hear some tanks revving their engines. Milton must be spreading the word."

Private Milton Silverman entered the command post with a worried look on his face.

"Only Sergeant Witkowski didn't believe me, sir. He told me to go back to bed."

"What's the password tonight?" asked Jordening. "Have they posted a guard yet?"

"Corporal Whip Johnson has guard duty, sir. The password is 'swordfish,'" answered Silverman. "Corporal Johnson woke Sergeant Witkowski, and Witkowski was madder than a wet hen."

"That's good, Milton," said Jordening. "You'd better help Wes get the equipment out of here. I'll take care of Witkowski."

After Jordening left, Appleby stepped into an adjoining room to get his musette bag. Appleby had no more than left the room than he heard Private Silverman bellow: "ATTENTION!"

Immediately Appleby returned to find Silverman standing rigid. Before him stood a full colonel wearing an officer's winter dress coat with the "chickens" in place on the shoulders. Appleby recognized Colonel Harold Quinn, his regimental commander.

In a quiet, mellifluous voice the Colonel said, "At ease."

Lieutenant Appleby had often pondered the nature of his enigmatic regimental commander. The man was difficult to figure out. Perhaps he was a career officer who couldn't quite make the grade. As a grey-headed man about fifty with fine, delicate features, he should have at least been a brigadier by now, considering his service record. Appleby had been told Colonel Quinn had graduated first in his class from some famous military college. Of average height and build, and of mild manner, Colonel Quinn always backed and warmly received Lieutenant Appleby. Of course, Appleby had heard the snide remarks about "queer" Quinn, the bachelor; but there was never anything suggesting out-of-line behavior in his dealings with the colonel. In fact, Appleby liked and respected what he thought Colonel Quinn to be, a cultured and highly intelligent person.

"I'd like to speak alone with Colonel Quinn, Milton. Maybe you and Wes can busy yourselves outside," said Appleby.

"Yes, sir, Lieutenant, I'll help Wes finish loading the three-quarter-ton."

"I'm sorry, Colonel, I can't even offer you a chair."

Colonel Quinn took out a package of Camels and offered Lieutenant Appleby one, then withdrew his arm. "Sorry, Tom, I forgot; you don't smoke, do you?"

"Just something left over from my football days, Colonel."

"I like your self-discipline, Tom, and more than just with smoking." After lighting a cigarette with his Zippo, Colonel Quinn said, "I can guess you probably think the command has gone nuts with this pullback."

Smiling, Appleby said, "I have to admit, Colonel, I'm a little confused."

"Off the record, Tom, we're hoping to trap Dietrich. We believe the panzer leader is only a few miles from here. The Resistance believe they can lure Dietrich's battle-group out into the open by our withdrawing from the Siegfried Line. At Division General Clay is calling it 'Operation Trojan Horse.' And you know how General Clay will take chances!"

Appleby shrugged, "What's to stop Dietrich?"

"Combat Command 'A' will soon be hunkered down in our place. At this moment, with their equipment muffled, they're moving up by a different route."

"Does that mean the end to 'Operation Queen'?"

"No. Just, maybe, a head start. . . . I guess it depends on what Dietrich does."

"I thought S2 told us that units of the 'Hammer' and 'Lightning' divisions were opposing us?"

"They are. But we believe the SS is now calling the shots. Not that it matters, but we've heard Himmler's made Dietrich a general just to give the SS control over General Bartholomaus at Puffendorf."

"Well, in that case, I had better see that my men are on the move."

"Just a minute—Lieutenant. Are you really a confirmed bachelor, as I'm told? Or is that another false rumor—like so many others I know of."

"Whoa, Colonel!" Embarrassed, Appleby said, "No, that's not true. I've just put my profligate life on hold. . . .Or I thought I had."

"I hate to get personal, Tom, but do you know some Red Cross doughnut girl whose family is as rich as Rockefeller's?"

"No I don't, Colonel Quinn."

"Well then brace yourself, soldier. In fact, that's why General Clay ordered me up here. To personally command you to attend this dance he's throwing in Heerlen tonight. Before its over, your company will be right close by. She wants to meet you, and she's got gobs of pull with the General. It's an order, Tom."

"I've already heard about the dance. Please give the General my regrets. . . . What Red Cross women?" Suddenly he remembered the good-looking girl who he'd briefly held when the Luftwaffe strafed the L5s. "Oh, I believe I remember her now. You say she's as rich as Rockefeller?"

"Interested, huh. The family has money, Tom, but I've heard she's an outcast—a black sheep."

As Colonel Quinn departed, his last words were: "See you at the dance, Tom, by 2100 hours. Let your XO (Executive Officer) command Company 'D.'"

WHEN LIEUTENANT JORDENING arrived on the scene, he let Sergeant Witkowski know that a withdrawal had indeed been ordered. Witkowski then charged into action. "You'se don't blame me for doubting something Peewee told Johnson, do you'se, Red?"

Sergeant Witkowski quickly became a bear with corporals Jenks and Johnson. He didn't like their book talk nor the fact they'd both been instructors at the Armored Replacement Training Center. Those cadre from Fort Knox all thought they were a bunch of smart sons of bitches. As he'd found out from experience, they didn't know shit from Shinola about combat. Now that he had a fresh chew of tobacco, he demanded speed in loading the tank. From the top of the stairwell he hollered, "Get your's butts in gear you'se guys, Jenks and Johnson, Nate's already got the dozer goin."

Private Hank Henry, who was having difficulty packing his duffle bag, said, "Don't let Polack get on your nerves. He's just that's way."

"Why are we pulling out, Dale?" Whip asked.

"Remember John Smith quoting Tennyson's 'The Charge of the Light Brigade,' VD? . . . 'Theirs not to reason why. Theirs but to do and die.'"

"I heard you, Jenks," growled Sergeant Witkowski, having descended into the basement. "You'se guys won't die if you'se do what you'se told. Now get your butts in gear!"

"It's me, Polack. I had some trouble getting my junk in the duffle bag. The corporals were helping me," said Hank.

THOUGH GROUND FOG shrouded the retreat, it could not hide the sound of roaring tank engines and, like a thousand squealing pigs, the noise of countless track-laying vehicles simultaneously on the move. Pathfinder jeeps driven by MPs showed the iron titans the way on this cool, moist evening, with temperatures near freezing. The driving lights on the tanks had been purposefully dimmed, but it was mostly a case of follow-the-leader. Nevertheless, in such mass movements of men and their equipment in fog, some were bound to go astray. But who would have expected that it would be a vehicle under the command of one of the most experienced and decorated tank commanders. Not until a huge explosion lifted the dozer off the road, throwing one of its tracks, did a droopy

Witkowski and a nonplussed driver, Nathan Talbot, realize they were alone somewhere on a dirt road near the Dutch-German border. The convoy had vanished.

Nate turned off the engine and Sergeant Witkowski with a flashlight jumped to the ground to assess damage to the dozer.

Sticking his head in the turret Witkowski said, "We'se okay. Everybody out."

When the crew gathered around him on the ground he said, "I'm sorry as hell about this. It's all my fault. Here's the situation: We'se took a wrong turn and lost the company, and we'se run over a land mine. Fortunately, we'se only received a slight blow. We'se did throw a track, but Nate and Hank can get it back on in short order." Wilkowski paused, and Whip instinctively knew what was coming.

Sergeant Witkowski proceeded: "I don't mean to be a smart ass, but Jenks and Johnson, look at that sign." Witkowski trained his flashlight on a sign along the road which read: *Meinen*. "It's my guess Jerry didn't have time to remove the warning signs when he retreated. I doubt if there are any other mines other than where a sign is posted." He paused again. "Now not intending to be a smart ass," he repeated himself, "you'se guys both know something about clearing mine fields. And I don't think this is a big deal."

Corporal Jenks asked, "Do you have any bayonets in the tank, Sergeant? For probing the road."

"Yeah."

"And another flashlight?"

"A couple."

"Good. VD and I will clear a path."

While the others maneuvered the dozer back on to its lost track, Whip and Dale cautiously probed the road ahead with the two bayonets. Wherever there were warning signs they found clusters of German Teller mines buried in the road, which they defused without incident. At Fort Knox Whip had always warned the trainees about booby-traps attached to the likes of watches, dead bodies and land mines. With his stomach in his throat Whip worked gingerly, fearing just such a wicked device. Nor did he share Witkowski's analysis of why the warning signs remained in full view. He figured it was bait for booby-traps. But after he and Jenks had advanced about seventy yards to the last warning signs, he at last breathed a sigh of relief.

"You'se guys are wonderful," said a grateful Witkowski from his commander's seat in the turret. "Come on, VD. You'se too, Dale. Let's get the hell out of here before the Krauts spot us. I've got a map, and I now know where we're at."

True to his word Sergeant Witkowski guided Nate back to the line of traffic, and before long found the bivouac area assigned to Company "D." Because Heerlen had not been the scene of any fighting, all its buildings stood undamaged. Furthermore, because Holland was one of the Allies, the army did not force civilians out of their homes to house the troops, as was the case in Germany. So it was back to shelter-halves for the tankers.

A concerned Lieutenant Jordening stood waiting for the crew to dismount from the dozer as Nate shut down the engine.

In relating the whole misadventure to Jordening, Sergeant Witkowski said, "Lieutenant, that VD Johnson and Dale Jenks deserve the 'bronze.' As cool as cucumbers they cleared that road of mines. I'm satisfied to have them in my tank."

HAP HARDESTY WAS NO LONGER Staff Sergeant. Shortly before the evening evacuation, Colonel Quinn had called him to Regimental Headquarters in Heerlen and promoted Hap to Master Sergeant. He also removed Hap from the 1st Battalion and made him Chief Kitchen Steward for the entire 67th Armored Regiment.

Upon learning of Hap's transfer out of battalion, Major Burk, somewhat miffed because he had not been involved in the promotion or transfer, hurried to his battalion kitchen to offer his congratulations before Hardesty left his jurisdiction.

When Major Burk established 1st Battalion Headquarters in Ubach, Germany, Hap had found a gymnasium where he'd set up the battalion kitchen. As he and Joe, alias Please-Joe, were packing their personal belongings, a smiling Major Burk walked up to the two. Suddenly, Burk noticed Little Joe and his expression turned grim.

Since Joe had come under the tutelage of Sergeant Hardesty, the boy had been exposed only to the kitchen staff of the battalion where he was an instant hit and everyone's doglike mascot. But gruff Sergeant Hardesty allowed no fooling around either by Joe or the kitchen staff with him. The boy could never have had a more protective overseer than Hardesty. Even though Joe was a "street-smart" urchin, he did not appear to chafe under Hardesty's restrictions. And he still wore his replica of an American army uniform—though with a unit patch missing.

Major Burk growled, "What's going on with this kid here, Hardesty?"

"Crap," mumbled Hap to himself. Here he was almost out of the grasp of the army's number one martinet and asshole. Nor did he feel like being very obsequious to Major Burk. On the other hand, he didn't want to be "busted" either. So, briefly, Hap retold the story of Joe.

Joe watched with anxiety showing in his eyes and face.

Major Burk starred at Joe with growing disapproval.

When Hap finished speaking, Major Burk snarled, "I should bust you on the spot, Hardesty, for bringing this brat on board! Man, you know the regulations. This isn't back in France someplace. We're about ready to go into action!"

In a rage, his lower lip turned down, Little Joe said, "Sergeant Hardesty forgot to tell you, sir, Major, that Lieutenant Appleby approved of my helping Sergeant Hardesty until he could find Sergeant Sullivan for me."

"Oh, so now we have Lieutenant Appleby to blame for this indiscretion, if indeed what this brat says is true. Is that right, Sergeant?"

Hardesty looked straight ahead. He had said all he was going to say about this matter to this chickenshit.

It dawned on Major Burk that he'd worked himself into a ticklish situation. And Burk was a very politically correct person. Lieutenant Appleby, unfortunately, was the most popular officer under Burk's command, and Sergeant Hardesty was a favorite with the men, as well as with the general. But as so often happened with Major Burk, lady-luck helped him out. He'd read that the most prized possession of a Nazi Hitler Youth was a dagger inscribed in German: "Blüt und Ehre" (Blood and Honor). The dagger was awarded following the successful completion of a "Mutprobe" (test of courage).

As Major Burk carefully scrutinized Joe, he noticed a telltale bulge in Joe's pocket. Major Burk wondered? Then sarcastically he asked, "Hardesty, did you ever search this kid for some kind of identity?"

"No."

Catching Little Joe by surprise, Major Burk grabbed the boy and spun him around until he grasped him in a bear-hug. Inserting his right hand into Joe's pocket, Major Burk withdrew a dagger from an inside sheath. Releasing Joe from his grasp and without looking at the dagger, Major Burk handed the weapon to Sergeant Hardesty. "I can predict what it says on that knife, Sergeant. It says: 'Blüt und Ehre.' Right!" Triumphantly Burk proclaimed, "It's the knife of the Hitler Youth."

Rolling the dagger in his hand, Hardesty looked sorrowfully at an ashen-faced little Joe. "Is that right? Are you a Hitler Youth?"

Crying, Little Joe pleaded, "Honest I ain't. I found it."

"Sergeant Hardesty, I'm going to have to take this kid to S2 for interrogation."

Grabbing Joe by a hand and jerking him toward his waiting jeep, Hardesty said, "First, I'm taking the kid and his story to General Clay. I've been ordered to report to him anyway. If you want to have me court-martialed, Major, I'll be at the General's headquarters." Sergeant Hardesty gunned the jeep as he burned rubber heading for Heerlen and the Secondary Technical School.

NICOLINE KNEW BEP RIEKSEN only as her lover. She had no inkling he was Rieksen of the Resistance. She thought he had been involved in social work with the coal miners before the German occupation and was a close friend of her late husband. Her abduction had occurred while she was returning home from shopping. Gagged, blindfolded and stuffed into the trunk of a car, she had thought she was going to be raped and possibly murdered. She'd read about such things.

Upon awaking in a drug-like state, she slowly oriented herself as to what had happened. She heard no sound other than her own slow breathing, which increased rapidly as she began remembering details of the kidnapping. She suffered only a mild headache and a few bruises from having resisted her captors. Perhaps it was a dream, a nightmare. Finally she sat up on a torn leather couch. Dim light entered the room from a small translucent window over the door. Perhaps it was a transom for ventilation. She could not tell if it were daylight or electric light. She had no idea of the time. The room had an antiseptic smell, like in a hospital, but it was comfortably warm considering the chilly weather. Other than the ancient leather couch, the only furnishings were a dilapidated rocking chair and a straight-back chair shoved under a small writing desk, something like tourists find in cheap hotels.

Then she heard someone coming down a corridor toward her. The steps seemed to resonate as if made upon terrazzo flooring. Fearfully she waited.

A gentle knock followed the turning of a key in the door. A German officer walked in. The gold braid of the epaulet offset his immaculate grey uniform. Breeches, polished jackboots, a Sam Browne belt, German war-eagles stitched to the breast pockets, organizational patches on the collars of the blouse, and an iron cross around his neck, all bore witness to the exalted distinction of the wearer.

Nicoline rose to face the formidable-appearing officer.

A tanned face suggested he was a field officer as compared to a staff officer. Streaks of grey in his hair implied middle age. Red hair and blue eyes suggested a Nordic origin. His physical bearing pointed to self-discipline. Softly in English he lectured her: "Mrs. Lindemann, I am General Kraus. It was not my idea that you were kidnapped and brought to my headquarters. I do not fight terror with terror, which may surprise you for a Waffen SS officer. I am a battlefield general; I do not ask for quarter nor do I give it. But I don't wage war against women and children as is being done by the Allies in their air-war of extermination against German cities."

Nicoline was transfixed. Most of Holland remained in German hands. Throughout the German occupation she'd nearly succumbed to Goebbel's propaganda about Nordic racial superiority until she'd fallen in love with Bep and adopted his anti-Nazi views. In their appealing uniforms with their war-eagle emblems, iron crosses and high-visored military hats, she had considered the German army officers very attractive. And though she had not told Bep, she felt sorry for all the Dutch girls who were now being rounded up by the Resistance in the liberated parts of Holland and having their heads shaved, and sometimes worse, all because they had befriended German soldiers.

"Why do you want me, General Kraus?" Nicoline asked.

General Kraus looked puzzled. "It is not I, it is the Gestapo."

"I haven't done anything against Germany," said Nicoline.

"Do you know a Bep Rieksen?" asked Kraus.

"Yes. He's my friend," said Nicoline openly.

"Do you know what he does?"

"He's a social worker."

"You do not know of his activities in the Resistance?"

"What are you talking about?"

Nicoline was so genuine in her answers that General Kraus believed her. "Listen, Mrs. Lindemann, I'm not supposed to be your interrogator. The Gestapo will do that. Your friend is thought to be a leader in the Resistance. The Gestapo kidnaped you as a hostage. This Rieksen will be informed of your circumstances."

"Resistance leader?"

You do not know that your government in London has praised your friend over the BBC?

"No."

Too many emotions were confusing Nicoline, and she felt faint. General Kraus saw unabashed bafflement in her face and helped her to the couch. "Lady, I do not have the power to free you, but I do have the power to keep you in my custody and see that you remain unharmed. Perhaps all will end well for you." As kindly as he could make his voice, he said, "Persevere, Mrs. Lindemann."

TWO OF HIS AIDES AWAITED General Kraus in his office when he returned from his interview with Mrs. Lindemann. He had only commandeered one small section of the hospital for his headquarters. His SS "Lightning" Panzer Division was bivouacked in the woods. His reserve division was for counterattacking any early successes the Americans might achieve at Puffendorf, when and if they should attack.

"Be at ease," General Kraus told his aides as he sat at his desk. Major Krugger and Captain Snodgrass likewise found chairs. Lighting a cigarette General Kraus said, "Help me, gentleman, to brainstorm and ponder our predicament."

Major Krugger and Captain Snodgrass also helped fill the room with cigarette smoke as they patiently waited upon their general to establish the line of thought. After some minutes with a furrowed brow, General Kraus said, "First, consider the little lady down the hall. Why did her kidnappers bring her to my headquarters?"

"Her abductors said the Gestapo and the SS were one in the same. They were Dutch collaborators and seemed in a hurry to have her off their hands," answered Captain Snodgrass.

"You then notified the Gestapo in Amsterdam," General Kraus stated.

"Yes," replied Captain Snodgrass, his voice somewhat unsteady.

"I have no problem with that. In my absence you did what you had to do, Captain. Let me tell you something. I'm impressed by that little lady; and we do not sanction the methods of the Gestapo. They may question her, Captain; but they are not to lay a hand on or remove her from these premises. You see to that, Captain Snodgrass."

"Yes, sir."

More smoking and again a furrowed brow. At last, in a measured voice, General Kraus said, "What's going on with the 'Hammer' Division, Bartholomaus, and Dietrich? Any ideas, gentlemen?"

For the first time Major Krugger spoke: "It's a case of the old Prussians against us in the SS, General Kraus. It's Stein and Bartholomaus making a last ditch stand. Himmler probably sent Dietrich to put an end to their sway in the Wehrmacht."

"Have you considered, Major Krugger, only such a limited role for the querulous panzer leader? I think there's more."

"May I ask, sir," responded Major Krugger, "what the General has in mind?"

"What about another 'Blitz' in the West? I hear Manteuffel is also on the way to join us."

"God in Heaven, General! Wouldn't that open the floodgates for the Tartar swine?"

"May I remind you, Major Krugger, in the SS we never second guess the Führer."

MUCH LATER LYING IN BED General Kraus continued to muse about the lady who inadvertently had become his captive. Inexplicably, he felt warmly and concernedly about her. The image of his two young, motherless children and his poor wife who had died of tuberculosis appeared in his mind. Because of his military career, he had married late. His last thought before going to sleep was: "I must get to know this Mrs. Lindemann."

CHAPTER 4

DURING THE EARLY EVENING hours the Hitler Youth, Arnd, learned of "Operation Trojan Horse" and the trap set for Major Dietrich's battle group. Immediately Arnd set off for the German lines on a borrowed bicycle. At the moment Arnd had no way to contact Samson, and Mr. Lintens, now petrified after being publicly accused of being a Nazi collaborator, was incapable of decisive action.

During his stay at Mr. Lintens' home, Arnd had familiarized himself with the city of Heerlen, and with the help of a map had studied the route from Germany that Samson had followed when they'd made their way through the American lines. Now, Arnd knew he possessed vital information. Even though it was dark and fog had moved in, he had to take whatever risks were necessary to warn Major Dietrich.

Very soon Arnd discovered that the road to Puffendorf was no problem to find. All he had to do was backtrack along the flow of American armored vehicles. If Arnd had needed any confirmation of what he'd learned, this jam of military traffic proved its veracity. As he biked past the pillboxes and dragons teeth of the 'West Wall,' he knew he was in American occupied Germany and under curfew restrictions. The MPs he'd seen guiding the tanks from their jeeps and standing at most road crossings would shoot him on sight.

His map studies proved indispensable. Arnd found a road with a pittance of traffic and free of MPs. But the distance he'd come and the dodges he'd executed to evade the MPs left him exhausted and out of breath; yet he had to keep pedaling as he cursed the swine Americans. Once he reached the front lines, getting past the American sentries and safely into the hands of his countrymen would be no easy matter either. He was laboriously pumping the bicycle when he was suddenly sideswiped by a speeding jeep.

"Take the flashlight and see what I hit, Joe," a deep voice said.

Blinded by the light, Arnd felt the bicycle being removed from on top of him and heard a child's voice ask in broken German if he was hurt. Abruptly the light was doused. As he picked himself up, he faced the outlines of two figures standing next to him. One looked to be a boy and the other a large American soldier. Though he puzzled about the French accent of the child's voice, Arnd had been trained for such encounters. He played dumb.

After brushing himself and feeling certain he wasn't hurt, he suddenly grabbed the bicycle from the boy and mounted it. But the soldier caught a handlebar before Arnd could take off.

"Give me the flashlight, Joe," the soldier said.... "Look what we have here! A blond-haired, blue-eyed Hitler baby.... You don't look like you're much hurt, baby Kraut. What's the matter? Couldn't you understand Joe's German?"

Arnd stared at his feet.

"Maybe we'd just better take you to an aid station and see if you really did get hurt. It's pretty nippy weather to be wearing just shorts and a flimsy shirt. Your knees are bleeding and you do look pretty messed up, kid."

As the soldier began to tug on the bicycle, Arnd suddenly screamed in German, "Leave me alone, pig!" He yanked the bike free and pumped away into the dark with the boy trying to catch him.

"Let him go!" called the soldier to the boy.

Shortly, Arnd left the two in the darkness.

A HAZY MOON and the glow from the Milky Way seemed to part the ground fog. Still, Arnd could barely see his way. As he gathered speed on the flat, blacktop road, grotesque ruins of homes and factories flashed past like dark silhouettes in a shooting gallery. At last, completely exhausted, he could not avoid the collision of his bicycle into the rear of an iron behemoth, an M-36 tank destroyer. It blocked the road. He rolled into the ditch and lay as still as a dead man.

"Halt! Give the password," a voice squeaked.

Arnd did not answer; but his eyes detected motion. Slowly a figure rose from out of a nearby foxhole and soon loomed over him. Simultaneously Arnd was blinded by a light and struck a jolting kick. He grunted slightly and coiled into a ball, his hand clasping his Hitler Youth dagger. Through squinting eyes he watched the soldier bend over him. Suddenly the soldier cried in pain as Arnd's two feet struck the soldier's groin toppling him over backwards. Quickly Arnd plunged into the curtain of darkness toward what he believed to be the German lines. But the American soldier recovered fast and with an automatic weapon sprayed the night in the direction of Arnd's departure—and not without effect. A bullet grazed Arnd knocking him to the ground.

A jabber of voices erupted from the vicinity of the tank destroyer. Then a terrified voice croaked, "I saw him—Crofton, Sweeney. I saw him with my own eyes. It was that Nazi werewolf that S2 warned us about—that Hitler Youth bastard with the yellow hair and blue eyes. He tried to slit my throat with his dagger."

"Crazy Dick's gone off his rocker, Lieutenant. He says he was shooting at a werewolf."

"Sweeney. I've had all I can stand of 'Crazy Dick.' Take him back to the aid station, and get back up here—pronto. I'll deal with that 'nut' later."

As THE AMIS (AMERICANS) made no further conversations or movement toward him, Arnd rolled on his side and ripped off a piece of his shirt which, with the help of his teeth, he wound around his bleeding arm. Rising, he stumbled in the direction of the German lines. Before long, a guttural voice demanded that he halt to be recognized. In German Arnd rattled off the oath of the Hitler Youth:

> *I promise in the Hitler Youth to do my duty*
> *at all times in love and faithfulness*
> *to help the Führer—so help me God.*

"I heard the shooting. God in Heaven! How is a Hitler Youth coming from the Americans?" A light quickly revealed the bedraggled and wounded Arnd. "You must be taken to the aid station."

Arnd protested: "I'm a German agent. I must quickly see your Kampfgrüppe Führer. Tell him it is Arnd, and he comes from the American lines."

"God in Heaven. You must be the Hitler Youth praised by Goebbels! Come, I'll take you at once to our leader. His tent is only a few meters from here."

Shortly a Tiger tank displaying a kind of blue radiance appeared, its mighty Mabob engine purring, warming in the early hours for the move back to the "West Wall." Following a "Heil Hitler" greeting, Arnd spoke softly and calmly as he warned a black uniformed Major Dietrich about the trap.

Stroking his lips reflectively and seriously listening to Arnd, Major Dietrich finally said, "My orders from Field Marshal Stein are to proceed and reoccupy the 'West Wall' which the Americans have evacuated."

"If you move forward Major Dietrich, you will find not a deserted 'West Wall,' but one bristling with American soldiers with their antitank weapons. The American air force is also ready to catch you out in the open at the break of dawn."

"Arnd, my patrols and reconnaissance units have reported a withdrawal of American units. Intelligence has confirmed it."

Smiling, Arnd said, "Mein Herr Major Dietrich. It is all part of the big trick. The 'West Wall' is supposed to become your 'Trojan Horse.' Check again before you move your tanks from their concealment. The American Combat Command 'A' lies in wait for you. It was not a ghost which shot me!"

One of Major Dietrich's adjutants stepped forward and whispered, "I believe we ought to get medical care for this boy." Turning to Arnd he asked, "How do you feel?"

Again smiling, Arnd answered in American slang: "Okie-dokie." Then back to German. "Perhaps an aid man may bandage my arm. . . . I must soon return to my post."

The adjutant bowed to Arnd, "You are an honor to the Fatherland. The Hitler Youth must be praised for producing the likes of you. However, it is my duty to inform you, young man, that the one whom you call Major has since been promoted to Brigadier General by our Führer."

Arnd never missed a beat. Bowing and clicking his heels sharply, he said, "I am honored to serve SS Brigadeführer Hans Otto Dietrich."

Removing his own Iron Cross from his shirt collar and pinning it on Arnd, General Dietrich said, "Arnd, consider this a battlefield award. Our Führer, Adolf Hitler, will personally hear from me about what you have done for the Fatherland on this night, I swear."

Blushing, Arnd removed the Iron Cross and looked at it proudly. Then he handed it back to General Dietrich. "Save it for me, General Dietrich. I must return to Heerlen." Anticipating a negative reaction, he raised his hand. "I have my assignment, General. Please have someone escort me beyond your lines; I'm like a dog, I can find my own way back."

Stunned, General Dietrich and his adjutant stood speechless. Finally, General Dietrich said, "We're not dealing with a mere child here, Alfons. See after his needs." Turning to Arnd, "If either you or I don't soon go to Valhalla, I should like to meet you again sometime."

Both then clicked their heels, bowed to the other and executed snappy "Heil Hitler" salutes.

MASTER SERGEANT HAP HARDESTY found Brigadier General Brighton D. Clay, his mentor and friend, looking amused at Joe while once again Hap retold the saga of Please-Joe to a commanding officer. From the pain showing on Joe's face, it was an ordeal for him. Standing next to Hap before General Clay's desk, Joe fidgeted and seemed on the brink of panic.

"Hold it," General Clay said to Hap. Turning to Joe, he said, "Hey, Little Joe. Look me in the eyes. Don't look so damn scared. No matter what the truth is in your case, I don't hurt children. We'll work out something good for you that you'll like. Relax. You'll find I can be a good friend." Looking at Hap he urged the Sergeant to continue.

Hap never left anything out that he could remember, including Major Burk's discovery of the Hitler Youth dagger and Major Burk's threat to bring court-martial proceedings against him.

General Clay rose gradually from the chair behind his desk. He walked to an upholstered couch in the room and motioned Joe to approach him. "Would you mind, Little Joe, sitting on this couch with me and talking over your problem?"

The minute General Clay began speaking, Joe felt at ease. He quickly regained his composure and cockiness. "Sure," he answered, plopping himself down on the couch beside the general.

"You helped a Sergeant Sullivan in a supply outfit. Is that right?"

"Yeah."

"Was it in Belgium?"

"Yeah."

"Could the supplies you have in mind be food supplies?"

"Of course, General Clay."

"Not clothing or gasoline or something else—just food?"

His eyes brightening, Joe said, "Yeah."

"Was the name of the Belgium city, Charleroi? And were there pyramids of food boxes, covered with tarpaulins, and stacked for blocks upon blocks?" General Clay cast a sweeping motion with his arm.

"Yes. German prisoners of war unloaded the freight trains that brought the food boxes from Antwerp and loaded other trains with the food boxes."

"Then your supply outfit, Little Joe, had to be the 98th Greyhounds," said General Clay almost triumphantly. "And the hundreds of German POWs working at that railhead could explain how you happened to find a Hitler Youth dagger.... Why didn't you tell this to Sergeant Hardesty?"

With a straight-face, Joe said, "Sergeant Hardesty and Lieutenant Appleby only wanted to know the name of my outfit. And

I couldn't remember it. And I still can't remember that it was what you said."

"The 98th Greyhounds."

"Yeah."

"But you do know the location was Charleroi, Belgium?"

"Yes."

"Jack," General Clay called to his operations officer who was entering the room. "Get on the phone tomorrow and see if you can locate a Sergeant Sullivan with the 98th Greyhounds. Some of them are presently stationed in Liege. Right now, go find Voss and tell him I must see him immediately. He's somewhere in the building. Hurry! We have to get to the dance."

Returning to the leather chair behind his desk, the General began, "Little Joe, Hap, it may take some time to check this out...." He paused and scratched his head. "Little Joe, I want to help you all I can. That's a promise. For the time being, I think I'm going to place you with a Dutch foster family. You can see Hap every day if you fellows want to get together.

Philip Vossmaar entered and saluted.

"Voss, I've got a problem for you. You see that little 'bugger' standing next to Sergeant Hardesty." Clay laughed and shook a finger at Joe. "He needs a temporary lodging in the vicinity. As I understand it, that's your specialty, Voss—locating sanctuaries for displaced folks."

Philip Vossmaar smiled good-naturedly as he scanned Joe. "Sure. The boy could stay with the parents of my friend Karel Konijn. They live in this same block."

"Good. Take care of Little Joe.... Now, I have to get on some other matters.... Oh, I almost forgot. I wouldn't worry, Hap, about Major Burk's court-martial. I doubt if we ever hear anything about it. If we do, it will be taken care of without any bother to you."

Susan Montgomery knew that relationships with soldiers during wartime were not like relationships during peacetime. There was the ever present factor of uncertainty. Uncertainty about a whole range of subjects, not the least of which was availability. As a consequence, the whole game of girl-meets-boy had to be put in high gear. Of course, Susan believed she could have any man she really wanted, and at twenty-five she was ready to make her *pick*; and in Lieutenant Tom Appleby, Susan saw her *pick*.

As she and Sally waited for Jimmy Malloti to come and drive them to the Casino, she decided that a lot of the usual preliminaries would have to be waived. She would have to take a chance on boldness not intimidating Tom. "Wow," she exclaimed. She hadn't met the guy yet and was already fantasizing a first name basis. Watching Sally primp for the occasion, she at last decided not to be too rushy.

In their comfortable hotel room, Susan lowered herself into a chair, drawing on her cigarette while she watched Sally put on brown, leather-soled "dancing shoes." Susan considered her co-hostess an adult Shirley Temple: blond curls, dimples and outstanding dancing ability. One exception, the real child movie star was much brighter. Hearing the unmistakable V-for-victory-honk: da, da, da—daaaaaaaa—of General Clay's jeep, she rose. "Come on you, curly-headed, 'broad'; get your ass in gear. There are men waiting to be . . . had."

Minutes later, as the two girls jumped into the jeep, Sally in the back and Susan next to Jimmy, Sally quipped, "Cripes, Susan. You're getting to be almost as vulgar as me."

After he shifted into high, Jimmy let his hand fall on Susan's thigh.

Susan's reaction was a quick slap to the face of the dark hoodlum.

Sally said, "Hey, what's with you guys?"

"Heck, my hand slipped off the gearshift, and Susan can't take a joke."

"I can take a joke, baby, but only a 'pass' from the right guy."

Knowing General Clay's fondness for Susan, Malloti bit his lip and stepped on the gas.

Soon all was forgiven and forgotten as the sound of Glenn Miller's music reached their ears. Both girls' feet began moving to the rhythm as they loved jitterbugging. After the jeep had stopped, Susan thanked Jimmy for the lift. "I'm sorry about my flare-up, Jimmy, but I have so many things on my mind."

THE CARPETS HAD BEEN ROLLED UP, the gaming tables pushed aside and a bandstand built. The Casino was decked out in red, white and blue bunting to honor the American liberators. The musicians in their army uniforms, with a few informally dressed Dutch musicians among them, swayed with the beat they were producing. Neatly clothed Dutch girls in rippling skirts and American army officers in dress uniforms bobbed to the music. If the front lines were only a few miles away and the girls spoke only broken English, who cared? It was almost like Saturday night in hometown, USA. Booze and barkeeps, food and waiters stood ready in the back of the Casino. A cluster of various sized tables with wooden chairs ringed the large dance floor. Colored lights were turned low. The place was a jumping.

At one small table near the entrance Major Richard C. Burk III sat alone brooding over the unfortunate turn of events in his life. Sure, the festivities were not lost upon him. With the help of a gin and tonic he lamented his recent defeats: No sand table lecture before brass from SHAEF, no heading up Combat Command "B," no consultation about the pullback or this stupid dance, problems with some of his personnel and affronts by division staff officers. But Major Burk never wallowed in self-pity for long. As the expression has it, he held his cards close and waited.

He didn't have long to wait. She landed unceremoniously in his lap as she tripped over his outstretched legs. What might have been a most satisfactory accident from Major Burk's perspective, Major Jack Collins quickly nullified. Appearing out of nowhere, he grabbed the girl by an arm and pulled her off Major Burk's lap, whisking her away in the direction of General Clay's table near the dance floor. Wistfully she turned and took one long look at Major Burk before confronting the general and the guests seated at his table.

Another girl trailing behind stopped, smiled and said, "Sorry, Major, but you know how it is when you're in a rush. Maybe we'll meet out on the dance floor if you know how to jitterbug." Then she followed the others toward the general's table.

Coming to his senses, Major Burk rose and followed until he saw General Clay look disapprovingly at him. Quickly he dropped into the first vacant chair he could find. On closer scrutiny Major Burk could hardly believe his eyes. Seated next to General Clay was Lieutenant Appleby. He was surprised because he knew Tom was not a carouser and doubted if he even knew how to dance. Certainly he was not reputed to be a ladies' man. That he was seated at the general's table, in itself, galled Major Burk.

Also at the table was a young appearing captain who Major Burk had never seen before. He was embracing the first girl like she was some relative. For the first time it struck him that the two girls were not Dutch. He saw they were dressed in short-skirted Red Cross outfits worn by doughnut girls. "Holy Mackerel," it at last registered on his alcohol benumbed brain: Those two girls were both exceptionally good looking, each in her own way, and they were undoubtedly Americans. The one who had landed in his lap reminded him of Milton Caniff's "Dragon Lady." Dark and voluptuous! The other girl would satisfy as the dumb-blond type.

Focusing on the Dragon Lady, he was drawn to her peridot eyes, coal black hair extending down her back and resting on her shoulders. She had high cheek bones and an infectious smile that exposed bright white teeth. A slightly pointed chin tilted up in good humor; and then his eyes were diverted to slender, seductive fingers on surprisingly long arms leading his glance to her equally long legs. Observing her movement, he felt her effervescence. From his vantage point, it appeared she wore no makeup, no rings, nor earrings, necklaces or bracelets. She was wise not to do so, he thought. In her case such adornments could only have distracted from her natural mystique..

On the other hand, her blond companion had carefully highlighted her features. Mascara lined her round eyes. Powder and rouge tinted her face. Red lipstick emphasized her sensuous lips. Thick enlarged glasses added to her bouffant-blond good-looks, and an assortment of bracelets encircled her wrists. Both girls were slim, tall and well stacked. Major Burk considered them both dynamite, but he preferred the Dragon Lady.

Soon, to his envy, Major Burk saw Tom get up, with the Dragon Lady in tow, and take to the dance floor. The band was playing Glenn Miller's bouncy "Pennsylvania 6550." As the two joined the other dancers he could hardly believe Tom was such an expert dancer. His big Company "D" Commander and this mystery woman moved among the other hoofers like two bobbing corks on a fishing pond, weaving in and out of the mob of bouncing couples. They were oblivious of the other dancers and were obviously enjoying each other.

Dragon Lady had to have a real name. Major Burk decided to find out what it was. He might as well raise a few eyebrows as easily as Tom, for he was a pretty nifty dancer himself—and cuttin'-in was a time-honored American tradition.

As soon as he stepped on the dance floor, though, he found himself in the arms of the Dragon Lady's blond companion. With a wink of her eye she brazenly embraced him and snuggled up close. The band was now playing "Moonlight Serenade." A young Dutch musician took the mike and gave a Johnny Desmond rendition of the number. This was not the way he'd intended to meet the Dragon Lady, but it might just workout better this way; so he clutched the blond as he led them near Tom and his partner.

When the Dutch vocalist concluded Glenn Miller's famous theme song and the dancers began returning to their tables, Dick Burk called out, "Hey, Tom. I had no idea you were such a good hoofer?"

Thus confronted by his battalion commanding officer, Tom Appleby smiled in recognition.

The two girls exchanged understanding looks. Then the blond said, "Major, I think you're a party crasher. But that's okay by me. My name is just plain, Sally Brown. This is Susan Lavet Montgomery, and it appears you already know Lieutenant Tom Appleby. "

"I'm Dick Burk, and I'm very happy to meet you girls," Major Burk said gallantly.

Susan suggested, "Rather than stand around out here, let's get back to our drinks. Why don't you join us, Major Burk? I'm sure it will be all right with General Clay."

The invitation was what Dick Burk had hoped for, but as they approached the general's table, Burk saw Jack Collins' face turn livid; whereupon, Burk half expected the explosive operations officer to reproachfully sound off. But General Clay lay a hand on Collins. "Be seated, Dick. First, I'd like to introduce you to Captain Don Montgomery, Susan's brother. Captain Montgomery is Ike's right-hand man at SHAFF. He'll be observing your briefing at the sand table and reporting back to Ike."

A flurry of thoughts entered Major Burk's mind. Just when he thought "Operation Queen" was dead, the general's statement would appear to suggest such was not the case. Perhaps the opportunity to make a name for himself was still viable.

Offering his hand, the young captain stood, saying, "General Clay gives me too much credit. I'm really just an errand boy for Ike."

"That reminds me," said General Clay. "I think it's about time for your announcement, Don." Rising from the table, the lean one-star general walked to the bandstand and grabbed the microphone. In a resolute Midwestern twang the general introduced Captain Montgomery and then ordered both Captain Montgomery and Lieutenant Appleby to come front and center. Next he ushered Captain Montgomery to the mike and stepped back beaming like a father at his son's high school graduation.

The slightly built, delicate featured captain did as he was instructed. Dark-haired like his sister, his bloodshot, baggy eyes suggested to Burk either a hard-working officer or a rich playboy. From the man's serious expression, he figured the former was the more likely.

In a high pitched, unsteady voice the captain said, "At the request of General Eisenhower, it is my pleasure to declare the promotion of Lieutenant Tom Appleby to the rank of Captain, and, also, to award him the Distinguished Service Cross. . . ."

Susan Montgomery let out a scream of delight when her brother pinned the DSC on Captain Appleby, bringing a roar from the happy crowd and a crimson face to Tom. Never had Dick Burk felt so disgusted. He thought he might puke on the spot. He hurriedly excused himself from those who remained seated at the table and left the Casino.

Major Burk's hasty departure was not lost by a pair of shifty eyes standing in the shadows at the back of the ballroom. Jimmy Malloti smiled in satisfaction.

FIELD MARSHAL MANFRED STEIN at Army Group "C" headquarters did not know what to make of the report he'd just received from Puffendorf. Apparently Dietrich, in disobedience to his orders, was holding fast and not advancing his battle group to reoccupy the "West Wall." True, it was inexplicable behavior on the part of the Americans. But all reliable intelligence reports indicated that this indeed was just what General Clay had done with his "Fighting" 15th Armored Division. He had pulled his division back into Holland, vacating that part of the "West Wall," which the 15th had overrun following the German collapse in France. Stein knew many British generals considered American generals to be dumb about strategy. Perhaps they were right. Of course, that wouldn't explain Dietrich's disobedience. Even though Dietrich was of the Waffen-SS, he knew better than to disobey a direct order from a commanding officer and Field Marshal of the Wehrmacht.

Shortly an aide-de-camp announced the arrival of General Bartholomaus. The two Prussians greeted one another with a shake of hands. "Damn. What's going on at Puffendorf? Why didn't Dietrich obey my orders?" asked the infuriated Field Marshal.

Removing his monocle and smiling weakly at his perturbed commanding officer, Gerd Bartholomaus responded, "Sorry to come running to you again, Manfred—and so soon—but this time the Americans appear to have broken our security."

Apparently playing for time and acting as if he were here for an extended stay, Gerd Bartholomaus leisurely removed his grey field coat, neatly folding it over a handy oak chair, and deliberately removed his parade cap, placing it in an adjoining chair. Manfred Stein observed these actions of his elderly compatriot with less than enthusiasm. Now was not the time for renewing old friendships.

Field Marshal Manfred Stein was of the old Prussian General Staff. Of late, his star seemed to have waned with the rise of the SS with Hitler—but so too had the military fortunes of the Reich.

Adjusting the monocle in his one good eye and glancing at the map table before sitting, Gerd Bartholomaus' said, "It turns out, Manfred, that General Clay's 'West Wall' was a 'Trojan Horse' setup for us." Moving his hand to forestall an interruption, Bartholomaus went on, "We have a mole in our security, Manfred. I know it would look good with Hitler to have the entire 'West Wall' once again in German hands. But Hans Dietrich was right this time; and he almost got burned."

By now Manfred Stein knew that the two were in for an extended session, and he realized the necessity of Gerd's taking his time. His only interruption of the old soldier's monologue was to offer Gerd a cigarette. Manfred leaned back in his upholstered chair to hear the rest of the story.

After Gerd lit his cigarette and took a few puffs, he said, "For the history books, Manfred, remember this name. The name is 'Arnd.' Yes, it is that Hitler Youth that Goebbels has boasted about over the radio. According to Hans Dietrich, this knabe was captured by the Americans, but escaped from them. Shot and wounded, the fourteen-year-old made his way through the front lines to warn Hans that the 'West Wall' had become a Trojan Horse for us. Afterwards the knabe vanished into the night supposedly to return to Holland. We have no idea of the boy's source of information. He would not reveal this even to Dietrich. The boy did say he was on a mission in Holland for Skorzeny. What do you think of that Herr Generalfeldmarshal?"

Sitting up abruptly, Manfred said, "That's a very remarkable boy, if it's true, even for a Hitler Youth. But I'm more intrigued by the mention of Skorzeny. The last time I heard about Skorzeny, he'd rescued Mussolini from his captors. What in the hell is Skorzeny doing here? Something must be up, Gerd. I've learned that Manteuffel's entire army is on the move from the East to the West. Skorzeny and Arnd? Maybe they're after big name hostages like Eisenhower or Churchill, but why would Manteuffel be coming West unless a major military operation has been planned? Whatever it is we're still being kept in the dark."

"I suppose you know Hitler made Hans Dietrich a general," said Gerd ominously.

"Ja. But you remain in command of the 'Hammer' Division. I've heard nothing to the contrary. Please remember, Gerd, your forces far outnumber and are more significant than Dietrich's relatively small battle group. His responsibility is to make breakthroughs or to counterattack penetrations by the enemy. Cooperate with him. But you still have the responsibility for holding on at Puffendorf, Gerd. You didn't get the sobriquet 'Old Badger' for nothing; and don't forget, you have General Kraus backing you up with the 'Lightning' Division."

"Where does General Rheinhardt fit into this equation?"

"As long as I'm the Group Commander, I'll take care of Rheinhardt. You take care of General Clay and his 'Fighting' 15th Armored Division. . . . But it appears that skinny dummkopf, General Clay, nearly caught us with our pants down. Or was it Rieksen and his Dutch Resistance that nearly did us in? Unfortunately, it looks like I will have to call on the Gestapo to find out what happened to our intelligence. But that's not your problem, Gerd. What I want you to do is get back to Puffendorf. I don't believe we have long to wait before the Americans attack."

ABOUT THE TIME Brigadier General Bartholomaus departed from Field Marshal Stein's group headquarters, newly commissioned SS Brigadier General Hans Otto Dietrich was arriving at III Panzer Corps Headquarters to report to SS Lieutenant General Franz Rheinhardt.

General Rheinhardt was a little man. Although he wore all the paraphernalia of a high ranking Waffen-SS officer, he appeared about as threatening as a clerk in a small shop. After "Heil Hitler" exchanges, the pallid faced, thin lipped corps commander extended a limp hand to his underling. A dour appearing adjutant brought the two generals coffee and quickly departed. Franz Rheinhardt began, "I must congratulate you on your long deserved promotion, Hans. Knowing the fond affection the Führer has had for you, I could never understand why you were so often passed over."

"Thank you, Franz. I believe until now the Führer had special assignments for me which did not require high rank."

As General Rheinhardt lay his wire-rimmed glasses on a table, he asked, "Where is Gerd?"

Smiling and bowing, his right index finger touching his lips, Dietrich said, "You should know, Franz, that blood is thicker than water."

Not pleased, General Rheinhardt answered, "One day soon we're going to have to remove those two Prussians. I understand it is only days before Hitler ousts the 'Fat-One' (Hermann Goering) and names Himmler, Reichsführer."

"Why even put up with them now?"

"You, better than I, know about the coming Ardennes Offensive. We still need the Prussians to protect our back door. . . . Enough of that talk for now. Why didn't you obey Field Marshal Stein's order to take back the 'West Wall?'"

At length Hans recounted the saga of Arnd and his revelation of the "West Wall" being a Trojan Horse. Lugubriously Dietrich added, "General Clay's ambush was probably planned by Rieksen. I'm sure the Gestapo will have its revenge, though; for I understand we now have Rieksen's mistress as a hostage."

"You know the story on that, don't you, Hans?"

"What do you mean?"

"The Dutch collaborators who kidnaped the women mistakenly turned her over to Fritz's people at the 'Lightning' Division. Now Fritz says he doesn't know the whereabouts of the women."

"What happened to her?"

"We're puzzled. The Gestapo even has Fritz under surveillance. They assured me they'll soon kill or capture Rieksen, but I hope he's captured alive so we can discover the traitor among us."

"What is your opinion, Hans? Now that you didn't fall for General Clay's trap. Will Clay return to 'Operation Queen' or will the American attack come elsewhere?"

Touching his lips with his finger Hans Dietrich said, "'Operation Queen' will now proceed as planned."

"If you are so certain about that, have you read the intelligence report on a Lieutenant Tom Appleby, supposedly the Americans foremost tank commander? He probably will lead the attack on Puffendorf," said Franz.

In a rare burst of laughter Hans Dietrich had trouble stifling his outburst. "Mein Herr General," he said familiarly, "I must tell you something funny. I was so outraged about being duped by General Clay that I had to have my own immediate little revenge. On my field telephone I called the Stuka pilot, whom the Amis call 'Bed-Check Charlie.' As you know, the Luftwaffe drops a few bombs every night. I directed him to the Casino in Heerlen where he could lay his egg on General Clay. Unfortunately, a Mosquito 'nightfighter' shot him down."

"I have trouble seeing any humor in that, Hans."

"Ah yes. Well, the pilot returned unhurt to our lines. But before the Mosquito got him, he dropped a parachute flare containing a message from me to 'Daredevil-6,' Captain Appleby's radio number. I told him we had a warm welcome awaiting him when he led his forces in 'Operation Queen.' Incidentally, Lieutenant Appleby is now 'Captain' Appleby."

General Rheinhardt was not pleased. "With your painted tank and this new nonsense, Hans, you're too theatrical. The Americans will surely attempt to trick you again, and I fear your vanity may get you killed. No, Hans, I don't like your message to Captain Appleby. And be reminded, your grounding is a direct order from the Führer. Maybe another officer could command your tank? The Fatherland needs you alive not only for Puffendorf, but to lead this coming Ardennes offensive. . . . If anything happens to you at Puffendorf, Manteuffel will have my hide, to say nothing of the Führer."

ON PASSES INTO HEERLEN, following their clearing the mine field, corporals Steve "VD" Johnson and Dale Jenks, along with their friend, John C. Smith, easily found Heerlen's most popular gathering place, The Beer Garden. It was a democratic hangout. American brass and enlisted men commingled with Dutch civilians. At a small table near the entrance, Steve and John attempted to resume their philosophical discussions, but Dale Jenks cut them short.

"Son-of-a-b....!" said Dale, whose dark eyes had lit up. In a conspiratorial whisper he said, "Don't look yet, but our famous company commander just sat down with a most luscious looking brunette. They're sitting near the entrance."

For the next half hour, ogling Tom Appleby's female companion became the preoccupation of the corporals as philosophy gave way to instinct. Immediately they spotted the new railroad bars on Tom's shoulders. Next they observed that, contrary to rumors, their popular company commander behaved more like a lover-boy than a wallflower. If petting was a criterion, their cuddling commanding officer qualified. Confirming the sobriety of their CO, the corporals noted Captain Appleby drank a straight fruit drink while his female friend spiked her's from a purple flask. Captain Appleby appeared to grin approvingly.

At that exact moment the air-raid alarm sounded. Someone said, "Oh, it's just 'Bed-check Charlie.'" The warning went unheeded. Far off an explosion sounded, and briefly the lights went out. As they flickered back on the chatter of voices resumed. But Captain Appleby was gone! His brunette sat alone at her table. Moving quickly, Dale Jenks said, "So long to philosophy; I'll see you guys later."

Approaching Susan Montgomery, Dale introduced himself, "Hi, I'm Dale Jenks from California. May I get you a drink? .... I see my company commander must have been called away, or else why would he abandon someone so lovely as you?"

The tall, dark and handsome corporal had a line Susan was used to. Ordinarily she would have enjoyed a riposte; but every time she got close to Tom Appleby, fate stole him from her. She was mad. "Get lost, Corporal. See that shifty-eyed private standing by the door. He's a New York gangster. He'll slit your throat if I tell him to."

Sitting in Tom's chair, Dale said, "Don't be so hard-hearted, lady. I don't mean any harm." Noticing her Red Cross uniform as if for the first time, he said, "Aren't you supposed to cheer lonely soldiers."

Somewhat taken by his audacity, she said, "Okay, soldier. What's your problem?"

"Thank you, Miss. . . . There's this girl whose boyfriend was suddenly called away. She looks so forlorn. I'd just like to cheer her up. But she won't let me. What am I to do?"

"Okay. Didn't you say your name was Dale?"

"Yes."

"Okay, Dale. I don't want to dillydally here any longer; and I do need to get back to my hotel. If you wish to walk me back there, I'll let you. We can talk along the way." Lighting up another cigarette, Susan winked at Dale and said coyly, "Don't forget, Corporal, there's no 'Roll-Me-Over-In-The-Clover.' That Mobster guy," Susan tilted her head again toward Jimmy, "will be closely following us in a jeep."

CHAPTER 5

"Shit out of luck again, good ole Sally Brown, shit out of luck again," Sally Brown said ruefully, lamenting the desertion of her companions. First, Major Dick Burk III had suddenly excused himself during the ceremonies decorating Tom Appleby. Then Tom and Susan had taken off for who knows where. Later "Bed-Check Charlie" had dropped his nightly bomb and the lights had gone out. When they had come back on, there was Colonel Quinn speaking with General Clay. Next all four officers had apologized and left. Then the dance had started up again. Now alone at the general's big table and under a spotlight, Sally said softly to herself, "I'm pissed-off. I'm leaving this joint."

Light ground-fog gently veiled the city, though the taller buildings penetrated the wet cloak. Plunging through the blackout curtains into the inky damp night, Sally wished Jimmy Malloti were still around. Of course, that hoodlum was undoubtedly watching over Susan. "Christ," she thought, "Susan always gets the breaks." Nevertheless, Sally was sure she could find the hotel by following the railroad tracks. Their hotel lay kitty-corner to the main passenger depot. Over the boulevard from the Casino, a narrow brick sidewalk followed parallel to the tracks. To get to the sidewalk Sally had to make her way through an array of jeeps, personnel carriers, three-quarter-tons, meat wagons, and a few "liberated" German staff cars. Once on the brick sidewalk, she hurried her steps toward the depot, still at least a mile away.

The cold air made her shiver and she wished she had had

her trench coat on. She also thought her leather soled "dancin' shoes" announced her approach. To her ears they sounded like the clip-clop of a shod horse on pavement. "Damn," she swore, "I should have had General Clay find me a ride." She knew she had only a vague sense of the direction to the hotel; and considering the late hour and being a young woman alone on the street, she felt vulnerable.

At least the first sounds she heard were nonthreatening. Off in the distance the loud shrieks of drunk GIs and their girl friends reassured her that she wasn't alone in the darkness. Further, giving her a sense of security, she saw MPs in jeeps accompanied by city cops. Occasionally they flashed bright lights on civilians and soldiers as they coursed through the area. But at the very moment she was feeling most secure, she was without warning struck on the head and wrestled into some bushes; and before she could utter an outcry, her assailant had gagged and bound her.

Then the man's hands began to grope. Sally could feel her attacker was huge and powerful. Suddenly a light was flashed on the bushes and the tense body of the man lay crushing her to the ground. The light moved on and then was closed. After what seemed endless time, she felt the man relax.

Sally had seen the man's face. A face she'd never forget. She thought it was more animal than human. Hearing strange sobs and feeling moisture on her face, she trembled. Then a guttural, quaking voice said, "I'm gonna free you, lady. Don't scream or yell. I'm sorry." In an instant the man was gone.

Soon Sally regained her feet and began wandering the blacked-out city in a daze; when at last the depot loomed out of the darkness, she ran across the boulevard to the hotel. Partly regaining her senses, she tore through the lobby and down the hall. Her room light was on when Sally burst through the entrance.

Susan cried, "Holy, God, Sally! Look at you! What happened?"

Like a mother Susan embraced Sally who sobbed faintly. After awhile Sally settled down and gushed forth as much as she could recall. "Susan, I can't forget the utter sadness in that man's face. He looked like a wounded animal . . . I feel kind of sorry for him."

"For God's sake, Sally, what are you talking about? A beauty and the beast? I'm going to call Clay and get the MPs after that son-of-a-bitch."

With red eyes flashing and blond curls shaking, Sally grabbed Susan's arm. "No, Susan! There was something pathetic about him."

"Like shit," said Susan, brushing away Sally's hand. "That pervert's a menace. It could be me next. He raped you, didn't he! Look at the lump on your head and your cuts and bruises! . . . If the MPs hadn't flashed a light in your direction, you'd probably be dead now."

Looking Susan squarely in the eyes, Sally said, "Susan! I know most everything about you and you know most everything about me. Don't forget, we're supposed to be bosom buddies. Leave the guy alone. Maybe he has some destiny to fulfill."

"Sally, you're not just a caricature of a 'dumb-blond.' You are a 'dumb-blond!' I'll do what you ask, but you're crazy."

Later, to ease Sally's mind, Susan recounted her own evening with Tom until the coming of 'Bed-Check Charlie.' In conclusion she said, "Figuratively speaking, Sally, it appears we were both fucked one way or another."

SLEEP DID NOT COME easily to Tom Appleby. To say that the day had been one of the most pleasant in his life, might be an understatement. The promotion to Captain and receiving the DSC all in one-helping was really humbling. He thought it would be tough living up to the honor.

And talk about frosting on the cake. This Susan Montgomery, chick, had it all: looks, brains, family connections, and fun to be with. That she tried so hard to please him was really amusing. He wondered how long that could last? The fact she was a Red Cross girl might make her accessible if she didn't get transferred; but having her little brother at SHAEF might help in that respect.

As Tom crawled out of his sleeping bag, having lain on an army cot with wide open eyes, he noticed his watch showed 0200 hours. Though his men were sleeping in their tanks or on the ground in their shelter tents, the Division had requisitioned a house for him and his headquarter's staff. As sleep seemed impossible, he decided to heat some water for coffee; earlier he'd discovered the kitchen had a small gas burner. He thought, "The natives are amazed at the American's instant coffee; and as substitutes go, it's not too bad."

He never had to dress, just slipped into his size 14A combat boots. The house was not heated and with the exception of his field jacket, he'd left his woolen clothes on. Approaching the kitchen, he saw light. To his surprise his executive officer, Red Jordening, sat at a table seriously gazing at an empty flask of Old Granddad.

Though Red hadn't attended the dance, he knew what had happened. Colonel Quinn briefed him after Tom and Quinn arrived from Division Headquarters. Red spoke first, sounding like John Wayne. "I'm not surprised you can't sleep, Captain. A DSC leaves only room for the 'Congressional.' You're on a roll. All of that, and this Rockefeller babe. What more could a patriot ask?... Maybe a transfer back to the states?"

Knowing his XO had a fine-tuned sense of humor, Tom laughed. "Pardon me! Her name is Montgomery not Rockefeller. And if you think I have good reasons not to be sleeping, what is the cause of your insomnia, Red? Old Granddad?"

"I was worried someone might have stolen my liquor ration. I was just checking to see that my case hadn't been opened."

"Pardon me!"

"All right. I know I'm a lowly 'second louy,' but I keep thinking about this son-of-a-bitch Dietrich. Do you still have the message 'Charlie' dropped?"

"Yes." From his pocket Tom produced a crumpled sheet of yellow paper. He handed it to Red. "I guess you can say I'm lucky that the parachute and its message were found so soon. The German pilot who dropped it was shot down."

From scrawled writing in English, Jordening read:

> *Greetings to Captain Tom Appleby, Daredevil-6, of the 67th Armored Regiment of the 15th Armored Division. We have a warm reception waiting for you in Operation Queen.*
> *Hans Dietrich*

Dumfounded, Red asked, "What is Dietrich up to?"

"He's playing a game. Some Germans are like that. Remember the Red Baron of World War I? I've heard Dietrich's tank is painted a special kind of blue," said Tom.

Looking incredulous, Red said, "Why would Dietrich want to draw attention? We even hide our rank at the front."

Stroking his chin and looking owlish, Tom said, "Interesting isn't it. But we can't deny it's got Dietrich this far, though, can we? . . . Perhaps there is some way to exploit his desire for notoriety. Maybe we should give that some thought."

"What really bothers me, Tom, is how could Dietrich possibly know your radio number and your promotion?"

"How? I suppose Jerry monitors our communications. S2 does his. And he interrogates his prisoners. . . . Let's give the devil his due; Jerry's no fool."

"It still beats the shit out of me why he would send this fucking message addressed to you?"

Tom Appleby chuckled. "Maybe some spy in our outfit passed on the information that Company 'D' is to lead the attack in Operation Queen? Then, again, maybe Dietrich hopes to confuse us by pretending to know the plans for 'Operation Queen.'"

"Christ, Tom. That isn't possible is it?"

Winking at his executive officer, Appleby said, "You know, I have an idea, Red. Maybe I ought to have one of our pilots drop a note to the Herr battle-group Führer challenging him to a personal duel—he in a Mark IV—but not his Tiger tank—and me in a Sherman."

No longer amused, Red said, "I never thought I'd hear my CO go off his rocker." The half-inebriated Second Lieutenant rolled his bloodshot eyes: "If our brass had even a hint you were entertaining such hogwash, they'd bust your butt—not pin the DSC on you. . . ." Lieutenant Jordening appeared about to throw up. His face briefly blanched, but color quickly returned. "Even if you were stupid enough to do what you say, you would have no right to put your tank crew at risk!"

"Hold it, Red. Just a 'demolition derby' with only the two of us involved."

Captain Tom Appleby had never heard his XO talk to him with such vigor. He knew that the brass had their eyes on John "Red" Jordening. Off the record, General Clay had said that Jordening was the best executive officer in the Division and would soon be upgraded to captain and given a company to command.

As a minister's kid, John Jordening was impious. As a teenager he'd cussed, smoked, drank, danced and messed around with the girls. Anything to disquiet his parents and prove his independence to his pals. Although older and wiser, he was still a free thinker, which presented no problem to Captain Appleby.

Red's rejoinder convinced Tom that Red thought he was serious about dueling with Dietrich. Impishly continuing his charade, Tom said, "They say Dietrich's fluorescent tank refracts light.... Did you ever spear for fish, Red?"

"No," said Red in disgust.

"Well, I've speared carp in the Platte River in Nebraska. It depends on the depth and the angle of both the sun and the fish, but usually you hurl your spear below the image of the fish. If '6' ever encounters the 'blue-one,' I'll have my gunner shoot low."

Irritated, Red said, "My God, Tom. That's more bullshit. If Dietrich's *blue* tank has any credibility at all, it's purely psychological.... Of course, a Tiger shoots farther and has more armor than a Sherman."

Suddenly, Private Milton Silverman's squeaky voice intervened. "Lieutenant Appleby, sir, is there anything wrong? You and Lieutenant Jordening are arguing, and I can't sleep."

Before Tom could answer, Red said, "No, Milton. We're just celebrating. Go back to bed, Milton."

"Yes, sir, Lieutenant." Private Silverman turned and walked back to his cot.

"Let me get something straight," said Red. "'Operation Queen' is now on track seeing that Dietrich didn't swallow 'Trojan Horse.' Burk is to give his briefing at Division at 1400 hours tomorrow. Company 'D' will still lead the attack for Combat Command 'B.' Is that right?"

Nodding his head and laughing, Tom said, "You're always on

the ball and correct . . . most of the time, Red. I'm a lucky CO to have you as an XO. Get some sleep! . . . See you in the morning."

AFTER RED RETIRED to an adjoining room, Tom occupied Red's chair and abruptly stared at Red's empty whiskey bottle triggering thoughts about himself. He had long worried some about his own contradictive behavior—being spontaneous and gregarious one moment and the next withdrawn and sad; then a psychology course in college had convinced him he had manic-depressive tendencies. However, he had rationalized that unconventional traits resided in nearly everyone and his were minor. Nevertheless, knowing his weakness, he had fought his gloom and doom days by immersing himself in sports, especially football. When the war came his ROTC training launched him into the officer corps and soon the responsibilities of leadership and danger surprisingly appeared to have allayed his inherent demons.

Also contrary to the front he now projected to his men, a teenage life of dissolution and rebellion, arrogance and bluster had nearly ruined his life before his high school football coach had guided him to a reconciliation with his elderly and religious parents and to a path of stoic sobriety and self-assurance. It had worked—until now. Though he hadn't let on to Red, their rebellious backgrounds were similar, but maybe Susan Montgomery was now tempting his resolve and reformation.

THE THREE DUTCHMEN of the Resistance found a table in the far rear of the Beer Garden. Samson appeared sullen and worried. His blinking eyes nervously scanned the room. The blinds were closed to shut out the afternoon sun, and among the few customers there were no American soldiers. Bep Rieksen was deep in thought. He produced a briarwood pipe and a small pouch of tobacco from his tweed jacket, and soon was puffing thoughtfully. Karel Konijn ordered a pitcher of beer, waiting on the others to begin the conversation.

At last Bep said, "We know Dietrich had orders to move to the West Wall and was preparing to do so; then suddenly he stopped. His patrols either discovered the movement of Combat Command 'A' or Dietrich was warned of the trap."

Samson guessed he was a suspect. "You know where my loyalty lies, Bep. I took the risk and personally told Dietrich of the American's retreat. I was lucky not to have been detained or I'd have been shot by now. I dare never face the German again."

As if not hearing Samson, Bep continued: "I spoke with General Clay this morning. He said the first disturbance reported at the front was a claim by a soldier of seeing a Nazi werewolf. Shortly afterwards, German patrols discovered the presence of Combat Command 'A.' At that point, according to General Clay, 'Operation Trojan Horse' was kaputt." Bep noted a change of expression on Samson's face. "Did I say something, Samson?"

Too late, Samson realized he must have shown surprise at the mention of a Nazi werewolf. Hastily he said, "I saw night patrols being formed before I left Puffendorf. That's all."

Doubting Samson's alibi and looking him squarely in the eyes, Bep said, "So you believe you've burned your bridges with the Hun?"

"They'll kill me. I set them up for this . . . this—'Trojan Horse.'"

"Not you alone, Samson. There were other hands in this pie." Pausing for a swallow of beer and then putting the pipe to his mouth for a few more puffs, Bep's grey eyes turned bright and friendly. "What will now happen to Janeane and your relatives?"

Tears welling in his eyes, Samson replied, "You know the Gestapo. . . Why ask? . . . If nothing else, this should have shown my loyalty to the Resistance."

Carefully laying his pipe on the table, eyes narrowing, Bep inquired, "Crocodile tears? Not if 'The Great Samson' was the one who warned the Hun."

An indignant expression appeared on Samson's face; his fists clenched and his muscles tightened; he sat ramrod straight. Gulping air he puffed out his chest like the hood of a cobra. Scornfully he asked, "Have you forgotten Nicoline?"

Bep and Samson exchanged evil-eyes, like boxers waiting for

an opening. Neither man made a move and time passed. Finally the two men began to relax, and Karel Konijn put a derringer back in his coat pocket.

"You win, Samson. I believe you," said Bep. Then he grabbed his pipe from the table, relit it and puffed briefly.... "No, I haven't forgotten Nicoline, even though the Gestapo doesn't know of her whereabouts. Nor have I forgotten your people.... But I do have a plan." Gently laying the pipe down again and drumming on the table with his fingers, he said, "Carefully consider this, Samson: If you gave the Hun 'Operation Queen' along with the body of Bep Rieksen, do you think you would be redeemed in the eyes of Dietrich and the Gestapo?"

Samson respected Bep's intelligence. He knew there was a ploy in the making.

"How?"

"A body burned beyond recognition, shot up by the Gestapo, having the identifying papers of Bep Rieksen on it?"

"The Gestapo has many Dutch informers. You'd have to disappear from the face of the earth."

"I believe that could be arranged. If not exactly the 'face of the earth,' at least with a disguise and a temporary visit to England."

After mulling over the idea, Samson probed, "Whose body?"

"I have a Nazi collaborator in mind. The Resistance decided upon his execution some time ago. His body will be transported to the Hague and disfigured. You will notify the Gestapo about a Resistance meeting at which Rieksen will be present. A firefight will ensue. Later the Gestapo will discover the body of the notorious Bep Rieksen. You will call them. If it seems they believe they've really found my remains, you can appear in person and give them the new 'Operation Queen.' . . . You will then have fulfilled your obligations to both the Gestapo and Dietrich. Of course, there are details which must be worked out. What do you think?"

By holding his breath in intervals, Samson hoped to conceal his raging emotions. However, he thought Bep's plan feasible. If only a last straw, it offered a slight hope for freeing Janeane if it were not already too late.

"Again I ask, Whose body?"

"A collaborator by the name of Lintens. The man has turned in many Resistance fighters to the Gestapo. It is about time justice be done to that traitor. But this is of no concern to you, Samson. However, you must remain in Heerlen, so I can instruct you at the right time."

Samson bit his tongue to hide his emotions.

After drinking a beer and giving Bep his room and telephone number at a cheap hotel, Samson deliberately and slowly left The Beer Garden.

THOUGH SAMSON WAS DRESSED for the season and the early November sun was warm, his blood ran cold. He quickened his pace toward the railroad station. Upon approaching the concrete steps of the depot, he lurched his cumbersome body forward two flights at a time until he gained the entrance. Hurriedly he walked to a public telephone. He called the number of A. W. Lintens. A deep-voiced woman answered. Samson identified himself and asked for Arnd. After the boy answered, Samson said, "Listen carefully, Arnd, and do exactly as I tell you. You are in danger! Great danger! Without alarming the Lintens, gather your belongings and meet me at the downtown railroad station. I will be waiting for you near the number one ticket booth. That is all. But Hurry."

Finding a bench and seating himself, Samson was aware of bustling activity all around him. A passenger train had just steamed to a halt, and people rushed by without a glance in his direction. Outside most of the pedestrian traffic were either walkers on the sidewalks or people on black bicycles. American army vehicles crowded the streets. Since the American liberation in September, Dutch transport trucks and a few civilian cars were only recently beginning to reappear on the streets. Samson knew it would be awhile before Arnd arrived, so he lit a cigarette and let his mind wander.

It had been a shock when he had first seen the boy-spy. The boy was Arnd, his very own nephew. His sister Eva's son. She had married Herman Hauptmann of Essen, Germany. Samson had been told that the entire family had been killed in an American air raid. It turned out that during the attack Arnd had been at a Hitler Youth rally in Nuremberg.

Furthermore, it had not taken Samson long to discover the extent of Arnd's indoctrination by the Hitler Youth. After spending only a brief time with the boy, Samson had no doubt Arnd would have betrayed his own parents if he thought they were not loyal to Hitler.

The fanaticism of Arnd created a problem for Samson. Samson's sympathies lay with the Allies; circumstances forced him to spy for the Gestapo—but he had become a "double-agent"—passing information to both the Resistance and the Gestapo. Samson knew Arnd considered his uncle an unquestionably loyal Nazi. And Samson realized the danger Arnd posed if he should ever learn of his uncle's connection with the Resistance. But, still, Arnd was family and blood, which always meant so much to Samson. And he fondly remembered playing games with the youngster when his sister visited their home in The Hague.

Before long, a worried expression on his face, Arnd bounded into the railroad station and immediately located his uncle. Removing a bulky knapsack from his back and sitting beside Samson, Arnd gasped for air. After catching his breath and speaking in English, Arnd said, "I ran most of the way. What is the matter, Uncle?"

Again Samson was impressed with Arnd's childlike appearance and his mastery of American English. He asked, "How old are you, Arnd?"

"Is that what you scared me for? To learn my age. I'm fourteen. I know I look younger."

"There is a big problem." Glancing furtively around the depot, Samson said, "We're going to my hotel room. It's on the second floor, but I want you to enter by a fire-escape. I'll go by way of the lobby and then let you in."

Studying the serious expression on his uncle Hans Spoor's face, alias Samson, Arnd realized this was no game, and without speaking did exactly as he was told.

When they had at last settled themselves on wooden chairs in

Samson's dingy hotel room, Samson said, "Arnd, I have knowledge that the Resistance knows about Linten's spying. He will soon be executed."

"Shouldn't we warn him?"

"No. His house is already being watched by the Resistance. I only hope no one paid serious attention to your departure."

"How do you know this, Uncle?"

Smiling, Samson said, "I can't reveal my sources."

Arnd was already sophisticated enough as a spy to accept his uncle's answer without question. "Lintens is no problem for me. He's a coward and a dummkopf. His wife is an old hag. And their two brats should never have been born," said Arnd matter-of-factly and with a shrug of his shoulders. "But where should I stay now?"

"I will take you to your Grandpa and Grandma Spoor at the Hague. They would love to have you."

With a look of horror on his face, Arnd threw up his hands. "No! No! I cannot leave Heerlen?"

Dumbfounded, Samson asked, "Why?"

"My mission! My Special Force's assignment!"

"What is your assignment?"

"Why, Uncle Hans! As an agent, you know I am not to reveal my purpose unless authorized to do so," Arnd remonstrated.

Samson was flabbergasted. From a package of American cigarettes given him by Karel, he took one and lit it.

Looking innocent, Arnd asked, "May I have one?"

"Oh, so the Hitler Youth taught you to smoke too. . . . Here, I'll light it for you."

Arnd replied coyly, "No. The Special Forces."

"You know, nephew, you border on being a 'weisenheimer,' kid."

"I believe the Amis call it being a 'smart-ass,' Uncle."

Reaching for a bottle of cognac, which he'd stashed away in the dresser, and with his back to Arnd, Samson asked, "Are you the werewolf who warned Major Dietrich?"

"Yes, Uncle. I could not find you. And I learned at Puffendorf that the Kampfgrüppe Führer is now a Brigadeführer."

With the bottle in one hand, Samson faced Arnd and asked,

"How did you know about the trap?"

"You mean General Clay's 'Operation Trojan Horse'?" Looking like a cherub, Arnd replied, "Remember what you told me, Uncle. We cannot reveal our sources."

Suddenly a thought electrified Samson. "Do you know General Dietrich very well? Do you know the real reason he's at Puffendorf?"

The earnestness of his uncle's questioning confused Arnd. "Don't you know? Are you teasing me?" But Arnd was now on guard; and he decided upon his return to Germany to ask more questions about his uncle's work with the Gestapo.

Peering pensively out the window at the traffic below, Samson placed the cognac on a small writing table. As he inhaled on his cigarette, he noticed shadows of buildings beginning to crawl and darken the street. He was now convinced his nephew had become privy to important secrets of the German High Command. It appeared, as well, that Arnd had a source close to General Clay. As he continued to watch the tentacles of night reach over the narrow street, he made up his mind. He would call Karel Konijn and have him locate a place for Arnd to stay. Then, as kindly and pleasantly as he could, he would try to get his fourteen-year-old nephew drunk—and see if that would loosen the young fanatic's tongue!

THE FLIGHT IN THE SMALL German reconnaissance plane had been fearful and upsetting for Nicoline Lindemann. A north wind had slowed and buffeted the little aircraft. The pilot of the grey-black Storch, and the plane's only other occupant, was SS Brigadier General Fritz Kraus. Hedgehopping close to the ground, General Kraus had piloted the monoplane out of Holland and to a safe landing at his hunting lodge near the Arnsberger Wald (forest), about 130 kilometers from where his "Lightning" Panzer Division was presently positioned.

The order that hostage, Nicoline Lindemann, was to be executed in revenge for the activities of the Resistance had dismayed Fritz Kraus. Later information that Gestapo agents were already on their way to carry out the execution had prompted General

Kraus to return immediately to Germany for a long-delayed eye treatment. A Russian shell had nearly blinded him in one eye. Because the front was momentarily quiet, General Rheinhardt had approved of his taking a brief medical leave.

Fritz thought no one in his command, not even his adjutants, Major Krugger or Captain Snodgrass, knew of his complicity in spiriting Mrs. Lindemann from her room to a vacant house near a landing strip. Major Krugger, on the other hand, had reported her gone and General Kraus had correctly notified higher command. A halfhearted search for the woman had turned up nothing. General Kraus figured Major Krugger and Captain Snodgrass might have their suspicions, but he considered them loyal subalterns.

General Kraus did not announce the time and method for his departure. Orders were displayed on his desk for his staff officers until his return. He also left "homing pigeons" if anything exceptional at the front should develop in his absence.

WHEN THE PLANE LANDED, his children and their spinster aunt stood waiting next to a small, metal hangar. He had hardly cutoff the engine than the towheaded children rushed toward the airplane. Max, an aggressive ten-year-old, and Felicia, a shy eleven-year-old, had not seen their father for over a year. Fritz thought the children resembled their mother, Margarete. They were both slender and had Margarete's bright smile.

Climbing out of the plane, he was hugged by Max who blurted out, "Father, did you bring us any sweets."

Kneeling and gathering his blond son in his arms and kissing him on the lips, Fritz laughed, "So, Max, you still have the sweet tooth. Yes, I have Swiss chocolates for you and Felicia in the plane. . . . Come, Felicia, my shy one; let me look at you and hug you and kiss you too. . . . My, my what a beautiful young swan you're turning into."

Fräulein Gertrud Schultz, the portly sister of his wife, stood to the side viewing the scene critically. She'd never liked the general. She'd warned her poor sister against marrying a soldier at a time when Germany was again beating the war drums. But her younger sister was beguiled by the flashy uniform. Though Margarete had always been sickly, she felt Fritz Kraus was the cause of her sister's contracting tuberculosis and dying of the disease. At hardship to herself, Margarete had followed Fritz from camp to camp.

And unlike the usual slow progression of the disease, in Margarete's case its onset had claimed its victim almost before the disease had been diagnosed; and as Gertrud was the only available relative, she had cared for the children while the general made war for that madman, Hitler. Now Fritz's sudden appearance with a strange women aroused her suspicions; by now, Gertrud had come to regard the children almost as her own.

General Kraus' family was of the landed gentry. He was the sole inheritor of a considerable fortune and estate. Even in defeat, if he survived, he would be able to claim land and position—that is, in a non-Communist state. Fortunately, his land lay in the path of the Allies. To be sure, he'd heard of the Morgenthau Plan to turn Germany into an agrarian nation and later of a plan to divide Germany between the Allies. But he knew the war wasn't over; Hitler had something brewing to offset recent defeats and maybe yet bring about victory.

General Kraus' views about Hitler, the Nazis, even his own Waffen-SS, had, in recent days, undergone a transformation. Though he wasn't an intellectual, he was an honest man. Perhaps his fellow officers still viewed him as a fanatical Nazi. Certainly he had given them no reason to think otherwise. Yet he could not banish from his mind what Hitler had done to the Polish and Russian people, and what Hitler was now offering to the German people—a kind of Götterdämmerung. And he knew he could not wash the blood from his own hands; he too had danced too often to the music of the Führer. But at all costs he must try to save Max and Felicia for the world of tomorrow.

Nicoline on her part was still in a near state of shock. The entire episode involving her abduction and detention at General Kraus's headquarters was beyond her comprehension. Even General Kraus's lengthy explanations had left her confused. Nicoline in all reality was apolitical. She did not like what the Nazi's were doing to her country, but she harbored no hatred toward the German people.

Nor was Nicoline so perplexed that she did not recognize the unusual respect and accord General Kraus was showing her. If she were indeed a hostage based solely on her relationship with Bep; and, as General Kraus had informed her, the Gestapo had now ordered her execution because of something Bep had recently done, why then would General Kraus, an SS General, risk his own standing to save her life? She could not even begin to guess an answer.

PLEASE-JOE HAD PRETENDED to be an amnesia victim wandering the streets of Charleroi, Belgium, when the Americans arrived. As he had told Sergeant Hardesty, he couldn't remember anything prior to the coming of the American soldiers. When he finally did begin to remember, he said, he was sleeping in the locker room at a local coal mine. As the American army was busy constructing a food depot and prisoner-of-war camp, he had begun hanging around these soldiers.

Sergeant Kevin Sullivan, a battalion supply sergeant, had first noticed Joe running from one soldier to another imploring, "Candy, cigarettes, money... Please, Joe... Please, Joe... Please, Joe." Dirty and disheveled, the youngster had looked cute to Kevin Sullivan. Kevin called, "Hey you, 'Please-Joe,' come here!" After the boy told Kevin he had no home or parents, Kevin asked him if he wanted to stay with him. The army had just rented an abandoned warehouse for Sergeant Sullivan's platoon and the boy jumped at the chance to be with an American soldier. When the lad insisted that he didn't have a name, Kevin said, "Okay. In that case, I'll call you, *Please-Joe.*" Soon Kevin had a uniform made for Please-Joe and at night placed a cot next to his own for Please-Joe to sleep in.

But Sergeant Sullivan was a crude man, and he and his buddies soon amused themselves not only by teaching Joe American-English but, also, by showing him how to cuss, smoke and drink. They made jest of getting Joe drunk and having him retell dirty stories. They doubled over in laughter at his French accent. As a result, the soldiers were quickly turning Joe not only into an All-American brat but a dissolute child as well. Luckily for Joe, Sergeant Sullivan's commanding officer was made aware of what was going on, and Sullivan was told to get rid of the kid. So Kevin issued Joe a bogus pass and fake assignment.

When Little Joe returned, Kevin had moved to a new location within the city. Hurt and scared, Joe looked and asked for Sergeant Sullivan who, he was told, had been transferred to Liege, Belgium. Then to Little Joe's further disappointment, the army truck in which he stowed away didn't stop at Liege; rather it ended up at Hap Hardesty's kitchen in Ubach, Germany.

FOLLOWING GENERAL CLAY's instructions, Philip Vossmaar took Joe to the home of his friend Karel Konijn. Joe was most satisfied with the arrangement. Mr. and Mrs. Konijn immediately fell in love with the winsome, dark-haired youngster. Guessing the round-faced lad to be about twelve years old, the Konijns did all they could to lure the cheerful boy away from his obsession with American soldiers. It was all to no avail. Joe was up in the morning and gone before the elderly Konijns ever got out of bed. He did not return from being with Hap Hardesty until nightfall. Then he told jokes and volunteered his services for any kind of odd jobs. Karel, the Konijn's's youngest son and Resistance fighter, rarely returned home anymore; and Joe was such an engaging youngster that the Konijn's even discussed the possibility of adoption before they realized that Little Joe was irrevocably committed to the Americans.

Joe was perceptive. Since Hap Hardesty had entered his life his legacy from Kevin Sullivan was nearly forgotten. He knew he'd been an object of amusement for Kevin and his buddies. That had been all right by Joe because he thought he had no hope for a good life without Sergeant Sullivan. So he obliged the GIs by doing whatever they asked from him, even when his immature judgment told him it was wrong. But in gruff Sergeant Hardesty he knew there was genuine affection—nor did he dare perform any of the bad things he'd been doing for Sergeant Sullivan and his friends. He returned Sergeant Hardesty's love by becoming almost a paragon of virtue—the exact opposite of his previous behavior. Fortunately, Joe was still young and pliable.

As the morning sun shown through the bedroom window, fourteen-year-old Arnd Hauptmann sat on his bed reviewing what had become a complicated situation. A soft-spoken man by the name of Karel Konijn, a friend of his uncle, Hans Spoor, had brought him here for boarding, a Mr. and Mrs. Konijn. Later, the elder Konijn had escorted him to this upstairs bedroom. The previous night Arnd had spent in his uncle's hotel room.

Arnd smirked when he thought about his uncle's bungling efforts to get him drunk. German boys drink early in life, but they usually don't get drunk. He had recognized his uncle's game and played along. When his uncle's back was turned he'd poured the liquor down the sink and cupped his hand over his drinking glass.

Based on the sensitive questions his uncle had asked, however, Arnd was becoming more suspicious of his relative's loyalty to the Fatherland. Consequently, until his growing doubts were resolved, he'd decided to be ever alert and careful. One of Colonel Skorzeny's agents would soon be making contact, and he would then learn more about his uncle and how much he could trust him.

And just who were these Konijns with whom his uncle had arranged for him to stay? Uncle Hans had warned him they were not Nazis like the Lintens. In fact, Uncle Hans had told him to say that he was a refugee. No questions would be asked.

At least the Konijns lived next door to the Secondary Technical School. This should make it easy for him to maintain his association with his American officer friend, the main reason he was in Heerlen; but the Konijn's would hardly allow his friend to remain alone with him at night. Such a problem would have to be worked out.

Further complicating matters was the fact he would now have a roommate. Another refugee kid like himself. Arnd laughed at that thought. It wouldn't be long before he'd send that brat packing—one way or another.

Also, the Lintens lived across the street. Arnd wondered if the Resistance had already disposed of Mr. Linten? Would the family then remain in the neighborhood? He didn't worry about Linten's kids. They were already scared to death of him and, furthermore, had been trained to keep their mouths shut.

From his bedroom window, Arnd spent most of the day observing the goings and comings of American soldiers to the school building. He had told the Konijns that he needed to rest from his ordeals.

ALONG WITH THE SHADOWS of evening, Joe returned to the Konijns' home after having spent most of the day in Sergeant Hardesty's jeep going from one mess kitchen to another, as Master Sergeant Hap Hardesty was making sure all the men of the regiment were being fed. Joe was now relaxed and reassured by the pledge of General Clay that he could accompany the division in the days ahead; and Joe knew he had found more than a friend in Hap Hardesty. He at last had someone who was as concerned about his welfare as a father would be; and Joe dared hope that after the war a way would be found for him to go to the States. He wanted to become Hap's adopted boy, a brother to Hap's boy, Virgil.

After greeting Joe with a playful slap on the back, Mr. Konijn informed Joe that he now had a roommate upstairs. A refugee boy from the war about his age.

Quickly Joe bounded up the stairs and opened the door to the bedroom. In shocked recognition Joe's mouth dropped open and his eyes bugged out. Instantly he recognized Arnd. He recalled Hap shining the flashlight on the bicycle rider they'd hit and saying: "*Look what we have here! A blond-haired, blue-eyed Hitler baby. What's the matter, baby Kraut? Has the cat got your tongue, or couldn't you understand Joe's German?*" Then the boy had grabbed the bicycle and rode off into the night toward Puffendorf.

In Arnd's case, he had already been told some of the circumstances about his roommate, Joe. But Joe's silent staring at him was annoying. "What's the matter, *Frog*? Are you dumb or something?" snarled Arnd.

The German slang word for Frenchmen angered Joe. "No, *Boche*, just trying to remember if I've seen you someplace before."

The fearless comeback and hint of recognition by Joe dramatically changed Arnd. The importance of his mission and his danger in a strange household caused him to remember his Special Force's training. He said, "I'm sorry, Joe, for acting rudely." Rising from his bed and offering a hand, he said, "My name is Arnd Hauptmann. And, by the way, I'm only part *Boche*, as you called me. My mother was Dutch. Can we be friends?"

There was something phony about Arnd's sudden politeness, thought Joe; and only reluctantly did he take the proffered hand. His first inclination was to put Arnd in his place by revealing that he and Hap had already met Arnd on the road to Puffendorf. With a second thought, however, he replaced that impulse by silence. Tomorrow he'd tell Hap about Arnd, the *"Hitler-baby,"* being his roommate.

"I hope you don't mind, Joe, my taking the bed next to the window," said Arnd; "I love to watch the American soldiers. They're so relaxed compared to the stupid German soldiers who look like children's toys with all their rigid goose-stepping."

Joe was fascinated by what he thought to be playacting. That first growl from Arnd was more in character than this feigned friendliness. Why had the chameleon suddenly changed colors? Scratching his head and taking the other bed against the wall, Joe said, "No. I don't care. I see American soldiers all day."

Both boys were about average height. One was light in appearance, the other dark. While Joe wore his frequently washed replica of an army uniform, Arnd was clothed in a blue sport shirt, a wrinkled, wool suit coat and dark shorts with brown stockings and scuffed brown shoes. Only, with Arnd, the onset of pubescence could be discerned. Nearly invisible blemishes dotted his forehead and face. Both boys flopped themselves on their frame, pull-down beds.

Locking his fingers behind his head and staring at the ceiling, Arnd said, "Joe is a funny name."

"Not any more than Arnd."

"Mr. Konijn tells me you have an American soldier friend you spend the day with. Why?"

"So what?"

"Did this Sergeant Sullivan or Sergeant Hardesty ever do anything personal to you?"

Rising on his bed, his brow wrinkled, Joe asked, "What do you mean by that?"

Also sitting up, Arnd said, "Would you like a cigarette, Joe. Mr. Konijn said smoking was okay if I were careful."

"No! Hap says I'm too young to smoke."

After lighting up and taking a few puffs, Arnd said, "You speak pretty good English, Joe. How old are you?"

"Your English is good too. How did you learn it? I'm twelve."

"In school. I'm fourteen.... You know, I, also, have an American soldier friend. He might come to visit me this evening. Would that be okay with you?"

"I don't care."

"The problem is I need to see him privately. We talk about... things. Maybe you could go to the movie. They're showing American films now."

Joe sensed the drift of the conversation. He stared at Arnd until the older boy's blue eyes looked away. Joe noticed for the first time what a handsome boy Arnd was. "But beautiful like a Viper—and just as deadly," thought Joe. He would not sleep easily at night with this Boche in the same room.

"That's okay if I'm still here tomorrow or some other time. But not tonight. Hap told me to get a good night's sleep. Tomorrow we may be moving back to the front."

At that moment grey-haired Mr. Konijn knocked on the door and entered. In his younger days he had worked down in the mine and had inhaled a lot of cold dust. Now his breathing was labored. "Well, I hope you boys have gotten acquainted. My wife has something ready for us to eat. Perhaps you two should wash and go to the water closet."

After the evening meal and the boys had returned to their shared room, Arnd said, "I'm going for a walk, Joe Why don't you go to sleep? I'll be really quiet when I come back."

"Okay."

After Arnd left, Joe was in quandary about what to do. He felt misgivings sleeping in the same room with Arnd. He thought about going to General Clay or telling some officer at the school about Arnd, but he finally rejected these ideas. He couldn't trust Arnd, but he wasn't scared of him either. Anyway, Hap would know what to do, and he would come early in the morning. Thankfully, he hadn't revealed to Arnd the circumstances about their first meeting. And, apparently, Arnd had no idea they had met. But just to be careful, he decided to sleep with his Hitler Youth dagger in his hand, thankful that Hap had returned the weapon as a vote of confidence.

Contrary to Sergeant Hardesty's order to get a good night's rest, Joe didn't sleep a wink—and with good cause.

Arnd did not return until the early morning hours, and he did so with shoes in hand and on tiptoes. Moonlight beamed under the window curtains into the room. From a hole in his blanket, Joe watched Arnd sitting on his bed smoking another cigarette. Joe pretended to breathe deeply as if he were asleep. Then alarmingly he made out the form of Arnd slowly moving toward his bed. Without waiting to learn Arnd's intentions, Joe tossed the blanket back and sprang to the door, simultaneously turning on the light switch.

Both boys were startled to see the other in his underwear, crouched and grasping a dagger!

Arnd was the first to recognize the similarity of the daggers. "God in Heaven, another Hitler Youth," he said. Quickly Arnd rattled off in German the oath of the Hitler Youth. Then rapidly he spoke in German. At first puzzled that Joe stood mute and on guard, Arnd then reverted to English. "I know we are never supposed to speak

German. But can you identify yourself as a fellow Hitler Youth? The handshake or something?"

Without thinking, Joe mumbled, "I know you're the werewolf who gave the alarm about 'Operation Trojan Horse.'"

As Arnd mulled over Joe's reply, he gradually began to relax and smile. "Only another werewolf could possibly know of that. . . . I understand we cannot talk about our assignments, and I know there are French Hitler Youth from Alsace-Lorraine. . . . Are you from there?"

Sensing an opportunity, Joe shrugged his shoulders and turned both hands upward, while still holding on to his dagger.

With his azure eyes fixed on Joe, Arnd finally said, "Yes, I trust you."

Cautiously both boys lowered their daggers. Arnd stepped forward and put his arm around Joe, as an older brother might, and said, "I like you, Joe. I really do. I hope we can meet again after we have completed our work." Stepping back to his own bed, he saluted in a whisper, "Heil Hitler." Then he jumped into bed and was soon asleep.

But Joe took no chances. Though he returned to his bed, he never closed his eyes.

With the light of dawn Arnd was still asleep when Joe hurried to Hap's waiting jeep. But Hap would not listen to Joe. He said, "Tell me your story later, Joe. Orders just came down to move back to the front. It won't be long now." And every time Joe attempted to talk, Sergeant Hardesty shook his head. Everything had to be packed. New kitchens established. Regular supply lines formed. He had too much on his mind to listen to the kid this morning.

When they at last got to Hap's quarters and Hap had turned off the jeep, Joe grabbed Hap by the arm. In desperation Joe screamed, "My new roommate back there in Heerlen is that Hitler Youth, the werewolf, who warned the Germans about 'Operation Trojan Horse.'"

Suddenly Sergeant Hardesty was all ears. Even before Joe finished his story, the jeep was again burning rubber toward the Secondary Technical School. The MPs motioned Sergeant Hardesty into the courtyard. In minutes Sergeant Hardesty and a breathless

Joe stood before General Clay. Shortly, the Konijn residence was surrounded by MPs and other military personnel.

But the mouse was gone. Hurriedly a conference was held in the General's office with Mr. Konijn, Karel Konijn, Bep Rieksen, Second Lieutenant Philip Vossmaar, Samson, Major Jack Collins, Master Sergeant Hap Hardesty and Little Joe, and other staff officers.

In a husky voice Mr. Konijn said, "Just after Sergeant Hardesty's jeep drove away, there was furious knocking at the door. When I opened it, I was confronted by an American colonel who asked for Arnd. He seemed in a hurry. They stepped outside and closed the door. But I could still hear them whispering in German. Shortly, Arnd hurried upstairs and got his knapsack. He gave me some dollars and thanked me. Then the two walked down the street and were soon out of my view."

General Clay asked, "What did the American officer look like?"

Mr. Konijn said, "He was a tall man, at least six-foot-four with a nasty scar on his face."

Bep Rieksen asked, "What did they say in German?"

"I couldn't make it out."

Unnoticed, Colonel Quinn had entered the room. He approached Mr. Konijn and asked, "On what side of his face did this officer have the 'nasty scar'?"

Thinking a moment, Mr. Konijn replied, "On his left side. It was a bad one. Perhaps a dueling scar."

"American officers don't fence without face masks," boomed Major Collins. . . . "And very few have ever fenced."

"What was the officer's bearing? His general impression upon you, Mr. Konijn?" asked Colonel Quinn.

Under the rapid fire interrogation Mr. Konijn was beginning to get uneasy. Sweat appeared on his forehead and face. His son Karel noticed this and interceded. "I think my father has answered all your pertinent questions. He is not in very good health, and I believe he should be allowed to go home and rest."

Mr. Konijn put a hand on Karels' arm and looked squarely at Colonel Quinn. "A great Teutonic Knight." Then he walked out of the room with Karel.

Colonel Quinn's finely etched face at last turned to General Clay. "The description fits Skorzeny, sir.

Irritably General Clay asked, "Are you suggesting, Quinn, that the number-one German commando, Otto Skorzeny, the one who rescued Mussolini, is here in Heerlen?"

"From what I just heard, it's likely, sir."

"I would agree, sir," interjected Bep Rieksen.

"Then what in the hell are we waiting for?" bellowed General Clay. "Let's get the bastard. Jack, have all combat units alerted. Everyone else must search for this guy and that kid. Get the civilian government in here, pronto. What the hell's going on? First Dietrich and now Skorzeny! Is Hitler planning to throw his whole army at the 'Fighting' 15th Armored'? Jeesus Christ, Jack, see that Corps knows about this."

"We'll also get our people searching, General," said Rieksen as he, Samson, and Philip Vossmaar hurriedly departed.

To himself Samson whispered, "I wish the Americans had caught Arnd. Then he wouldn't get hurt." But Samson was certain neither Skorzeny nor Arnd would ever be found in Heerlen. In going after Skorzeny, the Americans and the Resistance were up against the master commando of all time. Hell would freeze over before they caught Skorzeny. And it struck him that his nephew must be highly regarded by Hitler to send the likes of Skorzeny, himself, on a rescue mission of a mere child.

CHAPTER SIX

Surveying his work, Sergeant Nick Whipple, division artist and camouflage expert, stepped back satisfied. He'd scaled the sixteen by six foot sand table to show the two miles of front assigned to the "Fighting" 15th Armored Division. From road maps, aerial photos and reconnaissance reports, Sergeant Whipple had molded the sand into a topographical map. Assembled in a lecture hall at the Secondary Technical School, the four-foot high sand table, along with a cluster of charts supported by a metal tripod, would provide the visual aids for Major Dick Burk's briefing.

Standing beside Nick and pleased with Nick's creation was Major Burk. Based on his recent overflight of the battlefield and his own sketches, Major Burk noted that the principal features marked in his drawings matched those depicted on Sergeant Whipple's sand table, especially Hill 102.6 and the big industrial structure southeast of Puffendorf. Major Burk knew the sand table would be a big help in his briefing of the officers of Combat Command "B"—which was scheduled to begin shortly at 1300 hours.

"Good job, Nick. Your work matches almost perfectly the drawings I made after I flew over the area."

"Thank you, sir."

As Major Burk sat on a folding chair dragging on a cigarette, the thought occurred to him that the title of the song, "What a Difference a Day Makes," certainly applied in his case: Clay's on the spur of the moment, harebrained "Operation Trojan Horse" had backfired, which pleased Major Burk. He detested officers who did not follow standard operating procedures, officers such as General Clay. But he usually kept in mind that General Clay was his commanding officer and, therefore, his resentments were best not expressed; for it was not lost upon Major Burk that some of the high brass admired Clay's unconventionality, though they probably hoped Clay wouldn't blunder himself or them into major trouble.

On the other hand, and music to his ears, had been Major Collin's disclosure that before the briefing this afternoon, he, Major Burk, would be formally promoted to lieutenant colonel. Feeling no appreciation whatsoever toward General Clay for this, Major Burk suspected that any support for his promotion must have originated at Corps Headquarters. Nor did his being chosen over Colonel Quinn to head Combat Command "B" come as a surprise. He considered Quinn a fruity, gutless wonder who should have been cashiered out of the army long ago.

After completing a mental review of his battle plan, Major Burk's thoughts turned to Susan Montgomery, the "Dragon Lady." Just recalling her alluring features warmed his blood, renewing his determination to someway undermine her infatuation with Captain Appleby. A fleeting premonition of doom about Sergeant Witkowski occurred to him. Fortunately, Witkowski had apparently kept his mouth shut about St. Lo.

WITH RESPECT TO THE BRIEFING, Major Burk did not have long to wait; soon the large, semicircular room was filled with over a hundred alert bodies all focusing their eyes on the large sand table. The rows of desks in elevation provided all the men, even those in the back, with easy vision for following Major Burk's depictions.

From a side door a staff officer suddenly appeared and commanded, "Attention!"

Generals Eisenhower, Bradley, Simpson, Clay, and other high ranking officers filed into the lecture hall. Major Burk immediately spotted two stars on Clay's shirt collar in place of the one of a brigadier general. "So," thought Dick Burk with no pleasure,

"Clay got promoted too." Then the friendly, familiar face of Ike, beaming like a benign grandfather, gave the command to be at ease.

The presence of Ike presented a rare opportunity for Major Burk. Feeling he was in his element, Major Burk immediately sought General Clay's eyes for the command to proceed.

Instead, General Clay walked briskly to the sand table, faced the assembled officers and in his sonorous voice said, "Officers of Combat Command 'B,' the importance of 'Operation Queen' to bringing about the defeat of Germany and the end of the war is underscored today by the presence of the Theater Commander." He paused as all eyes centered on Ike who nodded at the recognition.

General Clay quickly resumed, "Before beginning the briefing, it's my pleasure to announce the promotion of Major Burk here to lieutenant colonel, as it is Colonel Burk who will be responsible for this presentation." After calling Dick Burk "front and center," General Clay had an aide remove Burk's gold oak leaves from his shirt collar and replace them with the silver oak leaves of a lieutenant colonel. A snappy salute from Colonel Burk and polite applause concluded the brief ceremony.

General Clay continued, "Colonel Burk and his staff plotted most of the details as soon as Division received the objectives and timetable for the attack. At high risk to himself, Colonel Burk personally viewed the battlefield from an artillery spotter plane; also, up front in his light tank, he personally reconnoitered Jerry—and even a bit on foot, though a Kraut mortar crew attempted to lay an egg on him while he did." General Clay paused in acknowledgment of good-humored chuckling, casting a smile at Colonel Burk. Concluding his introduction, General Clay said, "Mark his words!"

General Clay and the other high brass remained standing but moved backwards toward a wall. The moment belonged to Colonel Burk. And he was ready!

Colonel Burk's wire-rimmed glasses and wrinkled brow suggested a certain schoolmasterish first impression; however, a haughty sneer on his face soon belied a pedagogical disposition, as the upward thrust of a cleft chin, drawn, thin lips and yellow-green eyes displayed more the appearance of a hungry hawk than that of a beloved teacher.

Wearing a tanker's field jacket and dressed in khaki woolens, he strode to the front of the sand table, dropping small chunks of dry mud off of his combat boots on to the wooden platform. As he scanned the faces of his audience, he ran the fingers of his right hand through his close-cropped sandy hair, and then in a hoarse voice said, "Well, Peg-Leg and Googly-Eye (General Dietrich's wooden leg and General Bartholomaus' monocle) didn't swallow 'Operation Trojan Horse.' Let's hammer them with 'Operation Queen.'"

As Colonel Burk paused, there was a nervous stirring. Most of the officers doubted that Ike and the other "high" brass had even been consulted about "Operation Trojan Horse." Ike whispered into General Clay's ear and General Clay nodded and winked at Ike.

After clearing his throat, Colonel Burk began speaking in a slow, Midwestern drawl: "If the weather holds, day after tomorrow, November 16, American and British bombers will soften up the zone in front of XIX Corps, and just before 1300 hours our Combat Command 'B' will launch the general attack." Warming to his subject he began speaking forcefully. "The Command will be divided into Task Force 1, Task Force 2 and Task Force X."

Colonel Burk, displaying a three-yard, wooden pointer, which he flourished like a conductor's baton, turned to the sand table and briskly moved the pointer from town to town as he said, "Task Force 1, on the right, has as its objectives the villages of Loverich and Puffendorf, including hill 102.6. Task Force 2, in the center, will take Floverich and help with Apweiler. Task Force X, on the left flank, has as its first objective the village of Immendorf, and then will help with Apweiler. Setterich is the responsibility of the 29th Infantry Division. After we have achieved our objectives Combat Command 'A' will enter the battle through us and continue the attack."

Lowering his voice a decibel, he said, "All of these little towns are about a mile apart. The ground in between is scarred with antitank ditches and presumably crisscrossed with interlocking machine gun, mortar and artillery. As you all know, because of the rain, snow and sleet, mud is everywhere, making for poor trafficability. Other than that, it's good tank country with a gently sloping plain toward the Roer River."

COMBAT COMMAND "B" & OPENING PHASE OF "OPERATION QUEEN"

On November 16, 1944, the front lines of the "Fighting" 15th Armored Division extended for about two miles from Waurichen to Beggendorf. "Operation Queen," the big push to the Roer River, was about to begin.

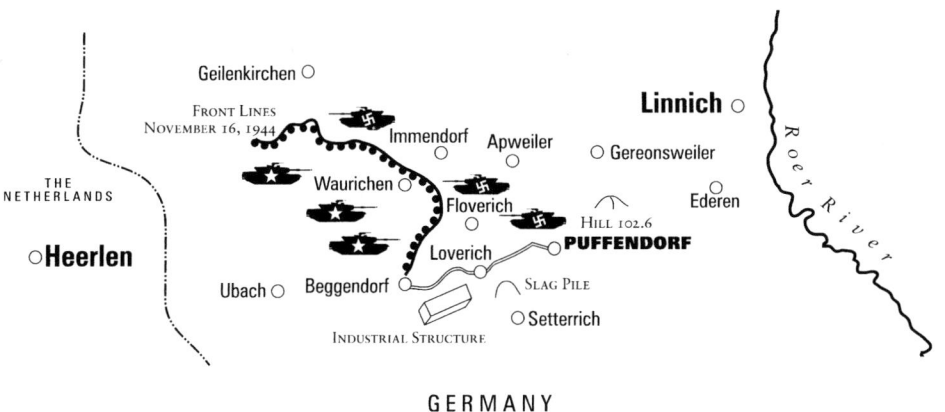

PAUSING TO CLEAR HIS THROAT again, Colonel Burk focused his eyes on Captain Appleby, sitting directly in front. On Appleby's right, Lieutenant Jordening was hunched over taking notes on a clipboard while to Appleby's left, Lieutenant Joe Nicholson momentarily made eye contact with Colonel Burk's hawkish eyes. Nicholson blinked, and Colonel Burk droned on: "Task Force 1 will be comprised of the 1st Battalion, the 2nd Battalion, a platoon from the 17th Engineer Battalion and "B" Company of the 702 Tank Destroyer Battalion and the 2nd Battalion of the 41st Armored infantry. Captain Appleby will be in command of Task Force 1."

Using the pointer he pinpointed on the sand table the immediate objectives of Task Force 1: "They are to take and secure Loverich and upon attaining it to be prepared to attack Puffendorf and the high ground to the north of it, designated as Hill 102.6.

"The Assault Guns and Mortar Platoons of the Division will be massed and coordinated centrally by the Field Artillery. At 12:15 air strikes and artillery barrages will be laid down on known or suspected strong points and emplacements."

Getting the special attention of Lieutenant Jordening by kicking his foot, Colonel Burk said, "H-hour will be 12:45. 'D' Company tanks under Lieutenant Jordening here will jump off from the 'line of departure' at the southern tip of Beggendorf at the command from Captain Appleby...."

On and on the raspy voice of Lieutenant Colonel Burk detailed the specific problems and objectives of Combat Command "B" and the opening phase of "Operation Queen." After Colonel Burk, others continued the briefing, and it was close to 1600 hours before the officers of Combat Command "B" were dismissed to return to their individual units. The "high brass" had long since departed.

AT HIS GESTAPO HEADQUARTERS in The Hague, police chief, SS Lieutenant General Hanns Albin Rauter, lived in fear of retribution. He knew his policies, aimed at suppressing the Resistance, would cost him his life if Germany lost the war. But now with Allied armies already in parts of Holland and fearing an uprising by the population, Rauter resolved to squelch it in the bud. His directives included executing three Dutch nationals for every German killed, forbidding all travel between provinces and imposing curfews throughout Holland. Dutchmen were also pressed into service as laborers digging trenches for the Wehrmacht, and public gatherings of more than three people were forbidden.

Rauter, however, required "hatchet men" to do his blood letting. The Gestapo thug assigned to track down the infamous underground leader, Rieksen, was a psychopath, Count Siegfried von der Schulenburg. Usually dressed in a dark suit and looking like a respected business man, the Count got his kicks from torturing his victims. During his childhood, the parents of the Count had been aghast at the predilection of their young son for tormenting his pets. Only in time did corporal punishment teach the boy to conceal his cruel nature. Now Rauter had given this monster free-rein in the tracking down of Rieksen.

DRESSED IN A SMUDGY white shirt, dark tie and faded blue suit, Herr Graf, as the count was sometimes called, sat in his dingy office drumming his fingers on a worn desk, mulling over the information that his men had just killed Rieksen at one of Amsterdam's brothels. What a pity, he thought. Of all his enemies, he had wanted this one captured alive.

The double-agent Samson, who was responsible for Rieksen's entrapment, had negotiated a kind of quid pro quo with Count Siegfried which the Count had no intention of fully honoring: a conjugal visit by Samson with his mistress, Janeane Mitterand, and the release of Samson's sister and her husband—and also the release of Frau Lindemann, Rieksen's mistress.

After bargaining with the Count over his private telephone, Samson had pinpointed Rieksen at the Waterfront Hotel, a nefarious brothel. Unfortunately, the underground leader had been found with accomplices; gun fire had erupted, the hotel had been set afire, and Rieksen's body had been discovered in a smoldering room of that building.

Continuing to drum his fingers on his desk, the Count now impatiently awaited the arrival of Samson even as he instructed an aid to telephone SS General Dietrich. Samson had promised to deliver a revised version of "Operation Queen." But before the general could be brought to the phone, Count Siegfried's office door opened and two of Siegried's armed men escorted the bulky Samson before him. Count Siegfried hung up the receiver.

"Ah, 'The Great Samson,'" the Count began amiably as he remained seated behind his desk.

As if drugged, Samson's blank, dark eyes blinked rapidly as he gradually lowered himself onto a metal stool before the Count's desk, feigning stupefied unconcern.

"Are you tired, Samson, or should I address you as Hans Spoor?" asked the Count in a heavy, threatening voice.

The mention of his Christian name by this idolatrous Nazi, brought Samson to attention. He had no illusions about the danger he faced from the blood thirsty count. Slowly he sat up and focused his eyes on the jaundice face behind the dilapidated desk. "Maybe I am tired, Herr Graf. It's been a long night. The sun was just rising when I entered your headquarters."

"Let's get down to business. Did you accompany Rieksen to Amsterdam?"

"No. He gave me the plans for 'Operation Queen' in Heerlen."

"Did you know that Rieksen was surrounded by a gang of his men?"

"No."

"Have you any idea where Rieksen is now?"

"Probably in Hell."

Count Siegfried's bloodshot eyes starred implacably at the brutish, scarred face of Samson, whose somber eyes dilated as several of Siegfried's men moved in closer, the massive hands of Samson clinching as they rested on his lap.

MOTIONLESS, COUNT SIEGFRIED was allowing the minutes to drag when his telephone rang. An assistant answered and gave the receiver to Siegfried, who turned away. Though the Count spoke rapidly and in a muffled voice; Samson heard his name mentioned.

When the Count hung up, he again turned to Samson. The tight lines in his yellow face had vanished. In a soft voice he said, "That was General Dietrich. He's having a courier flown to Amsterdam for the plans; he expects 'Operation Queen' to begin at any moment and is preparing for any eventuality. However, he wants to look at whatever Rieksen gave you."

Not convinced that all had gone as planned, but hoping not to alert Count Siegfried either, Samson removed from his shirt a white envelope and placed it on Siegfried's desk, blandly inquiring, "Did you keep your part of the bargain? Have the hostages been released?"

Smiling, knowing he had no idea of the whereabouts of Frau Lindemann, Siegfried said, "You really don't give shit about Frau Lindemann, do you, Samson? Your concern is mostly for Janeane Mitterand. Am I not correct?"

Samson eyed the Gestapo chief without replying.

Siegfried continued, "Too bad, Samson. I lied. As long as you are allowed to be a 'double-agent,' we must hold these people to ensure your loyalty. But they will be well treated. And they are lucky to yet be alive. General Dietrich thought you might be the one who set the trap for 'Operation Trojan Horse.'"

Samson resignedly relaxed and awaited his fate.

"However, Samson, by helping us eliminate Rieksen and by acquiring the plans for "Operation Queen"—if they prove to be real—you may have partially redeemed yourself," said the Count. "So I've decided to reward you, Samson. Mademoiselle Mitterand awaits you at the Waterfront Hotel.... Perhaps, though, I should inform you that we found the body of Rieksen in a burned room of that building...." The Count let his words sink in, then said,

"But I don't hold it against you, Samson, that Rieksen was escorted by his men. I kind of expected that."

Samson thought, "*Damn. Maybe Bep pulled it off again. But I must be cool.*"

"Thank you," said Samson.

"Before I allow you to depart, a word of caution. We now know of your relationship to the 'wunderkind'—Arnd Hauptmann. In the future we trust your loyalty to the Reich will never falter, for through the boy we do know about your parents in The Hague." He paused to allow that disclosure to also sink in. Then in a hollow voice, he added, "Be assured, for now they will not be detained. But never let us down, Samson. . . . You may go."

FOLLOWING HIS MEETING with Count Siegried, Samson hitched a ride with a Gestapo agent to the Waterfront Hotel. He had not seen Janeane since her abduction some months past.

The smell of the briny sea and the clamor of ravenous gulls always gave Samson a lift; but the sight of vacant wharfs and useless cranes revealing that the Germans had destroyed the port facilities of Amsterdam, pained Samson.

After expressing thanks for the ride, his eyes scanned the front of the red-bricked hotel, once a Mecca for sailors. Old men with fire hoses lingered before the rambling structure, but only a few rooms had been burned. Still, it was business as usual: a few patrons, women and liquor. Samson was baffled that even though a fierce war raged nearby and Holland was plagued by severe shortages, a weird sense of normalcy prevailed. Because he had been to the Waterfront Hotel many times, he knew where to look for Janeane.

After climbing a flight of stairs, Samson directed his steps toward a particular door he well knew. But just as Samson neared that door, it opened and he was in the arms of his beloved. Quickly they stepped into the room, Samson closing and locking the door behind them.

A purple, velvet curtain draped one wall of the room, and on the others hung erotic paintings. There were no windows and from the fire the smell of smoke suffused the stale air. "Mon Cheri,

Mon Cheri," whispered Janeane. Clad only in a silk, flowered negligee with matching cotton house slippers, the young, svelte, dark-haired girl, her face rouged and powdered, her lips soft and red, led an eager Samson to bed. They only spoke briefly and passionately. But their bliss was short-lived.

The sounds of automatic weapons and the clamor of someone climbing the narrow stairs alerted Samson, who began pulling on his clothes while leaping from the bed. Staccato pounding on the door caused Samson to instinctively hold Janeane as her shield. Then he heard his name being called by a familiar voice.

Cautiously opening the door, Samson was confronted by Bep and Karel, both holding German machine pistols in their hands.

Laughing, Bep said, "Let's get the hell out of here. The Gestapo figured out the identity of their corpse. The Herr Graf is on his way."

Before anyone could move, a Gestapo agent, who'd been operating a movie camera, stepped out from behind the curtains firing a Luger. Janeane screamed as mortal shots struck her in the back.

Instantly Bep riddled the body of the Gestapo agent.

Anxiously removing the dead woman from Samson's arms and laying her on the floor, Karel pleaded with Samson to hurry from the building. Soon both Karel and Bep were tugging and forcing a distraught Samson down the narrow stairway.

Several of Bep's men covered the retreat of the three into an idling Citröen. Karel took the wheel with Bep beside him. Samson was shoved into the rear seat. As Karel sped away, he swerved to avoid colliding with an army staff car carrying Count Siegfried. A wild chase caromed through the streets of Amsterdam. At length Karel veered into a depository district and escaped into a labyrinth of streets, finally parking the Citröen inside a large warehouse.

When the three emerged from the car they were greeted by other armed, Resistance fighters. Into a warm, dimly lit room the three hurried. Much to his surprise and concern, Samson saw his elderly parents seated on a bench. After greeting them, Samson turned to Bep who had unbuttoned his trench coat and was again puffing on his pipe. "What now?"

"Too bad we couldn't pull it off. Tonight we go on to Eindhoven, avoiding the main roads and bridges. British soldiers are waiting for us near the front where we'll abandon the car."

"What about my sister and her husband?"

Bep looked away. Karel said, "We couldn't get to them." Slowly raising his right arm and gently patting Samson's sagging shoulders, Karel said, "I'm sorry, Hans, my friend."

The grey, bareheaded parents embraced, sobbing.

"We must leave at darkness. The Count will soon have swarms in here," said Bep emphatically.

Speaking firmly to his parents so all could hear, Samson declared, "I'll not leave my sister to that madman, Siegfried. I'll kill him, even if I must die. I'll remain in Amsterdam!"

Over the cries of Sampson's parents, Bep struck his pipe against the side of his heel. At length he said, "All right, Hans. I can give you a chance to get at Siegfried, but it will probably be a martyrdom."

"Life without Janeane means nothing to me, Bep."

Thoughtfully Bep said, "You might gain access to Count Siegfried's headquarters by posing as a maintenance worker. I can get the necessary pass and a blueprint of the building." Briefly interrupted by more Resistance men entering the small room, Bep said, "Unfortunately your size and looks make even a suicide mission difficult, Samson."

FRÄULEIN GERTRUD SCHULTZ had not welcomed the telephone call from her brother-in-law, General Fritz Kraus, summoning her to meet him at his hunting lodge with instructions to bring his children, ten-year-old Max and eleven-year-old Felicia. He had informed Gertrud that he would be accompanied by a refugee woman for whom he wanted Gertrud to prepare a temporary place at his hunting lodge. The thought that there might be a relationship between Fritz and this woman alarmed Gertrud.

While waiting for the plane, Gertrud had conjectured that she would die if the woman in some way meant removing the children.

She loved them. How could Fritz possibly forget that for the past years, since the death of Margarete, the children had become the whole focus of her life?

And now, after the landing of Fritz's plane, as she watched Fritz lend a steady hand to the strange woman emerging from his aircraft, Gertrud was struck by the woman's unique beauty, even though only a blue, silk scarf tied around her head, displayed any bright color or elegance. Furthermore, this woman's ordinary cotton blouse and skirt, her ankle length stockings and tattered coat were all shades of grey, just like the day.

But Gertrud noticed something different about the woman, an unusually thin and angular neck, somehow reminding Gertrud of a swan; and as Fritz introduced the woman to the children, Gertrud gaped at the gentleness and friendliness emanating from the woman's face. Strangely the children seemed to gravitate toward the intruder when she gracefully bent at the knees to be at their level. And contrary to the children's usual reserve toward strangers, they eagerly approached this stranger; and shocking though it was to Gertrud, each child sparkled at the woman's embrace.

When the children and Fritz, with the woman in grey by his side, walked toward her, Gertrud imagined a funeral procession. She could not help feeling a deadly antipathy toward this interloper. As they all stopped before her, Fritz said evenly, "Gertrud, I want you to meet Frau Nicoline Lindemann. Nicoline, Fräulein Gertrud Schultz." Nervously Fritz cleared his throat and speaking directly to Nicoline said, "Since Margarete's death, Gertrud has been staying and caring for Max and Felicia at my town house in Warstein. Gertrud was Margarete's older sister, and as I have no close relatives, I'm very much indebted to Gertrud for caring for the children these past years." There was a certain authority, perhaps ominous finality, maybe a sense of guilt, in Fritz's voice that Gertrud had never noticed before. He sounded different, but she wasn't sure how to interpret it.

For her part, Nicoline quickly sensed Gertrud's resentment, and she recalled General Kraus saying on the airplane that he hoped Nicoline would be friends with Fräulein Schultz. Remembering what the general was risking on her behalf, Nicoline was determined to try to please everyone.

Bowing to the stout and matronly Fräulein, guessing that she must be at least in her forties, Nicoline said, "Fräulein, please consider me your humble servant."

Nicoline's self-abasement was not what General Kraus had in mind, though he had warned Nicoline that she must not reveal her true situation to Gertrud. Therefore, General Kraus interrupted, "Gertrud . . . Frau Lindemann comes from a distinguished Dutch family. Circumstances relating to the war brought her to my command, but I have asked Frau Lindemann for the time being to remain silent about her situation." His commanding eyes locked with the stubborn eyes of his sister-in-law. "Frau Lindemann will be considered a guest for as long as she remains."

Not in the least camouflaging her feelings, Gertrud said unctuously, "Well, of course, Fritz." Looking directly at Nilcoline and curtsying, she said, "On behalf of all of us I bid welcome to Frau Lindemann. If it were in peace time, we would hold a party, right, Fritz?" Then dramatically thrusting her left arm out, she said expansively, "Let's have a party anyway. The manner by which Fritz's great Führer is winning the war for the Fatherland, it could well be the last party for all of us."

The irony in Gertrud's voice and its suggestion of doom surprised and annoyed General Kraus. But he had not seen Gertrud recently, and he too noticed a change. Usually a meticulous dresser, today the fur stole around Gertrud's wide neck was soiled, as was her red, woolen coat. Bracelets and earrings were missing. Gertrud's luxuriant hair, streaked with grey, was held in place by a simple black, ornamental comb; and her hair seemed dull and unwashed. What had happened to Gertrud? Fritz knew Warstein had not been bombed; and all along he had seen to it that scarce necessities, such as food, clothing and coal, had been carefully acquired for Gertrud and the children. He had also dispatched such items to the maid and gardener who helped Gertrud with the house and yard work. At a glance, the children appeared scrubbed, happy and well dressed. Had the stress of the war unnerved Gertrud? He would soon find out!

Smiling at Nicoline, General Kraus said, "You know, Frau Lindemann, defeatist talk is against the law in Germany. But I know these are difficult times." Turning to his sister-in-law, he said, "Come now, Gertrud. Cheer-up. We don't want to let our guest get the wrong impression about our love and confidence in our Führer."

"I see, Fritz, you are still the fanatical loyalist. I hope your optimism stems from knowledge I know not of. "

"Be confident, Gertrud. It does."

At that moment out of the overcast sky a flight of seven pigeons appeared. Momentarily each bird hovered as it descended to a perch on a small wooden out- building. The birds then tripped a one-way door opening to a pigeon loft near the rafters of the building. But the first pigeon to alight, a snow white one, remained on the wooden perch until Fritz held out his arm and cooed softly. The pigeon dropped from the perch and glided toward Fritz's outreached arm just as a diving falcon noticed the humans and aborted a strike. As the falcon screeched an alarm and banked away, the white pigeon veered and returned to the safety of the loft.

Urgently Fritz said, "Max, get me the shotgun."

Hurriedly the husky blond boy ran to the log cabin and within minutes returned with an over-under twelve gauge which Fritz grabbed as his eyes focused on the falcon. The predatory bird had found a dead tree limb from which to survey the situation. As Fritz stalked the bird, it suddenly realized its own peril and flew out of sight.

Returning to the group, Fritz said, "That for-damn falcon nearly got Snow White. She'll probably never fly to my arm again."

"Don't worry, Fritz. I'm sure the bird knows the source of its danger was not you." Pointedly Gertrud went on, "You have more important things to worry about anyway. I certainly know you're not at fault."

Confounded by Gertrud's remarks, Fritz asked, "At fault for what?"

Avoiding Fritz's eyes, she said, "The way the war is going, of course."

By now Max had had all of this adult talk he could take. Excitedly he asked, "Can we go partridge hunting, Father? We brought Hektor from town. He's in the cabin."

Fondly Fritz thought of Hektor, his roan, and white-ticked German Shorthaired Pointer, the last present Margarete had given him on his birthday over three years ago. "First things first, Max. Remember, we must look after Frau Lindemann's welfare. See that she is comfortable in our cabin. Then I have to determine if the pigeons brought any messages. After that, if all is well, Hektor, you, and I will see if we can bag some partridges for the pot. How's that?"

"Wonderful, Father!" said the towhead.

"Let father and son go their way," urged Gertrud. "I'll see to the comfort of Frau Lindemann, and Felicia can help."

"Of course, Father, Max has been a little devil waiting for you. Go with the brat. I'll help Aunt Gertrud and make the acquaintance of Frau Lindemann."

"Please do not worry about me, General Kraus," interjected Nicoline.

"Thank you. Thank you all," said General Kraus. "You, Max, it's tingly weather. Put something on for the briars, and bring me my hunting clothes—and Hektor. I'll be at the barn."

AFTER MAX HAD RUN to the cabin and General Kraus had left for the outbuilding, Nicoline stood transfixed staring at the imposing log cabin. Though just one-story high, the building appeared to ramble over the landscape, probably having multiple rooms. A red tiled roof slightly distracted from the rustic appearance of the structure, she thought. Set in a clearing within the pine forest, scarlet leafed vines clung noticeably to the logs like the tentacles of some marine creature, and white-chipped rock covered a path leading from the small metal hanger to the front doorway of the cabin. With few exceptions, noticeably the mowed grass on the landing strip and a narrow, blacktop road and parking place for automobiles, natural vegetation nearly surrounded the cabin. "There should be little need for yard work here," surmised Nicoline.

"Frau Lindemann, allow us to get out of this chilly dampness and go inside the cabin," said Gertrud.

"But of course. I guess I'm overcome by this fairy-tale-like setting—the forest, the log cabin. It reminds me of a picture in *Grimm's Fairy Tales*."

"Well, now, Frau Lindemann!" snickered Gertrud. "Let me assure you that the house is not made of gingerbread. I'm really not the wicked old witch, and Max and Felicia are not *Hansel and Gretel*."

Smiling, Nicoline said, "You're teasing me, Fräulein. Yes, let's get out of the chill; I see by the smoke from the chimney there is a fire in your fireplace."

Nicoline had correctly guessed the hunting lodge would be in masculine décor. Sturdy wooden chairs and tables and couches were scattered about a large room whose principal feature was a huge stone fireplace now aglow with yellow leaping flames. A metal screen confined crackling and exploding embers. The room smelled of pine and smoke. Trophy heads and various guns clung to the walls, as did several large paintings of hunting scenes.

As Nicoline warmed her hands by the fireplace her eyes settled on an oil painting of a dog pointing a partridge in a bush. It hung prominently above the fireplace.

Felicia said, "That is Hektor, Frau Lindemann. Max must have taken him out by the back door."

"He is a beautiful dog."

With Fritz temporarily removed from the scene Gertrud was determined, in spite of Fritz's admonition, to learn the relationship of this woman with her brother-in-law. She said, "Felicia, go make the bed in the north room and tidy it up for our guest."

"Yes, Auntie."

Following Felicia's departure, Gertrud asked, "For how long, Frau Lindemann, have you known Fritz?"

Nicoline recognized Gertrud's intent. "Not very long, Madam."

Conspiratorially Gertrud said, "For your information, Frau Lindemann, Fritz is different from most men. He was raised as a pampered only-child by a domineering mother." Gertrud's face contorted in pain. "Poor Margarete had to suffer the consequences of such a spoiled child becoming a man."

"What do you mean?"

"Oh, I can't go into details. You heard what Fritz said to me. But this marriage was pure hell for poor Margarete. Please say nothing to Fritz, but for your sake, Frau Lindemann, I felt compelled to warn you before anything might happen."

That "anything" could happen between herself and General Kraus had not entered Nicoline's mind in spite of General Kraus' unusual solicitations for her welfare. But after what Fräulein Schultz just said there was no doubt that that was just what concerned this lady.

Still smiling at Gertrud, Nicoline said, "My first husband is dead, Fräulein Schultz. But I have a new love to whom I'm engaged to be married when the war is over. Have no fears."

Somewhat taken back, Gertrud bluntly asked, "Then why did Fritz bring you here?"

Not knowing how to answer the question, Nicoline changed the subject. "Why does General Kraus raise pigeons?"

"Frau Lindemann, you are avoiding my question."

"Really, I don't know. Perhaps it is to protect me."

"Protect you from what?"

"I thought I asked you, Gertrud, not to interrogate our guest!" remonstrated General Kraus as he walked to the fireplace. Dressed in the brown of his hunting attire, he had entered the cabin from a side entrance.

"Even though I'm a German woman, Fritz, I find it difficult to quell the nature of my gender."

"All right, Gertrud. First, let us sit a moment."

"Where are the children?" asked Gertrud.

"They are tending to Hecktor and the pigeons."

General Kraus smiled at Nicoline before directing his gaze at his sister-in-law. He then recounted the events leading up to his decision to hide Nicoline from the Gestapo (of course, excluding the attraction he felt toward Nicoline).

Fritz's amazing revelation of being at odds with the Gestapo and thereby his beloved Führer opened the door of opportunity for Gertrud. She breathed a sigh of relief as General Kraus concluded his story.

But General Kraus' monologue was not yet over. Still with a steady eye on his sister-in-law and a firm tone in his voice, he lectured: "Any compromising of me or Frau Lindemann would adversely affect the children. I'm sure you can realize that, Gertrud. You know what the Gestapo does to the families of those who have opposed them! Think about it. . . . If only because of the children, I know I can trust you."

After a strained silence Gertrud said, "I would never have believed, Fritz, you of all people, could ever do anything like this. You have already compromised yourself. But don't worry about me. I'm forever faithful."

The confident ring to Gertrud's voice did not exactly please General Kraus. He believed he might have made a mistake in being so candid, realizing his sister-in-law had never held him in high esteem. But the deed was done. He still felt Gertrud would never harm the children in anyway.

At that moment the children and Hecktor bounded into the house. In a mighty leap that nearly bowled the general over, Hecktor was immediately on the lap of his beloved master, all eighty pounds of him, his wet tongue scouring the general's face.

"Enough, enough, my loyal-one. Down, down—sit—my-beauty. Max!—Let's get the heck out of here before Hecktor tears the place down! I heard partridges drumming in the forest when I came to the cabin. Come on!"

Out the door hurried the three hunters, leaving the three females smiling and absorbed with their private thoughts. Gertrud wondering how to get rid of Frau Lindemann, Nicoline wondering why General Kraus was protecting her; and Felicia wondering what kind of person Frau Lindemann would really prove to be.

LIKE A SOLDIER ON DUTY Fritz Kraus was up and about before the crack of dawn. As Gertrud had brought provisions when she drove his black Mercedes to the hunting cabin, he was preparing himself an English breakfast of coffee, bread with jelly, and bacon and eggs. He knew Gertrud was a night reader and would sleep late. He only hoped that the children would sleep too, so he could have a little time alone with Frau Lindemann. He had already quietly knocked at her door.

The hunt the previous day had been a success. The incomparable Hecktor had pointed and retrieved partridges and was now curled up on his Persian rug before the fireplace. A bonding with Max had been strengthened. The young boy already shared his father's love for the out-of-doors, fishing and hunting. And for the moment Fritz longed for a time of peace when Max would be older and he could teach him all these skills. He already could see that Max would be an eager and willing student.

Felicia likewise occupied his thoughts. She with the beguiling smile and delicate features, and mind as sharp as a tack. What could happen to her if the armies of the enemy should prevail and overrun this region? He was worried by the thought. He knew what his own troops had done in Poland and Russia, but he hardly considered the Slavic peoples as being on the same plane as the Germanic races.

And that was where Frau Lindemann came into the picture. Frau Lindemann was the girl friend of the Resistance leader, the legendary Bep Rieksen. If Frau Lindemann could be prevailed upon to protect his children, if worst came to worst, it would greatly relieve his fears. Max and Felicia must be protected at all costs; and, like himself, they both appeared attracted to this unusual woman. Of course, he had not given up hope. The tide of misfortune for Germany must soon change. Any moment he expected a pigeon to bring news of the American tank attack necessitating his immediate return to the front; so this morning he must act quickly to prevail upon Frau Lindemann for the well being of his children.

NICOLINE HAD HEARD the anticipated knock on her door as the general had requested an early morning breakfast. Perhaps she would learn the reason for her being brought here. Quickly she dressed in her robe and opened the door of her bedroom to the pleasing aroma of frying bacon, recalling a food she had not eaten in years. Tucked in one corner of the large room was a cast iron cook stove and there a frying pan sizzled with bacon and eggs. Resting next to the frying pan on the stove was a percolating black coffee pot dispensing another memorable aroma in the cabin. A rectangular table covered by a flowered oil cloth revealed an array of plates, cups and silverware already set up. Four oak chairs were pushed under the table. The general was dressed in a grey, leisure sweat suit.

Hecktor announced the arrival of Nicoline by a deep-throated growl. "Good morning Frau Lindemann. Perhaps you would like to freshen yourself in the water closet. We do have modern conveniences out here thanks to hoarded gasoline and an old generator. There is also a basin of water and cotton cloths and towels waiting for you. See you in a few minutes."

After a brief breakfast with only a little small talk, the two seated themselves on the couch before the stone fireplace, again fired to break the chill. Nicoline spoke first, "General Kraus, please call me Nicoline. Your kindness amazes me."

"And you, Nicoline, address me as Fritz. But in embarrassment I must tell you that there is a selfish motive behind my, what you call, kindness."

Nicoline looked puzzled, but offered no reply.

Swallowing hard, Fritz gently took Nicoline's soft, white hand in his tan, leathery hand. "Don't be alarmed, Nicoline. But I need you. I need you for the sake of my children."

Nicoline was surprised to discover that the touch of Fritz's hand did not alarm or offend her. Looking into his blue eyes, she was drawn to the older man. But if his was an advance, it was hardly the place for it, considering the nearness of Gertrud and the children. Yet she was pliant, and said nothing, smiling demurely at his pleading, facial expression.

"I do like you. I believe I liked you from the moment I first saw you at the hospital. But I know you are committed, and I respect your situation. Yes, I do envy Rieksen. And he is why I might need you more than ever."

Puzzled by Fritz's allusions, Nicoline said, "How is it possible that I could ever help you?"

Continuing to squeeze Nicoline's soft hand and peering into her doe-like eyes, Fritz said, "If Germany should lose the war and the Allies overrun us, who is there to look after the safety and well-being of Max and Felicia? No one whom I trust. Not Gertrud!" Fritz saw the look of surprise on Nicoline's face. He released her hand and stood. "I had a dream. It was a foreboding one. Nicoline, I have not been an angel. As I search my soul, there is blood on my hands I'm ashamed of. I did it for my Führer. Remember, I'm an SS general. I'm obliged to do my duty."

Glancing out the window, Fritz saw that the light of dawn was struggling again with an overcast day. Surely the pigeons must come. Finding a chair by the fireplace he again gazed at the remarkable Dutch beauty who silently appeared to hang onto his every word. "Nicoline, I don't know how to make this request after such a brief time together, but would you consider caring for Max and Felicia if the war goes badly or I am killed? You could return with the children to your own home in The Netherlands if you wish."

Startled by such a request and needing time to digest its implication, Nicoline, nevertheless, promptly replied, "Of course, Fritz. Your children are so nice." Pausing and staring at her hands, she said, "But aren't there problems?... Gertrud?... And I hope you survive the war, Fritz; what with all your obvious wealth, you can do wonders for your children."

"That will be taken care of, Nicoline. For now, stay and get to know Gertrud and the children. Will you do that for me?"

"How could I not?" Nicoline starred compassionately into the eyes of Fritz Kraus.... "Know that I will do so with love, Fritz."

As the word "love" echoed and reechoed in Fritz's mind, his peripheral vision caught a shadow flashing by the window. Looking toward the barn, he saw the pigeon he had been expecting— and he knew certainly that the American tank attack had begun.

CHAPTER 7

AGAIN WHIP JOHNSON found himself standing in the tank commander's hatch eating a freshly plucked apple, but unlike a few days past he knew this would be no practice run. This would be the real thing: his baptism of fire—and his guts churned. He could be dead or maimed in the next few minutes. Suddenly the same old "Why me?" scrolled by his mind's eye in bloody technicolor. For the moment his young life seemed reduced to kill or be killed. How could life suddenly turn so vicious and final?

Scanning for his tank crew, Whip saw them grouped under one of the apple trees. Dale Jenks appeared to be speaking and gesturing as Nate Talbot, Hank Henry and Sergeant Witkowski laughed at whatever he was saying. For the moment Whip wished he could be like Dale who under pressure was the coolest person he'd ever known. Dale always said his life or death was up to God; but as long as God gave him life, he'd be looking for ways to have fun. With such a hedonistic attitude, Whip wondered why Dale had ever teamed up with pessimists and cynics such as John C. Smith and himself.

Then he recalled that since Dale and he had cleared that mine field, Sergeant Witkowski's attitude toward them had undergone a dramatic about-face. Witkowski had already recommended them for the Bronze Star, and he never spoke disparagingly to them anymore. Evidently Witkowski's initial grumpiness stemmed from a belief that each replacement had to prove himself. Even so, Whip knew the mine field thing, though dangerous, wasn't anything like looking the enemy square in the face—with either you killing him or he killing you. Yet it did give Whip some comfort to know he was in a tank commanded by an experienced tank commander; one who had survived numerous tank battles all the way from the beachhead in Normandy.

On the other hand, the bad side in being with Witkowski was that Colonel Burk had only recently ordered Witkowski to take over the bulldozer tank—a highly regarded target for German gunners. As Whip understood it, this placement of Witkowski in the dozer had overruled Captain Appleby. One guy had even hinted that Burk's action was ominous for Witkowski.

That idea set Whip's mind running rampant. Damn, he wished he were still at Knox arguing with Smith instead of crammed into this cold tank inhaling toxic fumes from its idling motor. He cast away the apple core and grasped *The Story of Philosophy* from under his sweater. Holding the book steady in his gloved hands, he said, "Shit. Come to think of it, most philosophers are prophets of doom." As Whip saw it, the only advantage philosophy had over religion was that it didn't sugarcoat reality. In essence, most of the philosophers said, "You're screwed, buddy, and there's no way of getting out of being screwed in this God damn, fucking world."

Then Whip recalled reading that one should develop a philosophic attitude. Find equanimity in the struggle of life. In other words, have the guts to take whatever comes your way without whimpering, and certainly don't live a lie by swallowing some dogma and then pointing at the heavens proclaiming you now know the only universal truth. "Shit," he murmured, "I'm really getting cynical just like Smith."

Truthfully, reflected Whip, he had no quarrel with any of the world's religions, and freedom of religion is a great thing. Maybe the greatest thing on earth. If a particular religion or denomination can comfort, reassure or make one feel good in this brief life—wonderful! It just angered him when the zealots of any faith, or political organization for that matter, attempted to force their beliefs on others by edicts, laws or whatever. "Really—since the beginning of history the fanatics have been the source for most of the wars and most of man's inhumanity to man," concluded Whip. On second thought, Whip admitted greed and lust must be contributing factors.

"Thank God for the American Constitution and the protection of minority rights in the U.S.A," sighed Whip; because he believed that tyranny by the majority could be just as bad as tyranny by a dictator like Hitler, and so had most of the Founding Fathers. That's why Whip felt he was fighting this fucking, damn war against the Nazis—to save the world from the fanatics of all stripes who, if they could, would sculpt everyone in their own image.

At that instant, the air bombardment of the enemy began. In quick response, Whip replaced *The Story of Philosophy* beneath his army sweater and prayed, "Please, Oh God, protect me!"

The Battle of Puffendorf had begun!

Lieutenant Colonel Richard C. Burk III, the Combat Command "B" leader, viewed the arrival of "H" hour from an entirely different perspective than Whip Johnson. He wasn't worried so much for himself at all. In his case, he saw a chance for fame and glory and returning home a war hero. That was important to Dick Burk in light of his future ambitions. Regardless, since Saint Lo, where he had been made a battalion commander, he now saw more behind-the-lines duty; not that his present status was without risks, just that the risks were usually much less than that of a frontline company commander. Keeping this in mind, he hoped for the success of his battle plan even as he directed the driver of his light tank to a defilade position on the edge of Beggendorf. From there he would have a good view of the jump-off of Company "D" at "H" hour.

CAPTAIN APPLEBY, the Task Force "1" leader, was entirely engrossed with the problems at hand as he, too, positioned his command tank, a medium Sherman, on the outskirts of Beggendorf. Next, he made sure he had radio contact not only with Colonel Burk, but with all the other tank commanders in Task Force "1," and especially with the "air tank"!

Important for the success of "Operation Queen" was having good radio communication between all elements participating in the attack. In a tank designated as the "air tank" rode an officer of the tactical air force assigned to support "Operation Queen," and on this day the air officer was also accompanied by an artillery officer. The air officer maintained radio contact with the pilots in the flights of P47s cooperating with the ground offensive, being able to call in or call off air strikes at most any time. The artillery officer could do likewise for artillery barrages.

At the beginning of the attack, the air tank was located in a defilade position between the command tanks of Burk and Appleby. Because of radio monitoring and jamming by the enemy, much of the language over the radio was in code. However, at the behest of Captain Appleby, his own command tank remained designated as "Daredevil-Six" in spite of his knowledge that the Germans were aware of his radio designation.

SECOND LIEUTENANT "RED" JORDENING was also mentally preparing himself for the battle. His 1st Platoon of "D" Company would initiate the first wave of the attack. On his immediate right would be the second and third platoons. At the outset of the battle each platoon would have either four or five tanks; and, thanks to the replacements, "D" Company was now nearly at full strength. However, he knew the company would not be at full strength by day's end. Like all the veterans, he only hoped the "law of averages" wouldn't catch up with him and that the objectives assigned to Task Force "1," taking the villages of Loverich and Puffendorf, as well as Hill 102.6, could be obtained on day-one.

As planned by Captain Appleby, Second Lieutenant Joe Nicholson's 2nd Platoon and Second Lieutenant Fred Kipping's 3rd Platoon would follow the 1st Platoon tanks out of Beggendorf, eventually fanning out to the right of the big industrial structure. Red, on the other hand, would lead his 1st Platoon left of the building, but to the right of the Beggendorf—Puffendorf road, just as other units of Task Force "1" would be attacking on the left side of the road. At the same time units of the 29th Infantry Division would attempt to take Setterich.

With respect to his own contribution to the plan, Lieutenant Jordening had determined to form a wedge with four of his tanks and put Witkowski and the dozer some 75 yards back, but allowing space between the lead tanks for Witkowski's guns to also fire forward.

AT LAST, CAPTAIN APPLEBY was calling in over the radio net to make sure Task Force "1" was on line when a strange, guttural voice interrupted. "Is that you, Captain Appleby or should I say 'Daredevil-Six'? From the pounding your air force and artillery are giving us, this must be the hour of your big push." The voice clicked off, followed by an eerie silence. Then Jordening heard Captain Appleby ask higher command for a fix on that last radio transmission. Appleby added, "It sounded strong like it was right among us." At once Appleby warned all units that the radio net was being tapped by the enemy. "Take care what you say," he ordered.

DURING NOVEMBER OF 1944 the Allies usually had total air supremacy over the battlefield. The only break the German ground forces got from aerial harassment by the Allies was "Adolf Hitler" weather, as they called it. It was the worst weather western Europe had experienced during the century, nearly nullifying Allied air power. Overcast skies, damp, cold sleet and snow followed day after day. November 16 was no exception. But shortly after noon there was a break in the skies, and through it, like enraged hornets, funneled planes from the American tactical air force strafing and bombing Puffendorf and the surrounding area. Then at 12:45, "H" hour, Lieutenant "Red" Jordening, on command from Captain Appleby, gunned his 1st Platoon past the "line of departure" at Beggendorf.

Just ahead the armored artillery laid down a curtain of fire that preceded the tanks like a wall-cloud before a Dakota thunderstorm.

The enemy doughs had no chance to raise their heads. To the rear of Jordening's mediums, the light tanks protected the armored infantry as they harried enemy doughs out of their foxholes.

With one last nervous glance out his periscope, Whip Johnson went into action. As in the rehearsal every gun mounted on the dozer opened fire. Though he was preoccupied loading the 75, he was struck by the oddness he felt, as if he were in a dream. Even the humming of the radio had other worldliness about it until abruptly, the profane voice of Lieutenant Nicholson erupted, "God damn antitank shell hit 'Seven.' . . . Tank burning. . . . Get the God damn bazooka man in the fire-trench. . . . Oh, my God. . . . That fucker won't fuck anymore. . . . 'Six,' we have casualties. . . . Get artillery on Setterich, we're catching hell from there. . . ."

At once Captain Appleby's voice said, "'Three,' get your guns on that haystack west of Setterich. There's your tormentor. His shell just ploughed the earth next to me. . . . Good, you got 'em."

"Score one for John C. Smith," thought Whip, knowing his Fort Knox buddy was the loader on Lieutenant Nicholson's tank.

Eight minutes after crossing the line of departure, Lieutenant Jordening's 1st Platoon of five Sherman tanks crashed into the apple orchard overlooking Loverich. Four of the tanks advanced on through the orchard then wheeled to the orchard's western edge and stopped. The barrels of their guns poked through the trees toward Loverich. But the bulldozer tank was not among them!

Even though he was strapped into his seat, the body of Whip Johnson lunged forward as the dozer smashed through a hedgerow bordering the orchard. Following a big bump, the tank stopped dead in its tracks.

Because of restricted vision, Sergeant Witkowski rarely "buttoned-up" (closed the turret hatch)—and then only when he was under the direct fire of the enemy. Consequently, his voice coolly announced a "play by play" over the intercom: "We fell into a tank trap. There are enemy doughs all around us, but so far they're quiet. Our light tanks and infantry should be here any second; afterwards, I'll roll the logs off. . . . I think we can get out of this hole on our own power."

Then urgently, Witkowski said, "Problems. Some Krauts are

playing with a bazooka. Who's got a tommy gun?"

Whip handed his gun to the tank commander who leaped from the tank. . . . Shortly, Witkowski reentered the tank. "There were two of them. They won't bother us any more." Handing the hot gun back to Whip, he next announced, "Here comes our own infantry. . . . The enemy is surrendering. . . . Nate, help me get these logs rolled off."

With the logs providing traction, Sergeant Witkowski guided Nate Talbot, who worked the dozer out of the ditch. Then Sergeant Witkowski resumed his commander's seat in the tank, and the dozer moved through the orchard in quest of the other tanks.

At that moment Whip recognized the voice of Lieutenant Jordening on the radio. "'Six,' this is 'Five.' Tell 'Thirteen' (the air and artillery tank) to lay off. Our own stuff is falling on us."

Glued to his periscope, Whip saw the dozer was surrounded by swarms of grey-coated German infantrymen with their hands in the air. One particular youth, hatless, the whites of his eyes pulsating in absolute terror, probably crapped his pants when Nate momentarily halted the tank and Dale leveled the 75 at the pit of the kid's stomach.

Witkowski warily motioned all the enemy to the rear where the armored infantry were collecting prisoners.

Immediately after joining the rest of the 1st Platoon, Witkowski quickly had the dozer collaborating in the shelling of Loverich. His first target, though, was at a church steeple, because, as Whip had been told, from church belfries German officers often directed their artillery fire. Nevertheless, it seemed almost devilish to Whip that churches should be the first to get clobbered; but then he philosophized, "Maybe that's only natural—with war being hell."

BAFFLEMENT REIGNED at the "Hammer" Panzer Division headquarters in Linnich. The "old badger," Brigadier General Gerd von Bartholomaus was in a rage. At an aide-de-camp he shouted, "Where in the hell is Dietrich? Where in the hell is General Kraus? I thought the God-for-damn 'SS' were so notably devoted to their beloved Führer. What are they doing? Deserting a sinking ship!"

Word had just arrived that artillery barrages and air strikes on Loverich and Puffendorf had lifted and American tanks were now streaming out of Beggendorf toward Loverich. Efforts to contact General Dietrich's battle group at Puffendorf had failed. It was as if they had disappeared from the face of the earth, he was told. "Impossible," he yelled, his washboard face contorted red, monocle dropping out of his one good eye. "Dietrich's battle group with all its Panthers and Tigers can't just disappear. And you tell me that General Kraus is somewhere in the Reich for an eye treatment. . . . I can't believe it!"

At that delirious moment General Bartholomaus was handed a phone with a call from Army Group "C" headquarters. Field Marshal Stein wanted a situation report. "Gott im Himmel, Manfred. This is it, I'm certain. The opening of the big offensive we've been expecting. Manfred, I've attempted to reach Rheinhardt at III Panzer Corps, but he refuses to talk with me. Dietrich has disappeared with his battle group, and General Kraus is supposedly back in the Reich for an eye treatment. What are your orders?"

Field Marshal Stein replied, "Calm down, Gerd. Kraus has broken bivouac and will be counterattacking the Americans in the morning. He will be in Linnich quickly to help you prepare the counterattack." After a pause, Stein said, "Forget about Dietrich. Those are the orders from OB West." (Field Marshal Beck, at OB West, was the Supreme Commander of all German forces on the Western Front.) "Beck thought two panzer divisions along with their attachments could halt, or at least slow the advance of the Americans in the Puffendorf area . . . I hate to burden you at a time like this, Gerd, with drivel, but I was ordered by Beck to reassure all of my subordinates that the Fürher is planning a move that will soon wipe out any temporary successes of the enemy."

Field Marshal Stein spoke with ironic emphasis. Gerd Bartholomaus well understood and totally sympathized with the disdain Field Marshal Stein had for the "military savvy" of Hitler. "Do the best that you can, Gerd, in a bad situation. Keep me informed and I'll do whatever I can to help you."

Shortly after the call, General Kraus himself hurried into the "Hammer" Division's operations room. Raising his right hand at the wrist, he said, "Heil Hitler."

Of all the SS generals, Fritz Kraus was the only one Bartholomaus really liked. Even though Kraus was as fanatical about Hitler as the rest, Bartholomaus had discovered in Fritz a gentleness and humanity lacking in most of the SS generals, but because of his SS "blood oath" to the Führer, even Fritz could not be entirely trusted.

"Heil Hitler. I thought you had deserted us," lamented the old general, rising somewhat slowly from a chair next to his map table.

"Sorry. I don't blame you if you're put out with me, Gerd. What are your latest reports?"

With a wooden pointer General Bartholomaus noted various positions on his war map. "The Americans are attacking on a ten mile front, all along their XIX Corps area. For the moment we're holding, except it appears that units of Clay's 15th Armored Division may be making a breakthrough in the Loverich area and in the direction of Puffendorf."

General Kraus pondered General Bartholomaus's reply even as he carefully studied the war map secured to a large flat table. Then he said, "My division is fresh, though still understrength. We were just refitted." Pointing a finger at the war map, he continued, "Why don't I move my panzers to Gereonsweiler during the night and begin a counterattack before dawn on the 17th. You could come in on the 18th with your reserves, Gerd. Is your infantry in condition to follow my panzers?"

"As you well know, Fritz, my front line positions are mostly held by Volksstrum and Hitler Youth. I'm ashamed to do this to our old men and boys. However, there are a few veterans scattered among them to stiffen their spines; but at the moment, though, most of my veterans are being held in reserve to plug the gaps. . . . I know this should not be the time for complaining, Fritz, but answer me: Why does the Führer continue this war with such a rag-tag army? There's nothing left to scrape from the barrel."

"I understand how you feel, and, frankly, you just expressed some of my own concerns. But you are misplacing the fault if you blame the Führer for our predicament. Rather it lies with Roosevelt and his Jewish advisor, Morgenthau, who intends to enslave the German Nation by plowing up the country and permitting only pastoral activities. . . . Considering that alternative, Gerd, we can only fight on. . . . Maybe a miracle will occur. Such ones have often happened in the life of our Führer."

General Kraus's statement struck a nerve. "Speaking of miracles, General Kraus," asked Bartholomaus, "where in the hell is that great miracle worker, SS General Dietrich and his famous battle group? They have vanished. Only the day before yesterday I saw him at Puffendorf. Now at this critical moment I can't even reach him by radio—I already tried the telephone."

"I don't know. You and I may have to fight Clay alone. We can do it for I know you've created one hell of a good defense, Gerd, having antitank ditches dug, crisscrossing the whole area from Loverich to the Roer River with interlocking machine gun, mortar and artillery." Reaching for a pencil, General Kraus pointed at the map and said, "Your hedgehog defense is brilliant, Gerd. I see that each village on this Roer plain is within direct firing range of two or more similar towns, and the Amis will have to take them separately. I see that these villages are mutually supporting strong points. It will be impossible for the enemy to attack without our forces seeing them coming across the flat lands. The Amis must surely pay dearly attempting to go through here, Gerd.

"Also—let me tell you this, but keep it to yourself. Manteuffel and his 3rd Panzer Army are being plucked from the East and brought West even as we speak. I'm told the Führer has a surprise in store for Eisenhower; and you and I will eventually be part of that surprise, too! For now, we must blunt and halt 'Operation Queen.' . . . And about Dietrich . . . Most likely Dietrich's secrecy has something to do with the arrival of Manteuffel. Remember, Dietrich is a protege of Hasso's."

After several moments of reflection, General Bartholomaus replied, "I wish to thank you for taking me into your confidence, Fritz, even though I'm not SS. From my vantage point, you're young and I'm old. I've got the experience and you've got the energy. I feel very comfortable fighting this battle with you by my side. Maybe we can yet do something that future generations of Germans may remember and honor."

General Kraus accepted the compliment with a nod. "In recent weeks I've done some soul searching, Gerd. I'm not pleased with everything I've been associated with in this bloody war. But for now, we are both soldiers. No matter what we believe about anything, the uppermost thought in our minds must be to do our duty to our Fatherland. I know you can not feel any differently, Gerd."

"Of course, Fritz. All Germans must do their duty for the sake of the Fatherland!"

IT HAD NOT TAKEN John C. Smith long to realize he was in a tank with two psychos—Lieutenant Joe Nicholson and Private Morbid Morris. At first glance the lieutenant looked as innocent as a cherub in a painting by Raphael and the private as evil as the monster in *Frankenstein*. The lieutenant revealed his warped mentality by ceaseless profanity and a kinky view of life—like he was going to fuck the first fräulein he could lay his hands on and he'd kill every Kraut trying to surrender, which John C. Smith did not doubt in the least.

The grotesque-appearing private was mute most of the time, with the exception of his encounter with "VD" Johnson. In response to most questions, Morbid would lift his bushy eyebrows and say mysteriously, "My day's a comin', man." Even Lieutenant Nicholson had once shook his head and cried, "How in the fuckin' God damn hell did I ever end up with you, Morbid?" Morbid had looked glassy-eyed and repeated, "My day's a comin', man." John Smith thought, "How did both these misfits ever get by the induction center, let alone one of them becoming a commissioned officer?"

John C. Smith realized that Lieutenant Nicholson at first did not have a much higher regard for John C. Smith than he had for Morbid Morris. John remembered Lieutenant Nicholson's first comments when he was assigned to the tank. "My God, Lieutenant Appleby, you're not really giving me this bespectacled, dried up, pimple-faced kid are you? God, the shithead doesn't look like he's out of adolescence. How in the hell can he load the 75?" At that time John could not understand Appleby shaking his head and saying—not to Lieutenant Nicholson but to himself, "Sorry, Corporal, but someone has to go here." Now he no longer had any doubts about Appleby's misgivings. But John was stoical and hoped for the best. He knew that nothing lasts forever, but it was still too bad he couldn't be in the same tank with "VD" and Dale.

ON NOVEMBER 16, 1944, Lieutenant Nicholson was uncharacteristically quiet and serious faced as he lead his 2nd Platoon of four tanks in the wake of Lieutenant Jordening's 1st Platoon. As they passed the line of departure, he headed for the east side of the rectangular industrial structure. Lieutenant Kipping's 3rd Platoon quickly followed the 2nd Platoon. Both platoons then fanned out to the right of the immense building. Light tanks covered the advance of the mediums protecting their flanks as armored infantry followed the light tanks on foot. Effective fire from the field artillery continued to fall just ahead of the attacking force, keeping the enemy doughs pinned down until the tanks and the armored infantry overran their positions.

Exactly three minutes after the start of the attack, enemy outposts began yielding prisoners. Whenever opposition developed, the tanks opened fire with all weapons. Some of the enemy doughs carried bazookas, but few ever had a chance of putting them into operation. The two medium platoons and a light tank platoon on the right flank crossed several fire trenches without incident. Entangled concertina wire proved ineffective. At 12:49 the second platoon began receiving antitank fire from the east in the direction of Setterich, and at this point, Sergeant Pagano's medium tank hit a mine, putting it out of action. It was then hit repeatedly by antitank fire, killing three of the crew and severely wounding the other two.

Captain Appleby moved to the front and drew antitank fire thereby locating the enemy gun. He then directed the fire of the two right flank platoons on the enemy position, and by 12:51 the gun was silenced.

Shortly thereafter units of the 90th Armored Infantry Regiment and light tanks of "A" Company cleared Loverich of all opposition. The medium tanks of "D" Company now shifted to the east of Loverich from where they could see their next objective, the high ground north of Puffendorf known as Hill 102.6 They were soon joined by the light tanks of "A" Company.

THE ATTACK ON Hill 102.6 jumped off at 1400 hours. At about the same time, medium tanks from the 2nd Battalion and their attachments were directly attacking Puffendorf. By 1500 hours both Puffendorf and Hill 102.6 had been captured. However, enemy fire did prevent the occupation of the ridge top of Hill 102.6, but the tanks commanded it from the draw.

All units of Combat Command "B" were then ordered to secure the ground gained and dig in for the night; the offensive was to be resumed at 0800 of the 17th. Infantrymen of the 90th Armored Infantry Regiment moved up and outposted the tanks. Colonel Burk, after satisfying himself that the positions of the tanks and infantry were adequate for night defense, moved into Puffendorf to set up his command post in the basement of a house on the main street. Combat Command "B" had mostly achieved its objectives on this opening day of "Operation Queen."

As he outlined his plans for the next day's attack, the Colonel expressed his gratification at the manner in which his subordinates had thus far carried out their assignments. From General Clay and Colonel Quinn came congratulations. Colonel Burk passed the praise along to his battalion and company commanders and platoon leaders.

AS DARKNESS SETTLED Captain Appleby sought out Colonel Burk for a private discussion. "I'm apprehensive, Colonel," said Captain Appleby, "what tomorrow will bring. We took no prisoners from Dietrich's battle group, and we had no encounters with any Panthers or Tigers, yet Dietrich was supposed to be encamped in the vicinity of Puffendorf. . . . About the voice on our radio net just before the jump-off. Did our technicians ever report a fix on that transmission?"

His raspy voice indicating annoyance, Colonel Burk said, "I was told it might have come from the industrial structure. I've ordered a platoon from Recon. to check out the interior of that building. Anyway, Captain, I've always doubted there is a battle group or a Major or General Dietrich. I believe the results of today's fighting bears me out." Superciliously pushing his glasses back on his nose, he asked, "Why should you be singled out above any other officer?"

Captain Appleby recognized the rebuff. He smiled and said, "I shouldn't be." Then he turned and without another word left the Colonel's CP. After mounting his command tank, Captain Appleby surprised his driver by ordering a return to Loverich.

A narrow salient had been driven into the German lines from Beggendorf to Hill 102.6 about 2.5 miles deep. Enemy artillery and mortar fire continued to rain down from Setterich, which the 29th Infantry Division had failed to take, as well as from Apweiler, Gereonsweiler and Ederen; and Jerry was hammering the Loverich—Puffendorf road. Though traffic bringing ammunition and gasoline were bumper to bumper, the flare of burning vehicles intensified as darkness closed in.

In fading light while standing on his tank commander's seat, Captain Appleby studied two interesting features with his binoculars: the slag heap and the gigantic industrial structure to the southeast of Puffendorf. He knew they'd been bombed repeatedly, but even in the twilight, they both stood out like islands in an American river of military vehicles flowing toward the front. From his lurching tank, he couldn't make out much. Nevertheless, considering what he'd just heard from Colonel Burk, his guts told him to be wary. However, before ordering his driver back to the front line where his Company "D" was positioned on the side of Hill 102.6, he was determined to take a look for himself on the inside of that building which he thought might have been a large steel mill.

Approaching the structure from its northwest side, Captain Appleby ordered his driver to stop opposite a broken window from which he might peek inside. He had no more than climbed out upon the turret than he was confronted by a black uniformed soldier who poked a pistol into his gut. He saw the tank was surrounded by similarly dressed soldiers. Another soldier leaped up on to the turret holding a grenade. In perfect American English he said, "Order your men to surrender and to come out with their hands up, or I'll drop this 'egg' in on them."

Captain Appleby knew he'd been had, and did as he was told. Hurriedly the black dressed soldiers rounded up the five Americans and hustled them through a side door into the spacious building. Though the lighting was poor and apparently coming from lanterns, Tom could hardly believe his eyes at the activity going on within this huge shell. Like ants swarming around a disturbed ant hill, white-coated men were moving every which way as Panther and Tiger tanks, looking like prehistoric animals, were being pulled from a subterranean basement by winches. Some of the tanks were parked and had their motors idling. The smell of exhaust fumes and gasoline pervaded the air. Then he saw it! It was just being pulled from the basement—and it did radiate a kind of bluish glow. It had to be General Dietrich's own Royal Tiger tank. Suddenly the five American tankers were shoved into a small, dimly lit room. Grim faced SS soldiers, armed with machine pistols, confronted them.

As his eyes gradually adjusted to the light, Captain Appleby saw standing at a small table a formidable appearing SS soldier about whose identity he had no doubts. The pale scar, the metallic eyes, the determined set of the face and the artificial leg, which the soldier revealed when he limped from behind the table, pinpointed a legend. After the soldier halted directly in front of Captain Appleby, the latter whispered, "It didn't take you long, General Dietrich, to bring me down."

"I can't believe my eyes. How could the great Captain Appleby fall so easily into my hands." Slowly scrutinizing Captain Appleby, who was dressed in a tanker's winter outfit, General Dietrich said,

"You are a very large man to fit into a Sherman tank. How can you do it, sir?"

"True, General Dietrich, I do have to suck my gut in."

Looking sad General Dietrich said, "A pity we meet under these circumstances. I had hoped it would be tank to tank on the battlefield. But maybe . . ." His voice trailed off. Then he said, "I'm very sorry we have so little time to talk." General Dietrich suddenly seemed unsure. After a moment of indecision, he said, "Killing you and your men now would be unsportsman like, wouldn't it?"

With a nod of his head the five American tankers were roughly gaged, hog-tied and rolled into a corner where they bumped into other American soldiers likewise so trussed and immobilized.

Gently nudging Captain Appleby with his foot, General Dietrich said, "You know, and I know, that under these difficult circumstances, most officers on both sides would be inclined to take no prisoners. But I'm not a butcher, as I don't believe you are, Captain Appleby; therefore, you and your men should live to see another day. . . .

"Oh, if you should talk with General Clay soon, tell him turnabout is fair play, and that this is my little 'Trojan Horse.' I hope it proves more successful than his. However it goes, Captain Appleby, there's a chance we may meet again." General Dietrich drew himself up and said, "Auf Wiedersehen."

EVEN THOUGH WHIP JOHNSON hadn't had a bite to eat all day, he felt no hunger pangs. Deliberately he scanned the landscape with his periscope. Darkness was setting in and fires burned on the rim of the ravine. Maybe the fires were burning vehicles or just vegetation, Whip wasn't sure. It appeared Witkowski had found a defile within the ravine to park the dozer. The tank seemed surrounded by stunted trees and thick undergrowth. But Whip was still on edge, all his senses magnified.

Sergeant Witkowski asked Whip about the state of their ammunition. The AP was gone. Some Smoke remained and only three

HEs were left in the ammunition racks. Following the departure of Sergeant Witkowski and Dale Jenks to look for ammunition and jerry cans of gasoline, Whip allowed himself a can of "C" rations—diced potatoes and ham.

Later someone tossed his duffel bag down the turret hatch, and he pulled out of it a recently issued sleeping bag. All the crew's duffel bags had been secured to the top of the tank. When the company had first been issued the sleeping bags, there had been a lot of experimenting with the zipper. Most of the tankers finally agreed that in combat they'd never use the zipper for fear of being trapped inside their sleeping bag if the enemy should attack. But now with the motor turned off, the inside of the tank was becoming cold—damn cold; so Whip decided to worm his way into this cocoon, combat boots and all, though he remained in an upright position on his loader's seat. He was just becoming more or less comfortable when Witkowski stuck his head in the hatch and asked him to come top side and help bring ammunition and gasoline back to the tank.

Emerging from the tank for the first time since having left the point of departure at the apple grove in Beggendorf, Whip was struck by the surrealistic setting he was in:—the free burning fires on the rim of the ravine cast flickering, forked light and grotesque shadows everywhere. Tapping him on the shoulder, Sergeant Witkowski pointed to a half-track some hundred yards or more down the gully. "Our guys just came in. Go bring back all the shells you'se can carry."

Whip replied, "Okay," and set off on a dead-run toward the half-track which he would never have been able to see had it not been for the fires. Perhaps he'd covered half the distance when an apparition with vacant eyes leaped up directly in front of him jabbing his gut with a pistol.

"Identify yourself, soldier!"

Whip gave the spiel he'd been taught during basic training.

His interrogator, who somehow looked like an officer, was enraged. "Where's your sidearm, soldier?"

"Back at the tank. I'm after ammunition, sir."

"Are you so block-headed, soldier, you can't understand this place is crawling with the enemy. The way you were running I nearly put a bullet into you. Damn it, soldier, remember this, you never leave your tank in combat unless you take along your sidearm. What is your sidearm?"

"A tommy gun, sir."

"Then get the hell back to your tank and get it!"

The ghost vanished just as suddenly as it had appeared, but Whip did as he was told.

Finally, with his tommy gun slung over his shoulder, Whip carried out Sergeant Witkowski's orders. However, in the process of fetching shells and gasoline, he soon discovered he felt like a turtle out of its shell, highly vulnerable. Even though the tank was numbingly cold, Whip was surprised at how anxious he became to again have its steel hide over his head.

Once, though, Whip came upon John C. Smith likewise lugging ammunition, and the two buddies were delighted at having encounter one another. Briefly they stopped and talked in whispers. Nevertheless, one thing that John told Whip chilled Whip to the bone, and it had nothing to do with the temperature. John said he had overheard Lieutenant Nicholson and Morbid Morris conspiring to have someone in the outfit killed and make it look as if the Germans did it. John wanted Whip to know about this in the event anything happened to him.

Remembering Morbid's earlier threats, Whip asked nervously if he was the one on their hit list. Because of Lieutenant Nicholson's involvement, John said he was certain that Whip was not the intended victim. Furthermore, John said he'd keep his eyes and ears open as this was treachery at its worst; he detested having to associate with such vermin, especially in combat. Then uncharacteristically he said, "Maybe, VD, it's Divine purpose my being where I'm at."

IN FOG AND MIST on the morning of the 17th of November, 1944, and considerably before 1800 hours, the Germans launched their counterattacks from what appeared to be every direction of the compass. The 2nd Battalion tanks were just lining up with those of the 1st Battalion on the side of Hill 102.6 for the resumption of the offensive when the radio net crackled: "Tigers and Panthers appearing out of the mist and prowling east of the Loverich—Puffendorf road picking off supply vehicles like ducks in a shooting gallery. . . . In the direction of Gereonsweiler enemy infantry attacking supported by tanks."

All hell was breaking lose along the Puffendorf Salient.

CHAPTER 8

Susan Montgomery was looking for General Clay at the Secondary Technical School when she bumped into Colonel Quinn. Her face was drawn and anxious as she asked, "Would it be possible to talk with General Clay?"

"No, Susan; he is very, very busy."

"Has Captain Appleby been hurt?" she asked bluntly and without hesitation.

"I don't believe so. I heard General Clay say Captain Appleby's command had advanced to its objectives. But fighting is tough and ongoing, and Captain Appleby is usually out-front leading his men."

Even though he wanted to allay Miss Montgomery's fears, Colonel Quinn chuckled inwardly as he recalled the GI's labeling her "hot-pants Susan." At Division Headquarters it was open knowledge that Susan's "hot pants" were now pretty much reserved for one officer.

And Colonel Quinn understood the reason for Susan's concern. The purposeful bustle and activity of American soldiers on the 15th had indicated the "big push" was at hand. On the 16th the deafening roar of low flying war planes at full throttle, the chatter of their machine guns and the concussions of their fat bombs together with the punctuating booms of heavy artillery told the undeniable story—it had begun! And by the 17th of November the streets of Heerlen were crowded with red cross marked vehicles carrying the dead and wounded.

"Did you get a ride here with Corporal Higgins (the driver of the Red Cross clubmobile)?" asked Colonel Quinn.

"No, Jimmy picked me up. But he has to stay here."

"Then will you accept a ride back to your hotel from an old, discarded soldier?"

As with most of the personnel at Division Headquarters, Susan was aware of the high regard which General Clay held for Colonel Quinn. However, at fifty, Harold Quinn, white-haired and distinguished looking, would have much preferred a command assignment for the "big push." Instead, he remained a regimental fixture, and Susan had even heard a rumor that Lieutenant Colonel Burk would soon replace Quinn as commander of the 67th Regiment with Quinn being kicked upstairs as a staff officer to General Clay.

Susan observed that the colonel, his "chickens" pinned to his open shirt collar, was ready for the road. He had coat, gloves and hat in hand. She said, "I'd be very honored to catch a ride with you."

As the colonel drove his jeep out of the courtyard, Susan turned toward the fine-featured man and wondered at the irony in his voice and his choice of the word "discarded." "You appear to be downcast, Colonel. I know you can't talk about the battle, but I hope you haven't heard bad news from the front," said Susan.

Glancing at the beauty by his side, Colonel Quinn smiled wanly and answered forcefully, "Perhaps. An old war-horse hates to be stabled when the din of battle rages."

Before they had gone a block and before Susan could reply, the jeep stopped before one of the new, three-storied Dutch houses. Out bounded a child attired in the uniform of an American soldier. Without hesitation, the black-haired, round-faced boy hurled himself into the back seat, carelessly brushing past Susan who protected herself from the little tornado by holding her arms before her face. "What in the world!" she exclaimed.

Turning to the boy Colonel Quinn said tartly, "Little Joe, you'd better say hello to Miss Montgomery and ask her forgiveness. I believe you scared the wits out of her."

Joe had recognized Susan immediately. Refusing to meet her eyes, he muttered, "I know Miss Montgomery."

"Well, our acquaintance isn't mutual, kid. Who the hell are you?"

Colonel Quinn interjected, "If I may spare some of the details, Susan, this is Joe. He came to us as a stowaway on one of our food trucks. He is an orphaned Belgian boy who is now the mascot of the Division—General Clay's in particular; and his supervisor is Sergeant 'Hap' Hardesty to whom I'm delivering him."

Peering skeptically at Joe, Susan said, "That's a mouthful." And not feeling particularly compassionate, Susan added, "Why don't you stay with your own kind, kid?"

"What do you think I am?—a pervert," responded Joe saucily.

Turning to Colonel Quinn in wonderment, Susan asked, "What does he mean by that?"

As Colonel Quinn drove away from the curb, he said, "Just GI talk, Susan. He's around those guys all day."

"Well I think he ought to be with children his own age."

Wishing to change the subject, Colonel Quinn, asked, "What are your plans for the day, Susan?"

"Sally and Josh should have the clubmobile ready when we get to the hotel. I believe we're going to the 98th Field Hospital to try and cheer up the wounded . . . By the way, could we have lunch with your headquarters company? Maybe you could tell me about the battle, whatever's not censored."

"Sure. It will be our pleasure."

PUFFING ON A PIPE, a gift from his friend Karel Konijn, twenty-year-old Philip Vossmaar sat alone in his second floor bedroom, again looking out upon the grassy square in front of the Secondary Technical School, just as he had done a few short weeks past when Sergeant Beck Jones had shot the two German soldiers—and right from the doorway of his house. That was on the 17th of September, the day the American 30th (Old Hickory) Infantry Division liberated Heerlen. Now on the 17th of November, according to Berlin radio, the largest tank battle of the war raged near Puffendorf, Germany, only 10 kilometers away. He wondered if Sergeant Beck Jones was participating in that battle?

Because Sergeant Jones' company had briefly been detached from the 30th and assigned to the 15th Armored as security at the Secondary Technical School, the two had become good friends. Frequently Beck and he had smoked American cigarettes, drank American whiskey and talked late into the night. Though he really liked Beck Jones, Jones was still the typical American: boastful, arrogant, narrow-minded and chauvinistic almost to a fault. Were there any Americans anymore, like Jefferson, Mark Twain or Jack London, Philip wondered? Surely there must somewhere be an intellectual among all these American soldiers stationed in Heerlen. But if there were one, he had yet to meet him.

Next, Philip's thoughts drifted to his recent conversations with Karel. From behind German lines, Karel and Bep had just returned from Amsterdam where they'd left Samson. Apparently, their actions represented a desperate gamble by Bep to rescue Nicoline from the Gestapo, and they had apparently failed.

Philip's musings continued, but as he was more inclined to smoke cigarettes, he doused the pipe and lit a Lucky Strike. After a long drag, he thought about the killings of the underground, and he was glad he worked for the Intelligence branch. No matter how stupid and traitorous that man Lintens, his assassination by the Resistance appalled Philip.

After a while, Philip considered the complicated affair of the two youths who had stayed next door with Karel's parents. Even now he had a hard time believing that one of them was the famous German wunderkind, Arnd Hauptmann, a favorite of Hitler's. That this kid could also be Samson's nephew and also be rescued by the famous Otto Skorzeny seemed incredulous. And now the Americans had made the Belgian boy a kind of mascot, even as that kid continued to reside with the elder Konijns! How peculiar the Americans; and what a strange world, made even stranger during war time! Putting out his cigarette, he thought he'd better be getting back to Division Headquarters where there'd most likely be more refugees waiting for him to question.

CORPORAL WESLEY "WES" WILLOW and Private Milton "Peewee" Silverman had remained behind at Ubach, pending word from Captain Appleby that he had established his new command post. They had packed the three-quarter-ton truck with the company's communication and office equipment and parked it along the side of a main road. Wes had the vehicle idling and ready to roll.

The relationship between Corporal Willow and Private Silverman was bad. It was worse than that between Private Silverman and Sergeant Witkowski. But there was a difference. Witkowski aimed his insults at all the new replacements until they proved themselves reliable; whereas, Willow's slurs at Silverman were insidious and mostly racial. Once when he had overheard Wes degrading Peewee's race, even Sergeant Witkowski had spit out his tobacco juice and said, "Wes, your uniform is the wrong color. It should be black with a swastika wrapped around one arm." Sergeant Witkowski could not have known but that was the way it nearly had been.

Before the war Corporal Willow's father had been a low-level American diplomat stationed in Berlin where Wes had attended school and had been exposed to strident Nazi views. After the infamous *kristallnacht* of November 1938, Peewee's family had luckily escaped to the United States. On the other hand, Wes's father had not been called home until after the end of the so-called *phony war* in 1940. By then thoroughly indoctrinated with Nazism, Wes had wished to remain behind in Germany, but his family had firmly decided otherwise. Back home in the states Wesley Willow graduated from high school in 1942, but by then Pearl Harbor had occurred. Shortly following his graduation, the U.S. army drafted and sent him to Fort Knox; and in due time, Wes wound up as a clerk with Company "D," where he prudently concealed his Nazi sympathies—but not his loathing for Jews. With Milton Silverman joining the company Wes now had a convenient target for venting his prejudices.

Not desiring to play the role of Milton's protector, Captain Appleby had ignored the situation. Appleby had hoped Wes would become bored with his little game, or that Milton would defend himself. Instead, Milton ignored Wes and cheerfully went about his work. Soon after Milton joined the company, Captain Appleby had assessed the negatives Silverman had going against him: his new immigrant status, his minority race and religion, and his diminutive size. He thought the latter alone should have kept the five-foot Silverman out of the service. What Captain Appleby did not know was that the influence of Silverman's relatives in Washington was considerable. It was they who had decided that nothing should stand in the way of Milton being inducted into the U.S. army if that was what Milton wanted. And, of course, that was just what Milton had wanted!

Other than his size, Milton Silverman not only had a stereotypical Jewish look with his angular face, dark complexion and hooked nose, but he was also Jewish in thought and deed. Since the day of his bar mitzvah, he had devotedly performed the rituals of his Jewish faith. Now only quietly and in seclusion did he continue to do so, but like many introspective young men, even he was beginning to rethink his position on doctrines he had once embraced without reservation.

Nevertheless, at this moment, both Corporal Willow and Private Silverman anxiously awaited the call from Captain Appleby to proceed to the front. From inside the cab of the truck both men silently smoked. The radio, tuned to the company's frequency, seemed to hum expectantly. On this chilly, overcast day both men looked out gloomily on the steady stream of olive-drab vehicles flowing north, with neither man appreciating the other's company.

At last Wes said, "Jew-boy, go back and get some more cigarettes. I'm about out."

"Okay," cheerily replied Milton.

As he climbed over the tailgate Milton noticed the filing cabinet had fallen over, and when he attempted to right it, one of the trays spilled some folders. The first he retrieved had the name of Sergeant Witkowski on it. Curiously he opened the folder even though he knew it was supposed to be confidential. It included Witkowski's service record, but what caught Milton's eyes was a hand-written note signed by Captain Richard C. Burk III, Company "D," Commanding Officer. He read it and was flabbergasted. According to the note, Burk claimed Witkowski had committed treason at St. Lo by refusing to obey a direct order from his commanding officer. The note stressed that Sergeant Witkowski had jeopardized the safety of Captain Burk's command. It was dated July 30, 1944.

As Milton pondered the meaning of his discovery, a quick glance toward the cab revealed he was being observed by Wes. Hurriedly Milton returned all the folders, closing the filing cabinet and returning to the cab with the cigarettes. As everyone in the company knew, Willow was Colonel Burk's added eyes and ears.

"What were you snooping at, Jew-boy?" snarled Wes.

"I wasn't snooping. The filing cabinet overturned."

"Don't lie, Jew-boy. I saw you reading someone's personnel record. Whose was it?"

"Sergeant Witkowski's."

Wes's face lit up like a 200-watt light bulb. He smothered his cigarette. His eyes appeared owlish and he pursed his lips. "I suppose you read Colonel Burk's note."

"Yes. What does it mean?"

"It means, Jew-boy, that you're in a hell of a lot of trouble."

"I didn't do anything."

"Oh, yes, you did. By not minding your own fucking business, you found out what a chickenshit Witkowski really is."

"So what? I don't see anything bad has happened to Sergeant Witkowski."

"You think just like a Jew-boy, Jew-boy. You're so logical. I should have said Witkowski is a chickenshit 'coward.' That note is insurance for Colonel Burk."

"What are you talking about, Wes."

"Knowing you're a Jew-boy with a Jew's curiosity, I'll tell you what happened—for I was there! And if you know what's good for you, you'll keep your fuckin' mouth shut—Jew-boy!"

Wes glared triumphantly at Milton and launched into an emotional declamation: "Company 'D' was separated from the rest of the battalion during the 'breakthrough' at St. Lo., and Witkowski was the driver of Captain Burk's tank. At that time I was his loader. But our tank hit a land mine and blew a track. Captain Burk then ordered the rest of the company to proceed and link up with the battalion while we got the track back on. We didn't know exactly where we were, though we knew several German divisions were in retreat in our general area." Wes stopped to catch his breath, his eyes ablaze.

"When we nearly had the track back on, what do you know! But out of a grove of trees stepped several German soldiers holding something white." Nervously rubbing his hands, Wes said, "It didn't take us long to tie their hands and frisk them for weapons. But of course we found none because the bastards had obviously hidden them." Suddenly the pitch of Wes's voice rose.

"We were isolated, in unknown country, where the enemy could be hiding behind any bush or tree. Therefore Captain Burk ordered Witkowski to march the Germans back into the woods and shoot them. But," Wes snarled, "Witkowski refused a direct order from his commanding officer."

"You mean kill the prisoners in cold blood?"

"Listen, Peewee, Jew-boy, I didn't know your kind had a big heart for Nazis—though I certainly don't quarrel with what they're doing to your people. But in this situation, it was either them or us."

"That's not right."

With a leer Wes concluded, "Well, I did what Witkowski was too chicken to do. I took them back into the woods and shot them. After I was done, the others had the track back on the tank, and we got out of there toot-sweet."

BEFORE GENERAL FRITZ KRAUS flew back to the front, he made several decisions regarding Frau Nicoline Lindemann and his children, most of which greatly angered Fräulein Gertrud Schultz. The substance of his decisions was that Nicoline, Felicia and Max were to remain at his hunting lodge. General Kraus left it up to

Gertrud to decide for herself if she would stay at the cabin or return to his town house in Warstein. In any event, Gertrud was to keep the trio supplied with fresh food and to continue supervising the housekeeper and gardener at his Warstein residence, which was less than an hour's drive from the cabin. Because Fritz had admitted he was protecting Frau Lindemann from the Gestapo, Gertrud convinced herself, if for no other reason, that Fritz had betrayed not only herself, but the children as well in shielding this female fugitive, Frau Nicoline Lindemann.

Because November 16th was another chilly, overcast day, Fritz knew he'd have to keep the Storch close to the ground in his return flight to the front. He would fly at tree-top height directly to Linnich toward which his own units already would be moving. At General Bartholomaus's headquarters, Gerd and he would then plot the counterattack for the following day.

As the small monoplane warmed up on the grass runway, Fritz said his good-bys. He warmly hugged both the children and bade them be good and do as Aunt Gertrud and Frau Lindemann told them. As neither had yet been taught to swim, he warned both not to go near the forest pond unless accompanied by either Aunt Gertrud or Frau Lindemann. He said they should continue with their studies, and perhaps Frau Lindemann would help them if they were nice.

To Max he said, "Feed and water the pigeons and take good care of Hektor, but let Aunt Gertrud return Snow White to Warstein in case I need to send a message from there."

"Don't worry, father. I will take care of the pigeons and Hektor just as you would," said the ten year old, delighted with the responsibility.

Turning to Gertrud, Fritz said, "Please don't think I'm ungrateful, Gertrud. I'm aware of your sacrifices. I shall never fail to see after your welfare, but please understand, the children come first in my thinking."

If that were so, Gertrud thought, then why had he brought this woman here? Not at all convinced that Fritz even remotely understood his own motivations, Gertrud uncharacteristically took Fritz's hand. "Be careful, Fritz. I know you mean well and that you can not always help yourself. Remember, I remain your humble servant and the guardian of your estate and Felicia and Max, and I look forward to your safe return."

To General Kraus the tone of Gertrud's voice was strained and unnatural, as were her words.

Next, he took Nicoline's smooth, white hand and pressed it firmly. Looking into her worried eyes, he said tenderly, "I'm also grateful to you for what you have promised." Nervously he squeezed her hand repeatedly. "These are fretful times, and, as I told you once before—have confidence and persevere."

Now that Fritz was preparing to literally fly back into the thick of the fighting and danger, Nicoline was surprised at her own feelings. They were as if she were about to part from a lover. Dressed in the black field uniform of a general of the Waffen SS, the blue-eyed officer looked younger than the middle age suggested by the streaks of grey in his red hair; and she found his slightly freckled nose, tan skin and trim build attractive. In Nicoline's eyes Fritz was extremely handsome.

Suddenly she was overcome by feelings of guilt, as before her mind's eye flashed the taut face and slim figure of Bep. She saw him pale and frail, wearing his grey trench coat and smoking his constant pipe. She saw him dressed in leisure clothes at the piano playing Mozart, and she remembered his soothing voice and gentleness after her husband had died. Then she recalled their nights in bed in one another's arms.

"Is something the matter, Nicoline? You look ill. Are you sick?" inquired Fritz, showing alarm.

Shaking her head and looking Fritz in the eyes, Nicoline said, "Sorry.... As Gertrud said, do be careful for the sake of all of us. I'll help Gertrud with the children and the work, and I, too, look forward to your safe return, Fritz."

Quickly Fritz gave Nicoline a kiss on her cheek and climbed into the cockpit. Soon he was airborne and lost to view in the light fog. Sadly and without speaking the group on the ground returned to the cabin.

For the remainder of the day everyone at the hunting lodge was heavy hearted. Even Hektor looked downcast lying on his Persian rug before the crackling fireplace, and the children stayed in the house until bedtime mostly reading and coloring books. But almost immediately following Fritz's departure, Gertrud declared she would remain at the lodge until it was absolutely necessary to get fresh food, as there was an underground cellar abundantly stocked with provisions. "In reality," she said, "we can all stay here almost indefinitely." The cabin itself was off the beaten path and visitors were unlikely. Of course, they had firearms and Hektor, and the Mercedes automobile if someone should get sick. Also, in case of an extreme emergency, there was a foot path leading through the woods to a farm about five kilometers away. Furthermore, the farmer, Herr Lüdwig, came periodically to mow the runway and look after the place.

As the day wore on, Gertrud made bread and Nicoline tidied the cabin. In the evening Max proposed that he, Nicoline and Felicia go fishing at the forest pond the next day, but Gertrud said the weather was too nasty. Felicia said she, at least, could show the beautiful pond to Nicoline if it were not raining in the morning, to which Gertrud made no reply. At dusk all four retired to their beds lulled to sleep by the hum of giant airplane engines. In other parts of Germany that night, death and destruction would soon be raining down from the skies.

THOUGH MOST OF WESTERN Germany continued to be overcast the morning of the 17th of November, 1944, the Arnsberger Forest was bathed in sunshine, just what Felicia had hoped for. Following a breakfast of coffee, fresh bread, butter and jelly, she grasped Nicoline by the hand leading her out the door, but only after both had retrieved woolen jackets. Though it was a clear day, the morning air was brisk, and a sullen Max, explicitly forbidden by Gertrud to accompany the two, had already slipped out the back door with Hektor.

Ever since Fritz had first informed Nicoline about his first wife

Margarete, Nicoline had had a yearning to know more about this woman. At first she had been tempted to address her inquires to Gertrud, but, on second thought, figured Gertrud would probably present a prejudiced version of her younger, deceased sister. On the other hand, Nicoline felt that a few judicious questions presented to the bright and lively Felicia could elicit the naive truth of a child.

The path leading to the forest pond wound through a spectacle of nature. Even though "colorama time" in the Arnsberger Forest was nearly over, a few gaudy leaves of poplars and maples remained to shimmer in the breeze. But mostly the path tunneled through a forest of tall, fragrant evergreens. Topping a rise, Nicoline was briefly blinded by the reflection of the sun upon a jewel. When she could at last focus her eyes, a sparkling diamond set in a ring of yellows, reds and greens nearly took her breath away. Shaped like an arc and measuring about a city block in length, though only a few hundred yards or so wide, the crystal waters of the forest pond, constantly replenished and drained by a an inky looking creek, barely revealed a ripple on this day.

"Oh, my goodness!" said Nicoline.

"Father calls this place his 'Crown Jewel' and says this is where the Lady of the Lake lives. Of course, he is joking."

"Is your father referring to the English King Arthur?"

"Of course. I already have read about Lohengrin, Roland and King Arthur. I even read to Max about them. . . . Let me take you to a bench father built where we can sit and talk. It is on the other side from where we now stand."

After crossing a little rustic foot bridge spanning the creek, they followed a path to a clearing overlooking the pond. The bench was made of rough timbers. Settling themselves on its sanded surface, Nicoline noticed that Felicia, whose blond hair was combed down all around her head and cut short, had the beguiling look of one very satisfied with what she was doing. Nicoline thought, "What a splendid child."

After a moment or so of silent communing with nature, Nicoline asked the question she'd had on her mind. "What did your mother look like, Felicia?"

"She was very beautiful, Frau Lindemann, just like you, but not so strong as you," answered the child with alacrity.

"Do you mean I'm fat?"

Placing her hands to her face and exploding in a girlish laugh, Felicia said, "Oh dear no! You are tan and just look so big and strong. Mama was so pale and thin and weak; and after she got sick she seemed to slowly evaporate." With tears welling up, Felicia went on, "It was so sad." Then abruptly Felicia perked up. "She was kind and gentle, like you, and very wise."

"Was she anything like her sister, your Aunt Gertrud?"

Again Felicia giggled. "They were as different as night and day, Frau Lindemann."

Feeling a little guilty interrogating the child when the aunt was not around, Nicoline changed the subject. "How well do you and Max get along?"

Puckering her nose and thoughtfully bringing a finger to her chin, she said, "I love him, but I don't dare let him know it. He is almost impossible to live with. He is a rough boy who wants to do everything his way."

Suddenly they heard a stentorian voice from the opposite side of the pond scolding, "Max, you little devil. Go to your room."

Max rose from the grass along the opposite bank from where he had been eavesdropping. To Nicoline, Max suddenly appeared to lose his balance, toppling toward the pond.

Gertrud screamed as Max splashed into the water below.

All was reflex action with Nicoline. Off flew her jacket and shoes as she jumped up and stood on the bank before the cold water. She dove, then swam toward the flailing boy. He was at least seventy yards away—too far she thought to save from drowning.

But other more sensitive ears had heard Gertrud's scream. Off chasing a butterfly, Hektor raced back to the pond. With only a brief pause, the shiny 80-pound dog leaped from the bank toward his master. Having retrieved many ducks from this pond for Fritz, Hektor was a strong swimmer. In seconds he was next to Max who flung his arms around the powerful dog's neck. By the time Nicoline reached the pair, the boy and the dog had reached shallow water;

Max was standing in his clothes, dripping wet. After coughing up a bucketful of water and looking totally abashed, the boy suddenly realized he was in the arms of Nicoline who had bent down to embrace him. Both had sopping wet clothes clinging to their bodies—as they remained shivering and standing in the water.

At last Max stammered, "Swimming isn't so hard. . . . Why are we standing in the water?"

THAT EVENING BEFORE A GOOD FIRE, Nicoline and the children reflected on the day's big event. Max had his night clothes on and with a blanket draped over his shoulders, sat in a chair, his feet soaking in a tub of hot water. He appeared to have the sniffles, so Nicoline had prepared this treatment as a kind of palliative. She said it was a family remedy for warding off pneumonia.

To Max, Nicoline said, "You see what happens when you're a bad boy and don't do as your Aunt Gertrud says. You get punished one way or another."

Sheepishly Max replied, "I know you're right, Frau Lindemann, but if Aunt Gertrud hadn't scared me, I wouldn't have lost my balance."

"That is no excuse for your misbehavior," said Nicoline sternly.

"I know it, and I apologize to Aunt Gertrud."

Nicoline had never seen children at this age so mature.

Gertrud had not yet recovered from her own shock, going about the house still in a daze. She merely nodded at Max when he apologized.

Sitting on a couch with a demure expression on her face, Felicia said, "You were very beautiful, Frau Lindemann . . . in the water with your clothes clinging to your body." And again she giggled. "Where did you ever learn to swim so fast?"

"It's a long story and someday I may tell you."

"Frau Lindemann, can Hektor sleep with me tonight?" asked Max.

"Of course. He probably saved your life."

"Frau Lindemann, will Hektor be with me in Heaven?"

"Pshaw. Don't talk about Heaven. You have a life to live."

THE FOLLOWING MORNING Nicoline took it upon herself to do Max's chores of caring for the pigeons, as she insisted that he remain in the house for at least another day. Upon approaching the barn, she heard the characteristic cooing of the birds. She thought having homing pigeons must be a hobby for Fritz because, she had read, modern armies communicated by telephone and radio. Of course, before the war pigeon fanciers the world over raced their birds in competition. She decided the next time she saw Fritz she would try to remember to ask him about his birds.

When she entered the barn a musty odor nearly floored her; and she wondered if Max had been attending to the birds properly. Their cages were full of droppings. But she had no trouble locating the sacks of bird seed, grit and a hand water pump. Thankfully it was possible to fill the food trays and the water retainers without opening the cages.

After satisfying her chores, she surveyed the scene. She counted about thirty birds, mostly grey and barred in color. Some were paired and in separate cages with a few of the birds sitting on nests. She noticed some had bands around a leg with numbers; perhaps the bands were carriers for messages, she guessed. Some of the cages also had numbers. She was sure it was all thought out with a purpose in mind. Next, she paid particular attention to the wings of the birds. She knew they could fly for hundreds of miles without resting. Some had bulging wing muscles. These must be racers.

Then she saw the exception. It was alone and had a separate cage extending to an outlet near the rafters. Because it was the only white pigeon in the loft, it had to be Snow White, the bird that had flown to Fritz when they had arrived. Nicoline could hardly believe that she had almost missed seeing the bird, let alone feeding and watering it. Snow White's enclosure was located in the dark side of the barn and the bird must have been secluded behind its nest. Nicoline noticed that a metal lever was attached to the side of the white bird's cage. Curiously Nicoline touched it. She heard a clicking sound. Then a guillotine door lifted at the rafters and a shaft of light revealed an opening to the outside. With a flutter and a flurry Snow White disappeared out the opening.

Running outside, looking upward she cried, "What have I done?" There she saw Snow White already perched on the top of the grey stucco barn preening her feathers.

Unfortunately, Fritz had been right about the falcon remaining in the area. With the patience of the predator, the grey falcon now launched itself from a pine tree for the second time toward Snow White. But again before the raptor could sink its talons into its prey, human intervention saved Snow White. The blast of a shotgun shattered the air. However, the light load of Max's firearm did not bring the falcon to earth, and both birds flew away in different directions.

As bird feathers fluttered to the earth, Max shouted triumphantly, "I hit the falcon."

Overcome by the chain of events, Nicoline could only say, "You shouldn't be outside, Max!"

"I saw the falcon from the window, and I had forgotten to tell you about Snow White. It is lucky I came when I did. Snow White is Father's pet."

"But Snow White is gone. Where will she go?"

"She will soon return. Father's hunting lodge is her home. But as Father said, Aunt Gertrud must soon take Snow White back to our pigeon loft at Warstein."

"But you have that gun in your hands and you're such a little boy. How can you know how to use it?"

Laughing, Max said, "Father and I shoot targets a lot when he is home. But I am never to take the gun unless I am with him. This was an emergency."

Not being able to think of any logical response to the boy, Nicoline finally said, "Let's get in the house before you catch your death of cold."

As always this November, Amsterdam, "the Venice of the North," saw little sunshine, and on this particular day and early morning hour the fog was especially thick and dripping wet.

Samson, wearing a fisherman's rubber parka and hat, handled the oars of a small rowboat in expert fashion. Invigorated by the smell of salt air, he cautiously wove the boat in and out and along the sides of canals, slowly making his way to a predetermined destination; and other than hearing the dip of his oars and the ripples made by his boat, the only sounds he heard were the lapping of water against various obstructions and the squabblings of a few raucous gulls in the distance. He was alone, and that's the way he wanted it, for his was a mission of death—and likely his own.

Beyond a doubt, Count Siegfried must be turning the city upside down looking for Bep and himself, conjectured Samson. But Samson smiled knowing Bep must by now be safely back in British occupied Holland or maybe he'd already returned to Heerlen. True, in the past there had been differences between Bep and himself; and only in recent days had their purposes fully united, mainly because of Samson's growing hatred for the Nazis. Presently, he only hoped that the success of this venture might atone some for his past failings.

When the deserted houseboat for which he had been looking appeared out of the fog, Samson quickly fastened the rowboat to the dock and walked up a gangplank onto a dilapidated vessel. His stay would be only for the day, preparatory to his entry into the Count's headquarters.

The last word from Bep's informant, one of Bep's moles within the Amsterdam Gestapo, was that Count Siegfried had recently moved his headquarters to a common, five-storied grey, brick building—a former police station. As promised by Bep, a blueprint of this building, explosive charges and weapons would be placed for him within the houseboat, along with a key admitting his entry to this Gestapo station through a rear door; however, Samson considered the blueprint unnecessary, for he recalled having been detained in that very building years before on a charge of rowdiness. On the other hand, he thought, maybe the Gestapo had remodeled it to fit their sadistic pleasures.

Quickly he went below deck and found spread out on the cabin table the promised blueprint and key. In a red box, marked explosives, he found dynamite, fuses and primer caps. Several German Lugers and machine pistols with ammunition lay wrapped in oil rags on the floor next to the red box.

A wall switch turned on a dim overhead light, and he hurriedly discarded his rain wear. Finding a chair he sat at the table and began studying the layout of the Gestapo building. For now Samson's close-cropped black hair belied his name, and his dirty face concealed his unseemly pock marks. Soon after reaching for pencil and paper, he began taking notes; and as he squinted at the worn blueprint, his dark eyes no longer blinking, his calloused hands repeatedly closed and opened in nervous anticipation.

Among other things, Samson decided that he would leave around midnight dressed as a janitor, carrying himself like an elderly hunchback, his face soiled beyond recognition; and he would wear gloves, and if challenged, speak in a falsetto. At the rear entrance to the Gestapo station, he would find janitorial equipment and a place for planting his bomb.

Preparing the bomb presented no problem for Samson. Even before the war he had been a demolitions technician in the coal mines; nevertheless, it took most of the morning and the early afternoon hours before Samson was satisfied with his creation which he dubbed, "King Kong."

Afterward, he paced the cabin and smoked a cigarette. Chances were good that his sister and brother-in-law were already dead. The escape of Bep and himself from the whorehouse probably decreed their deaths. He knew the Count never delayed disposing of his hostages once their deaths had been decreed—but he didn't know this for certain.

Then his whole frame shook as he remembered the limp body of Janeane in his arms. For his sake, the poor girl had prostituted herself for the Gestapo. Thus, concluded Samson, death would be a liberation from guilt and a penalty for failing to protect his loved ones—and taking the Count with him would be his bittersweet revenge.

From his shirt pocket he withdrew a newspaper clipping about Japanese kamikaze pilots. Intently he reread what they had written.

One was quoted as saying, "Think kindly of me and consider it my good fortune to have done something praiseworthy." Another sadly reflected, "Every man is doomed to go his own way in time." Still another pilot concluded the last page of his diary: "Like cherry blossoms/In the spring/Let us fall/Clean and radiant." Samson was impressed, filled with a sense of camaraderie. He wondered why the Germans hadn't done something like the Kamikazes in attacking the American's Flying Fortresses, but then he knew, the German was cut from different cloth than the Japanese.

Later, and without trying, he fell asleep on the couch. When he awoke it was dark. He checked his watch and discovered the sentinel in his mind had indeed awakened him at the appropriate hour. The day had passed and he felt some what refreshed. With the exception of "King Kong," he gathered his gear into a duffel bag and slung it over his shoulder. In his other hand, he gingerly carried his lethal suitcase.

According to his personal papers, he was now Jan Triestram, an old crippled janitor. When he limped from the wharf onto the deserted street, the curfew in effect, he felt confidence in his plan. But before he could reach a sidewalk, a police car pulled in front of him, and a uniformed Dutchman wanted to know why he was on the street at this forbidden hour, the man volunteering that the Germans would probably have shot him on sight.

Samson fumbled for his papers like an old arthritic man and in a high-pitched, scratchy voice explained his situation. He said he'd just been hired. As Samson's papers were in order, the policeman insisted on personally driving him to his destination.

However, the intervention of the policeman represented disaster to Samson, as the Count's headquarters would no doubt have a passel of Gestapo men standing around; and if he were accosted, his duffel bag and suitcase would most certainly be searched. He had to think of some excuse for getting out of this police car—and fast!

Suddenly old, arthritic Jan Triestram went into a paroxysm of coughing. He yelled for the car to stop. He had to return for his medicine explaining that he would call for someone to come and get him. Alarmed, the policeman turned the car around and returned Samson to the houseboat. But it was some time before the fool drove away. Thus it wasn't until around 2:00 A.M. that Samson finally reached the back door of the Gestapo station. By this hour, Samson felt, the Count had probably gone and was now safely in his bed.

Nevertheless, Samson proceeded with his plans for blowing up the building. After silently unlocking the door and stepping inside, he saw what he was first looking for—a door to a tool room. A quick glance indicated the room was vacant. Discarding his gloves, he went to work, a master at the task before him. Expertly and precisely the main charge of dynamite, enough to blow this building to smithereens, was armed and set to detonate in one hour. With his arms now free, he next proceeded up a back stairwell to the top floor where, he'd been informed, the Count had his office.

But so far, he had encountered no one, and this gave rise to nagging suspicions. Since he had entered the building, everything had gone almost too perfectly, but once he reached the top floor, he heard voices coming from what he surmised must be the Count's office.

Stealthily Samson approached it. Suddenly the door swung wide open and in the middle of the room looking directly at him stood Count Siegfried von der Schulenburg, somber-eyed and now impeccably attired in a white shirt, black tie and blue-striped business suit. Of medium build with black, parted hair, Count Siegfried appeared almost harmless. Other than for his yellow complexion, he did not look to be the villain.

Now Samson saw that all the doors in the hallway were slowly opening, armed men stalking him from different directions. Other armed men suddenly appeared next to Count Siegfried. Then all movement toward Samson halted as if on cue.

The Count said affably, "Ah, 'The Great Samson.' We meet again—and so soon! Perhaps I should call you, Jan Triestram, the old janitor. . . . You are having quiet a few aliases these days, Hans Spoor!" Looking grim, the Count said, "But I doubt you will need anymore aliases, Hans."

Realizing his end, Samson straightened, uncoiling like a trained cobra answering to a snake charmer, while slowly aiming the Luger inside his loose work coat at the Count's heart. "How did you know?"

"You must surely realize by now, Hans, that every man has his Judas."

"And who was mine?"

"Rieksen."

"I don't believe you.... And my sister and her husband?"

"I had no alternative. You betrayed us. Too bad you didn't think of them."

At those words, Samson squeezed the trigger of the Luger. It clicked on a dud.

As both men stared at each other, the Count lamented, "You don't think we would allow you real ammunition do you, Hans? And, so sorry, Hans, but your bomb has already been defused too. You've been had, Samson!"

Samson lunged for the Count as bodyguards pressed the triggers of their firearms perforating Samson's body.

ACCOMPANYING THE COUNT on his night of requital was a ranking Waffen SS officer who had just come from the front. That officer was Captain Snodgrass, adjutant to General Kraus. As Samson's body was being removed, Captain Snodgrass offered a kind of benediction. "I thought the word in the Christian bible was that Samson's strength rose from his long hair. This monster's hair is short."

"Ja," said the Count with a smile of satisfaction, "though Samson never suspected, he also had his Delilah." Clearing his throat, the Count said, "Let's go to another room while this mess is being cleared and cleaned."

After the two were settled at a small table, the Count said, "Captain Snodgrass, before our interruption, you said that you had information of a nature that was only for my ears."

"Ja."

"The hour is very late. You have traveled a long way, and as I understand you must immediately return to the front. What is your information?"

"Am I not correct in saying that the Gestapo is looking for a Nicoline Lindemann?"

"Ja.... Most definitely."

"I can tell you where she is at."

"Oh, how interesting."

"She is being protected by SS General Fritz Kraus, who is the commander of the SS 'Lightning' Panzer Division and who is my immediate superior officer."

"Well now.... Where is the woman?"

"General Kraus is hiding her at his hunting lodge in the Ansberger Forest near Warstein."

"Why do you volunteer this information, Captain Snodgrass?"

"I'm Waffen SS. Isn't that reason enough?"

"If what you say is true, it must not have been reason enough for General Kraus.... Of course, we will look into this matter, Captain Snodgrass; and, depending upon the results, you will be informed. Obviously, you will say nothing about this to your general, and we do appreciate your stepping forward—even though we know it is your duty."

After Captain Snodgrass had departed the Count whispered, "What a day! Ja, every man has his Judas—and his Delilah."

PHILIP VOSSMAAR WAS CATNAPPING. He could see the light of dawn under the blinds on his bedroom window and knew is was time to get up. Late last night General Clay had mysteriously spoken of a special mission. He hoped he didn't have to find girls for another dance, but that wasn't likely with the American full-scale offensive in progress. But the general had refused to disclose his assignment until the following day. Well, this was the following day.

He had no more than put on his pants when there was a soft knock on the front door. He peeked out the blinds and saw Karel. Hurriedly he went downstairs and opened the door.

"Philip I can't come in," said Karel in a precise, clipped voice. "I stopped to inform you that Bep and I are again going behind the lines—but this time far into Germany. Bep just learned that Nicoline is alive and being held at Warstein, but she is in grave danger; therefore, we are risking a very dangerous rescue attempt, and you are to remain by your telephone for instructions."

"But I'm under orders from General Clay today," protested Philip.

"Forget them. General Clay has temporarily released you from his command. He knows we need you."

CHAPTER 9

CAPTAIN APPLEBY did not remain General Dietrich's captive for long. One of the hog-tied American soldiers slipped his bonds and freed the rest. But of the freed Americans, only Captain Appleby remained in the huge industrial building. The others found a side door and made toward American lines.

Captain Appleby, however, sought information. Chancing upon a catwalk in the dark, cavernous structure, he climbed to an elevated perch from where he saw the white-coated technicians, guided by flickering lanterns and dim flashlights, swarming over their panzers like honey bees attending to their queen. They were readying their behemoths for combat. The Tigers and Panthers were being greased, gassed and armed even while riding on a flat car which was slowly being winched from underground. The work proceeded as if at a Detroit assembly line. At the northeast end of the building each tank was being driven off of its flatcar and out through an opening.

Climbing back down the catwalk and hugging the wall, Captain Appleby worked his way toward this exit. If he could, he wanted to learn the exact destination of these Panthers and Tigers. At last, behind a stack of wooden crates, he positioned himself less than fifty feet from the exit. As a Panther slowly drove off its flatcar Appleby marveled at its low silhouette, wide tracks, four inches of steep slopping frontal armor and two machine guns. Intelligence reports indicated the Panther, weighing 44 tons, was capable of speeds in excess of thirty miles per hour—that compared to his own Sherman tank weighing 34 tons and reaching a top speed of 26 mph. Another discomforting intelligence report was that the high-velocity, long-barreled, 75-millimeter, main gun of the Panther could outdistance his own 75 and still penetrate 4 inches of steel.

Next to roll before Captain Appleby's eyes was an awesome Tiger tank. At 66 tons this leviathan, like the Panther, was protected by 4 inches of steel on its front side—compared to the 2 inches on his Sherman tank—and 3 inches on its sides; more importantly, it mounted an 88 millimeter main gun which at 500 yards reportedly could penetrate 7 inches of steel. This cannon was the bane of all Allied tankers.

SUDDENLY GENERAL DIETRICH's dusk-blue Royal Tiger appeared. This was Germany's most recent improved tank. It featured torsion bar suspension, overlapping road wheels, extended wide tracks and 7 inches of frontal armor!

In the shadows Captain Appleby slid along the wall until he was outside. He wanted to estimate the panzers numbers and destination. Using bushes as cover, he continued to watch the procession. He observed that the tanks were headed in the direction of the slag pile, most likely seeking cover in the evergreens which bordered this ugly scar on the landscape. So placed, they would be out of killing range from Sherman tanks within the Puffendorf salient.

Clustered around the exit were several gray half-tracks, staff cars and sidecar motorcycles. With keen interest Captain Appleby observed that the blue panzer was not following the other tanks, but instead was being parked in a grove of evergreens just beyond the exit. He guessed Dietrich might be planning to direct his ambush from this location—perhaps because of its better view of the Beggendorf-Loverich-Puffendorf road.

Alarmed by what he was observing, Captain Appleby knew he had to act fast if he were to prevent the annihilation of Combat Command "B." Stumbling through thorny bushes and stunted evergreens, keeping the wall of the industrial structure to his left, he at last bumped into his own Sherman tank, only to find it had been disabled by incendiary devices. Surprisingly, though, its radio still functioned. But for some reason, he couldn't raise the air or command tanks. On a hunch, he tried for the company truck.

SLEEP WAS OUT OF THE QUESTION for Corporal Wesley "Wes" Willow and Private Milton "Peewee" Silverman during the early morning hours of the 17th of November, 1944. The big-push for ending the war had begun and Combat Command "B" of the "Fighting" 15th Armored Division was spearheading the attack. Sitting in the cab of the Company "D" three-quarter-ton truck midway between Ubach and Beggendorf, Wes and Peewee were companions by circumstance. In a twist of fate: the war, the army and random orders, they had been brought together.

It was now over an hour after midnight and it suddenly appeared that Wes had parked in the middle of artillery which was relentlessly shelling the enemy. Blinding muzzle flashes, ear splitting reverberations and the occasional swoosh of answering artillery called for sporadic ducking into a foxhole.

Yet even in all of this bedlam Corporal Willow found time to feed on his hatred for Peewee Silverman, and he now felt he had had about all he could take of that Jew-boy. He considered it especially unfortunate that Peewee had discovered Colonel Burk's note in Witkowski's personnel file; and for the umpteenth time, Wes scolded himself for ever having blurted out the truth to Peewee about his killing those German POWs; because now, Peewee-Jew-boy would want to know more about that unfortunate event; and Wes just knew that Jew-boy would go poking his long, hooked nose more and more into this incident—and it wasn't out of the question but what Jew-boy might even get Colonel Burk into trouble. Well, Wes decided, he'd just have to think of some way of taking care of the little Jew-boy, too. With Jews, it was screw them before they screwed you. . . . In truth, Wes never had nor never intended to kill any Germans.

ON THE OTHER HAND, Private Silverman considered Wes an enigma. Wes was an American, and yet Wes was extremely anti-Semitic. Couldn't Wes realize that anti-Semitism was at the heart of Nazism, their common enemy? This constant harassment by Wes on racial grounds had nearly prompted Peewee to fight back. But being a recent immigrant and not wanting to cause trouble for anyone, especially Captain Appleby, Peewee had swallowed his pride. To be sure, he had no fear of racial insults; his people had been hardened by centuries of oppression; and no matter what happened, he was comforted in the knowledge that he was among the chosen. He had his religion to reassure him in all of life's trying situations.

FOR HOURS NOW, or so it seemed, they'd been stopped by the side of the road. Wes estimated they were only a few miles from where Company "D" must have dug in for the night; and as the truck carried some of the communication equipment of the company, Captain Appleby must surely require it. However, the radio receiver linking them with Appleby's command tank had gone dead around midnight; but before it had, they had learned that the first day of fighting had gone pretty much as planned, with units of the company having reached their objectives with few casualties; therefore, Wes and Peewee expectantly awaited Appleby's call.

"Stay with the truck, Jew-boy; I'm going to see if the MPs will let us drive on to Beggendorf. Be right back," said Wes.

Corporal Willow had no more than disappeared than the surrounding area was bracketed once more by an enemy barrage. But this bombardment turned out to be a farewell-for-now punctuation mark; abruptly, German artillery shifted to pounding Puffendorf. Nevertheless, the minutes dragged by and when Wes did not return, Milton grew nervous. After nearly a half hour, Milton was inclined to look for Wes, but knew he'd catch hell if he left the vehicle unattended. Suddenly the radio receiver crackled and came alive. "Daredevil '2.' Are you there?" asked a steady, but intense voice sounding like that of Captain Appleby.

Milton turned on the mike. "Yes, sir."

"I recognize your voice."

"So do I, yours, sir."

"Good. Is your partner there?"

"No, sir."

"Do you know the location of yesterday's 'point of departure'?"

"Yes, sir."

"How far away are you?"

"About a half mile, sir."

"Get here fast. It's an emergency."

"I don't know if the MPs will let me pass, sir. . . . That place is being shelled isn't it?"

"I have one order, Milton. Get up here—toot sweet! Don't let anything or anyone stop you. So move!"

"Yes, sir."

Milton Silverman knew Wes would be angry. If Wes hadn't been wounded or killed by that last barrage, he'd go berserk finding himself abandoned. But Milton would never considered disobeying a direct order from Captain Appleby.

Therefore, Milton slid into the driver's seat and shifted the truck into low. Shortly he wheeled the three-quarter-ton past MPs and on to the far shoulder of the Beggendorf road, speeding alongside ammunition and gasoline hauling deuce-and-a-halves and half-tracks. These vehicles crept northward in single file to avoid running over land mines. Driving with only their "cat eyes" (bumper lights), they barely illuminated the roadway. Milton, on the other hand, drove by the light of wildfires, exploding shells and muzzle flashes, some of which were directed his way after he careened past the MPs. His main concern, however, was that he might drive over a mine. However, his luck held. In minutes Captain Appleby jumped on to the running board, motioning Milton still farther off to the side of the road.

Captain Appleby opened the door on the driver's side, grabbing the mike as his big butt shoved Milton into the passenger's side. "Daredevil-thirteen, can you read me?" He repeated this call several times to the "air" tank before getting a positive response.

"Tigers and Panthers in the area of the slag pile," said Appleby evenly. "Have our artillery set their coordinates for the surrounding area and pepper it. I repeat: Tigers and Panthers in the area of the slag pile. Do you read me?"

"Yes, Six, we read you."

"Also, get aircraft in here as soon as possible. Tell the flyboys there's a beehive of Panthers and Tigers if they can just come in under the clouds when it gets light." Though Captain Appleby's men never heard him use any expletive stronger than "Judas priest," he unloaded, "Hell's going to cut loose here directly."

A rasping voice interrupted the transmission.

"Six! This is Daredevil-One!! Where in the hell are you?"

Recognizing the voice of Colonel Burk, Captain Appleby said, "I'm not near 102.6, but I will be shortly: Roger—Over—And—Out!"

Captain Appleby promptly turned off the radio; turning to Silverman, he said, "Hold on to your britches, Peewee. You're about to have a bronco ride, and if I hit a mine, both of us will have a high-ride to eternity."

As Captain Appleby predicted, the ride was wild and woolly; often they were mired in shell craters, but soon they had rejoined Company "D" in the draw leading to Hill 102.6. He parked next to Lieutenant Jordening's tank.

"Red," he called. The lieutenant popped up and out of the turret, scrambling to the ground next to the small truck.

"I don't have time for explanations, but listen carefully. Dietrich has about fifteen or more Panthers and Tigers in the trees around that slag pile we passed yesterday. They'll be hitting us from the side and rear. Besides that, a tank and infantry attack will be coming at us out of Gereonsweiler. I know it's still dark, but get our tanks out of this Judas-priest ravine and get them moving. Our only chance against Dietrich's monsters is to find room to maneuver and get in close. Y'all are sitting ducks here. Also, get a tank ready for me while I go find Burk."

"He just returned to his CP in Puffendorf."

"Okay. I'll be right back after I report to the colonel. We have only an hour or less before dawn. You're in command, Red, both of Company 'D' and Task Force '1' until further notice."

For the second time Captain Appleby found Colonel Burk's CP, which was located in a bombed out stone house on the main street of Puffendorf. It had a deep basement and that was where he found the colonel, who was at first enraged when he saw Captain Appleby. But as Tom explained the situation, the expression on Colonel Burk's face changed to one of grave concern. Immediately recognizing the threat to his whole command, Colonel Burk wasted no time in broadcasting a succession of orders bracing Combat Command "B" for the coming German counterattack.

While Colonel Burk was thus preoccupied, Tom retreated to the three-quarter-ton and raced back to Company "D." While he was mounting a tank borrowed from the 1st Platoon, he instructed the commander of that tank to ride with Milton back to Ubach and await further orders.

DIRECTING THE TANK DRIVER back alongside the Puffendorf-Loverich road and in the general direction of where he thought the slag pile was located, Captain Appleby hoped to surprise General Dietrich. Looking southeastwardly from Hill 102.6 he thought he could dimly make out its towering, volcanic-like features. And this concerned him, because he wanted his own tank shut off and concealed before Dietrich began his ambush.

As the tank engine roared, its tracks churning through the wet earth, Captain Appleby replayed in his mind his escape from the industrial structure, attempting to recall the lay of the land. Now dawn was fast approaching, not with shafts of dazzling light, as fog and drizzle had set in, but by degrees of illumination. Beginning directly in front of Appleby's nose, blurs gradually became things, and as more seconds passed, things became recognizable objects.

By the time Captain Appleby could clearly make out the tip of the barrel on his 75, he ordered the driver of his Sherman tank to shut off its engine. They had parked in a wooded area with thick underbrush at the northwest corner of the industrial structure. Hurriedly, Appleby instructed his gunner to level the 75 on a similar cluster of trees where he'd last seen the blue Tiger being parked. That grove was only about 40 yards from his Sherman. Then he clutched the 50-caliber machine gun and swung it toward the exit from the industrial structure. With a lump in his throat, sweat rising on his brow, the minutes passed; and as no hostile action was taken against him, Appleby assumed, therefore, he'd gone unobserved by the enemy.

Even if his tank had been heard in the semidarkness, what with the artillery, mortars, burp-guns and "screaming meemies" contributing their unique sounds to this tempestuous night, his tank might have been regarded as friend rather than foe.

Suddenly, his request for artillery was answered. Shell bursts began illuminating the slag heap and its rim of evergreens ignited in ever spreading yellow flames. This must surely indicate to General Dietrich that his plot, if not foiled, was at least discovered, thought Captain Appleby. And certainly counter measures would be forth coming from Dietrich.

Then, like ghosts, Captain Appleby saw infantry appearing and disappearing and tanks crawling from under the trees. Their suppressed muzzle flashes indicating Dietrich's ambush was getting underway.

Though he didn't know if the blue tank remained where he'd last seen it, Captain Appleby temporarily traded places with his gunner and settled himself onto the gunner's seat. He made certain that that particular undergrowth was in the middle of the cross-sights of his 75.

Within minutes a 700-horse powered engine, discharging ear-splitting roars and billowing exhaust clouds, powered the Royal Tiger from the grove that Appleby had zeroed in upon. Like a specter, the blue tank began lumbering out, crashing and crushing the trees to its front, tracking onto the trail leading to the mountain of slag. In jerks, its driver turned the steel leviathan's backside to the Sherman. Captain Appleby could even makeout General Dietrich's torso, standing in the tank commander's hatch.

Even the General's leather jacket and high-visored officers' cap were distinct from Appleby's position.

Uncharacteristically, Captain Appleby shook. At a distance of about 40 yards, he aimed at the Tiger's thin-skinned, motor compartment. Slowly his left foot pressed the firing button. Inside the turret of the Sherman there was a loud explosion and recoil of the breach. Instantly, an armor piercing projectile burned a hole through the Tiger's thin skin and exploded in its engine compartment. A ball of fire engulfed the Tiger.

Peering out his periscope, Appleby's loader exclaimed, "Up his asshole, Captain! You shot right up the Tiger's asshole!"

Quickly Appleby returned to the turret hatch and again grasped the 50-caliber pointing it in the direction of the burning Tiger. Only one crewman emerged from the flaming wreck. He stopped, sneering at Captain Appleby before limping into the industrial structure.

"Shoot any survivors," Captain Appleby ordered. "I'll take care of the one in the building."

He dismounted from the tank and quickly spotted the German lying on the floor. It was General Dietrich.

Covering the general with his .45, Captain Appleby demanded, "General?"

Like a cat, Dietrich rolled on to his back, attempting to level a Luger at Captain Appleby.

The Luger went flying as Appleby's foot struck Dietrich's gun hand. Then with great difficulty the legendary Hans Otto Dietrich rose, defiantly brushing the dust from himself.

"It seems as is if the tables are turned. . . . I should never have been so soft as to allow you to live, Captain Appleby. . . . Obviously, you're not a sporting man, what with your shooting my tank in its rear and kicking me when I'm down."

Captain Appleby smiled. "If I stay around and listen to you, General Dietrich, I fear your rescuers will nail me again." Captain Appleby holstered his .45 and turning his back on General Dietrich walked toward the opening.

"You shouldn't make the same kind of mistake I did—by leaving me alive, Captain. Otherwise, you may live to regret it too. . . .

However, I take back what I said about your not being a sporting man."

Stopping and again facing the general, Tom said, "If my superiors were ever to learn I permitted the famous General Hans Otto Dietrich to return to his battle group, I would be court-martialed."

For the second time this night, General Dietrich straightened and said, "Auf Wiedersehen."

When Captain Appleby had again returned to his Sherman tank, his tank gunner said, "I suppose you took care of your prisoner."

Before replying, Appleby had the Sherman headed toward Beggendorf, but he turned his head in time to see a German staff car race out of the industrial structure, driving in the direction of the slag heap.

Over the intercom Appleby grunted, "Un huh."

SS LIEUTENANT GENERAL FRANZ RHEINHARDT resembled Heinrich Himmler in appearance and size. Frail, cleft-chinned, nearsighted, preferring, like his chief, a pince-nez eyepiece, the black uniformed general, Commander of the III Panzer Corps, stormed into Brigadier General Gerd von Bartholomaus's operations room at Linnich. No Heil Hitler, no introductory greetings, just a peremptory— "What are you doing? Where is Dietrich?"

The two generals to whom he addressed his curt questions were bent over a war map studying the progress of their counterattack. Aides were coming and going, moving symbols on the map, updating the battle. Both looked up, startled by the surprise intrusion of their corps commander.

The time was around noon of the 17th of November and formations of both Bartholomaus's "Hammer" Panzer Division and Brigadier General Fritz Kraus' "Lightning" Panzer Division were successfully counterattacking against the salient won by General Clay's 15th Armored Division on the 16th. Both generals had received their orders directly from Field Marshal Manfred Stein, their Army Group "C" Commander.

Rheinhardt's III Panzer Corps, of which both Bartholomaus'

and Kraus' divisions were a part, was under the authority of the Group "C" Commander. In following Stein's orders to counterattack, both Bartholomaus and Kraus had assumed Rheinhardt had a hand in making that decision. Now they were about to learn differently, as well as of a change in the hierarchy of command.

Because he was SS and a long-time close friend of Rheinhardt's, General Kraus spoke up first. Clicking his heels and bowing to his corps commander, he said, "Mein Herr General, Heil Hitler. . . . We our counterattacking against the American offensive, and we received our orders directly from Field Marshal Stein. . . . We had assumed your hand was in on that decision. . . . We have just learned that General Dietrich, in an operation which he personally calls 'Trojan Horse II,' is now attacking the American salient from the rear and side. All our actions are going very well with numerous American tanks burning and all their forces in full retreat."

Eyes flashing, the frail general, whose torso seemed longer than his legs, said, "I'm surprised, Fritz, you didn't first clear this operation with me." Pointedly ignoring Bartholomaus, Rheinhardt declared, "Himmler has replaced Göering as Reichsführer, and Himmler has decreed that all SS forces shall take their orders only from ranking SS officers. Stein is not SS! . . . Both of you are now being ordered by me to disengage your forces!—and that includes General Dietrich."

"Begging your pardon, Herr General. We have the Yankee reeling. We may very well be able to push him out of Germany completely if you permit this attack to continue," pleaded the redheaded Fritz Kraus.

"Sorry. The Führer has decided. The 'Lightning' Division is to go in reserve for now. He has other plans for it."

General Bartholomous, exasperated, said sarcastically, "Of course, you will give me additional well-trained Volksstrum and Hitler Youth along with their mighty panzerfausts?"

Turning to General Bartholomous for the first time and mimicking the old soldier's sarcasm, General Rheinhardt said, "How did you guess, 'Old Badger.' They're already on the train from Berlin."

"Humph. I didn't even know the trains ran anymore from Berlin."

"You tell a lame joke, old man. But the truth is the Führer expects you to hold at the Roer. In this sector we will fight a defensive, delaying action. Don't worry 'Old Badger'; and, mark my words, the Americans will soon be running for their lives out of all of Germany."

Though Fritz Kraus knew Hitler was planning a major counter offensive somewhere in the West and was aware that Hasso von Manteuffel was on the move to the West, that didn't rule out his being sent to the Russian front as Hasso's replacement. Therefore, he quizzed, "And me—Russia?"

General Rheinhardt answered crisply, "No," and left the room as abruptly as he had entered, his "Heil Hitler" barely audible.

Wrinkling his nose contemptuously and sneering, General Bartholomaus was determined to call Field Marshal Stein when this swine Rheinhardt was gone. Manfred always knew how to get around the slimy SS. Nevertheless, even though the "Lightning" Division, and probably Dietrich's battle group, would now be withdrawn, the Americans had suffered enough so that he could delay their getting to the Roer River—and apparently that was all Hitler wanted.

As GENERAL RHEINHARDT LEFT the Operations Room, he motioned General Kraus to accompany him. Once outside the building, General Rheinhardt stopped suddenly and laid a friendly hand on Fritz Kraus's shoulder. Looking the red-haired general in the eyes, he spoke to him like a concerned brother.

"Before I left my headquarters a disturbing message was laid on my desk. That message concerned you. It was from the Gestapo in Amsterdam—Count Siegfried to be exact. Apparently, and stupidly to my way of thinking, you are under investigation for harboring a Dutch woman, the mistress of an underground leader being sought by the Gestapo, I believe. Can you shed any light upon this matter, Fritz?"

These unexpected remarks and that direct question hit Fritz Kraus in the gut. His light complexion, though tanned, turned crimson. For a moment he was both stunned and alarmed for the sake of Nicoline—and the children.

Bowing before the questioning gaze of his mentor, he answered honestly, "Yes, there is something to it."

Astounded, General Rheinhardt replied, "Then you're a careless fool, Fritz." For a brief moment General Rheinhardt looked at the ground. At last, almost compassionately, he said, "I suppose you're involved romantically with the woman?"

"Yes."

"Where is she now?"

"At my hunting lodge near Warstein."

"I believe the Gestapo knows that; for if I remember correctly, the message said something about Warstein—but I was in a great hurry when I read it."

General Rheinhardt, though frail and nearsighted, in contrast to his vigorous and athletic friend, was a quick thinker. Though he was more political and fanatical about Hitler and National Socialism than was Fritz Kraus, he was not devoid of human qualities. Friendship and loyalty ranked high on Rheinhardt's scale of values. Both generals had forged their friendship on the battlefields of Russia, and briefly General Kraus had been General Rheinhardt's Chief of Staff.

Removing his pince-nez, General Rheinhardt paced up and down beside his staff car, pausing only to kick at a clump of dirt with a polished black boot. Suddenly he stopped. Conspiratorially he whispered, "Give the necessary orders to disengage your troops. Fly back to Warstein and bring this woman to my headquarters. I'll protect her if she hasn't done anything harmful to the Reich. I'm sure my influence with Himmler is as great as that of Count Siegfried's." Then he cleaned his pince-nez with a cloth and said, "I can't believe you would be protecting her if she had done anything harmful to us."

"Believe me. She has not, my general," said Fritz Kraus seriously.

"Good. . . . I have a pressing matter to attend to with General Dietrich, if I can find him. . . . Then I hope to see you at my headquarters with your lady friend—that is, if you can beat the Gestapo to her!"

THE GREYISH, RED TENT occupied by General Dietrich covered a quarter the size of a football field. The psyche of Dietrich was beyond the comprehension of General Rinehardt. Sometimes he considered the man to be mad, but if madness didn't negate his being a successful battlefield commander, so be it.

During the ride to the front he had heard and seen the results of the successful counterattack. Armored personnel carriers and transport vehicles clogged the roadway, making it almost impossible for his staff car to move forward. Dazed American prisoners staggered along beside the road under the scrutiny of bayonet armed, steel-helmeted German soldiers. It was almost like the days of Blitzkrieg. Oh, how he'd like to see that return!

Thankfully, the sky remained grey and only very daring American aviators dived through the clouds to bomb and strafe. And rather accurate antiaircraft fire took its deadly toll of these courageous ones. He could only hope that this Adolf Hitler weather would hold on into the next month. But he knew, as only a handful of SS officers knew, Hitler himself was planning a major offensive in the Ardennes; therefore, he was confident storm fronts would persist.

HIS HAND WAS BARELY SENSITIVE to the texture of the greyish, red tent when a soft melodious voice remarked, "It is damask from jacquard looms covered with water repellent; it is invisible from the air. This was the tent of a sheik."

Jerking his head up, General Rheinhardt saw standing before him the scar-faced myth. Startled, he said, "At least General Dietrich, you heeded my order and are not in your Tiger panzer at the front."

Bringing his right index finger to his lips and almost sheepishly avoiding Rhinehardt's steady gaze, General Dietrich apologized. "No. I left it burning at the front."

His voice rising a decibel, General Rheinhardt asked, "You what?"

At this, Dietrich's eyes burned into Rheinhardt's, and the latter looked away.

Dietrich said, "I'm compelled to give the Devil his do. The Ami's do have a great tank commander, a certain Captain Appleby. He put a hole in my tank."

Taking a breath and gathering the courage to look into the steel eyes, the frail one replied imperiously, "So you did disobey my order—and the Führer's order!"

"Not really, my general," said Dietrich letting his right arm drop to his side. "Rather, I planned a trap for the enemy behind his lines, sort of like a Trojan Horse, if you know what I mean. My presence was required to begin the attack. Pursuant to your's and the Führer's order, I had no intention of personally engaging enemy tanks—nor did I!"

Again Dietrich's index finger found his lips as he continued: "The trouble, my general, is that I confronted a clever and resourceful enemy. One who fired upon my panzer from concealment.... I'm fortunate to stand before you."

Dietrich glanced, flint-like, first at General Rheinhardt and then beyond him, dropping both his arms to his sides. "But when we go into the Ardennes, my general, let me assure you, Hitler himself will have given his permission for me to lead the attack."

Speechless, General Rhinehardt stared at the disheveled Dietrich, whose shredded uniform he had not noticed before. This harangue of Dietrich's confirmed to General Rhinehardt that Dietrich was indeed crazy. The man was obviously cuckoo. He would be happy, very happy, to send Dietrich packing. Maybe Dietrich was Hasso Manteuffel's protégé. He could have him.

"General, Dietrich, I'm ordering you to retire your battle group and to assemble in reserve."

Resignedly, almost patronizingly, as if he were speaking to a child, General Dietrich replied, "Yes, General Rhinehardt, I was in the process of complying when you arrived."

General Rhinehardt's "Heil Hitler" fell upon General Dietrich's back as the battle group leader limped into the hollows of his labyrinthine tent.

THE "OLD BADGER" WASTED little time in seeking succor and support from his fellow Prussian, Field Marshal Stein. General Rhinehardt and General Kraus had no more than left his Operations Room, than Bartholomaus was on the phone to Army Group "C" Headquarters. But before a connection could be made, an aide announced the arrival of Field Marshal Stein himself.

Of aristocratic Prussian lineage, the tall, blond Field Marshal was a product of Hitler's expansion of the Wehrmacht during the 1930s. As a handsome prototype of the German master race, many Nazis had considered it surprising that Manfred Stein had never become SS, though they did not know of the taint of Jewish blood that flowed in his veins. Hitler, however, did know. Nevertheless, only since the ascendancy of the Waffen SS had Stein's influence waned.

Seeing Manfred, Gerd grinned and relaxed. The two clasped hands, steady in their gaze

Monocle in place, the lines on his face wrinkled like a washboard, old Gerd said, "Did you know that Rhinehardt just left? He was blustering with this counterattack."

"Let him stew. We'll soon put him in his place, and at the same time rescue the German people from the carnage coming from the East."

"I don't understand you, Manfred?"

"Even with you, my friend, I can not go into detail. . . . Let me say this. Do you know Albert Speer?"

"No. Just that he is the Minister of Armaments."

"He is my friend, Gerd, and he is very close to Hitler. They were both architects, you know."

"So what?"

"Speer is requesting that all generals refrain from destroying the infrastructure of Germany in preparation for a postwar world."

"Does he mean bridges and the like?"

"Ja."

"Is he a defeatist? . . . That is treason!"

"Well. Ja, he believes the war is lost. But he desires to spare the German people from being raped by the Mongols."

"Even I know Hitler would never acquiesce to those views."

"Ja. But with Hitler out of the way, there are many who believe the West would stand with us against the Tartar hordes."

In a flash, Gerd knew of what Manfred was speaking. Gerd had come to hate the Nazis. Yet he remembered the failure of the attempt on Hitler's life last July. Indeed, Hitler almost seemed to have divine protection. But Gerd had lived his life and had only his country to think of. He responded, "Of course, you can always count on me, Manfred."

"I was sure of you, Gerd."

BY THE EVENING of November 16th, euphoria reigned at Major General Brighton D. Clay's 15th Armored Division Headquarters in Heerlen, Holland. The blackout-curtains were tightly drawn in all the windows of the Secondary Technical School, but the lights inside burned brightly. The mood was restrained ecstasy. Nearly all the objectives of the first day of fighting had been taken. The esprit de corps of the division had never been higher. The big push for ending the war was on, and the 15th Armored Division had earned the honor and opportunity of spearheading this final drive. Congratulatory messages were pouring in, including one from Ike himself. But the tall, wiry Clay cautioned his staff against overoptimism.

"You know 'Jerry,'" said the general to his operations officer, Major Jack Collins; "he'll counterattack like hell on the 'morrow. Have you checked to make sure Colonel Burk has his defenses in place and is ready to resume the offensive in the morning?"

"He has, General. I just talked with him on the telephone. . . . But there does seem to be some discrepancy with Task Force 1."

"That's Appleby's command. What kind of discrepancy?"

The short, stocky major snorted, "I'll tell you what Burk said, then I'll tell you what I think, if that's all right?"

"Shoot, Jack"

"Burk says he's filing an insubordination charge against Appleby and wants him relieved of his command. He says the captain was

AWOL for most of the battle. After he returned, Appleby gave primary battle orders without first consulting Burk. Supposedly, Appleby was captured by General Dietrich and then made good his escape all in a matter of an hour or two. After reporting to Burk, Appleby returned to Company 'D' on Hill 102.6 where he countermanded some of Burk's defensive arrangements, even appointing Second Lieutenant Jordening commander of Task Force 1, and then again fleeing the scene. Burk has no idea of Appleby's present location. Now, General, do you want to hear my interpretation?"

"Fire away."

"I believe this is nothing more than a personality clash. You and I both know that we're dealing with two very fine soldiers here. I believe the trouble lies with that Red Cross broad. Both soldiers have the hots for her. And in Burks' case, I wouldn't put it past him going so far as to attempt court-martial proceedings against Appleby."

General Clay appreciated Major Collins' candor. And General Clay thought maybe the Red Cross girl might have something to do with the squabbling between Burk and Appleby; and just maybe in the future he'd have to do something about it; but for the moment, he was concerned less with personality clashes and more with a successful push to the Roer River.

What startled General Clay during Collins' lively discourse was to learn of Appleby's capture and escape and his reported rearranging of defensive positions, only to disappear again. General Clay felt something ominous in all this.

"Jack, get Burk on the phone or by radio. I want to hear from him the details of what Captain Appleby reported. Also—raise Appleby if you can? I want the resumption of our attack to begin in the dark, before dawn, to meet head-on, at close quarters, any Jerry counterattack. Have someone rouse Combat Command 'A'—they too must be moving before dawn to continue the attack right on through Burk's Combat Command 'B.' Double-time, Jack!"

Moments later Major Collins returned, "Neither Burk nor Appleby can be raised."

"Damn!"

CHAPTER 10

EVEN BEFORE DARKNESS SETTLED on the evening of the 16th, the lack of fuel and ammunition shut down "Operation Queen," and Colonel Burk ordered his forces to dig in for the night. Sergeant Witkowski, relying on his combat instincts, directed his tank driver, T/5 Nate Talbot, to park the bulldozer tank in some thick undergrowth in the ravine just short of the summit of Hill 102.6. Looking around he grumbled, "Too damn many tanks in this gap."

IN WHIP JOHNSON'S CASE, his perspective remained self-centered. Ultimate fear and the possibility of destruction tortured his mind and knotted his guts throughout the night of the 16th. Morosely he sat on his loader's seat, fully clothed, covered like a moth in a cocoon by a flimsy, recently issued, sleeping bag, his teeth chattering—not from the cold, but from grim premonitions. The sleeping bag warmed and protected him from the frigid steel hull, but not from the fever in his brain, as he likened his sleeping bag to an Egyptian mummy and the dozer to his steel sarcophagus.

He reflected on the first day of his baptism of fire: At the last minute before leaving the apple orchard, the assistant driver, Hank Henry, had been replaced. Superstitiously, Whip had considered this a foreboding omen. Was fate, knowing in advance the bulldozer tank was doomed, expressly saving the life of one of its members, Hank Henry—and just in the nick of time? Maybe in answer to a devout mother's prayers? And if so, that probably meant that he, Whip Johnson, was done for; for he remained in the dozer as it passed the "line-of-departure." Yet the dozer had gone unscathed the first day, even after falling into a tank trap and being surrounded by enemy infantry with panzerfausts. But there was always the law of averages, and the battle would resume at the brink of dawn.

Whip shivered, breaking out in a cold sweat. Even a catnap was impossible. He wondered, "How can survivors fight day after day and not go crazy?" In his case, he felt it wouldn't take much to be pushed over the brink—and even after only one day of combat. Fervently, he remembered to praise God, as there was no atheist in Whip Johnson's body!

DURING THE NIGHT Nate Talbot, with his driver's hatch open and his senses alert, heard them. In spite of rumbling artillery, coughing burp guns, screaming meemies, droning airplanes and crackling wild fires, he heard them. He could distinctly make out the grinding sounds of track-laying vehicles, and not far off toward the north—the enemy's tanks and self-propelled guns! Nate knew the coming day would be hell.

FORTUNATELY, WHIP JOHNSON, being the loader, was insulated from most of these disquieting sounds by being cooped up inside the turret. But the voice of Lieutenant Red Jordening on the radio quickly received Whip's full attention. Red ordered Task Force "1" to start their engines, spread out, " . . . get the hell out of this depression." But there was not enough time!

Whip's first realization that dawn was breaking was the sound of American 30-caliber machine guns opening fire. Peering out his periscope, he saw his worst nightmares unfolding. Out of the morning mist beyond the top of the ridge he noticed human forms appearing and falling like ten pins—appearing and falling, appearing and falling, and looming ever larger and larger by the seconds. Canvassing the draw, he spotted both light and medium tanks on the move as armor-piercing shells plowed the soft earth between the tanks. Pockmarks materialized as high-explosive artillery and mortar rained down into the ravine. Suddenly, one of the tanks flared like burning celluloid, its crew popping out of their hatches and racing for cover.

Over the intercom Witkowski commanded the dozer into the battle, and all of the tank's guns opened up. No longer glued to his periscope, Whip armed and rearmed the 75, mostly with AP ammunition. "Our shots are either falling short or glancing off the enemy," said Witkowski, ordering the dozer back into the underbrush.

Whip again grabbed the periscope. The ravine had become a pyre for American tanks. Whip witnessed crewmen on fire, rolling on the ground, and then more armor-piercing projectiles, missing the dozer, but furrowing the earth next to the tank.

Buttoning his hatch and collapsing gloomily on his commander's seat, Sergeant Witkowski asked, "What should we do?"

Whip could hardly believe his ears. But without hesitation, as if he were Marshal Ney advising Napoleon, he said, "They've got this place zeroed-in. The only thing we can do is wait until a target comes close by. Then we can fight. To leave our hiding would be suicide."

Dale Jenks remained silent.

After momentary reflection Witkowski said, "I feel we'se should move to the front and fight, but your'es probably right, VD," and opening his hatch, he again stood on his commander's seat.

When Whip again grabbed his periscope, he was amazed at his own audacity in suggesting to Sergeant Witkowski the strategy in this hopeless situation.

Then from Whip's callow point of view an amazing turn of events ensued—for what seemed like hours—nothing happened! The tanks that had been hit continued to burn, of course, but the shower of death raining down upon Hill 102.6 and the gap leading to its summit gradually abated, and then ceased all together. And the human phantoms rising and falling on the skyline no longer appeared. Though the mists still clung persistently to the ground, a pall of bluish smoke drifted lazily into the chasm.

"What's going on?" Whip asked himself.

Suddenly the radio crackled and the steady voice of Captain Appleby, long absent, sounded, "All units return to Puffendorf; if you have infantry near at hand, alert them and allow for their evacuation before leaving your position. Make this an orderly withdrawal. Once in Puffendorf, officers position your tanks defensively. Tank commanders meet at the Colonel's CP as soon as possible."

With the dozer no longer engaged in combat and slowly slinking away from Hill 102.6, Whip again locked his eyes to the periscope. Past burning, demolished Shermans, the dozer tracked. Whip wondered at the status of their crews as well as the whereabouts of the enemy gunners who had picked the tanks off. Now that the dozer was moving among them, why didn't the enemy gunners shoot the dozer too? But apparently the enemy gunners had either been silenced or were now preoccupied; for, with only a half- to three-quarters of a mile to go, the retreat into Puffendorf went unchallenged; and Whip breathed a sigh of relief when Witkowski at last had the engine shut off, explaining they had taken up a defensive position on a side street in the town.

BECAUSE OF AN EXTRAORDINARY combination of inherited genes, Second Lieutenant Joe Nicholson recorded the highest IQ of any man in Company "D," and his brains had easily piloted him through OCS (officer's candidacy school). But just as impressive as Lieutenant Nicholson's high IQ was his ugly disposition, also the result of a genetic quirk. And as it happened, in Company "D," Joe Nicholson found kindred spirits in Corporal Wes Willow and Private Morbid Morris; in time, it was as inevitable as water seeking its own level that these three would coalesce.

Mainly they nurtured grudges. Nicholson hated Captain Appleby over some imagined slight; Willow hated Sergeant Witkowski as a result of Witkowski's involvement in what had happened at St. Lo; and Morris hated Whip Johnson because of his humiliation at Fort Knox. Among themselves the trio promised dire consequences to their three enemies.

While the company was stationed in Heerlen, John Smith had once observed them huddled, looking devious. Sidling within earshot, Smith had heard them shower curses and calamity upon Appleby, Witkowski and VD. At the time, John had dismissed their bile as the usual soldiers' griping and had never bothered to discuss the incident with anyone.

Of course, Wes Willow, Colonel Burk's lackey, always made it his business to keep the 1st Battalion Commander appraised of any interesting goings-on in Company "D"; and from his perspective, Colonel Burk considered the three malcontents as possible pawns for his own purposes. On one occasion he had even told Wes to stoke the fire of the cranks, but keep him well informed of their plotting.

But as "Operation Queen" was getting underway and only moments before leaving the orchard on the outskirts of Beggendorf, John Smith had again seen the three gathered together, speaking low with crafty glances. Suddenly, John's gut feeling had been one of apprehension—and not only because of the looming battle with the Germans. Shortly, Wes Willow had driven away in Colonel Burk's jeep. At that moment the time to advance to the "point-of-departure" had arrived and all crews had begun entering their tanks. Thus John Smith did not have a chance to vent his fears until he saw VD on the side of Hill 102.6 on the evening of the 16th.

NOW IN THE MORNING hours of the 17th, the German counterattack was forcing the surviving American tanks back into Puffendorf, and Nicholson's tank was among these. Deliberately Nicholson parked his tank in a shed near the outskirts of Puffendorf. When John Smith took a look out of his periscope he was puzzled to see that the bulldozer tank was front and center—about forty yards away. Then he saw that his own tank's 75 did not point toward the north or east, from whence the enemy was attacking, but, rather, was aimed directly at the dozer.

John mumbled under his breath, "I told VD wrong. He is in danger!"

From the moment Sergeant Witkowski parked the dozer in Puffendorf, time lost all meaning to Whip Johnson, events became kaleidoscopic:

1—Witkowski goes to and returns from the CP.

2—Whip is called upon to arm the 75 as the dozer begins firing at something.

3—Dirt and debris fall on the dozer as a near miss by a German gunner creates a crater in front of the tank.

4—A defective AP shell again ruptures and the warhead lodges inside the tube of the 75.

5—Witkowski dismounts and with the cleaning rod pushes the warhead into the breach and onto Whip's lap.

6—Cleaning the breach with his right, gloved hand, Whip rearms the 75.

7— A time lag.

8—Whip experiences hunger pangs for the first time.

9—From a "K"-ration carton, Whip prepares a cracker-cheese sandwich.

10—As he bites into it, his "lights" go out! When Whip regained consciousness he was inside an infernal. Like a blow torch, fire from the engine compartment was racing through the turret and out the turret hatch. His chest and right side ached as from a severe blow. Willing his eyes down, he expected to see his guts hanging out his side. Instead, he saw the pocket of his olive-drab field jacket brightly reflecting the raging engine fire. But Dale Jenks and Sergeant Witkowski had vanished. Whip jumped into the flame, his left hand engulfed by fire as it gripped the turret hatch. Frantically he leaped out of the turret, only to slip and fall, rebounding off the lower hull of the tank. Prostrate on the ground, his first thought was he'd broken his leg.

Regaining his feet, he looked wildly about. Just off the street and next to a brick house was a sandbagged machine gun nest, and coming down the street toward him was a tank destroyer. He ran toward it, shouting up at its commander, "Where are the medics?"

Peering at Whip as if he were a zombie, the commander pointed to a large, stone house. Following the man's hand, Whip saw a conspicuous red cross on a white background secured to the outside of the building. Whip sprinted toward it, stumbling onto the outside entrance to its basement. Opening the door, he descended a long stairway into a crowded cellar.

Medics, with needles of morphine, met him at the bottom. The bliss of the drug soon enveloped him, but he remembered saying something about war being hell, which did nothing to impress his listeners. Somehow he was aware of the sympathetic face and encouraging voice of Captain Appleby. "Y'all be okay, Whip." The man's big hand briefly touched Whip's shoulder as the aid men laid Whip onto a stretcher which they stacked, along with others, on a multiple bunk bed. Whip's stretcher occupied the highest slot, inches from the timbered ceiling.

By now the morphine was really kicking in: Whip had the sensation of suspended animation. Yet fear persisted, especially when a large enemy shell hit the house and debris fell on his face. No, he realized he wasn't out of the woods; nor could he tell how badly he'd been burned or if Puffendorf was about to be overrun by the counterattacking Germans? And what would the Germans do with the American wounded?

Time passed. And though Whip was never again checked by the aid men, who had their hands full with increasing numbers of wounded, he overheard bits of conversations: From Loverich, half-tracks and T2s were bringing needed ammunition and returning with the wounded. Though the Germans had come close to cutting the road, for now it remained open, though subjected to heavy shelling; and many of the half-tracks and T2s were not completing the dangerous round trip.

Finally, without a word, medics came for Whip, placing his stretcher, along with others, in a half-track. One man drove while another rode shotgun. Wheels turning and tracks churning, the vehicle roared out of Puffendorf. It swerved, groaned, slowed, roared, veered, raced. Whip threw up. Eventually, the half-track made it back to Beggendorf.

Shortly, as Whip was about to be examined by an elderly appearing doctor, corpsmen removed his heavy army sweater. In the process, out tumbled his hardbound philosophy book on to the damp ground. The hit to the tank had driven Whip's chest into the steel breach of the 75 forcefully enough to dog-ear the whole book. Luckily, the book had cushioned the blow to Whip's chest.

The gray haired doctor retrieved the text, thoughtfully inspecting it. "Second degree burns," he said reassuringly. "Like a very bad sunburn."

It seemed to Whip the doctor was more interested in his worn philosophy book than the nature of his wounds. Carefully the doctor turned some pages. At last out of the side of his mouth he said to the waiting corpsmen, "Take him to the 98th."

Handing the book back to Whip, he advised, "You'd better hang on to your Will Durant's *The Story Of Philosophy*, soldier. This book probably saved your life!"

Soon Whip was on a "meat wagon" headed for Heerlen.

Near him on a stretcher a young soldier sobbed, "They amputated my leg. . . . They amputated my leg."

A gruff voice replied, "At least you're alive and done with the fuckin' war. . . . You'll be a war hero back home."

WHEN CAPTAIN APPLEBY returned to Hill 102.6 with his borrowed Sherman tank Colonel Burk had just ordered the withdrawal to Puffendorf. By then the counterattacking German infantry, accompanied mainly by Panthers, had nearly wiped out Burk's Combat Command "B." All the way from Apweiler to Hill 102.6 the Germans were rolling the Americans back.

As the surviving tanks began their withdrawal, Captain Appleby dismounted from his tank and ran from foxhole to foxhole telling the infantry to fall back with the tanks; meanwhile, on the edge of Puffendorf, Lieutenant Jordening's tank fell into a ditch covered with trash. Dismounting, Jordening ran back and placed the remaining tanks of Company "D" in the best possible defense on the northern and eastern outskirts of the town. At this moment, Captain Appleby returned from the hillside and turned his tank over to Jordening. Then on foot Appleby sprinted for Burk's CP to try and secure additional help for his depleted forces, as well as locate ammunition, most of which had been expended.

As Jordening mounted his newly assigned vehicle, he spotted a Panther moving across his front from left to right. He had only one armor-piercing round remaining, two of smoke and six of high explosive. The armor-piercing shell missed, but his first high explosive round was close enough to force the enemy to retreat from Jordening's line of vision. Again the German tank approached, firing as it came, but obviously the enemy tank commander had not yet located Jordening. Shells went swishing down the street into town, crashing against a building. Jordening then fired two rounds of smoke and again the enemy retreated. The next time the German tank approached, Jordening let go with his last four rounds of high explosive, scoring a hit on the driver's hatch, once more forcing the enemy's withdrawal.

Appleby returned just as Jordending was dismounting to hunt for ammunition from one of the other disabled tanks—and he was most relieved to see his company commander! "Tom, get me some help!" he shouted.

"What do you think this little can opener behind me is?" Appleby inquired. Then Tom guided Lieutenant Roger Owen's command M-36 tank destroyer with its 90mm gun into position.

But Jordening didn't have to elaborate on the situation, for at that moment the enemy tank sent two shells whistling down the road within inches of the TD. Immediately Owens returned the fire, and with two well-placed rounds of armor-piercing ammunition set the enemy tank blazing; and the battle was over momentarily.

Appleby then took off to place the remaining three tank destroyers in positions from which they could best support the tanks, while Lieutenant Owens helped Jordening in extricating his tank from the ditch; consequently, when Appleby returned, Jordening gave his company commander's tank back over to him, along with a couple AP shells which he'd just scrounged from another disabled tank.

As his driver had been wounded and evacuated, Captain Appleby again left his tank at the edge of Puffendorf and made his way to the aid station where he learned that the dozer had been destroyed even though it had been in a defilade position when hit. Apparently, Sergeant Witkowski and his gunner were both dead, but the loader, Whip Johnson, though wounded, was at the aid station. While Appleby was still there, Witkowski's driver and bow gunner showed up—though just as Appleby was leaving. Quickly Appleby asked Nate Talbot if he was all right and capable of being the driver of his command tank.

T/5 Nate Talbot was a twenty-two-year-old Illinois farm boy. Dark complexioned, of average build, his husky voice often croaked like that of an adolescent's. With some tools and a little bailing wire, he could fix just about anything. He claimed that after all the cantankerous tractors he's driven down on his dad's Illinois farm, operating the bulldozer tank was easy.

After the dozer had been hit, Nate, sitting in his driver's seat, had been covered with blood and human flesh, but quickly he had evacuated the burning tank. However, the bow gunner, Hank Henry's last minute replacement, had been trapped by the barrel of the 75 protruding over his hatch. Screams from the man had caused Nate to reenter the fireball. After he had pulled the newcomer over the transmission, they had both then escaped out the driver's hatch.

Next, Nate had jumped up on to the turret and had attempted to peer inside. The heat and flames had scorched his face. He had seen nobody and had assumed from the blood and flesh still on himself that all the occupants of the turret must have been killed. At that moment, the dozer was jolted by another armor-piercing hit, and Nate had dropped to the ground. Within minutes, though, both he and the assistant driver had found the aid station where he had run into Captain Appleby.

When Captain Appleby asked Nate if he would be able to drive his command tank, Nate winced, remembering that Sergeant Witkowski had been his closest friend. Though Appleby's request was really an order, Nate was eager to comply. Both Polack and Nate had received their Bronze Stars for their part in the destruction of a retreating German column in Normandy. Now Nate sought revenge for the killing of Polack. In war such hate can be the source of heroism.

As Nate ducked from the aid station, he was taken under small arms fire. Cautiously making his way to the orchard where Appleby's command tank was hidden, he was surprised to find the tank deserted. But he was even more surprised to see a Panther emerging through the ground mist looking like a hungry shark. Dropping inside the turret, he settled himself on the gunner's seat, quickly sighting the 75 on to the Panther's right side. Inexplicably, the Panther came to a dead halt less than a hundred feet from the orchard. Nate pressed the firing button and the Panther exploded in flames. As panicking crewmen attempted to flee from their burning panzer, Nate dropped them in their tracks with the coaxially mounted 30-caliber machine gun.

"War is hell," he said grimly.

Sweat pouring off his brow and all feeling drained as if a suction tube had extracted the contents of his stomach, Nate slumped forward. Suddenly Captain Appleby's head was in the turret. "Nate, Nate—are you all right?"

"Yes sir, Captain."

"Well, don't try to win the war by yourself."

THAT NIGHT—on the 17th, Appleby parked his command tank next to Burk's CP on the main street of Puffendorf. All crew members remained in the tank. As darkness descended, German infantry attempted to infiltrate the village. Nate Talbot, standing in the driver's hatch, fired a Tommy gun at fleeting shadows disappearing down the street. His shots alerted the entire command to the danger; and subsequently the German night attack was repulsed. In the morning on the 18th, five dead German soldiers lay sprawled on the street in the grotesque agony of their deaths next to Appleby's command tank.

(Several months later, Nate Talbot was awarded the Silver Star for his heroic actions on the 17th of November, 1944, during the Battle of Puffendorf. He said, "Why me? Why not Polack?")

FROM HIS BESIEGED command post in the basement in Puffendorf, Colonel Burk was at last on the telephone with General Clay who wanted to know why "Operation Queen" was stalled. Colonel Burk concealed from General Clay that for the moment he felt like a prairie dog trapped in its hole by a rattlesnake. Instead, he took a deep breath and described the German counterattack. He had had to retreat or risk the annihilation of Combat Command "B."

"What about air and artillery support?" asked General Clay.

"Air support was difficult if not impossible due to low clouds, and the artillery, though helpful, had not yet slowed the German counterattack," said Colonel Burk.

"Can you hold out for a few more hours, before Combat Command 'A' arrives?" questioned General Clay.

"Yes. By a more aggressive use of our TDs," answered Burk. (*Though tank destroyers had little armor protection, because of their 90mm gun, they could duel on an equal footing with German tanks. But according to the army manual, TDs were supposed to be employed only in defense from a defilade position.*)

"Use the TDs as you see fit, Colonel Burk."

Just as Colonel Burk was concluding his telephone communication with General Clay, Captain Appleby arrived at the CP looking for help. At first Colonel Burk was cool towards his arch rival, but Burk now realized that if he'd not countermanded Appleby's order to disperse the tanks in the draw, his command might now not be in such a predicament. Therefore for the moment animosities had to be laid aside. Burk needed Appleby.

IN AN EVEN VOICE Captain Appleby asked, "Can you get us ammunition and support, sir?"

"There should be four TDs arriving at any moment. Put them in defilade around the perimeters. Combat Command 'A' has already arrived in Ubach, and ammunition is on its way from Loverich; also, Thunderbolts are going to try and come in under the clouds," stated Burk, also in a level, matter-of-fact voice.

"I've already put the TDs in defilade, sir," said Appleby.

ON THE EVENING of the 17th General Clay's eyes were more red than hazel and his face more spongy than leathery. Even though he had a cot placed in his operations room, he was doing without sleep. Standing by his side peering at the large sand table were Major Jack Collins and Colonel Harold Quinn. Aides were moving representations of both known American and enemy positions on the sand table.

Puffing on a Camel, General Clay said glumly, "It looks like the whole 15th Armored is bogging down. The 29th Infantry didn't take Setterich, and we're catching hell from there, making it impossible for Combat Command 'A' to wheel into action. Both Task Forces '2' and 'X' got beaten back at Apweiler, and Task Force '1' is just barely holding on at Puffendorf. 'Operation Queen' will be dead in its tracks if we don't do something fast."

Poking a pudgy finger at the table, stocky Major Collins opinioned, "In this open terrain with every square yard registered by artillery, we can't operate without air support, sir."

General Clay looked at Colonel Quinn. "What do you think, Harold?"

With brazen self-assurance Colonel Quinn said, "First—you do know, don't you, General, that Captain Appleby called in from Beggendorf confirming the presence of General Dietrich's battle-group and warning of a Trojan Horse attack from our rear?"

"Yes. That big industrial structure was supposed to be Dietrich's 'Trojan Horse.' But Appleby's warning probably checkmated Dietrich.... You still haven't answered my question, Harold."

SQUINTING HIS EYES at the sand table the mellifluous voice of Colonel Quinn began, "All right.... If Burk can hold on to Puffendorf during the night, I'd do two things, General."

Bumming a cigarette from Major Collins and lighting up, Colonel Quinn continued: "First, I'd order Burk to separate his infantry and tanks of both Task Forces '2' and 'X' that are still trying to take Apweiler. Send the infantry on the road and in the fields, and send the tanks up the draws where they'll be hidden." Retrieving a pointer, Colonel Quinn indicated the low places he thought the tanks might successfully negotiate, leading up to and behind Apweiler. "We might even be able to trap Jerry in a pincer's movement if our tanks can get behind Apweiler unseen."

"Second, we have to take Setterich. The 29th Infantry is stalled. Call General Amery and tell him Task Force '4' of our Combat Command 'A' will be coming through him. These people are itching to get into this battle. Their 'point-of-departure' can also be Beggendorf. As you see, most of their force is presently assembled at Ubach."

TURNING TO HIS OPERATIONS OFFICER, General Clay asked, "What are your suggestions, Jack?"

Tightening the muscles of his bulldog jaws and taking a deep breath, Major Collins exhaled and said, "With the weather preventing any decent air support, I think Harold's ideas have merit, sir. We no longer can deploy our tanks in the open around here, and Setterich has to be taken.... An inexplicable report just came in that Dietrich's and Kraus' forces are being ordered to withdraw, leaving only Bartholomaus' 'Hammer' Division opposing our advance to the Roer River. But we don't know the reliability of this report.... It could be a trap."

With hands clasped behind his back, General Clay paced up and down the length of the sand table. The tall, lean general had a worried look in his light brown eyes. Suddenly, he stopped his pacing and said, "Issue the necessary orders, Jack, for Harold's plan. Let's go to my office and have coffee."

DURING THE EARLY EVENING of the 18th, Colonel Quinn was relieved to learn that the strategy he'd suggested the day before had been successful. The tanks of Task Forces "2" and "X" reached Apweiler by 1430 hours and had secured the village by 1515. And as he'd predicted, they trapped the defending Germans in the fields between the town and the advancing infantry. Late that afternoon Setterich also fell to Task Force "4" of Combat Command "A." General Clay had then called Quinn to his headquarters at the school to praise his "tactical acumen," as General Clay had put it.

RETURNING TO HIS OWN 67th Regimental Headquarters, Colonel Quinn decided to find Hap Hardesty and Little Joe and perhaps have a bite to eat with them. He couldn't remember when he'd last eaten. He found his Chief Kitchen Steward already preparing to move some of the kitchen equipment on to trucks. Hap said, ". . . in preparation for the advance of the division." Colonel Quinn thought it might well have been in the opposite direction from what Hardesty probably figured.

Looking into the nearly deserted dining room, he was surprised to see the Red Cross girls sitting at one of the rectangular tables with Little Joe wedged in between them. Also seated at the table was T/5 Josh Higgins, the driver of their clubmobile. As Colonel Quinn approached the four, both Susan Montgomery and Sally Brown jumped up, anxious lines written on their faces. They wore no Red Cross outfits; both were dressed in GI fatigue clothes with an army field jacket for warmth. Their subdued GI appearance was a far cry from their usual bright "on-stage" display.

"We just came from the hospital," said Susan, "so we know there's a terrible battle going on. Are we winning?"

"It's hard going. The Germans are contesting every inch of their Fatherland."

Attempting to cover for Susan, Sally asked, "How's Captain Appleby?"

"As usual he's in the thick of it. So far so good."

As he sat down across from the girls and Little Joe, and next to Josh Higgins, who stood and saluted, Colonel Quinn winked at Little Joe.

At once smiling easily, Joe rose, rushed around the table and sat next to Colonel Quinn.

"Hey," said Sally, "it looks like you've got a new friend, Colonel."

His dark eyes sparkling, Joe said, "Colonel Quinn is finding me a way to the states."

Looking into the kitchen where Hap Hardesty was busy, Sally said, "I thought you were going to be Hap's boy."

Wrinkling his nose and sounding less than certain, Joe replied, "I think I am; 'cept Hap's boy, Virgil, hasn't answered my letter."

Laying a hand on Joe's shoulder, Colonel Quinn said, "Don't be so impatient, Joe."

"How do you fit into the picture?" Sally asked bluntly.

The graying, fifty-year-old colonel nodded his head. "I'm the catalyst, Sally. Through some friends in Washington I'll try to expedite Little Joe's acceptance as a displaced person if Hap and his wife will take Joe."

ALL THIS PALAVER ABOUT JOE was the furthest thing from Susan's mind. Even though she hadn't been much of a student, she remembered snippets from a high school course in English literature. Maybe it was Shelley or Keats; maybe it was Lord Byron. She couldn't remember whom, but the class had read the love letters and poems of some great English writer in which that writer had attempted to describe his feelings for his ladylove. At the time she'd thought the author's descriptions pretty gushy and silly.

But now her love for Tom Appleby was not silly. Instead, she found it ravenous. Day and night her hunger for Tom gnawed at her, demanding gratification. In fact, Tom Appleby consumed her mind. Her desire for him eschewed reason and caution, actually seducing her with the promise of ecstasy.

In recent days, Susan smiled, poured coffee, handed out doughnuts, parroted platitudes, wrote down names and addresses, consoled and laughed. But she did so as an automaton. The likeness of Tom Appleby's face and figure lived with her. His strong athletic build, wavy auburn hair, topaz eyes, smooth tan skin and that cute dimple, whenever he smiled, enchanted her; and remembering his speech and mannerisms captivated her, like his "Y'alls" and "Judas Priests." They were always said in such a kindly, funny way.

She had even used her influence with her brother, Donald, to try to get Captain Appleby removed from combat. But Donald had just laughed. The only time Donald had ever made fun of her that she could recall.

Abruptly she said, "Colonel Quinn, don't you think Captain Appleby could be better used as a staff officer?"

Just then a soldier on "KP" brought Colonel Quinn coffee and warmed over "C" rations. As he was still puzzling the foods' edibility, Colonel Quinn delayed responding. At last, looking Susan directly in her eyes, he said, "I'd love to trade positions with Captain Appleby. You're quite influential with the general, Susan. See if you can arrange it."

SERGEANT BECK JONES, Private Jimmy Malloti, and Second Lieutenant Philip Vossmaar had all gathered at Philip's home the evening of the 18th of November, 1944. As Philip's home was just down the block from the Secondary Technical School, the three were readily available for duty, though Philip was temporarily on leave, serving with the Dutch Resistance, and Beck Jones, at the request of General Clay, had just been transferred from his infantry outfit to General Clay's staff. Their gathering was for relaxation. The Americans provided the Scotch and cigarettes, Philip the dwelling.

Beck Jones didn't mind his changed status—rear-line duty compared to front-line duty. And Beck and Philip had been friends since Heerlen's liberation day—September 17. On several occasions, prompted by good Scotch, the swarthy, good-natured sergeant had unfolded the turbulent tale of his marital life to his Dutch friend. In his thirties, a Texan and a career soldier, he had fathered a boy and a girl before splitting with his school-age wife; and that was all before Pearl Harbor. If he survived the war, his goal was to look up his kids, and see if he could help them.

While Beck Jones was open and above board, dusky, shifty-eyed Private Jimmy Mallotti looked sneaky and dangerous. A New York Sicilian, he usually made a bad first impression. Somehow, General Clay had recognized the possibility for staunchness and loyalty in Mallotti. Tapping these virtues, Clay had made Jimmy his unranked alter ego. Besides being his chauffeur, he was General Clay's eyes and ears, and recently the watchdog over the Red Cross girls. But, of course, most everyone in the outfit believed Jimmy had a gangster connection back in the states.

With the Scotch beginning to take hold, Philip opened up, "I understand the news from the front is better today."

"Yeah, I believe we broke Jerry's counterattack," said Beck. "But I don't understand how the Germans can fight, considering what the Ruskies and our air force is doing to 'em. I thought they were kaput after St. Lo."

Inhaling deeply and thoughtfully on his Chesterfield, Jimmy suggested, "This is for their own land and families. The Reds never gave up to them in Russia either."

All three inhaled and sipped and then Jimmy said, "I wish those Red Cross broads would leave. I spend more time nursemaiding 'em than driving the general."

Bleary-eyed, Beck added, "I bet that blond bombshell would make a nice piece of ass."

Smiling, Philip couldn't resist, "I think Jimmy has one of our Dutch widows keeping him warm at nights."

"Shit, she has too many kids crawling over the house and on the bed to hardly get anything done."

All three laughed, smoked and drank more whiskey.

Philip considered how basically simple and kindhearted the two Americans were; yet, at the same time, so uneducated, gross and vulgar. One moment they'd give you the shirt off their backs and the next slit your throat if you crossed them.

As all three lapsed into silence, enjoying their high, Philip centered his thoughts on the "mission" of Bep and Karel. From an informant in the Resistance Bep had learned that someone not connected with the Gestapo was holding Nicoline at Warstein, Germany. Supposedly, this rescue attempt of Nicoline was a race between Bep and Karel and the Gestapo to get to Warstein first. As the Dutch Resistance had invented a technique for making long-distance telephone calls from behind German lines, bypassing German controlled switchboards, Karel had asked Philip to remain by his phone in case of help being required.

The expected call came just as Philip was saying his goodnights to Beck and Jimmy. The crux of the message was that Philip had to get to Eindhoven posthaste to bring a wounded Karel Konijn, Philip's best friend, back to Heerlen. The wounded Karel would be at the railroad depot. The caller divulged nothing else—just that it was pressing for Philip to get to Eindhoven posthaste. The unknown caller, after again stressing urgency, had hung up.

Problems raced through Philip's mind. How would he get to Eindhoven? That Dutch city had been liberated by the British; it was far away. But Beck and Jimmy still lingered at his front door!

Quickly and succinctly Philip briefed them about his problem. He didn't have a car, nor, for that matter, did he know how to drive.

"No problem," said Jimmy. "I'll get a staff car and we'll be on our way to see the fuckin' limeys. . . . We'll be back in Heerlen before dawn, or my name ain't Jimmy Malloti."

CHAPTER 11

WHEN AN AMBULANCE distanced Whip Johnson from combat, his fears of imminent extinction subsided, and he felt grateful relief. But when blisters on his face caused partial blindness, feelings of anxiety recurred. The mere thought of blindness terrified him. Nevertheless, considering his momentary unconsciousness while inside the burning tank, he realized he was very lucky to have escaped from that fiery infernal.

At the station hospital he was transferred from a stretcher to an army cot, briefly examined and drugged again. It seemed, however, like he was in a large gymnasium and was surrounded by other wounded soldiers who appeared to be placed helter-skelter about the room on army cots.

Seemingly interminable time elapsed from his arrival until he was lifted on to a gurney and taken into an emergency operating room. Remembering an aversion to ether, Whip warned the doctor about his vomiting and getting sick. Then someone inserted a needle into his arm and a soothing female voice said, "You have nothing to worry about, soldier; we're using sodium pentothal, the 'truth' serum. It won't make you sick. Just start counting." Whip counted to three.

When he regained consciousness Whip immediately wondered what hidden "truths" he might have disclosed while on the operating table. Recalling that his surgery had begun in the morning, he checked the Swiss wristwatch his parents had given him for his high school graduation and noted that it read 4 P.M. Apparently there was no recovery room at the front. You woke up on your own—if you woke up at all!

Noticing that his burned left hand had been bound repeatedly by rolls of white dressing until it looked like a boxing glove, he moved his non-burned right hand to his head and discovered his head was similarly encased, with slits having been made for his ears, eyes and mouth.

A gurgle in Whip's stomach and pressure in his groin caused him to remove a khaki army blanket and sit up. Nearly within arm's reach sat a German soldier on a cot. The man, who didn't look much like a superman of the Aryan race, appeared both old and distressed. Whip felt no need to communicate.

Still dressed in his brown, wool shirt and pants, Whip noticed someone had folded his field jacket and laid it beneath his cot, where he likewise saw his combat boots, stocking helmet liner and his now-precious *The Story of Philosophy*—the book that had probably saved his life. Rising rather unsteadily and looking around, he discovered that he'd guessed right. He was in a large gymnasium. Then he saw some GIs with trays of food, but first he had to locate a latrine. He asked, and one of the GIs pointed toward a door.

When Whip opened that door, he was startled to see a face out of the movie, "The Invisible Man." In that movie, the "Invisible Man" had wrapped his face with gauze to make himself temporarily visible. Moving up closer to a large mirror over a sink, Whip observed that his lower lip looked like raw meat. Finally, stepping back and scrutinizing his whole head, he concluded, "Maybe I look like a mummy, but at least I can see again."

Afterward, Whip located the kitchen and dining room where he quickly found out that acidic foods, like tomatoes, made for unbearable pain once their juices reached his lower lip. Struck by a wave of nausea, he dumped his food and returned to his cot where he lay back down.

Not long after, corpsmen moved him out of the building and on to another "meat wagon." This time the trip was long and tedious, but a medic had provided him with sulfa and aspirin tablets for preventing infection and reducing pain. In spite of the wearisome ride, Whip felt good. The doctor had assured him he wasn't going blind; and also important to Whip, he had experienced combat without having done anything particularly craven, brief though it had been; what's more, he had survived, receiving only minor abrasions and burns. In a short time he would be completely healed. Abruptly, the coward in Whip reflected, "Hopefully, not too short a time."

WHEN AT LAST the ambulance halted, Whip was taken into a huge, circus-like tent and helped onto a regular hospital bed that was one of many placed in neat rows. Medical charts hung on each occupied bed, and clean white sheets and heavy lavender blankets covered each patient. A white-coated nurse told Whip he was at the 91st General Hospital and they were located on a hill overlooking the city of Liege, Belgium.

The nurse was just explaining that he was located in the outside annex of the hospital when Whip heard the pulse-jet engine of Hitler's "V-1"—"the buzz bomb." Whip saw horror register in the eyes of the young nurse as she kneeled and ducked, seeming to pray, beside his bed. After the jet engine of the bomb shut off, the wail of its death dive was nerve wracking; finally, its detonation, somewhere below in the city of Liege, shook the ground with shock waves. Trying to appear collected, the nurse rose and said, "You'll get used to 'em."

Whip thought, "Oh, my God. It never ends."

What combat had failed to do, Hitler's V-1 nearly accomplished—that is, drive Whip Johnson crazy. Day and night buzz bombs targeted the railhead city of Liege, and sometimes more often than just two or three a day. But so far the hospital had been spared. Lying helpless in bed, shielded only by the cloth of a tent and the threads of an army blanket, Whip could never completely relax.

Probably less than a week after Whip's arrival in Liege, he was informed that he was being transferred to a burn hospital in England. Whip's relief was inexpressible. This time the ambulance took him directly to an airport where he was loaded aboard a DC2. But just as the plane taxied down the runway another buzz bomb, sort of a "good-bye present," Whip imagined, hit the runway. In swerving to avoid the crater made by the bomb, the pilot nearly lost control of his aircraft. Miraculously, though, he got airborne, and promptly flew into a storm over the English channel.

Having foolishly eaten a tomato stew before departure, Whip's lip briefly flared as if stung by a swarm of bees. But that was nothing compared to the airsickness he soon experienced. As the storm bumped and bounced the plane, it wasn't long before Whip's stomach expelled its contents. In the lull immediately following his stomach's upheaval, however, Whip looked upon the bright side. Lost in the storm, the defenseless aircraft wasn't likely to be shot down by some German fighter ace.

Nevertheless, it was dark when the plane penetrated the "soup" and promptly put down at a British airfield. Before long and in rain British medical personnel appeared with gurneys, and a limey soldier wheeled Whip into a Quonset lined with hospital beds. After helping Whip get into one of the large beds and making certain he was "tucked-in," the British soldier sauntered to the nurses' desk and attempted to get a date for a dance later that night. The nurse played "hard-to-get" and the soldier played "be-a-sport." Speaking with British accents, their casual bantering was like heavenly music to Whip's ears. At last having had nearly all his fears extinguished for now, Whip assumed a fetal position, snuggled into the warm blankets and was soon relaxed and fast asleep.

AFTER THE 18TH OF NOVEMBER, the battered remnants of Combat Command "B" pretty much assumed a supporting role as the "Fighting" 15th Armored Division pushed on to the Roer River in the next few days. On the 23rd the 1st Battalion moved back to the vicinity of Heerlen, Holland, to refit and train more replacements.

Obviously it would take several weeks before the Division would be ready to fight again. "Operation Queen" was over, and units of the Division now stood on the banks of the Roer River.

But the offensive was costly: over 200 dead, over 1,000 wounded, and 200 missing. The 15th lost 80 tanks, about half unrepairable. The advance into Germany of about ten miles was the toughest ten miles the Division had ever fought.

ON THE 24TH OF NOVEMBER, the day after Thanksgiving, John C. Smith believed he had little to be thankful for, even though he had just come through the Battle of Puffendorf unharmed. His closest buddies, VD Johnson and Dale Jenks were probably dead. What troubled John was that their deaths might not have occurred as the result of enemy action, but, rather, was the result of "friendly" fire. Most likely, Second Lieutenant Joe Nicholson had ordered and Mike "Morbid" Morris had fired the AP missile that had struck the bulldozer tank, killing his friends—and within the confines of Puffendorf. At least, these were John Smith's strong suspicions. Later that same day, John Smith learned that Witkowski and Jenks had indeed been confirmed killed, but that VD had escaped with burns and was expected to return soon.

WITH SOME OF HIS DIVISION DUG in on the west bank of the Roer River, Major General Brighton D. Clay ordered a meeting of regimental, battalion and company commanders at Division headquarters at 0900 hours on the first day of December, 1944, for a critique of "Operation Queen." Once again assembled in the Lecture Hall at the Secondary Technical School in Heerlen, Holland, the officers expectantly awaited the entrance of their commanding officer. At the appointed hour, the lean and leathery general entered from a side door, preceded by his bulldog appearing operations officer, Major Jack Collins, who promptly called, "Attention!"

Quickly stepping to the lectern, the general said, "Be at ease, men."

Scanning the faces of his officers, General Clay was impressed by the confidence in their eyes. Though the Division had taken a thrashing in getting to the Roer, his men showed no signs of having their tails between their legs.

"First, I want to commend you for your sacrifices, your bravery and your skill in executing your orders. It was tough going, but you hung in there. Convey my personal compliments to your veterans. Remind them to help get this winning spirit across to the new replacements—there are enough coming on!"

Looking again at the large sand table beside his lectern (Sergeant Steple was still in the process of creating a new scene showing enemy territory between the Roer and Rhine rivers), General Clay said, "The battle was won, but the war isn't over by a long shot. Our next objective will be the Rhine, certainly the most sacred river to the German people. As you can see, it's about thirty miles from our present positions on the Roer. Neither the code name nor the plan of attack have yet come down to Division, but you can sure bet we'll be in the thick of it."

General Clay scratched his face, collecting his thoughts. "First, a few general remarks: This was the most planned offensive the Division ever participated in. Yet a stubborn enemy surprised us with improved tanks and excellent battle tactics. In fact, elements of General Dietrich's battle group nearly recaptured Puffendorf, partly because of a breakdown in communications between Captain Appleby, who discovered General Dietrich and the ruse he had planned for us, and Colonel Burk, who countermanded Captain Appleby's order to disperse the tanks in the draw. I understand, however, Colonel Burk did not know of the proximity of Dietrich's force, but I fault both Captain Appleby and Colonel Burk for this.

"It must never happen again with any officers in this Division. The chain of command must be respected, but commanding officers must always allow their subordinates the leeway to act in a situation where there is little time to deliberate or communications have been jammed or cut."

Both Appleby and Burk blushed, theirs being the only names mentioned by the general. Afterwards the critique went on for most of the morning with Major Collins at the lectern and General Clay joining his men in the audience. Several other officers were called upon to contribute. Around noon General Clay summed up the main points and conclusions drawn, stressing that attacking tanks must always have room to maneuver; they must never be jammed close in a ravine or gully. Furthermore, he ordered his officers to conduct similar critiques throughout the command down to and including the last private. He also requested that all "After-Battle Reports," which were being prepared by each company and battalion, be quickly sent to his desk for collation and study.

As soon as his Hammer Division had been successfully extricated from the west bank of the Roer River, General Bartholomaus personally oversaw the destruction of several bridges and the defensive positioning of his troops. Now he was in the process of establishing his new headquarters at Bedburg when once again he was visited by his friend and commanding officer, Field Marshal Stein.

In the privacy of General Bartholomaus' office, the two Prussian generals exchanged warm greetings and both acknowledged that the bridges had to be blown, despite what Armaments Minister Speer was supposedly recommending.

After placing his officer's baton on a table and removing his black leather coat, Field Marshal Stein said, "Beautiful, beautiful. Your outnumbered forces, Gerd, exacted a heavy toll from General Clay's 15th Armored Division. It will not be 'fighting' another battle again so soon."

"I was told the BBC (British Broadcasting Company) is claiming a great victory for the Americans at Puffendorf. The number of our tanks they claim to have destroyed would equip two full-sized panzer divisions—ha, ha," said General Bortholomaus, his good, grey-blue eye sparkling, as he adjusted his monocle.

"With Hitler abandoning you during the middle of the battle by ordering Kraus and Dietrich to withdraw, I'm proud of you for holding off the Americans with your shrunken forces. It is you, Gerd, who is the true military genius," said the field marshal with genuine admiration in his voice.

"Thank you, Manfred. But do we now have sufficient forces to hold back the Americans in this sector while Hitler embarks on another one of his adventures?"

"I believe so. They are still keeping me in the dark as to the time and place, Gerd; but I'm certain Hitler will soon hit Eisenhower with a big punch. I'm guessing it will be in the Ardennes. Manteuffel and the others from the East should soon be in place."

Both men found leather chairs and lit up captured American cigarettes. Crossing his legs while blowing a smoke ring, Manfred said, "American cigarettes are all right , but I still prefer Turkish."

"Ja. The same with me."

"With Hitler's enterprise, what chance do you believe he has, Gerd?"

"As I said before, too little, too late."

"What about his V-1s and V-2s?"

"The same answer, Manfred. They are terror weapons that will not affect the outcome of the war. . . . Now, I will ask you: What about the Speer thing?"

Rising and retrieving his baton, the gold-braided, red-striped officer said, "It's on hold until we see what comes from 'Watch On The Rhine.' (Hitler's first code name for the planned 1944 Ardennes Offensive.) If Hitler's offensive is successful and the seaport of Antwerp should be recaptured, a negotiated peace might be salvaged. At least that is what they hope." Punching out his cigarette and speaking emphatically, Manfred said, "In my view, 'Watch On The Rhine' will never succeed. So be ready to help us, Gerd. I'll let you know the time."

A CHASTISED LIEUTENANT Colonel Burk returned to his 1st Battalion Headquarters following General Clay's critique. It was the middle of the afternoon and all was quiet on the western front. In Heerlen the sun even appeared briefly. This first day of December reminded him of the approach of Christmas. After the breakout at Normandy he had figured the war would be over before Christmas, but the Battle of Puffendorf proved otherwise.

He thought of his home in Omaha, Nebraska. His dad and his dad's cronies would probably be out pheasant hunting on their ranch in the sandhills near North Platte. Mother would be playing bridge while Dad was away. However, General Clay's admonition reminded him again that he had to be careful not to screw up his military career. He knew his dad had plans for him with a run at politics in mind; and he liked the political idea; but he knew it was about time at twenty-nine that he got married.

CORPORAL WES WILLOW was working on the "After-Battle Report" when Colonel Burk entered his headquarters in a rented Dutch farm house. The Nazi-educated corporal, son of an American diplomat, rose, and saluted, "Good afternoon, sir. In the 'After-Battle Report' I'm seeing you get good copy," he laughed.

Colonel Burk returned the salute and smiled. He recalled from his college history classes that both Winston Churchill and Lawrence of Arabia were serious about their press.

"I also put in there that in dereliction of duty Private Milton Silverman deserted his post when subjected to enemy fire."

Colonel Burk smiled. He knew of Wes' prejudice against Jews and his hatred of "Peewee" Silverman. "Cross it out, Wes. That kind of vendetta crap doesn't go in an After-Battle Report. I'll look into the matter later." He pulled a rickety, wooden chair up to a small dining table and sat down. "As I understand it, that was when Captain Appleby ordered Silverman on the radio to drive his three-quarter-ton to Beggendorf?"

"Yes. But I had ordered the Jew-boy to stay put until I got permission from the MPs to go forward. I took cover when Jerry sent in artillery, and when I returned, the truck and Jew-boy were both gone."

The thing Colonel Burk liked about Corporal Willow was his constant loyalty. Furthermore, Colonel Burk discovered Wes had a talent for writing. He made a much better office hand and radio operator than a tank loader, which had been Wes' original army assignment. What he didn't like about Willow was his continual whining.

However, Corporal Willow was the only subordinate in the battalion with whom Colonel Burk exercised any familiarity. Amused by Willow's feud with Silverman, Colonel Burk said, "Forget it, Wes. Silverman's got Appleby behind him on this one."

Corporal Willow wrinkled his flat nose, aimed his dark eyes at the ceiling and looking as serene as a bust of Buddha, said, "At least you don't have Witkowski to worry about anymore."

Willow's words troubled Colonel Burk. With a thrown track and lost behind enemy lines in Normanday, Burk had ordered Witkowski to take some captured German prisoners back into the woods and shoot them. Witkowski had refused calling it murder. But Willow had then carried out Burk's orders. War was war and Captain Burk had felt endangered if the Germans had been set free. At first Burk had worried that Witkowski might make trouble; but in time it appeared that all parties to that unfortunate event had let it lapse into their memories. No one ever mentioned it, though he had put a disclaimer in Witkowski's personnel records.

Biting his lip, Colonel Burk asked, "Was the dozer destroyed?"

"Yes."

"Knocked out by enemy fire."

"I don't know."

"Who saw it happen?"

"Lieutenant Nicholson and his gunner Private Morris."

"I thought Morris was the loader?"

"No."

"Who is the loader?"

"Corporal John Smith."

"Arrange for me to meet with this Corporal Smith."

" . . . You may also want to meet with Lieutenant Nicholson. He performed heroically during the Battle of Puffendorf. I'm including his exploits in the After-Battle Report. You may want to have him decorated."

Magnified by his glasses, Colonel Burk's predatory eyes, appeared blank as if he were deep in thought. Seemingly without giving the idea a moments regard, Colonel Burk's raspy voice echoed, "Of course."

"Oh by the way, Colonel, when Jew-boy and I were transporting the filing cabinets containing the personnel records, Jew-boy saw and read that note of your's in Witkowski's file."

Colonel Burk understood enough of what Wes said that Wes's statement immediately jerked Burk back to full attention. Looking Wes in the eyes, Colonel Burk asked, "Did you tell Silverman what order it was that Witkowski refused to obey?"

". . . No."

"Put Silverman on my list of those to see. Then get back to Company 'D.'"

"Yes, sir."

FOLLOWING THE CRITIQUE at General Clay's headquarters, Captain Appleby thought he had a thirst, so he drove his jeep to The Beer Garden. What he really thirsted for was the sight of Susan Montgomery. His thirst was quenched. She was sitting at the large table near the dance floor, accompanied by her usual retinue of Sally Brown, Josh Higgins and Jimmy Malloti.

When Susan looked up from her drink and saw Tom, she could have swooned. During the battle she had felt that her concern for Tom's safety was so great that had it not been for her Red Cross work she would have died from worry. Every ambulance to catch her eyes, she had imagined might be carrying the body of either a wounded Tom Appleby or a dead Tom Appleby. Every soldier she had looked upon in a hospital ward or upon a stretcher, she had tested for the familiar wavy hair, the genial eyes and the tanned face with the dimple. And each time a soldier had failed her test, she had breathed a considerable sigh of relief.

This time Tom Appleby never made it to the group. Susan headed him off, grabbing his hand and leading him to a remote corner. All he could do with respect to Susan's companions was to wave and smile in recognition.

Susan found an empty booth with beaded, transparent curtains and cuddled next to Tom. In a blur of embraces and kisses, they were as one. When a waiter appeared, Susan ordered a cognac and

Tom followed suit. Surprisingly, Tom had not tasted liquor since he had arrived in the ETO. It was one of his self-imposed disciplines. Next, Susan lit up a cigarette; and as Tom asked for one of hers, she realized another one of his resolutions was going by the wayside.

Susan pondered whether it was because of his battle experiences or the influence she was beginning to exert over him that Tom was loosening up. And the latter possibility thrilled Susan. Placing her hand on his thigh and spreading her fingers she said, "I know that battle was terrible, honey. You must have gone through hell?"

"I'm lucky to be here, Susan. . . . But we lost too many great soldiers out there." His head dipped and his voice cracked. "It's difficult reconciling my being alive. Sometimes I just don't get it, Susan." A tear formed at the corner of an eye and flowed down his cheek.

Susan Montgomery was moved as she had never been moved. Looking into Tom's face and seeing him grieve for his fallen comrades made her own life seem puny in comparison. She put out her cigarette and removed Tom's from his mouth, dousing it too. They were absorbed in another embrace when the waiter returned with their drinks.

"Honey, I don't believe you've ever seen Sally's and my room at the hotel."

"No."

"Can we go there? I have something to show you."

"Y'all shouldn't put yourself out, Susan, but I'd be real pleased."

"Come on, honey," said Susan, signaling to Sally. Meeting Sally halfway, Susan's limpid green eyes turned down as she whispered, "Tom and I are going to the hotel. Be sure and give us some time."

With a twinkle in her oval eyes, Sally returned, "You betcha, baby."

The chartreuse eyes of the two doughnut dollies met and they smiled. Sally returned to her table as Susan and Tom left The Beer Garden.

JIMMY MALLOTI WAS PHILOSOPHIC. "War is hell for front line soldiers like Captain Appleby, but I've got it made running General Clay's errands."

Josh Higgins emptied his glass of beer and asked, "Have you ever had any interesting errands, Jimmy?"

How T/5 Josh Higgins ever got the job as squire to the Red Cross girls and driver of their "clubmobile" might have something to do with his bland character, speculated Sally Brown when she returned from answering Susan's summons. If the term "slightly below average" applied to anyone, it fit the bill for Josh Higgins. Small, dark and twentyish, he was a mechanical genius. Asexual in instinct, almost like a eunuchoid, his love was motors. Sally considered Josh the perfect chauffeur for Susan and herself.

"Yeah," said Jimmy. "I just got back from rescuing some Dutch dude who was wounded in a shoot-out behind the Kraut's lines."

"You didn't go to the front did you?" inquired Josh.

"Naw. It seems that our Dutch interpreter, Voss, is a friend of this 'freedom fighter,' some guy named Karel or something. . . . Everybody over here is a Voss or a Karel or something. Ha ha. I don't see why they make their names so damn complicated, although this Voss guy seems like a pretty good Joe. Christ, he speaks better English than I do."

"You really don't have to be very exceptional to do that," said Sally.

Jimmy's dark, shifty-eyes flickered and he lay his hand on Sally's knee.

Ignoring the advance, the "doughnut dolly" continued, "Was this Karel hurt very badly?" Sally was dressed in her light-purple Red Cross outfit with the short pleated skirt.

Under the table Jimmy continued the slow, delicate advance of his hand. "Not really. His head was bandaged like he'd been kicked by a mule. But he and Voss chattered in their tongue like chipmunks."

"What do you know about a mule? Have you ever been on a farm?" asked Sally.

Smoothing his slick black hair with his inactive hand, Jimmy said, "Sure, back in Sicily when I was a kid."

Sally was certain she didn't love Jimmy. But even though there was something ominous about him, he was kind of good-looking. She knew him, she'd been around him, enough to consider him entertaining. He'd always been careful with both Susan and herself. She was in the mood; and she didn't see why all the good times had to go Susan's way.

Jimmy Malloti was elated. He could see by Sally's compliance that he could have his way. And maybe there wouldn't be another chance. Better act quickly while the bitch is hot, he thought. "Youse know, Sally. Youse never showed me those dolls youse been collecting over here. Could we go to yourse hotel room?"

"Yes. But it seems we have to queue up today."

IN HIS ROOM at the headquarters of the Otto Skorzeny commando organization, Arnd Hauptmann, the fourteen-year-old wunderkind, was practicing his American English in preparation for "Greif"—the code name for the commando actions being planned for behind American lines when the Führer launched "Autumn Mist." That was the real code-name for the Führer's surprise major offensive in the Ardennes region of Belgium and Luxembourg. Hitler himself was referring to his planned riposte with General Eisenhower as "Watch On The Rhine," suggesting a defensive posture to befuddle American intelligence as to his true intentions.

Arnd was physically and mentally changing rapidly. His youthful appearance was giving way to pimples, a fuzzy mustache and a breaking, lower-pitch voice; he was nearing fifteen. His innocence had long vanished. He'd killed before he could truly comprehend the meaning of death; he'd experienced sex before he knew what it was all about; and he'd been brainwashed before he had a chance to think for himself. This fanatic was happy in his work and ready to die at any time for his beloved Führer. Also, he now knew his uncle, Hans Spoor, alias "The Great Samson," had been a traitor and had met his just fate at the hands of Count Siegfried's Gestapo men.

But Arnd had one troubling thought. His Grandpa and Grandma Spoor had fled from Amsterdam to the British occupied zone to escape from the Gestapo. He loved his grandparents and had considered living with them at The Hague in Holland after the war if he survived. Why could they not see the greatness of the Führer? It was the Americans who had killed their daughter and grandchildren. Somehow he must soon go to his grandparents and make them see the light.

CHAPTER 12

THE 18TH OF NOVEMBER, 1944 was another bleak morning. The headquarters staff of SS Brigadier General Fritz Kraus' "Lightning" Panzer Division had worked throughout the night preparing for the divisions transfer to Bitburg, Germany. Unfortunately, from General Kraus' point of view, his division had been ordered to withdraw from the tank battle at Puffendorf just as the annihilation of General Clay's 15th Armored Division appeared imminent. At first resentful of the order to disengage, General Kraus had changed his mind after his Corps Commander, SS Lieutenant General Franz Rheinhardt, had explained the important role the "Lightning" Division would soon play in the Führer's coming offense in the Ardennes.

Later, General Kraus gave the subject more thought. A surprise attack in the Ardennes might be Germany's only hope for getting a just peace with the Allies. It could force the Allies into changing their commitment to "unconditional surrender" and implementing their "Morgenthau Plan" for turning Germany into an agrarian nation.

Furthermore, General Rheinhardt had given General Kraus specific leave to fly to his hunting lodge and bring Frau Lindemann to General Rheinhardt's headquarters at Münster where General Rheinhardt had promised to intervene with Himmler on Nicoline's behalf. In the mean time, General Kraus' "Lightning" Division would be transferring to the Ardennes sector. By flying his Storch, General Kraus hoped to both rescue Nicoline from the Gestapo and still be in Bitburg before the arrival of his division.

As GENERAL KRAUS' MONOPLANE was being serviced, he reviewed his division's travel plans with his aids, Major Kruger and Captain Snodgrass. The move was to be done at night. As Major Kruger and Captain Snodgrass were both assuring General Kraus that they would dutifully execute his orders, a telephone caller from Amsterdam rang General Kraus' headquarters and insisted on speaking only with the general. The caller, who refused to identify himself, said his message was of the utmost urgency.

Reluctantly, the beset general took the call.

"Kraus here."

A nervous, high-pitched voice said, "I cannot state anything but these facts, General: On the day before yesterday a Captain Snodgrass of the 'Lightning' Panzer Division revealed to Count Siegfried of the Gestapo that Captain Snodgrass' commanding officer, General Kraus, was protecting the Gestapo hostage, Frau Lindemann, at his hunting cabin near Warstein." The caller hung up.

General Kraus quickly asked that the call be traced; then, looking at the floor and gradually closing his eyes, he contemplated the caller's message. At last he turned to Captain Snodgrass who was still studying a map of the Ardennes.

General Kraus did not doubt the truth of the allegation. He knew Captain Snodgrass was an efficient but fervid officer. A former Hitler Youth leader, Captain Snodgrass had been accepted into the SS largely because of his zealotry.

"Captain," said General Kraus, "I believe you were on pass on the 16th. Where to?"

Worried by the question, as it followed General Kraus' conversation with a mysterious telephone caller, Captain Snodgrass nonetheless replied, "Amsterdam."

Avoiding Captain Snodgrass' eyes, General Kraus said, "I believe you returned to the division on the 17th after our counterattack had begun."

"Ja. Is something wrong?"

As if he did not hear the reply or the question, General Kraus sought Captain Snodgrass' eyes and stridently said, "You are to report immediately, Captain Snodgrass, to Captain Moulders. You are to command his lead panzer. I will issue the necessary orders."

The timbre of the general's voice and the nature of the order left no doubt in Captain Snodgrass' mind that his disclosure to Count Siegfried had just been passed on to General Kraus.

Staunch in his believe in Hitler and convinced it was the General who was at fault for shielding a fugitive, Captain Snodgrass proclaimed, "Jawohl, my General." Stepping back and extending his right arm, he shouted, "Heil Hitler."

Following the departure of both Major Krugger and Captain Snodgrass, General Kraus placed a telephone call to his gardener at Warstein. Upon learning that "Snow White" was in the pigeon loft, he dictated a message to be sent immediately to his hunting lodge.

BEFORE SUNRISE ON THE MORNING of the 18th, a restless Max Kraus rose from his bed, being careful not to awaken his sister, Felicia. He then dressed in his brush pants and brown knit shirt and tiptoed into the spacious, dark lounge where he retrieved a flashlight and his field boots. After lacing his boots, he found his camouflage jacket and Tyrolean sport hat. Then he stood on a chair and from the gun-rack lifted the "forbidden" twenty-gauge shotgun.

Even though he had been deliberate and careful in his movements, Max's every step was closely monitored. When Max hoisted the shotgun, all of his stealth for getting out of the house unnoticed nearly went by the wayside. With a mighty leap Hektor bounded to the chair and placed his front paws beside Max's boots, nearly toppling Max off the chair.

Reacting quickly, Max whispered, "No, Hektor! Down! Down!" Then bringing a finger to his lips, "Quiet! Quiet!"

The discernment between the ten-year-old and the bird dog was absolute. In apparent comprehension of the need for secrecy, Hektor instantly crouched beside Max and as if he were on cat's paws, retreated out the door behind his master.

Max loved Hektor, who had probably saved his life yesterday when he fell into the pond. That is what Nicoline said, though Max thought he could have swum to shore even without Hektor. But the point was, Hektor was there when he had most needed him. Therefore, much of the night he had pondered this question: What could he, Max, do to reward Hektor? In other words, what did Hektor enjoy doing more than anything? The answer was obvious: hunting! So on his own he'd decided to take Hektor duck hunting. He'd seen mallards in the pond, and his father's duck blind was always ready and snug—unfortunately, father was not here! And Aunt Gertrud, most assuredly, would never allow him to take a loaded shotgun without his father! So he'd decided to do it anyway, for Hektor's sake, and afterward take his punishment.

The morning was made for duck hunting. Overcast, brisk and damp. The battery in his flashlight was nearly kaput, but it hardly mattered. He knew the path by heart. Rustling in the brush never scared him either, for Hektor was with him. It could have been wild boar or Bismarck, the great stag his father had rescued when it was an injured fawn. Max had noticed that if his father could identify a particular wild animal, he would give it a name. In Bismarck's case, the deer had grown a great rack and was now quite old. Of course, his father never allowed his military friends to shoot at Bismarck when they visited here.

Now Max could see individual trees, and then he heard ducks quacking. Suddenly, all the ducks began quacking at once and their wings beat the water as one. For a second, their dim forms passed directly over him at tree-top height, the swoosh of their flight warming his young hunter's blood.

"Don't worry Hektor. They'll be back. They're just going out to eat from Herr Lüdwig's grain field."

Built alongside a cove, the concrete duck blind resembled a pillbox. Fritz had covered it with dirt, and natural vegetation grew from its roof and sides. Only the front and back entrances required camouflage. "Look at the brown swamp grass and reeds I put on the doors, Hektor. Don't you think I did a good job of camouflaging?"

Hektor barked his approval.

By the minute the forest pond and its surroundings were becoming clear. Max and Hektor covertly entered the blind, Max closing the camouflaged door behind them.

This was no ordinary duck blind, but a virtual bungalow with many of the amenities of a modern dwelling: leather couch, comfort chairs, sink, kerosene cook-stove and lanterns, water pump, cupboards and drawers with dishes and silverware, water closet, even a little writing desk and a clothes closet with hangers. Of course, among other things, Fritz had provisioned it with drink, food and reading and writing material. A bearskin rug covered much of its timbered floor. A separate chain-link compartment protected hunters from a wet dog. A revolvable periscope protruded from the blind, and a hinged wooden panel could be sprung, opening the blind toward the water, permitting hunters standing in a slightly depressed runway to shoot. Another panel could be separately triggered to release a dog for retrieving any downed ducks.

Obviously Fritz Kraus' duck blind promoted more purposes than just duck hunting. It was his retreat from a retreat. A place to go when he wanted to be alone. Having a penchant for writing, bird watching, nature study and photography, his elaborate duck blind served these interests as well. And, of course, for the past few years it had been the ideal place to bring his close friends from the army, and not only for duck hunting. Roe deer, wild boar and forest partridge were available to the gunners. For his military associates, taking a leave of absence with General Fritz Kraus had meant putting your worries aside and enjoying sport hunting and comradeship in the woods.

And wisely or unwisely, Fritz had suffused his young son with this adult, masculine environment, immediately whisking Max away from school whenever he was home on leave—much to the disapprobation of Aunt Gertrud. So, along with the dazzling colors of sugar maples, white birches and red ferns, the invigorating scent of a pine forest and wood smoke, young Max learned the excitement of the hunt and rowdy male bonding.

Upon entering the blind Max released the latch holding the shooting panel in place which then thumped down on the bank, exposing the grey cove. Next he jumped into the shooting trench within the blind and grasped elaborately carved wooden duck decoys which he flung into the water. Leaden weights splashed and plopped to the shallow bottom of the pond, anchoring the decoys. Cranking the handle of a small wheel attached to pulleys, he returned the camouflaged shooting panel to its closed position. Then he fell into an easy chair and pulled the retractable periscope to his eyes.

"The decoys look pretty good, Hektor. When the ducks come back from feeding, I hope to make some work for you. . . . I wonder what kind of punishment Aunt Gertrud will give me? Probably make me do all the dishes and clean the lodge for a week. That's all right by me."

Hektor wagged his stump of a tail in complete agreement.

Soon a few ducks returned early, making several passes before they dropped straight down into the middle of the pond, their wings and tails making a warning whistle. They chattered and warily swam toward the decoys. Max put a duck call to his lips and blew. Immediately the ducks took wing.

"Damn it! I was afraid I'd frighten them."

Hektor wagged his tail.

But two curious greenheads returned and hovered over the decoys, the beat of their wings thrashing the water into a white foam as they slowly descended. Almost in one action Max released the trapdoor and shot at one of the drakes. It splashed into the water dead. The other quacked an alarm and banked up and away. Hektor, who had not been caged, sprang out the opening and into the water. Almost before Max could catch his breath, Hektor laid the warm, gleaming greenhead into Max's waiting hand.

Examining the limp bird, Max said, "Damn it. Aunt Gertrud will make me pick the feathers and clean the duck. That won't be any fun, Hektor. . . . Did you have fun fetching the duck?"

"Woof," said Hektor as he shook water all over Max. Then the liver-and-white-ticked dog laid down on the bearskin rug as Max closed the shooting-panel.

Recalling the behavior of his father's guests after someone had shot a stag, Max triumphantly called, "Waidmannsheil!" Then for good luck he found a traditional oak-twig which he attached to Hektor's collar with leftover bailing wire. Throwing his arms around the startled dog, he said, "You are wonderful, wonderful, Hektor."

Max figured they had probably heard his shot at the lodge for the "crown-jewel" lay only a little over a kilometer from the house. They would be worrying, so he'd better get back and take his medicine.

As Max closed the door to the blind, he caught the sight of a white bird alighting on a birch tree. Focusing his eyes, he was surprised to see Snow White. Clucking to the bird as his father did, he suddenly saw the falcon streaking down from the sky. Dropping the drake, which he carried by the neck in his left hand, he brought the shotgun to his shoulder just as the falcon hit Snow White. But somehow Snow White managed to break free and fly toward the barn. As the falcon swooped to administer a coup de grace, Max shot, and the raptor fluttered dead to the water.

Max called, "Leave it, Hektor," and the dog stopped short of the water and returned to Max, who was now running toward the barn in pursuit of Snow White. The redheaded, blue-eyed boy found the pet pigeon in her separate pen. Bright red blood trickled from its back where the falcon's talons had struck. Then Max noticed that Snow White carried a message which he immediately retrieved and read. Though he didn't understand it all, he sensed that Nicoline was in deep trouble. Anxiously he ran to the cabin carrying the message.

The furor over his disobedience vanished the minute the message was read aloud by Gertrud: "*Nicoline—Danger—Gestapo—Hide In The Duck Blind—I'll Be There Shortly—Fritz.*"

Looking reproachfully at Nicoline, Gertrud said, "I knew Fritz' bringing you here would bring calamity upon us all."

The blast from the shotgun had aroused everyone at the lodge, and a fretful silence ensued as the children looked into the troubled faces of the adults, and read their concern.

Disregarding Gertrud's reproof, Nicoline coolly said, "I believe I should follow Fritz' instructions and go to the duck blind."

"Well, I'm not leaving this house," said Gertrud, "no matter what happens!"

Still holding on to the shotgun by his side, Max stepped forward and croaked, "Come on, Nicoline, I'll lead the way." Brandishing the twenty-gauge, he boasted, "I'll protect you from the Gestapo."

Noticing the gun for the first time, Gertrud shrieked, "Max, you little devil, hand me that gun—and right this minute!"

But Max was already heading for the door, beckoning Nicoline to follow.

Turning to Gertrud, Nicoline said, "Fritz will be here shortly and straighten out this matter; in the meantime, I believe I should do as he said." She quickly followed in Max's footsteps.

Gertrud slumped on the couch and began sobbing.

A wide-eyed Felicia slowly sank onto the couch next to Gertrud. Attempting to wrap an arm around her grieving aunt, Felicia softly said, "I'm staying with you, Auntie; please don't cry."

HAVING, ALSO, HEARD THE SHOT, four of Count Siegried's Gestapo agents, dressed in jackboots, light-brown knickers and black coats with swastika arm bands, now observed the movements of a woman, a boy and a dog into the woods. Quickly and silently they abandoned their staff car in the roadway from Warstein and attempted to follow the trio into the woods. But when they reached the "crown-jewel" and the end of the trail, they discovered their quarry had disappeared.

But the taller of the four, one with glasses and a crooked nose, saw the duck decoys and knowingly pointed. Nodding his head, he said, "There." With a wave of his hand, the four dispersed and approached the blind from different angles. As the tall one neared the blind, a child's voice cried, "Halt. We are duck hunting."

"Don't worry, my child. We just want to talk," said the tall one.

"I am forbidden to talk with strangers. Go to the lodge and talk with my auntie."

"We know there is a lady with you, my child. . . . Please speak up, lady."

"You must go to the lodge and speak with my auntie."

All four Gestapo agents jumped for cover as the shooting panel plopped on the bank and a shotgun discharged. Quickly the panel was again secured.

The tall one returned to the blind. He could hear the low, threatening growl of the dog. He warned, "We know you are in there, Frau Lindemann. We are from the Reichssicherheitshauptamt. You must surrender this minute, or we shall force our way in!"

At that moment, the tall one heard the drone of a low-flying airplane. Suddenly, out of the leaden sky General Fritz Kraus' Fieseler Storch monoplane roared, the black-on-white crosses on its fabric-covered fuselage and wings showing prominently as the plane circled the pond. So low and slow did the plane pass that even the swastikas on the tail fin were visible to the tall one. The pilot waggled the wings of the Storch.

The child shouted, "That is my father, General Kraus; go to the lodge; there he will talk with you."

The four Gestapo agents conferred. The tall one ordered two of his men to remain at the blind and to apprehend the woman should she come out, but not to harm the boy. Then he and an aid hurried to the airstrip to confront the general.

After General Kraus had taxied his plane to the front of its hangar, he shut off the motor and slowly and deliberately climbed out of the cockpit. When he turned to face the intruders he revealed the formal uniform of a decorated officer: gold braid, knickers with red stripes down the seams, iron cross at the neck, and a high-visor officer's cap. He removed thin buckskin gloves and unbuttoned his full-length black leather coat before confronting the two panting Gestapo men. And even the dull morning could not dim his bright red hair, deep blue eyes and tan facial skin. Smiling at the two as they stood out-of-breath before him, his perfect teeth gleaming milky white, General Kraus said, "One moment!"

Reaching inside the cockpit, General Kraus recovered an open package of cigarettes and his officer's swagger stick. Grasping the baton in his left hand, he offered the tall one, the one with the glasses and the crooked nose, his package of cigarettes.

"Nein, mein Herr General," said the Gestapo man, "You are in considerable trouble; now is not the time for amenities."

"Oh. Why so?"

"Let us not play games General. You are protecting a fugitive of the Reich."

"Then where is this fugitive I'm alleged to be protecting?"

Waving a Luger, Crooked-nose snarled, "Very amusing, General Kraus; I'm holding you in the name of the Führer until the criminal Frau Lindemann comes forth from your duck blind and is under my jurisdiction."

"I don't believe the Führer will approve of any detention of an SS general of the 'Lightning' Panzer Division," answered General Kraus, "even by a captain of the Gestapo." Angrily, his face flushing, General Kraus growled, "Your approach to a General, Captain, is one of insubordination. You know the punishment I can exact for you."

"In this case, General, I'm holding the Luger. And you are correct; I am Captain Spaulding, and I merely carry out the orders of my superior, Herr Graf Siegfried von der Schulenburg. Once I have Frau Lindemann, you are free to go and take whatever actions you choose against me."

At that moment pistol shots were heard coming from the duck blind distracting Captain Spaulding. When he turned his eyes again toward General Kraus, Captain Spaulding also faced a Luger, and a highly focused German general.

"We can both die this minute Captain, or we can live to fight the real enemies of the Reich. I have come to take Frau Lindemann to Münster, to the headquarters of SS Lieutenant General Franz Rheinhardt, Commander of the III Panzer Corps. You can tell that to Count Siegfried. If he or any of his superiors wish to trouble themselves with these 'small potatoes,' they may take it up with SS Reichsführer Himmler, himself.... So drop your pistol, Captain, or I shall shoot."

The tone of General Kraus' voice, the glint in his eyes, and the set of his face and body left no doubt in Captain Spaulding's mind that General Kraus meant every word he had spoken.

"You are an SS general; I am only a captain; perhaps you speak words of truth," said Captain Spaulding. As he shrugged his shoulders he said, "I'm sorry; I'm just following my orders." Dropping his Luger, Captain Spaulding took one step back, and extending his arm said, "Heil Hitler."

General Kraus acknowledged the salute with the nod of his head. Then looking in the direction of his duck blind said, "Let's go. You men lead. For your sakes, let's hope no misfortune has befallen a member of my family or Frau Lindemann."

The clearing at the entrance to the duck blind disclosed a spectacle. There stood two burly Gestapo agents with their hands held in the air. Covering them with a shotgun, stood Nicoline, and with nostrils flared, hair-on-end, crouched Hektor by the side of Max, a low growl rumbling deep from his throat. Two pistols lay on the leaf strewn ground at the feet of the Gestapo agents.

Instantly, General Kraus said, "You, Max! Steady! Grab Hektor and keep him under control! Nicoline, watch these men." General Kraus motioned all four Gestapo agents to enter the duck blind; whereupon, he proceeded to disarm and hog-tie each one with bailing wire. Upon completing the task, he said, "Captain Spaulding, I am sorry to inconvenience you and your men. Once I have taken care of my family and Frau Lindemann is safely on my plane, I'll return and release you."

Stepping outside to a waiting Max and Hektor, General Kraus asked, "What happened?"

Both Max and Hektor simultaneously charged Fritz Kraus, bringing tears to the general's eyes as he knelt and hugged both.

"Father," shouted Max, "your great stag, Bismarck, came charging out of the woods, and the Gestapo men were so distracted that Nicoline had time to cover them; and they were very scared of Hektor. Isn't that a miracle? . . . But I believe they wounded Bismarck."

"Quite a miracle," said Fritz, rising and resting his eyes on Nicoline, who still resolutely toted the twenty-gauge. Putting his arm around Nicoline, he said, "Let's go to the house. Our time is limited."

Wide-eyed Felicia met them at the door. "Oh, Papa," she cried, jumping into Fritz's arms.

Finally Fritz lowered Felicia to the floor and turned to his sister-in-law. They shook hands formally. Looking out the window at his waiting Storch, Fritz said, "Gertrud, I want you to take the children and return to Warstein. These next months will be dangerous times, and we must trust in God and pray for guidance and protection."

"Of course, Fritz," Gertrud replied sarcastically, and nodding her head at Nicoline asked, "And what about her?"

Disregarding the sarcasm and smiling at Nicoline, Fritz said, "Nicoline will fly with me to Münster where she will be protected. Trust me."

"That is wonderful, Papa," cried Felicia, embracing Nicoline.

"Come," said Fritz, " there is no time to lose. May God grant us the way to be together again in peace. . . . Max, do what Aunt Gertrud tells you; and do be a good boy."

"Yes, Father," answered a crestfallen Max. Then all of a sudden he perked up. "Father, Father—the falcon struck Snow White while I was in the blind, but I killed the falcon; then Snow White flew to the barn; that is how we knew you were coming. The falcon hurt her, but I do believe she will be all right."

"Very good. Take Snow White with you back to Warstein and care for her. . . . We all must leave quickly," said Fritz.

After the children had put Snow White into a carrying cage and jumped into the rear seat of the Mercedes with their pet, Gertrud drove off as the children waved a tearful good-bye.

Fritz gazed at the stuccoed barn and told Nicoline, "Herr Lüdwig will care for this place until someone returns."

MEANWHILE, BACK AT the duck blind, the Gestapo men were grumbling and cussing when General Kraus shed light upon them by opening the door to the outside. Covering them with his Luger, he shortly found wire cutters and released Captain Spaulding, who then released the others. Next he marched them to his waiting Storch, whose propeller was already turning.

"Captain Spaulding," said General Kraus, "again I express my sincere regrets at having had to treat you so rudely. When you explain everything to Count Siegfried, I'm sure he will understand. I would even be most happy to write a favorable commendation for you to the RSHA (National Central Security Office). By the way, you may recover your firearms at the duck blind. Heil Hitler!"

BEP RIEKSEN AND KAREL KONIJN, the Resistance fighters, passed through German checkpoints with no difficulty. They carried passes identifying themselves as Dutch foreign workers employed by the German war industry. Surprisingly, listed as supervisors and interpreters at various war labor camps, they could move about Germany even more freely than many German citizens. For the moment, however, the mobility of Bep and Karel was limited to two road bicycles. But they were in good shape and could do a hundred kilometers a day with only a little fatigue; and both Bep and Karel spoke nearly flawless German.

Bep had been both heartened and intrigued by the news that a German general was shielding Nicoline from the Gestapo. Bep, though, could hardly imagine such a situation—especially from an SS general! His informant had warned that Count Siegfried was sending agents to Warstein to bring Nicoline to Amsterdam, and her life would be spared only in exchange for the surrender of Bep Rieksen. Beb, of course, had determined never to be taken alive by the Germans.

HOWEVER, IT SO HAPPENED that when the two bicycle riders arrived at General Kraus' hunting lodge, General Kraus himself was just then roaring the Storch down the grass runway. Earlier, a big, black Mercedes, with two kids and a dog and a wild-looking old woman behind the steering wheel, had nearly run over them several kilometers back down the road. And only moments before, they had peddled by a grey wermacht staff car stopped in the middle of the road with its four doors wide open. Bep had considered it surprising that the big Mercedes had been able to negotiate around this roadblock.

As the Storch cleared the trees, Bep suddenly noticed two uniformed men running down the runway toward Karel and himself. Two others were running down a trail which led into the woods. "Do you have your pistol ready, Karel?" asked Bep. "It appears we've blundered into a hornet's nest."

"I'm ready, Bep."

Straddling their bicycles, both Bep and Karel readied German machine-pistols beneath their dark trench coats.

Captain Spaulding had sent the two husky Gestapo agents to get the car, while he and his aide retrieved the Lugers from the duck blind. Assuming Bep and Karel to be German farmers, it wasn't until the agents saw the resolute faces and eyes of the two men wearing black berets that they guessed at their own egregious mistake and mortal danger. But their fears were short-lived. A hail of bullets took their lives almost instantly.

Quickly Bep and Karel flung their bicycles aside and skirted the tree line, running toward the woodland trail where they'd last seen the other two Gestapo agents. Hearing the agents panting, trying to catch their breaths, Bep and Karel dove into bushes as Captain Saulding and his aide ran back up the path. As the two Gestapo men, both with Lugers in their hands, emerged from the forest trail, Karel yelled, "Drop your pistols."

The aide fired into the bushes wounding Karel as Bep shot the man dead. Captain Spaulding dropped his pistol and stood motionless with his hands raised in the air.

Crouching, Bep led the three toward some bushes near the barn. Karel poked Captain Spaulding in the ribs with his pistol and ordered him in German to follow Bep.

"Keep our man covered," said Bep in Dutch, "while I scout the house. If he makes a move, kill him."

Soon Bep motioned an "all-clear" from the back door of the hunting lodge, and Karel and his prisoner stepped quickly into the building.

Standing before the large stone fireplace with his hands held high, facing his captors, Captain Spaulding said, "I suppose you will kill me regardless."

"Not necessarily," said Bep. "Not unless your actions make us."

"You are Bep Rieksen."

"Yes."

"I suppose it won't hurt to tell you that the object of your quest was on that airplane."

"And what is my quest?"

"Frau Lindemann. . . . You must be deeply devoted."

"She is with General Kraus?"

"Yes."

"Where do they go?"

"How should I know? We were their prisoners, just as I am now your prisoner."

Bep could see he wasn't getting any more useful information from this Gestapo man. Pacing back and forth in front of the fireplace, he pondered his next move. Then he stopped and said, "I have a message for you to give to Count Siegfried. I will write it down."

The war will soon be over, Count Siegfried. Should you seize Frau Lindemann, however, if you will spare her life and protect her from torture, in your trial for "war crimes," I'll testify on your behalf. My testimony could save your life.

Bep Rieksen

"I will leave the note on the table," continued Bep, "and we will gag and tie you. Also, we will borrow your automobile. Within twenty-four hours the Gestapo will be notified of your predicament."

Captain Spaulding appeared relieved, but said nothing.

As General Kraus pointed the nose of the Storch toward Münster, Nicoline asked, "Fritz, did you see those two men on bicycles as the plane cleared the runway, just where the road from Warstein enters the clearing?"

"No. I must have been busy with the controls."

"There was something familiar about them."

"Hardly. That must have been Herr Lüdwig and his helper."

At first Fritz skimmed the tree tops with the Storch, but finally he took a brief long-glance at Nicoline who nervously viewed the passing scenery below the plane. In spite of her disheveled appearance, no makeup, dirt and dried mud on her brown cotton coat, a tear in her faded, blue headscarf, her soft dark eyes and angular neck again reminded Fritz of a beautiful swan in repose.

Finally, Nicoline asked, "Will I be treated as a prisoner by your general friend?"

"I don't think so, but it's the only way I can protect you from the Gestapo." More as a prayer, he said, "If we can just get through these next few months, I feel the war is about over."

"Who wins?" she asked.

"No one wins a modern war, but you can lose it. . . . Before spring, we will know if Germany lost it."

Above the roar of the plane's motor and vibrations of the fuselage, Nicoline inquired, "What will you do after the war, Fritz?"

"I cannot even begin to think about that now; I must stay focused for the big battle soon to be fought."

"I thought your last battle was the 'big' battle."

"Purely defensive."

"What about Max and Felicia?"

Looking into Nicoline's eyes, Fritz said, "If I live, you must come to Warstein. They love you, Nicoline—and so do I."

Gradually, Fritz had been gaining altitude, so he could give Nicoline, and not flying, more of his attention. Suddenly the Storch burst through the fog bank into dazzling sunlight. But a costly coincidence ensued.

HUNTING FOR ENEMY TARGETS, the pilots of two P47s saw the black crosses on the wings of the Storch flying at about a thousand feet below them; though the Storch wasn't really what they were looking for, it was the enemy. Therefore, they maneuvered their crafts so they could take potshots. Unbelievably to the second P47's pilot, his flight leader missed when he shot at the sitting duck. But the second P47 promptly sent the Storch flaming into a fog bank, and its pilot counted his fifth kill, making him an ace.

BACK IN THE ARNSBERGER FOREST, dressed in the uniforms of the Gestapo agents they had killed and now making their escape from the hunting lodge in the abandoned German staff car, the Resistance leader, Bep Rieksen, and his slightly wounded cohort, Karel Konijn, drove furiously out of the forest. But it was Bep who spotted the tail fin of the crashed plane sticking up from the ground, a fire smoldering in its vicinity.

Karel, who was at the wheel, braked to a squealing halt. As the two raced to the crash site, they saw the pilot had been able to glide his craft into a firebreak. Bep ran toward a figure in a rumpled skirt lying in the weeds about fifty feet from the wrecked plane even as Karel directed his attentions to a uniformed man. The impact of the crash had thrown the two from the airplane.

The woman was alive and moaning, bleeding from a gash on her forehead. Her lovely, familiar face and long slender neck revealed to Bep that he'd at last found Nicoline. A master of self-control, Bep knelt and spoke easily to Nicoline. Slowly her eyes focused and she instinctively embraced him. Encouraged by her responsiveness, he asked, "Where do you hurt, my darling?"

Without answering, Nicoline struggled to her feet. "Where is Fritz?" she stammered.

Karel had joined the two. "The SS general is dead."

Nicoline shrieked, "Oh, my God." Her furtive eyes searched for Fritz's body.

Recognizing Nicoline's anguish, Bep embraced her protectively, nuzzling her face and cooing, "My darling, my darling, if you can walk we must go to the car. We must hurry from this place." Gently, Bep nudged Nicoline toward the road, blocking her view of the smoking ruins of the Storch and the crumpled figure of General Kraus.

As the German staff car sped away with Karel at the wheel, Bep found a heavy army coat and wrapped both Nicoline and himself in it. "Oh, how awful! Whatever will become of Max and Felicia?" wept Nicoline, over and over.

FRÄULEIN GERTRUD SCHULTZ, Max and Felicia, Hektor, and the injured Snow White, did not return immediately to Warstein. Having nearly runover two strange bicyclists on their private road, slow-witted Gertrud Schultz waited until reaching the outskirts of Warstein before deciding to turn the Mercedes and go back to the hunting lodge.

Gertrud knew Fritz had left the Gestapo men bound and gagged and had ordered her not to return to the hunting lodge until the war was over. Those had been his last words before he had undoubtedly flown that woman—that Frau Lindemann—to another of his hideaways, trying to protect her from the Gestapo.

Gertrud made up her mind! She wasn't going to get the children into any more trouble by being a part of Fritz's conspiracy. She knew protecting an enemy of the state was a major crime. If Fritz had thought she would play his game, he was just plain crazy. Gertrud again remembered her poor sister, Margarete, the mother of Felicia and Max, whom Fritz had apparently forgotten. And Gertrud especially disliked the way Nicoline had buttered up to the youngsters. So . . . she would just drive back and free those Gestapo men and hope they caught the woman. If that got Fritz into trouble, he deserved it!

But Felicia and Max had other ideas. They had overheard their father's instructions to Aunt Gertrud and were well aware of Aunt Gertrud's dislike for Nicoline.

As Gertrud silently turned the Mercedes around and drove back toward the forest, Felicia, with a wrinkled brow, said, "Aunt Gertrud, I don't believe you should be doing this. Those men want to hurt Nicoline. We must give Papa time."

Wildly, Gertrud looked straight ahead and stepped on the accelerator.

Max threw a tantrum and said he would jump out of the car if she didn't stop.

Sensing trouble, Hektor emitted a deep-throated growl, even as Max unlocked the car door. Gertrud quickly pulled over to the side of the road.

"Remember those two strange men on bicycles? What were they doing on our private road? I've never seen them with Herr Lüdwig before. I believe your papa would want us to investigate them before they find the Gestapo men."

As Gertrud was speaking the grey, staff car of the Gestapo raced by them.

"Those were the men who were on the bicycles," shouted Max.

"I must learn what happened," said Gertrud again steering onto the road and stepping on the gas.

Soon they saw the tail of the Storch absurdly reaching skyward from the ground.

"Oh, Papa!! The plane's crashed," screamed Felicia.

Rushing to the crash, the children found their father looking serene in death. But they could not accept what they saw.

"Quick, Aunt Gertrud, we must take Papa to the hospital," cried Felicia.

Scanning the landscape, Gertrud grumbled, "Where is the woman?"

"Max, look for Nicoline," said Felicia, embracing and weeping tears onto the lifeless body of her papa.

"We can't carry your father. I'll go get the Gestapo men," said Gertrud.

"Hurry! Hurry!" sobbed Felicia.

After Gertrud had freed Captain Spaulding and aided him in placing the bodies of his men in the trunk of the Mercedes, they returned to the crash site only to find the children and Hektor gone. They soon found them, though, on the road crying and running toward Warstein, Hektor keeping pace.

After being squeezed into the front seat of the black automobile, Felicia turned to her Aunt Gertrud and screamed, "I hate you, and I will always hate you."

CHAPTER 13

AT HIS 1ST BATTALION headquarters, Lieutenant Colonel Burk smoked continuously and paced the floor as he waited for Second Lieutenant Joe Nicholson. A blue haze filled the dingy room that served as his private office. Lighting still another cigarette, he cracked the door to let in fresh air. He was troubled. That both he and Appleby had been singled out and openly rebuked by General Clay warned Colonel Burk that now was not the time for any show of hostility between himself and his popular Company "D" Commander. As a matter of fact, the appearance of goodwill between himself and Appleby might help the situation, and he wondered if he shouldn't do something conciliatory like even going on pass with Appleby. But he quickly rejected this idea. Their personalities were much too different.

Wiping his glasses with a khaki handkerchief, one thing was obvious: he must do nothing that would appear to be meddling in the ongoing affair between the Red Cross broad and the Captain. With respect to Appleby's future, fate would just have to have the last word there.

Such was not the case with Corporal Smith and Private Silverman. They both represented a new problem by evidently knowing something about the Witkowski matter.

Consequently, Colonel Burk had sent his executive officer Captain Krebs, and an aide, Sergeant Collins, to order both Smith and Silverman to battalion headquarters; and, to be sure, he wanted both Krebs and Collins out of the way when he spoke with Lieutenant Nicholson.

WHEN NICHOLSON DID ARRIVE, he, too, appreciated the privacy. The Company "D" 2nd Platoon leader had things on his mind only for the ears of his battalion commander. Following a cursory salute and the command to be seated, cherubic-faced Joe Nicholson quickly unburden his fears: "Appleby has begun an investigation into the loss of the dozer." Wrinkling his brow, Joe said, "Luckily, after Morbid's shot, the dozer was also hit repeatedly by enemy fire placing the blame squarely on Jerry. But I'm not sure of Smith; he was the loader. . . . It was an accident on Morbid's part. . . . Witkowski stupidly placed his tank in our line of fire. . . ."

BY THE TIME Corporal John C. Smith entered Colonel Burk's office, Lieutenant Nicholson had departed. Smith was apprehensive. One of his best friends, Dale Jenks, had been killed in the bulldozer. John had thought of Hamlet's wail: "There's something rotten in Denmark."

Colonel Burk was warm, nearly radiant in his greeting. He rose from behind a table and pulled up a chair for Corporal Smith, offering him a cigarette.

"Your platoon leader Lieutenant Nicholson has recommended you for the Bronze Star," began Colonel Burk, looking directly at Corporal Smith.

"Go along to get along" next flashed into John's head. "Thank you, sir," said John.

Looking like a schoolmaster pleased with the performance of a star pupil, Colonel Burk said unctuously, "As a reward for your actions during 'The Battle of Puffendorf,' I'm offering you a chance to return to Fort Knox where you can share your battle knowledge with the new recruits."

Svelte, pimply-faced Smith knew this was bullshit. His battle experience was nil. Yet a transfer from combat to stateside was about the best news John could ever have heard. He'd take it.

"Yes, sir."

"In that case, you are to pack and leave at 1300 hours for Liege from where you'll be flown to London for a flight back to the states. Your orders have already been confirmed," said Colonel Burk.

AFTER RETURNING TO HIS BIVOUAC John hurried to pack his duffel bag. He had learned that VD Johnson had survived, and he hoped that they might meet again someday to discuss everything about "The Battle of Puffendorf." He wished he now had VD to talk with, but considering the circumstances, it was best to let nature take its course.

WHEN PRIVATE SILVERMAN stepped before the Colonel, saluting and reporting as ordered, Burk's stern countenance was scanning a personnel file. Haughty eyes looked up over wire-rimmed glasses at the blanch-faced soldier.

A gravely voice began, "You were once the loader on Sergeant Witkowski's tank. . . . Is that right?"

"That was before I was wounded, sir," said the little, hooked-nose private.

"Well I'm making you the loader on Lieutenant Nicholson's tank."

"I'm Captain Appleby's orderly, sir," said Peewee meekly.

A crooked smile appeared on Colonel Burk's face. "You *were*, Private Silverman!"

"Yes, sir"

"Good. But first, on General Clay's order, I'm giving you an assignment in Liege. You are to do some personal investigating for General Clay. . . . I believe you know about General Clay's mascot, that kid they call Joe."

"Yes."

General Clay wants you to locate and talk to a Sergeant Kevin Sullivan with the 75th Greyhounds, a supply outfit. Find out everything . . . everything you can about how Sullivan found this street waif, Joe, evidently begging for handouts from the GIs at Charleroi, Belgium. Sergeant Sullivan has been informed of your coming. When you get back report directly to General Clay."

"Why me, sir?"

"I'm beginning to wonder also. Do you understand an order, Private?"

"Yes, sir."

"Then go get your gear. A jeep will pick you up in about a half an hour."

CAPTAIN APPLEBY KICKED THE DOOR. As usual Colonel Burk was pulling the rug out from under him: first, whisking Corporal Smith back to the states before the question of the bulldozer's fate had been settled, then sending Peewee off to Liege after ordering him into Nicholson's tank, and last but not least insisting that he, Colonel Burk, was so grieved by Witkowski's death that he was going to push for some kind of posthumous award for the deceased sergeant.

"What do y'all make of Burk's concern about the death of Sergeant Witkowski?" asked Tom, directing his words toward his redheaded executive officer, Second Lieutenant John "Red" Jordening.

The officers were alone at Company "D" headquarters where they had been writing letters to the relatives of fallen comrades. Corporal "Wes" Willow, who was writing up the 1st Battalion After-Battle Report, had left again on one of his numerous shuttle missions to battalion headquarters.

"Crocodile tears on the part of Burk. From what I've heard our battalion commander had some kind of a grudge going against Polack," Red offered.

"What about?"

"Something to do with the 'breakout' at St. Lo. Polack was Burk's tank driver back then. That was just before you took over the company and Burk made major and battalion commander. Do you have any ideas about it?"

"Maybe, Red, but it's best to let it be for now."

"Okay, I'll change the subject. Have you seen your Red Cross gal since we came back to Heerlen?"

Red observed that his question evoked a blush observable on Appleby's ears.

"Yeah.... Y'all can change that subject, too, Red.... Tell me about the new replacements and the refitting of the company."

"Okay. The replacements are generally better physical specimens than the last bunch, and Company 'D' is now nearly again at full strength. One thing amazes me, though, when you consider how out-tanked we are—and that is, how high morale remains with the men. Yet everyone wants to know when we'll be getting the new Patton tank. You know, Tom, we've gotta have that tank's 90mm gun to be able to stand up to Jerry's Panthers and Tigers."

"Clay says the division will soon be getting a few.... I believe brass thought the war would be over and an improved tank wasn't necessary.... Judas Priest, y'all know what date it is, Red? I've completely lost track of time."

"December 17.... It won't be long until Christmas. If the weather clears, it wouldn't surprise me none but what we're in action on Christmas day heading toward the Rhine; though I did hear this morning over the BBC that Jerry has made a penetration of our lines in Luxembourg."

"That's a long way from here, Red, even if it's true. No problem of ours."

PRIVATE PEEWEE SILVERMAN and Corporal John C. Smith both shared a ride to Liege. Their driver, Private "Jimmy" Malloti, humped over the steering wheel. "Do youse guys know that Jerry made a breakout south of here?" asked Malloti of his two passengers, whose knuckles were white from gripping their seats as Malloti wove the jeep recklessly in and out of traffic.

"How do you know?" shouted Smith.

"The General is in a tizzy."

Malloti's reply hardly answered the question, thought John, but if something was going bad in the ETO, he couldn't get his ass on a plane back to the states fast enough.

Private Silverman remained troubled about his transfer to Nicholson's tank. He disliked Nicholson. Among other things, Nicholson was a vulgar man. Peewee wondered if Captain Appleby could still change the move. In addition, his assignment to play detective and find out stuff about this little kid, Joe, was mind boggling. "Why me?" he had yammered to himself again and again. Then he suddenly remembered that Malloti was General Clay's personal jeep driver.

"Do you have any idea, Malloti, why General Clay wants me to snoop about Joe?" yelled Peewee. "How does that help us win the war?"

"A word of advice, Peewee. When General Clay gives youse an order, don't ask why. Just do it, if youse knows what's good for yourse ass," replied Jimmy.

THE RETURN OF ARND HAUPTMANN to Heerlen was fraught with great danger for the fourteen-year-old Hitler Youth fanatic, wunderkind of the Nazis. He was now known to the US Army as an Otto Skorzeny spy who was to be shot and killed on sight. Why risk a return to Heerlen?

As he had been told. It all had to do with the surprise attack in the Ardennes, planned by the Führer himself. And Arnd was part of "Operation Grief," to spread confusion and chaos behind American lines. Even now English speaking paratroopers dressed as American soldiers were being dropped in the rear of US lines. Furthermore, this time Arnd had not come alone, and he had been given a specific objective.

SLEET AND SNOW were making driving treacherous this morning, thought Hap Hardesty, Master Sergeant and Chief Kitchen Steward of the 67th Armored Regiment. He idled his jeep before the home of the elderly Konijns, as he waited for General Clay's little mascot, Joe, to come bounding out. He had sent his wife, Lucy, pictures of Joe. She had written that Virgil, their twelve-year-old, was excited about the prospect of having Joe as an adopted brother after the war. Hap considered how pleased Joe would be to receive a handwritten note from Virgil, which his wife had enclosed in her letter.

As Hap looked toward the front door of the Konijn house, he didn't see two German commandos suddenly loom out of the morning mist and approach the driver's side of his jeep. From beneath an American brown field coat, the more husky of the two produced a pistol with a "silencer," which quickly ended Hap's life without a struggle, barely a moan.

The two climbed into the back of the jeep, the larger one propping up Hap's lifeless body. When Joe came running out of the house he jumped into the front seat as usual, directing his attentions toward Hap's slumped over body. With a truncheon Arnd directed a blow to Joe's head that left him unconscious.

SOMETIME LATER, a throbbing headache directed Joe's hand to a lump on his head. As his vision cleared, his mind fought for reality. There sitting on a chair, dressed in Joe's army uniform, sat the Hitler Youth bastard, Arnd. Joe was lying on a couch covered by a blanket. Immediately, he sat up and noticed he had only his underwear on.

Smiling, and holding a cigarette in his yellow stained fingers, Arnd said, "Glad to see you come around, Joe. I would hate to have killed you after we've been bunk buddies. You're such a God damn little boy, too. I had a hell of a time fitting into your uniform."

"Where is Sergeant Hardesty?" questioned Joe. Then he saw a burly man sitting at a table dressed in Sergeant Hardesty's uniform. The man nodded and winked at Joe. He was drinking coffee. Suddenly an overwhelming sense of sorrow consumed Joe and he slumped to the bed crying disconsolately.

"Don't be a crybaby," mocked Arnd. "I was told what a tough

little monkey you were. Now you're crying just like a girl. I won't hurt you any more."

Arnd's words stung Joe. He rose and looked at his underwear and then at his GI uniform on Arnd. "Can I have my clothes back?"

"No. But I'm glad to see you're apparently coming to your senses. You're my prisoner. We had to kill your sergeant friend, and we'll kill you if you fuck with us. You know this is war, Joe. If I'm found out, I'll be soon enough tortured and killed; so, you see, how dangerous it is for me to even allow you to go on living."

Arnd put out his cigarette and stood before Joe, being only a little taller than the skinny Belgian boy. Arnd's handsome face and resolute blue eyes demanded attention. "If you don't become a shithead, Joe, and try to escape, you will be freed when it's safe for us."

Arnd pointed to a pile of children's clothing lying on a chair. "Sort through those and find something to wear."

His street smarts returning, Joe found some moth-eaten clothes and put them on. Eyeing Arnd suspiciously, Joe said matter-of-factly, "You're going to impersonate Sergeant Hardesty and me, aren't you, Arnd!"

"I was told you were a smart son-of-a-bitch, Joe. But don't get any bright ideas. Remember, I could have killed you. I decided to let you live. And don't give your jailers any shit, or they'll be forced into killing you anyway."

As NEWS OF THE GERMAN breakout in the Ardennes spread, the civilian population of Heerlen panicked. The appearance of enemy aircraft over the area in unprecedented strength on December 17, 18 and 19 forced the gradual realization that the enemy had indeed launched a major attack. The men of the "Fighting" 15th Armored Division sensed that they would soon be called upon to help contain this threat.

Rumors that the Germans had parachuted English-speaking soldiers wearing American uniforms behind the lines contributed to a state of the jitters. Sentries challenged everyone who ventured from their unit with questions about American trivia.

Nor was Major General Clay's headquarters in the Secondary Technical School immune to this alarm and confusion. Sitting behind a polished oak table in a former classroom, the gaunt-faced, grey-haired general studied a Field Order transferring his division to the south.

Turning to his Operations Officer, newly promoted Lieutenant Colonel Jack Collins, who stood at his side, Clay said, "This order calls for a blackout march at night going through Aachen, Verviers, Lonveigne, Aywaille and we're to close in bivouac near Hogne, Belgium.... It looks to me about 80 miles from here.... Issue the necessary orders, Jack."

"Yes, sir, General."

As Colonel Collins left the room, Colonel Harold Quinn entered. Ignoring Collins, he spoke directly to General Clay. "Sergeant Beck Jones, whose company is again guarding this building, reports that Sergeant Hardesty delivered an order from you to his company commander ordering them to pack up and return at once to their 30th Infantry Division. His company commander is now complying with your order, but the order didn't make sense to Sergeant Jones."

"It sure as hell doesn't, Harold, because I didn't give such an order."

"Get a company of light tanks in here, pronto, Harold. Have them surround this building.... Then cancel that order; if it's in writing, get it, and find Hardesty and bring him here!"

Colonel Quinn ran into Lieutenant Vossmaar as he was leaving the school building. Voss appeared concerned. After awkwardly saluting Colonel Quinn, Voss informed the Colonel that Rieksen and Konijn had just returned from deep behind German lines. They reported observing large movements of troops and armament heading toward the Ardennes.

"I think our high command already knows about it, Voss. By the way, have you seen Sergeant Hardesty and Little Joe?"

"I saw Sergeant Hardesty when he picked up Joe this morning. It was sleeting at the time, hard to see, and I was going to my office here.... I believe there were two others in the back of the jeep."

"Thanks, Voss."

When Quinn drove up to his regimental headquarters, he was surprised to see his people packing and making ready to leave the area. He had issued no such orders. When informed that Sergeant Hardesty had delivered such an order bearing General Clay's signature, Colonel Quinn realized that something was drastically wrong involving Hardesty. Failing to find the sergeant, he hurriedly drove himself back to Division headquarters.

The place had become a beehive of activity. In response to his earlier order, light tanks, manned by their crews, stood watch before the school. Armed sentries paced the boulevards to the front and rear of the building. Machine gun nests had been setup in the square. Sergeant Beck Jones's infantry company was at full strength in their bivouac. Even Colonel Quinn had to name New York as the city the Yankee's baseball team represented before being allowed to pass, the nervous sentry apologizing and saying it was an order.

When Colonel Quinn hurried into General Clay's office, he confronted a heated Lieutenant Colonel Burk laying it on General Clay. "I told you that kid was a Nazi, General. His disappearance and finding Sergeant Hardesty's body must now prove it. Face it, Brighton, the Nazis have made your Little Joe into one of Himmler's Nazi 'Werewolves.'" He and his American-speaking spies are turning your division upside down. They have to be found and shot."

"Maybe. But maybe you're rushing to judgment about Little Joe, Dick. Did you send Private Silverman to Liege to meet with this Sergeant Sullivan?"

"Yes. That was a couple days ago. So far Silverman hasn't returned; what's more, I'm sure he won't turn up anything good about that kid."

Biting his lip and looking dispirited, General Clay turned to Colonel Quinn. "Harold, Hardesty's body has been found shot at close range through the head. Little Joe has disappeared. False orders in my name have been issued throughout the Division. Someone looking like Hardesty and Joe are apparently doing this dirty work. . . . But I have other things demanding my immediate attention. I want you to take over security and get to the bottom of this matter. . . . And, you, Dick! Get back to the your command and have it ready to roll by darkness. Your 1st Battalion will be our guiding element; have Appleby's Company 'D' lead the way."

PRIVATES JIMMY MALLOTI and Milton Peewee Silverman and Corporal John C. Smith reached Liege, Belgium, on December 17, 1944. After dropping Corporal Smith off at the airport, the two privates toured the city searching for the 75th Greyhounds, Sergeant Sullivan's supply outfit. By the time they had found that unit quartered near the city's railroad depot, two V-1 "buzz" bombs had fallen on Liege. The fact that Liege was an important transportation center had made it a worthwhile target for Hitler's terror weapon.

After the second "buzz" bomb had sent the two ducking for cover, Jimmy Malloti said, "Let's find yourse man, Peewee, and get the hell out of this bull's-eye."

However, it was not to be. Sergeant Sullivan was away. They were told "Sully" spent the nights with a young widow woman and would not return until morning. Feeling far from comfortable, the privates spent the night sleeping on cots in a warehouse, courtesy of the 75th Greyhounds. When Sullivan did show up the next day, it was obvious to Peewee that Sullivan could never pass a General Patton spit-and-polish inspection because he looked more like a character out of a Bill Mauldin cartoon, bearded, unkempt and sleepy-eyed.

"So you're the guys who wanna find out about Please-Joe," said Sergeant Sullivan. "Cute kid. Smartass, though. He said he couldn't remember who he was, the lying little turd. Said he was in a bomb explosion and got amnesia. After the 'Old Man' got on my butt for having him around, I tricked Please-Joe into believing we were pulling out. That must have been when he stowed away on your truck. Anyway, shortly after that, Please-Joe's dad shows up at our headquarters. . . . That was in Charleroi. It seems

Please-Joe's real name is George DeRouk. He has a twin brother, Charles, who he didn't get along with. The little screwball just ran away from home and hooked up with us."

Both Peewee and Jimmy nodded appreciatively, delighted to get this information about Little Joe.

"At the front we don't have much time for fraternization," said Jimmy self-righteously

Peewee thought, "God, what a hypocrite Malloti is."

Malloti asked, "Youse wouldn't know how we could get in touch with Joe's family, would youse?"

Rubbing his dirty beard, Sergeant Sullivan said, "Yeah, I believe I have their address in my musette bag. Wait a minute, I'll get it."

Shortly, Sergeant Sullivan, looking satisfied, produced a dirty sheet of paper. Scribbled on it was an address in Charleroi, Belgium. "Our outfit works at both Charleroi and Liege," said Sullivan.

"How far is that from here?" asked Peewee.

"I suppose about 45 miles west of here. But if you got any ideas of going there, forget it. While I was getting that address, I was told Jerry has made a big breakout south of here. All passes and leaves have been canceled. We're going on 'full alert.' It seems Jerry's panzers are headed this way toward the Meuse river. Roadblocks are being set up every few miles. Even the fuckin' 'limeys' are coming down from the north to help us out. . . . You're with the 15th Armored, aren't you? You'd better be getting back to your outfit."

After a pumped-up Sergeant Sullivan left them standing by their jeep, Malloti said, "Looks like things are getting hot. But let's complete our mission; we've got General Clay's own written orders. Shit, the 15th Armored will never let Jerry reach the Meuse, and I can have us in Charleroi in less than an hour."

Though Jimmy Malloti got them through roadblock after roadblock by knowing about "Joltin" Joe DiMaggio, Vice-President Truman, "the splendid splinter," Ted Williams, Bugs Bunny, and more, they didn't reach Charleroi until afternoon.

Monsieur DeRuck, Little Joe's father, was short, balding, and round faced, just like Little Joe. Madam DeRuck was plump. Joe's twin brother, Charles, looked bright enough, but there the resemblance ended. Charles was blond and light complexioned. Monsieur DeRuck more or less confirmed Sergeant Sullivan's story. The whole family expressed remorse over Joe's alienation. They wanted him home right now. Monsieur DeRuck was an electrical engineer, university trained, and well-off financially.

Malloti and Silverman both assured the family they'd do everything to hasten George's safe return home. However, the two did not make it back to Heerlen, Holland, until the afternoon of the 19th; and Private Peewee Silverman did not gain an audience with Colonel Quinn until late that same afternoon, General Clay being absent.

ARND HAD LEFT Little Joe bound and gagged, but it didn't take the slippery little elf long to free himself. Joe soon discovered he was locked in a dank basement with minimum light seeping through one high, barred window. Standing on a table he was able to look out, but found his vision blocked by shrubbery.

Next, his roving eyes spotted the letter lying on the basement floor which Lucy had written to Hap. After opening it, he found Virgil's hand written note which was addressed to himself. Virgil wrote:

Hi, Joe,
Dad has written me a lot about you. You seem like a swell kid. I hope you can come and live with us after the war and be my brother. But I hate school and I like to fish and go camping.
                                                    Your friend, Virg

Again Joe was engulfed by sorrow. Sobbing, he said, "I'll kill Arnd someday."

Dim light still filtered through the bushes and window when two masked men unlocked the door. Without speaking they wrestled Joe to the floor, again gagging, binding and blindfolding him.

One of the men put a blanket over Joe, slung him over his shoulder and carried him to a waiting car. After driving numerous circles, Joe was rolled out of the car into an alley. Shortly, school-aged children found Joe and freed him. Much to Joe's surprise, he could see the outlines of the Secondary Technical School in fading twilight.

Gathering himself, he raced toward the building. But a sentry grabbed him before he could enter the courtyard.

Breaking free from the sentry's grasp, Joe shouted, "I must see General Clay. I have important information for him; I'm Joe, his mascot." When Joe reached the steps, the sentry fired his carbine. Joe collapsed, blood trickling from his mouth.

COLONEL QUINN and Private Silverman heard the shot and went to investigate. Several guards surrounded the boy. They made room for Colonel Quinn, just as General Clay's staff car drove into the courtyard.

Harold Quinn was aghast at the sight of Little Joe's lifeless body lying on the steps of the school house. He knelt by the boy and stroked Joe's olive-skin face, loving tears running down Colonel Quinn's face.

Boldly the sentry said, "The kid said he was Joe, General Clay's mascot. Then he ran from me. Colonel Burk ordered us to shoot that kid on sight. He's a Nazi 'Werewolf.'"

His teeth grinding, General Clay stood above Little Joe's dead figure listening to Harold Quinn relate the facts about Little Joe which Privates Silverman and Malloti had found out.

Finally, shaking his head and rubbing his face with his left hand, he said, "I was a fool, fool, fool, Harold. Life can be hell.... Have Malloti and Silverman return Little Joe's body to his parents. I'll write them and go visit them sometime.... That was a great kid. I wonder what kind of a person Joe would have grown into?"

GENERAL CLAY THEN HURRIED into the building, but came out directly after making a quick "about-face." This time he didn't look at Little Joe. Instead, he directed his resolute, hazel eyes upon his regimental commander. "Radio Berlin has announced that General Kraus was killed in an airplane crash back in Germany. SS General Hans Otto Dietrich has been given command of the 'Lightning' Panzer Division. Tell Appleby, personally for me, that in all likelihood he'll soon again be fighting against his old adversary in the Ardennes. . . . Let's get your outfit rolling, Quinn!"

CHAPTER 14

Whip Johnson convalesced at various hospitals in England through December 1944, until the middle of April 1945. Frequently Whip thought about the Battle of Puffendorf and the people he'd barely met before he was wounded. Above all, the charismatic Captain Appleby stood out in his memory. He recalled that some of the old tankers had once tried to entice him into drinking and Captain Appleby had intervened. "Judas Priest, y'all leave the kid alone. If y'all want to have some fun, pick on me." In the melee which had followed, Polack and two other hefty tankers had ended up scratched and bleeding on the ground, while Captain Appleby had hovered over them looking like a vulture ready to pick their bones. Then they had all laughed as if they had just made great sport.

In the faces of Appleby's men Whip had witnessed the reflection of the magnetism and appeal the Captain generated. In basic training Whip had been taught that familiarity breeds contempt, yet Whip had never seen another officer goof around with his men so much as Appleby had done.

Whip also wondered about Dale Jenks and Sergeant Witkowski. Would he ever see them again? They had occupied the two adjacent seats in the turret, but as he was escaping from the burning dozer, he had not seen either of them.

What about the driver, Nate Talbot and the new bow gunner, the one who had replaced Hank Henry at the last-possible moment before the attack had begun? Or was he, Whip Johnson, the only survivor of the bulldozer tank?

THE BATTLE OF PUFFENDORF

He longed for knowledge of what had happened, sensing that the sequence of events would be locked in his mind for as long as he lived. Searing images: The battle had waned and hunger pangs had gnawed at his stomach. He had just reached for "K" rations with its crackers and cheese when he had blacked out! Next, he had had the awful realization of stabbing pain in his right side and had seen yellow flames shooting like a blowtorch from out of the engine compartment and through the turret. He had recalled frantically grasping the hatch, his left hand enveloped by flames, as he had lunged out of the turret, and then had slipped and fallen to the ground.

Aware of a nearby machine-gun nest and a Tank Destroyer; he had shouted up at the commander of the TD for the medics; the mute commander had merely pointed at a red cross hanging on a house toward which he had run. After stumbling down into a cellar, corpsmen had met him with needles of morphine and had laid him on a stretcher. Graphic memories! Would he ever learn what really had happened?

By the middle of April, his burns having healed and the great swathe of bandages around his head and hand having long since been removed, Whip was sent to Birmingham, England. On the morning of April 13, 1944, a usually foulmouthed sergeant softly awakened the men creating unusual silence and a mood of gloom. "I have bad news for you, Americans," the sergeant sadly said. "Roosevelt is dead." The four-term President of the United States of America, Franklin Delano Roosevelt, had been the only president most of these GIs could remember. Also on that same day, Corporal Whip Johnson was reassigned to the 75th Greyhounds, a quartermaster outfit, at Charleroi, Belgium.

THE DAY BEFORE CHRISTMAS, 1944, found the Red Cross girls, Susan Lavet Montgomery and Sally Brown lost in their private thoughts as their driver T/5 Josh Higgins drove their rig toward Charleroi, Belgium, the location of their new assignment.

In the wake of the pullout of the 15th Armored Division from

Heerlen, Holland, the girls had been ordered to Charleroi, presumably for safety reasons. But that place hardly looked like a safe haven to Susan. Rumor had it that General Dietrich's rampaging panzers were already at Dinant scarcely 40 miles away and bearing down in the direction of Charleroi. So instead of feeling safe and secure this Christmas, eating turkey and cranberries with some rear-line outfit, the girls felt confused and fearful—confused by being caught in the massive redeployment of Allied forces attempting to stem and halt the blitzing Germans, and fearful because of the initial success of Hitler's surprise attack. No one in Heerlen had expected or had even thought it remotely possible that the weakened Wehrmacht could mount such a powerful offensive at this time. It had apparently caught the American High Command off-guard as well.

The best news of the day was the first appearance in weeks of blue sky and the warm sun. Hence, the Allied air forces were swarming to the rescue to be met head-on by a revived Luftwaffe. The "Battle of the Bulge" raged furiously both on the land and in the sky above.

Susan's main worry, though, was not for herself, but for Captain Appleby. She knew beyond a shadow of a doubt that at this very moment he must be in the thick of the fighting. She prayed and prayed for his survival and continuing good health. Yet even as she prayed for her captain, another curious thought intruded. Just before he had left Heerlen, Colonel Burk had approached her with an urgent request. He had asked if she would use her influence on his behalf. He sought a temporary pass to the states to visit his ailing father. Yet his coming to her hardly made sense. Surely Colonel Burk had higher contacts in the Red Cross than herself; on the other hand, maybe he believed her brother Donald at supreme headquarters could arrange it.

Then again, Colonel Burk may have had some other motive. Susan was well aware of Burk's intense interest in her. She was flattered. He was young, came from a good family, and without his glasses was attractive. She had never encouraged him—but had never rebuffed him either. She thought Colonel Burk an interesting person, and had said to him that she would see what she could do to help get him his "leave."

Sally's thoughts were also on men. Surprising to herself, one man more and more piqued her fancy—Jimmy Malloti. Ever since their night together at the hotel, Sally had acquired a whole new perspective regarding the Sicilian. Unlike others who viewed him as tough and threatening, she had found Jimmy kind and considerate, and the man really knew about making love.

For his part Josh mostly kept his mind on the road as he weaved the clubmobile in and out of the slow moving army vehicles; at other times, when the clubmobile was wedged and trapped within the convoys, he drove at an aggravating snail's pace, permitting his mind, though, to drift to his fantasy of one day owning his own "Josh's Automotive Repair and Body Shop"; he would probably build it just off a US Highway someplace in Louisiana. Thus daydreaming, he was critically supervising the placement of a business sign over his "hoped-for" shop when Sally suddenly screamed, "Stop! It's Jimmy and Peewee!"

Pulling over to the side of the road and braking to a halt, Josh saw the road ahead swarming with American soldiers brandishing weapons; among them, he spotted Malloti and Silverman.

Dressed in army fatigues and field jackets, gloves, scarfs and woolen helmet liners on their heads, the two girls piled out of their rig and ran toward Malloti and Silverman, who at once recognized them.

Jimmy Malloti grabbed Sally, "What in hell are youse doing here?"

"We're being transferred to Charleroi. Why aren't you with General Clay?"

"We were ordered to return Little Joe's body to his parents in Charleroi. We got held up in traffic and roadblocks, and we're looking for the outfit now."

Susan had overheard the exchange between Malloti and Sally, but her eyes settled on Peewee who grimly stared at a heavy-set soldier slumped over the steering wheel of a wrecked jeep. The soldier was obviously dead.

Noticing Susan for the first time, and seeing that she was looking at Peewee, Jimmy said, "Christ, youse should have seen Silverman go into action like he was Hopalong Cassidy. Peewee's the one who first seen the Nazi's pretending to be Hap and Little Joe. Shit, they were blocking the road in their jeep, just as big as youse please, directing all military traffic up a side road that led to a dead-end."

Cradling a carbine under his arm, a peaked Milton Silverman turned to Susan. "I never really thought I could do it, Susan, but I killed a Nazi." Peewee nodded at the burly soldier dressed in Hap Hardesty's uniform, just as the dead man was being drug from the jeep and laid in the mud and snow along the side of the road, a corpsman placing an identification tag on the bloodstained, khaki overcoat of the corpse. Coagulated blood streaked the dead man's face. "I don't like killing, but I finally feel good, not only for Hap and Little Joe, but for my people," said Peewee in a whisper.

"Christ, youse should have seen him," repeated Jimmy. "Before I could even slow the jeep, Peewee was out and runnin' at 'em. Carbine leveled at 'em. When the bastards tried to get away, Peewee didn't hesitate."

Looking around and seeing only the one body, Susan asked, "Where's the boy?"

"'That werewolf kid ran into the woods, but I think I hit him, too. They're tracking him now," said Peewee.

Reaching into his shirt pocket for a slip of paper, Jimmy again took hold of Sally. "This is the street address of Little Joe's parents in Charleroi. We didn't have much time with 'em. If youse can, youse girls go tell the parents what a great little kid Joe was. They're nice folks. They'll appreciate it." Thrusting the paper into Sally's hand, he gave her a big hug and a passionate kiss. Releasing her, he moved to go. "See youse soon, baby. Come on, Peewee. Let's go find the Division. Maybe youse kill some more Nazis bastards."

BRIGADIER GENERAL Gerd von Bartholomaus was feeling his 70 years this Christmas day of 1944. His "Hammer" Panzer Division, stripped of its Panther and Tiger tanks, now composed primarily of Volkssturm and Hitler Youth, no longer had the teeth that had helped stop the American tanks at Puffendorf. Thus his trip to the new headquarters of Army Group "C" at Bocholt was filled with despair. This maniac Hitler had brought Germanic culture to ruin, and it appeared too late to do anything about it. Not permitted to be part of Hitler's *Autumn Mist*, General Bartholomaus again sought the counsel of Field Marshal Manfred Stein.

Famous for his intellect and incisiveness in battle, at 55 years of age Field Marshal Stein did not show his years. Nordic in appearance, his blond hair and blue eyes matched the Nazi prototype for one of the Aryan race. His rise in the Wermacht had been fast until the SS found out that a taint of Jewish blood flowed in his veins; whereupon, his influence diminished, but by then he was the youngest Field Marshal in the service. Not made aware of Hitler's "Great Blow" in the west until the last minute, his orders were to: "Hold the line in the north with what divisions remain of your Army Group 'C.'"

For Gerd Bartholomaus, the Christmas of 1944 was just like any other day to him. A bachelor without family, military service was his life and love. On the other hand, Manfred Stein regarded this Christmas as being especially tragic. A devout Catholic, he had lost his one son on the Russian front, and he had recently moved his wife and his son's wife and small children to a rural town in central Germany.

Being admitted to his superior's office, Gerd saluted and inquired, "What's the news from the Ardennes?"

The two officers were alone, and Manfred uncharacteristically did not bother returning the salute of his fellow Prussian. "As you may already know, Gerd," said Manfred in mockery, "our dear little friend, SS Lieutenant General Franz Rheinhardt, with whom our beloved Führer entrusted the 20th Panzer Army, had to bypass Bastogne; and your scarface, peg-leg genius, General Dietrich, has made it to Dinant, maybe even over the Meuse river by now. But our other forces have ground to a halt. The sands of time are quickly running out on our delicate timetable, it would so appear."

Adjusting his monocle as he scanned the war map on Field Marshal Stein's desk, Gerd asked, "You have no hope?"

"SOMEONE MUST SOON CAPTURE one of the American petrol depots at Liege, Namur, or Charleroi; the panzers are thirsty; and it now looks as if only the scarface general has a chance of succeeding."

"What if our offensive falters, Manfred?" asked Gerd.

Shaking his head and pursing his lips, General Stein replied, "Our Führer, in choosing to vent his spleen on the Allies, is inviting the Mongols to tear down our eastern gate. I understand the 'Red hordes' are poised. The mighty force we have now assembled in the Ardennes should, at this very moment, be standing on guard in the east, rather than driving toward Namur. A vengeful rape of our country will surely occur if the Reds prevail."

"Have you heard from Speer?"

"It's too late. I feel it is *Guterdammerung*."

"It is Christmas, Manfred. As you say, Dietrich is still on the move," said the septuagenarian. "Perhaps if he can continue on toward Antwerp, the Allies will yet negotiate, and together we can face the Red menace." . . . Taking a long look at his somber friend, Gerd continued, "I have never seen you speak with such darkness, Manfred."

"You're a bachelor, Gerd. I have family."

Surprised at playing the optimist, Gerd said, "Let's forget our disappointments and the stupid SS. We have our duty."

"Ja wohl," said Manfred, at last returning the salute of his old friend.

AT 20TH ARMY HEADQUARTERS in Bitburg, Germany, it was indeed sweat time. SS Lieutenant General Franz Rheinhardt screamed at an aide, "Inform General Dietrich that all depends on him. Tell him he is the only commander who can now wrest victory from defeat."

It was in the late hours of Christmas day, and the falsetto voice of the little five-foot-three general left no doubt as to the urgency of the situation. As he studied his war maps through pince-nez eye glasses, an aide entered with a dispatch from OB West. Field Marshal Beck, who commanded all German forces in the west, indicated that Hitler had agreed to a pullback if General Dietrich wasn't successful in reaching the petrol depots at Namur.

But General Rheinhardt had not yet abandoned hope. He remembered the heady victories on the 16th and 17th. Everything had gone as planned, and the Americans were caught napping. Now on Christmas day the offensive was sputtering, mainly for lack of fuel. Unfortunately, the forecast calling for clear skies would open the heavens to Allied air armadas, probably forcing the panzers to seek the woods. Where was the Luftwaffe? was the question on every German soldier's mind.

At that moment an aide rushed into the room. "The spy known as the 'Weasel' has sent a message that the American 15th Armored Division is in the vicinity of Celles, and will begin an attack to recapture it at 0930 hours this morning. The American panzer commander, Captain Appleby, will be leading that attack. His radio number is Daredevil Six."

"Relay that message to General Dietrich immediately!" ordered General Rheinhardt. Then he studied his maps to digest the significance of that piece of information. It boded no good for Dietrich to have such a veteran armored division ready to challenge his advance on Namur.

BRIGADIER GENERAL Hans Otto Dietrich did not show alarm when Captain Alfons Rigor, his adjutant, informed him of the impending danger. But he did form a smile at the mention of Captain Appleby's name.

"Ah, my old adversary, the great Captain Appleby. What a splendid gentleman he is. However, on his day, my trusted Alfons, 'Daredevil Six' will be your problem."

"You know, Hans, for a long time I've wondered about your perfection. You apparently have no vices, or so it would seem. But at long last, I believe I've discovered your Achilles' heel."

"Oh, what is it?"

"You're a sentimentalist."

Laughing heartily and patting Captain Rigor on the back, General Dietrich said, "You may be right, Alfons. At least I hope there is method in my sentimentality. Look at the map. . . . How far is Dinant from Namur?"

"Probably between 15 or 20 kilometers, depending on where we find the petrol depots."

"Look at Celles."

"Ja."

"Alfons! You must not allow Captain Appleby to sever our supply line by recapturing Celles. On this side of the Meuse," said General Dietrich pointing at the map, "I'll blast up the highway toward Namur with my old kampfgrüppe leading the way while you check the 15th Armored with our 'Lightning' Division. . . . The General of the Luftwaffe, himself, has promised air cover all the way to Namur. His famous aces will fly this day; he has assured me of that. And after we're in Namur, with our reinforcements, like army ants, we'll engulf and then eat alive the American's 15th Armored Division. . . . Does that sound like sentimentality, Alfons?"

"No. It sounds unbelievable, given the reliability of the Luftwaffe these days."

"Tut, tut, Alfons. You can do it, and so can I."

"A question."

"Ja."

"May I use your blue Tiger into tricking Captain Appleby?"

"That's not very sporting, Alfons. But because you say I'm too sentimental, my answer is yes. . . . Don't let me down, Alfons."

ON THE 22ND OF DECEMBER, 1944, under the cover of darkness, the 15th Armored Division moved from the Heerlen, Holland, area to the vicinity of Ciney, Belgium. On the 23rd and 24th the various units of the Division deployed for battle. High Command ordered General Clay to engage General Dietrich's "Lightning" Panzer Division in the vicinity of Dinant in order to halt

Dietrich's advance toward Namur. Down the chain of command more detailed orders were issued.

Combat Command "B," commanded by Lieutenant Colonel Burk, was given the town of Celles to recapture, thus cutting Dietrich's supply line. Burk, in turn, ordered Captain Appleby to spearhead that attack with his Company "D."

BEFORE DAWN, while waiting with his platoon of tanks at the assembly area, Second Lieutenant "Red" Jordening discovered he'd left his sidearm, a .45 revolver, lying on a table at the company command post. When Colonel Burk happened to drive his jeep beside Red's tank, Red informed the colonel of his forgetfulness.

Without hesitating Colonel Burk said, "I'll continue to check our radio-net from your tank. Take my jeep and get your gun. But make it fast."

CORPORAL WES WILLOW was finally alone at the Company "D" command post, which was located in a chateau. Hurriedly he worked. After having hooked up his radio to an outside antenna, he'd sent his message to General Rheinhardt's 20th Army Headquarters at Bitburg, Germany.

Now the time had come for the "Weasel" to make good his escape while darkness remained and before the battle for Celles began. Quickly he stuffed his German uniform into a backpack; once in the woods, he'd change clothes and discard his American uniform. He'd already made arrangements for a German patrol to pick him up.

And he was glad that the days of the "Weasel" were coming to an end. He would never have left Germany and returned to the states if the Gestapo had not wanted it that way. His education in the German schools and the Hitler Youth had taught him the truth about Jews and Democracy; had given him a cause to fight for, a great man to admire and follow. But his biggest laugh was about how some in the outfit thought he had killed those German prisoners in Normandy; in reality, he had marched them into the woods and freed them, even as he'd emptied his firearm into the air.

Suddenly, just as he was about to leave the CP, someone tugged at the bolted door. He waited.

"God damn it, Wes. I know you're in there. Open the door!" ordered Red Jordening.

Wes cracked the door and stood silent.

Red shoved him aside and looked around the room suspiciously. He noticed the radio and the outside antenna had been tinkered with. He saw the backpack lying on the floor. He also saw his .45 resting on the table where he'd left it.

"Are you planning on joining the infantry, Wes?" joked Red as he reached into the open backpack. When he pulled out the grey German uniform he was dumbstruck. He spun on his feet to face Wes.

"Don't move, Red, or you're dead," said Wes, pointing the loaded .45 at his executive officer.

"What goes, Wes?" asked Red, his eyes narrowing and his voice soft.

"Belly down on the floor, Red. Hands behind your back. Any wrong move and I'll have to kill you."

With strips of telephone wire, Wes quickly bound Lieutenant Jordening's feet and hands. But just as Wes was attempting to gag the lieutenant, Private Milton "Peewee" Silverman returned. Holding his carbine in one hand, Peewee opened the door with his other hand and entered the room, having at last located his company command post.

Spitting the gag from his mouth, Red shouted, "Watch out, Peewee! Wes is a German spy! Shoot the son of a bitch!"

But Wes fired the first shot, and Peewee dropped to the floor.

Eyes on fire, like brimstone, Wes stood over Red. "I should kill you, too, Red. But you're Aryan, even if you don't realize it. Use your brains, Red. After Hitler conquers the world, and all the Jews and other misfits have been killed or castrated, we could use you to help build a greater, Nazi America. There would be law and order! There would be no crime, and everyone would have a job! I would even recommend you to Hitler myself!" After a reflective pause, he purred, "You and Burk are the only ones I've ever had any respect for in this God damn outfit."

Those were the Weasel's last words.

A bullet from Peewee's carbine entered Wes's brain.

BACK IN HEERLEN, Bep Rieksen was at Nicoline's house on Christmas morning 1944. He walked to the music room and soon was playing Paderewski's Piano Concerto on his baby grand piano.

From the bedroom, Nicoline called, "When you are finished with Paderewski can you play Chopin's Polonaise?" And suddenly the deep, dark depression again struck Nicoline, who began crying.

With a concerned look upon his face, Bep entered her bedroom where he found Nicoline sobbing and lying face down upon her bed. He lay beside her and stroked her head.

Bep knew what troubled Nicoline. She could not get General Kraus and his children from her mind. In the brief period the general had shielded Nicoline from the Gestapo by taking her to his secluded hunting lodge, Bep was convinced, something had happened between the two. Nicoline, however, denied any close intimacy whatsoever, and on this score Bep believed her implicitly. But she did admit of an attraction to the general and of a vow, which she had made to General Kraus, to protect his two young children, Felicia and Max. She spoke often of an urgent need to find and keep the children out of harm's way. "It's as if they were my own," she had pleaded, again and again. Bep had always replied, "Have patience, my love. We shall soon find them and keep your promise."

CHAPTER 15

CAPTAIN ALFONS RIGOR was a loyal and resolute paladin. The link between himself and General Dietrich had been forged in the wadis of North Africa and tested on the steppes of Russia. He would do anything for General Dietrich.

Of ordinary build and stature, Captain Rigor stroked his dark mustache, finalizing his plans for the ambush of Captain Appleby's Company "D." Planning for success, Captain Rigor had no trouble deciding who to place in the commander's seat of the dusk-colored Royal Tiger tank, the planned decoy in his snare. That vulnerable position would go to Captain Snodgrass, the Judas who had betrayed General Kraus to the Gestapo. Like General Dietrich, Captain Rigor detested cowardly informers, and he doubted not that the glory days of this Royal Tiger were numbered. Of course, he was also counting on Captain Appleby's removal to lead to the destruction of Company "D," thus ending the American threat to Celles and the cutting of General Dietrich's supply line.

FOR HIS PART and in direct opposition, General Brighton D. Clay had other ideas. His 15th Armored Division at last stood poised to halt the advance and wrest the initiative from General Dietrich. Holding Combat Command "A" in temporary reserve, General Clay ordered Combat Command "B" under Colonel Harold Quinn to recapture Celles. General Clay's plan called for the execution of a pincer's movement: Task Force "1," under Lieutenant

CHRISTMAS DAY BATTLE IN THE ARDENNES, 1944

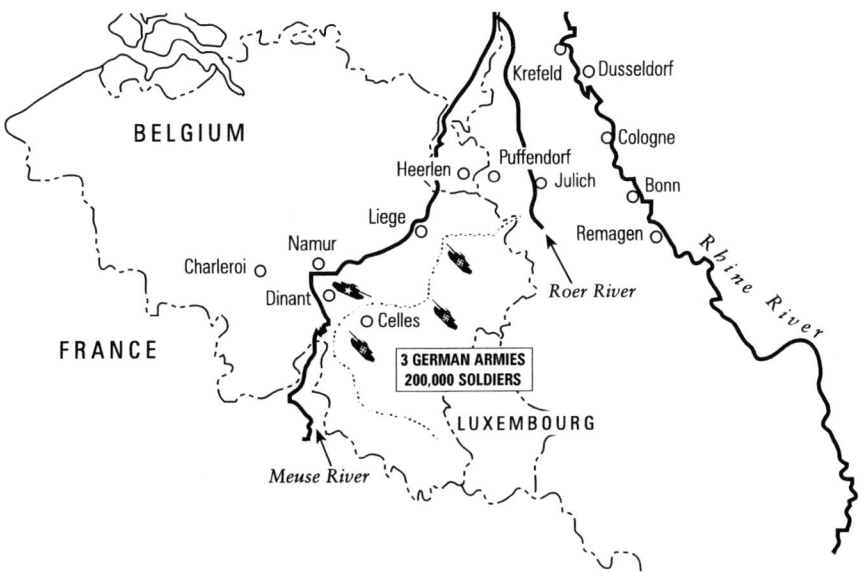

Colonel Burk, would strike from the northwest while Task Force "2," led by Captain Appleby, would attack from the northeast. Field Order 101 had designated 0930 hours of the 25th, Christmas day, as being "H" hour.

HOURS BEFORE at his Command Post and in his usual raspy-voice, Colonel Burk had given a last-minute briefing to his junior officers. He had stressed the necessity of getting on with the attack in an aggressive manner despite the opposition offered, emphasizing the fact that hesitancy and delay always resulted in higher casualties because the subsequent attack must then be made with depleted strength against an undoubtedly stronger defense, the element of surprise having been lost in the failure of the initial assault to get forward. "It is up to you company commanders and platoon leaders," he had emphasized, "to keep pushing your men forward; you'll be rewarded by faster attainment of your objectives with fewer casualties."

No one mentioned the problem that was uppermost in all minds—the difficulties entailed in negotiating the rugged ice-covered terrain, large areas of which were densely forested, broken up by innumerable ravines and draws, and added to these not inconsiderable obstacles were occasional meandering creeks, the approaches to which were often protected by yards of swampy ground offering no traction for the vehicles. In addition, the temperature hovered around zero, and the sun of the short December days was generally obscured by heavy mists or snow squalls. The only possible provisions for defeating the terrain had already been made earlier in Colonel Burk's oral orders to the units; foot reconnaissance must be utilized to the utmost and maintenance must follow the attacking echelons closely as possible.

LIEUTENANT JORDENING drove Colonel Burk's jeep back to the Assembly Area shortly before "H" hour. Dismounting from the tank an agitated Colonel Burk fumed, "What in the hell kept you, Lieutenant? . . . Was your .45 lost in a shithole?"

Waving the weapon, Red responded, "This revolver just killed Peewee Silverman, sir, but not before Peewee killed Wes Willow."

"Make sense, Lieutenant!"

"There isn't any sense to it, Colonel! . . . Wes was a German spy, and I caught him in the act of communicating with the enemy."

Quickly Red unfolded the events that had ended in the shootings.

Troubling thoughts raced through Colonel Burk's mind: Wes Willow had been his "boy." In Normandy, Wes had taken the German prisoners back into the woods and shot them following Sergeant Witkowski's refusal to do so. Then, as a clerk, Wes had been his eyes and ears within Company "D." He also had compiled the slanted 1st Battalion "After-Battle Reports." On the other hand, perhaps his death could be considered a blessing; but if there were ever an official inquiry, it could also prove devastating. Colonel Burk felt no emotion for the little Jew. War was war.

The flashes and concussions of the division's mortars and artillery ceased; dawn was breaking; already dogfights swirled and roared in the sky. It was make or break time for both the Germans and the Allies. "H" hour was seconds away.

Nodding his head up and down as if he'd made a final decision, Colonel Burk said, "We'll look into this matter when we get the time, Lieutenant. Are you ready to fight?"

"Yes, sir!"

"Good. Call 'Six' and let him and your platoon know you're back on line. I reported you missing." Then Colonel Burk turned and was soon driving his jeep toward his CP.

THE BATTLE OF CELLES would be no repeat of the Battle of Puffendorf, mainly because of the terrain. Puffendorf was good tank country where maneuverability was possible. In the Ardennes, the advantage lay with the defenders. Here the tanks would have little room in which to operate.

AT 0930 THE MEN OF "D" Company followed their Company Commander, Captain Tom Appleby, across the "line-of-departure," the first and third platoons deploying to the left of the Conjoux-Celles roadway, the second platoon advancing down the road supported by one platoon of infantry, while the other two infantry platoons proceeded to the right of the road. As "A" Company light tanks followed across the "line-of-departure," the enemy dropped a heavy concentration of artillery in the area. One of the shells scored a direct hit on Sergeant Travis' tank, killing him instantly.

The two platoons of "D" Company on the left flank soon ran into unlooked for trouble in the form of a friendly mine field. It was not very clearly marked. Valuable time was lost in making false starts through it, until at last Captain Appleby found a path, the rest of the tanks following in his tracks.

As the lead tanks approached Celles, they were joined by infantrymen from the right of the road who had found the going too rough in the woods. One platoon of them was still pinned down by heavy enemy fire. Lieutenant Jordening spotted two brick houses to his front, several hundred yards apart. As he approached the first one, his tank was struck by a bazooka shell, but the missile expended itself in the sandbags on the tank. Red then pulled off the road and stopped in a ditch. Machine guns to the front and flank opened fire. To his right, Red could see the enemy's tracers ripping the bedrolls on Sergeant Nathan Talbot's bulldozer tank; in a few minutes they were burning. Red warned Nate by radio. Only recently promoted to sergeant and given a tank to command, Talbot backed off 100 yards to be out of effective range of the enemy small-arms fire, then dismounted to kick the flaming bedrolls off.

All tanks opened fire on the two houses, and enemy fire ceased. Once more Company "D" tanks approached the rubble of the two houses and again the enemy panzerfaust became active, including enemy artillery that drove the infantry to cover.

When Captain Appleby informed Colonel Burk that the attack was being held up by bazooka men and it was necessary for the doughs to clean them out before the tanks could move on, Burk yelled into his mike: "'Six,' this is a direct order. Don't let a few bazooka men hold up your attack! I'm ordering you to get out front yourself! Get your men moving again!"

It was at that moment that Red saw what appeared to be a "blueish" Tiger tank lurking in the mist beyond the houses. "Oh, my God, Dietrich himself!"

Just then the radio sounded the voice of the second platoon leader, Lieutenant Joe Nicholson, who said, "I think the fuckin' houses have been cleared."

Suddenly Red saw Captain Appleby's command tank gunning by him. From the commander's hatch, Tom briefly turned toward Red, smiling and flashing the "V" sign.

Lieutenant Jordening warned, "'Six' there's a blue Tiger just beyond those houses! I think it's still alive!"

Captain Appleby's tank passed the first house from which Red Jordening had taken bazooka fire.

Lieutenant Pierce, forward observer for the Field Artillery, was following directly behind Appleby. As Pierce scanned the terrain in front of him for possible artillery targets, he was momentarily blinded by a sheet of flame leaping skyward from Appleby's tank; instantly, with a deafening roar, the turret blowed off.

Lieutenant Pierce then directed the fire of his tank on the house which shielded the enemy bazooka marksman; as he moved forward, he soon confirmed that all five occupants of the doomed tank were dead.

But then a remarkable, unpredictable human reaction unfolded: Following "Red" Jordening's lead, all thirteen of the remaining medium tanks of Company "D" fanned out as best they could along the hemmed in roadway, forming a wedge of steel, and "attacked"—all guns blazing!—in the manner of an old fashioned cavalry charge. Then the light tanks of Company "A" set out in pursuit of the mediums of "D" Company.

Luckily the enraged Americans caught Captain Alfons Rigor's Panthers and Tigers not yet deployed. Quickly black-crossed and white-starred tanks were milling about one another at point-blank range, and, abruptly, the advantage shifted to the speedier American tanks.

Red Jordening was the first to stick a Kraut. From twenty feet, Red's Sherman placed a shot into the innards of the dusk-blue Royal Tiger, exploding it into flames. Then Red's tommy-gun killed its escaping tank commander, Red's only regret being that the agile German officer was obviously not the peg-legged general.

Like king birds in the pursuit of crows the American tanks cut and wheeled until they could put a pot shot into the rear end of a German behemoth's light skinned engine compartment. Soon the day and the victory belonged to the Americans—though not without significant losses to themselves. Nonetheless, it was Second Lieutenant "Red" Jordening's impulsively led charge which resulted in the destruction of the "Lightning" Panzer Division's cutting edge.

With most of the Tigers and Panthers either burning or in full retreat, Red heard Colonel Burk's voice on his radio inquiring, "'Six,' what's your status?"

Lieutenant Jordening returned, "'Six' won't be with us any more." And there was a world of tribute in the unsteadiness of his voice.

As GENERAL CLAY'S COMBAT "A" tangled with Dietrich's kampfgruppe on the road to Namur, American P-38s, P-47s and British Typhoons could take most of the credit for annihilating Dietrich's force. Unfortunately for General Dietrich, the Luftwaffe general failed to deliver on his pledge of an air umbrella, and any hope the Germans may have had for achieving peace in the west died on Christmas day, 1944. Hitler had shot his wad. Henceforth, Germany must fight defensively.

FROM CHRISTMAS until the middle of January, 1945, General Clay's 15th Armored Division fought off and on in the "Battle of the Bulge" until that "bulge" had been significantly reduced. On the 17th of January the Division went into Corps reserve for a period of maintenance, rehabilitation and training. All companies were very much understrength, and it was hoped that replacements would be forthcoming before further offensive action was undertaken. The Division moved to an area in the vicinity of Aywaille, Belgium, where passes and other recreational activities were resumed. The men had a lot of sorting out to do.

Though deaths and mutilations are the contents of war, losses of comrades always hit the individual soldier hard. But the veterans callous themselves to this reality. When repose and reality finally allows it, they say to themselves, "I'm glad it wasn't me." Then they go on.

OF COURSE, the loss of Captain Appleby was deeply felt; his persona had come to represent the vitality of the Division. One of the first impressions a new replacement had, after joining the 15th

Armored Division, was its high morale. Even the privates and the noncoms of the outfit soon regaled newcomers with the exploits of Captain Appleby and spoke of his invincibility. Before his death, the veterans had always impressed upon the recruits how lucky they were to be in an outfit with such an exceptional, frontline leader. From the beachhead at Normandy up until the "Bulge," these stories, often whispered in confidence, had contributed to the "Fighting" 15th Armored Division's remarkable esprit de corps. And when the recruits at last saw the legend in action, they knew they had not been fed "a bunch of bull," and their own spirits soared. But now that the storied leader was gone; killed in action. How would the Division react?

At first Appleby's death had seemed unbelievable, but soon the officers began talking about his "spirit" living on in the actions of the Division that were still to come; and every new replacement continued to hear about the great leader and of his battlefield exploits. In death Appleby became larger than life. In a willingness to obey orders and give his life for his country, he was the example of the "ideal" soldier. That the Congressional Medal of Honor was never awarded Appleby, even posthumously, chagrined most who had personally known him. Of course, even Appleby was not loved by all!

Lieutenant Colonel Richard C. Burk III was secretly glad to be rid of the living legend. Appleby had been his arch rival not only for the love of his life, but for the respect of his men. For his part, Burk felt he had committed no wrong. He was totally convinced that other commanding officers under similar circumstances would have given the same order to Appleby that he had given to the Captain. Burk rationalized that Red Jordening's successfully led charge proved his appraisal of the battle. That some men of the Division felt resentment toward him, he understood. But he was confident, given time, such feelings would disappear and be forgotten. Yet, deep down, Colonel Burk well knew, he had been a lustful predator. "That's life," he said, shrugging his shoulders, and went on.

The other matter of Colonel Burk's concern centered on the possible investigation of Corporal Wesley Willow, the German spy, and how Willow had come to have such a favored position within the ranks of his 1st Battalion. Fortunately, nothing ever came of it. Not a word. Even Colonel Burk was surprised. In a reflective moment, he considered, "Is the army involved in some kind of 'cover-up' here?" It certainly wouldn't be the first time. However, he wasn't going to rattle any dishes over it.

The "Battle of the Bulge" also proved to be a watershed for many of the men of the 15th Armored Division. General Clay promoted Second Lieutenant John "Red" Jordening to First Lieutenant and made him Company "D" Commander, replacing Appleby. Clay offered "lucky" Sergeant Nathan Talbot a battle field commission of Second Lieutenant, but Nate declined the offer. He did, however, at the urging of Red Jordening, accept a promotion to First Sergeant and was given command of the First Platoon, replacing Red. At that point, Nate asked to be relieved from duty in a bulldozer tank. He now had had three dozers knocked out from under him since Normandy, and he felt his "luck" was running out. His request was granted.

Other changes soon followed. Washington recalled Major General Brighton D. Clay for duty at the Pentagon and at last promoted Colonel Harold Quinn to Brigadier General, at the same time making him the new Commander of the "Fighting" 15th Armored Division.

Some received bronze and silver stars for heroic actions, among them Colonel Burk and Lieutenant Jordening. Both men, along with Sergeant Talbot, received their Silver Stars at the same awards ceremony.

Yet the war was far from won. The Germans had just amply demonstrated that they still had clout. Following the "breakout" at St. Lo. in July, the men of the 15th Armored thought the war might soon be over, but Puffendorf and now Celles had dispelled their optimism. Considering that all future fighting would be on the sacred soil of the Fatherland, no one doubted but that the Germans would fight furiously for every inch of their land.

Red Jordening also had his qualms about attempting to fill Captain Appleby's shoes. But he need not have feared. The men of Company "D" looked upon him as the only one who could closely give them the outstanding leadership of Captain Appleby.

Nor could Red get out of his mind little Peewee Silverman. What a courageous little guy! After having been shot in the stomach by that bastard spy, Willow, Peewee had crawled to Red's side and freed him from the bonds with which Willow had tied him. Shortly after that, Peewee had died in Red's arms, mumbling something about "atonement." "Shit," swore Red, "little Peewee had nothing to atone for. Peewee's the one who should be getting all the medals." He'd have to see what he could do about that.

As SOON AS Susan Montgomery learned that the 15th Armored Division had been pulled off the line and was now in reserve and rehabilitation at Aywaille, Belgium, she and Sally Brown had T/5 Josh Higgins on the road again with their "clubmobile." No one had yet informed her of Captain Appleby's fate. At XIX Corps Headquarters, where Susan first heard the news, she broke down.

Collapsing into Sally's arms, Susan cried, "Tom is the only man I've ever truly loved, Sally. I'm such a horrible person. What is to become of me? Without Tom, life has no meaning. Let the Germans kill me, too."

As Sally embraced and attempted to comfort her friend, she was again reminded of their opposite backgrounds. Susan was the young, rich beauty who had gone wild; she, Sally, the blond bombshell, was from poor, rough, uneducated parents. In peace the two had lived in different worlds and would never have met. It took a war to bring them together. Now she was the only one Susan had to turn to in her moment of anguish.

Pushing Susan from her, Sally said, "Come on you weeping, broad. I know it hurts, so let's go get drunk: fuck the Germans, fuck the army, fuck the Red Cross and fuck this cruel life."

Sally's close presence and cavalier language helped. Wiping her eyes with her hand Susan asked, "Can I bum a cigarette?"

"You always do. You always do," echoed Sally.

SINCE THE "BATTLE of Puffendorf," baby-faced, foulmouthed Second Lieutenant Joe Nicholson and his conspiring crewman, Private Michael "Morbid" Morris, had maintained their silence about that battle. Until the loader on Nicholson's tank, Corporal John C. Smith, had been sent back to the states, Joe had been concerned that Appleby's investigation into the destruction of Sergeant Witkowski's bulldozer tank at Puffendorf might dredge up incriminating evidence. Now with both Willow and Silverman dead, and with the revelation that Wes all along had been a German spy, Nicholson saw more trouble ahead. Probably both Red and Tom had suspected that Morris, Willow, Burk and himself had something sinister going on. And Joe Nicholson knew Red Jordening was more of a hot head and even more likely than Appleby to push for an inquiry.

Still Lieutenant Nicholson didn't worry about it much. He really didn't give a shit about hardly anything. A brilliant person in some things, he did acknowledge that his animal survivalist instincts were in place, but that a lot of other things had gone by the board—a "conscience" for example. That's why he figured he made a good soldier. Killing and torture presented no problem for him. And for the most part he blamed his sadism on heredity. He thought it amazing how people's genes get scrambled and then the environment works upon the results. With some people, modification of behavior might be possible, he thought; with others it's definitely not. His family, by their moral standards, considered him a monster. Joe Nicholson knew his family had it right; but of course, he could care less.

Then there was the question of Michael "Morbid" Morris. That misfit amused Joe. He considered Morbid a throwback, for Morris looked like some anthropologist's sketch of a prehistoric man. Yet there was an almost pitiful response from the beast. For a morsel of friendliness, Morris responded with the devotion of a dog, and Nicholson presently had Morbid eating out of his hand. The man had interesting possibilities, Joe thought, because of the idiot's obsession of one day doing "great deeds" which would turn the world around and win for him respect and fame. Joe speculated on how to use Morbid's obsession for his own perverted pleasure. In this regard, Joe bided his time as he looked around for "great deeds" for Morbid to do.

COLONEL BURK ALSO BIDED his time with respect to approaching Susan Montgomery, but he tracked her every movement. One day, two weeks after the Division had gone into R&R, he found the clubmobile when the "doughnut dollies" were doing their thing.

"Oh, Colonel Burk," exclaimed Susan, flashing her bewitching smile, "did your leave back to the states come through yet? I put in your request."

Suddenly Colonel Burk's heart raced wildly as his eyes feasted on the "Dragon Lady." He had fantasized that she would seek him out. He also fantasized about her long, cold-black hair and naked breasts—and her "cool and limpid" green eyes.

"Colonel Burk. Oh, Colonel. I asked you a question." She understood all to well the gleam in the young colonel's eyes.

BURK'S ATTITUDE WAS CORRECT and humble, albeit out of character. "Ah, yes, Miss Montgomery, it did come through, and I thank you a jillion times."

"Don't tell me you've already been to the states and back again."

"Oh, no, Miss Montgomery. You see, my father got better and I decided not to take the leave at this time."

"Colonel, I've known you for awhile now. Please call me Susan if you don't mind. I believe you have in the past."

"Oh sure. Thank you, Susan."

Susan felt both amused and flattered by Colonel Burk's nontypical fumbling and posturing, as if he were experiencing an adolescent rite of passage. As other soldiers crowded around the clubmobile, she felt compelled to break off their discussion. Staging a demure posture, she said, "I believe I must end our conversation, Colonel Burk."

"Oh, yes. I understand, Miss Montgomery, I mean Susan. . . . I was wondering if you would want to come to the 1st Battalion kitchen for lunch tonight?"

"Of course, Colonel Burk. . . . See you then." Susan continued to pour coffee and hand out doughnuts to the impatient soldiers.

WHIP JOHNSON'S RETURN to Belgium, following his convalescence in England, caused him to recall his first stay in this small country. That was during the past October at a large bivouac on a rain drenched hill. Now it was April. The fears he had then felt, as he had waited to be assigned to a combat unit, now returned as a familiar uneasiness that would be associated with "war-recall" for years to come. Back in October, hearing the big guns in the distance and seeing the vast American bomber fleets flying toward Germany had convinced him, then, that he was about to become a part of the great battle going on.

Nor had he felt any compassion for the pitiful human beings on the receiving end of those weapons of war. "Pour it on baby!" had been his enthusiastic response. His only concern had been for himself. He had figured the sooner the Allies blasted the Germans into oblivion, the better off he would be. He had rationalized his "bloodthirstiness" by thinking the enemy would do the same to him if they could. Now was the time to kill or be killed, and the latter possibility had scared the hell out of him.

Incomprehensibly, it was on that hill that fate had again brought Morbid Morris into his presence, though on a stretcher. The nut had attempted to shoot himself in his foot. Nor had Whip forgotten the pfc with the crew cut and the limp who had vouched that Morbid would be quickly shot by a firing squad. Some prediction! Private Michael Morris had ended up with the 15th Armored Division, even days before Whip had been assigned to it..

But the worries that beset Whip the first time he entered Belgium had not been completely erased. Even though the war seemed to be winding down in Europe—there was still Japan! Nor was it beyond the realm of possibility but what the "Fighting" 15th Armored Division might even spearhead the invasion of that island country; therefore, Whip Johnson blessed whoever was responsible for assigning him to the 75th Greyhounds at Charleroi.

Located in a densely populated area in the Sampre-Meuse valley, Charleroi sprawled along valleys and ridges teeming with coal veins. Here and there a mountain of black coal dominated the landscape, and cobblestone streets and electric trolley lines followed the rambling valleys. The city seemed sooty and dreary to Whip.

As a railhead Charleroi was valuable to the Allies for keeping their millions of soldiers supplied with food coming from the important seaport of Antwerp. With that in mind the Allies had established a large prisoner-of-war camp near the city for the expressed purpose of using the POWs to unload and load food trains. Units of the 75th Greyhounds supervised this railhead and food supply operation.

Assigned to another Company "D," Whip quickly discovered this outfit was a far cry from his previous Company "D." The discipline of the 75th Greyhounds was virtually nonexistent, while the work in the food depot counted for everything. Whip soon had a regular eight to five job. Fawned upon by the civilian population as their "liberator" and with little physical danger to himself, it didn't take Whip long to feel he could get to like this kind of army life.

Throughout the city the army had leased buildings for housing its troops, and Whip was assigned a cot in what had once been a corner clothing store. The cots were scattered about a large room in disorderly fashion, and the ceiling lights were never dimmed. Sleeping in a darkened room was now out of the question. Soldiers came and went at all hours. Some to and from work in the depot. Many from shacking-up. Of those assigned to the building, less than twenty percent were present at any given time unless someone had given an alert that a roll-call was coming. This usually occurred only after some GIs had gotten into trouble with the MPs. Even punishment for being AWOL was mild. A weekend pass might be forfeited. All the buildings, built of grey stone blocks and dull red bricks, appeared to share a wall.

ON HIS FIRST DAY with the 75th Greyhounds, Whip found a building with a sign in its window declaring it to be Company "D" Headquarters. Shortly, he was giving personal information about himself to a pfc clerk who looked oddly familiar. Then it dawned on him that this guy was the smart aleck who had told him Morbid Morris would be shot by a firing squad.

"Say, I've met you before."

"Then you're a lucky soldier," replied the cocky pfc, who began to study Whip closely.

The clerk was wearing a good conduct and purple heart ribbon pinned on his shirt, along with the combat-infantryman's badge. "I see you've been a dogface," said Whip.

"You're perceptive, Corporal. Where have we met?"

Whip recounted the events of last October on the rain soaked hill.

"Yeah," said the pfc, "I like to kid new recruits. It sometimes gets me into trouble though." . . . Standing and extending a hand, the crew cut soldier limped from around the table. "I'm Nick Wolfe. As I'm more or less free, I'll take you down to our 1st Battalion Headquarters at the Depot, your new place of employment."

As WHIP STOOD ON A HILL overlooking the valley and the Depot, he saw myriad rails, stemming from a main railroad line, curving onto a siding, the tracks looking like the strings on a giant harp, while on both sides of the rails stood rows upon rows of symmetrically formed pyramids. From Whip's high vantage, the pyramids looked like something a colony of ants might have made.

Observing Whip's interest, Nick said, "Those mounds are formed by cardboard boxes containing canned food and by cartons of 'C' and 'K' rations. The boxes are laid on to a wooden floor and stacked into the shape of a pyramid, then covered with a tarp."

"Who does the work?" asked Whip.

"Mostly POWs—and some Belgians. But the POWs are always spoutin' off about the Geneva Convention, saying they don't have to work if they don't want to. Actually, the work isn't hard and most of them like it. They get extra rations for doing it."

"What do the GIs do?"

"We plan and organize this operation, and supervise and police the POWs. Each POW work crew has about a dozen workers and one POW supervisor who is made responsible for getting the work done. GIs roam the Depot and see that the crews are kept busy."

"Is it dangerous?"

"No. And the GIs carry no weapons within the Depot. But there is a problem—pilfering. When a GI isn't around the POWs break open the cartons and treat themselves to food and cigarettes. It's a big waste.... Actually, we have nearly as much trouble with our Belgian employees. The poor people were deprived for so long during the occupation that they steal from us like pack rats."

About halfway down a trail which descended into the valley, the two came to a level stretch of land which seemed to have been recently bulldozed out of the side of the hill. On it stood a rectangular building of new construction which resembled a US army barracks. Whip wondered if the army used the same blue prints to make these structures. The wooden edifices looked more or less the same whether built in Kentucky, England or now Belgium.

Nick continued, "This is our 1st Battalion Headquarters. Major Slick Draisy is our commander and is responsible for running this Depot."

As the two stepped inside the building, Whip saw more familiarity. The desks, chairs, and typewriters looked the same as in the personnel offices at Fort Knox. What was not the same was the absence of WACs. In their places behind the typewriters sat men wearing the grey uniforms of the Wehrmacht. Among the clatter of the machines, Whip heard the babble of the guttural tongue.

Suddenly Whip was stunned by a familiar looking figure walking toward him in the form of a young boy fitted into a clean German uniform. The face of that fair haired German soldier was a "dead-ringer" for the Dutch boy who had helped him with his duffel bag at Heerlen, Holland.

As the boy collected some papers from off a nearby desk, Whip noticed yellow-stained fingers on his right hand.

Spontaneously Whip said, "Haven't I seen you someplace before? . . . At Heerlen, Holland?"

The blond, blue-eyed boy turned and took a long look at Whip. Slowly he gathered his papers, smiled and said politely, "Sorry. I've never been in Holland."

Wanting to say more, Whip said, "Are those cigarette stains on your fingers?"

"Bingo! They're not a birth defect."

At that moment a Warrant Officer hurried back to his vacant desk. "Arnd, Major Draisy wants you." After the young German soldier had left, the Warrant Officer said, "Soldier, the war isn't over and fraternization with the enemy is forbidden even here." After finding and scanning through Whip's file, he pointed to a chair by the door. "Be seated. Sergeant Sullivan will be here shortly to take you to your work."

Before leaving, Pfc Nick Wolfe took Whip aside. "A word of caution, Johnson. Be on strict business terms with all these POWs, especially that office boy; he has become some kind of a sacred cow around here. He was captured in the Ardennes during the 'Battle of the Bulge' and had been wounded in the arm. He is an example of the Hitler Youth and how the Nazis are now scraping the barrel for man power."

Looking toward Major Draisy's office door, Whip said, "He's more than just that, Nick. He's more than just that."

CHAPTER 16

NEAR THE END of February, 1945, after more than a month of maintenance and training, the "Fighting" 15th Armored Division prepared to resume its delayed drive toward the Rhine River. On the 26th, with many of its men humming or whistling "Lili Marlene," the catchy German tune that Belgian daughters had taught them, the Division crossed the swirling waters of the Roer River at Julich, Germany. That river, now swollen by the blasting of the dams to the south by the retreating enemy, had special meaning to the veterans. They could remember the frenzied tank battle fought at Puffendorf, scarcely six miles away, where last November the Division narrowly escaped annihilation.

By contrast to the bitter fighting to reach the Roer, the crossing went uncontested as infantry elements of XIX Corps had previously taken Julich and were now rapidly expanding their bridgehead. But some forty miles to the northeast stood the Division's next objective, the "Adolf Hitler" bridge spanning the Rhine at Krefeld-Üerdingen. Taking it would be a race to surprise the enemy before he blew it up.

BY 0430 HOURS on the 28th, the assembly area east of Julich was a scene of bustling activity: crews warming up vehicles, heating coffee over small gasoline stoves, making last-minute checks of vehicles and equipment to insure readiness for combat. The veterans joked about the old combat soldier's bogey, the law of averages, while most of the replacements, wound tight, quietly waited to see if their preparation and training would measure up to the task that lay immediately before them—"their baptism of fire!"

FORTUNATE FOR THE NEW replacements, according to intelligence reports, the enemy standing in the way no longer had the sting of those at Puffendorf and Celles. Mostly they were the Volkssturm (Civil Defense) and their weapons were the panzerfaust and 20 and 40 mm flak guns now leveled at tanks rather than pointed skyward at bombers.

As the battle unfolded the intelligence reports proved correct. Here and there fire-fights on the outskirts of towns only briefly delayed the attacking force. Though the Division was not without losses, it overran infantry, machine gun and antitank emplacements, and destroyed virtually every enemy tank that dared to venture forth from hiding. American and British fighters controlled the skies and they rocketed, bombed and machine-gunned everything with a black cross on it. Fighting all day and half the night, elements of the 15th Armored were in the outskirts of Krefeld-Üerdingen by March 2. Unfortunately, on March 4 the Germans blew up the bridge before it could be taken intact. Under the penalty of death to his commanders, Hitler had ordered all bridges on the Rhine destroyed.

Consequently, on the 5th of March the Division settled into garrison routine, this time in the vicinity of Pesch, Germany, close to the Rhine River. In the period that followed, the personnel enjoyed the longest stretch of blue sky and warm sun since landing on the continent. Taking full advantage of it, a comprehensive sports schedule was set up. Volleyball courts and softball diamonds were laid out, and officers and men participated in an intensive athletic program. Passes were resumed, although quotas were small.

Most of the interest centered around the continuing action along the Rhine, especially in the Remagen bridgehead seized by the Ninth Armored Division. Speculation over the inevitable trans-Rhine-action was rife; all agreed that the last big push was imminent. As the days passed, aerial activity increased; the softening up process was well underway.

AFTER THE RACE to the Rhine had been accomplished, the High Command praised the new Division Commander, Brigadier General Harold Quinn, for his excellent leadership; he, in turn, found plaudits for those of his command who had distinguished themselves, among them the new Company "D" Commander, First Lieutenant John Jordening and his 1st Platoon Leader, First Sergeant Nathan Talbot.

IT WAS STILL IN EARLY March with a hint of spring in the air. On such a calm, sunny day, the temperature in the upper sixties, newly promoted Corporal James Malloti was happy. He had General Quinn's jeep, and, snuggled close to him, he had his girlfriend, Sally Brown. "What a wonderful day to be alive," he thought.

Jimmy was glad he had chosen to remain with the Division rather than return to the states with his mentor, General Clay, following the general's reassignment to the Pentagon. Jimmy would gladly have accompanied the general, but it would have cut short his romance with the woman he had come to love. As it turned out, General Quinn was as pleased to have Jimmy as a driver and alter ego as General Clay had been before him; the loyalty to those Jimmy served was as staunch as that of a Swiss guard.

Sally no less than Jimmy appreciated the love grown between them. Jimmy had become her man, and the fact he had been willing to forego a return to the states to be with her had cemented their union.

Today, though, she hardly appreciated driving all the way back to dingy Charleroi, Belgium, where she and Susan had been assigned during the "Battle of the Bulge." But Jimmy had wanted to go there; so here they were, both on pass, speeding down the autobahn as if no war existed and they were just carefree tourists. Sally said, "What a crazy, screwed up world!"

Pensive, Sally pressed her hand on Jimmy's thigh, and asked, "What do you make of what's going on between Colonel Burk and Susan?"

"I'll tell youse this, honey. The Colonel ain't been the same since Appleby's death. Lots of the guys blame Burk. He knows it. In fact, he's no longer the skunk he used to be. Or maybe it's Susan who's changing him?" Pausing to reflect, he asked, "Does she love him?"

Moving her hand back to her lap, Sally hesitated. "I don't know. We don't talk about it much. She loved Captain Appleby dearly, but I do know she doesn't blame Colonel Burk for Tom's death. She believes that kind of thinking is stupid."

The autobahn was packed with troops and supply vehicles; checkpoints were everywhere. However, attached to the bumper of their jeep was a metallic standard of a brigadier general. Their papers were in order and a few words always opened the gate.

"Jimmy. Is it important to you that we wait until the war is over to get married?" Sally's face glowed.

Slowing the jeep, Jimmy said, "Youse do know something about my background, don't youse? . . . I would first like youse to meet my family."

"In New York City?"

"That's the big problem between youse and me, Sally. The Family!"

"Who cares? I wouldn't be marrying your 'family.' Just you and me."

Jimmy looked bleak. "Where do youse think we'd live after the war?"

"Why not Peoria? My brother could get you a good paying job there."

"I don't want ever to see youse hurt one way or another, Sally. . . . I'm different. I'm already sworn to a kind of blood-brotherhood. Youse could never understand it, Sally."

Jimmy looked down the road and stepped on the gas. Suddenly without warning he pulled over on to the shoulder and braked to a halt. Dismayed, Sally watched in awe as he jumped from the jeep and ran to a building that looked like a greenhouse. Soon he was back, out of breath, grasping a loose bouquet of flowers which he thrust into Sally's hand. "There's a piece of wire in the back seat. Tie them together, Sally"

Shaking her head and obeying, Sally asked, "Did you pay for them?"

"Youse knows better, honey; they're spoils of the enemy."

Thinking the flowers were some kind of love token, Sally rested the bouquet on her lap and awaited a further explanation. But they were miles off the autobahn and traveling on a narrow, two-lane, cobblestone road when Jimmy again pulled over and stopped.

With a sudden rush of memory Sally recognized the place. It was where Peewee had killed the German commando.

Helping Sally from the Jeep and taking the flowers from her, Jimmy said, "Youse know, I'm not a good man. Where I grew up, we didn't get along none too good with Jews. But I was a kid."

Fashioning the bouquet into a kind of garland and gently laying it by the side of the road, Jimmy removed his helmet liner and with bowed head said, "Be in peace little guy. Youse a better man than I am—Peewee!"

A while later, back in the jeep, and nearing Charleroi, Sally said, "You are different, Jimmy. And I love you for it."

IN CHARLEROI the shadows of the late afternoon crept over the hilly, narrow streets, lined on both sides by attached buildings that housed either small shops or dwelling places. The DeRuck brick and stone house abutted a corner where two such streets met. Both Jimmy and Sally had been there before.

In response to Jimmy's knock a plump lady opened the door.

"Hello. I'm the American soldier with a message from General Clay for Monsieur and Madam DeRuck."

"Je ne comprends pas Anglais. . . . Charles!"

A pleasant-looking, light-complexioned boy appeared at the door.

Jimmy repeated his introductory statement, and the boy, who looked about thirteen, translated for his mother. The boy then asked, "What do you want?"

Quickly Jimmy reminded the boy that he was one of the American soldiers who had returned the body of Little Joe, or George.

"Oh." Then with many gesticulations the boy spoke a rapid fire of words to his mother. Both began to cry.

Appreciating their feelings, Jimmy waited. Finally, the two stopped their tears and the lady spoke to the boy who, offering his hand, said, "I'm Charles, George's twin brother. My mother, Madam DeRuck, invites you inside our house."

Jimmy pointed at his companion. "Sally Brown is my friend. She is with the American Red Cross."

"Of course, she is invited also."

Once they were seated at a large dining table, Madam spoke to Charles who then translated. "My mother apologizes for not recognizing you, as do I. We were so shocked at seeing George's body, we saw nothing else; and you were here so briefly. Where is your fellow soldier?"

"Youse mean Peewee. He was killed in action."

"Oh, I am so sorry." Then Charles translated again for his mother.

Jimmy decided he had to get his message delivered and get out of here; Sally and he wanted to get a hotel room before dark. "As I told youse once before, George was the mascot of our Division, especially General Clay's. The General admired yourse little brother, and he asked me to give his regrets over Little Joe's—George's—unfortunate death and to deliver a personal letter for yourse family."

Looking toward the street, Charles asked, "Is General Clay here?"

"No. He had to return to the states. But he hopes to meet youse and yourse folks someday. Maybe in the United States. He wonders if it would be all right to write. I have his address here." Jimmy handed Charles a sealed envelope containing the general's letter to the family.

Charles passed it on to his mother and translated Jimmy's words.

Madam DeRuck smiled broadly and spoke to Charles.

"My mother says thank you, and we will reply to the general. She wishes Monsieur DeRuck were here now, but he's an engineer at the electrical plant." Looking wistful, Charles said, "George was very, very rebellious. For twins we did not get along too well. As you can see, we do not look alike at all. I am much taller than George, who appeared younger than he really was."

Suddenly, the unmistakable sound of marching men filtered into the house.

Noticing the changed expressions on his guests' faces, Charles said, "Those are German POWs marching to work in the food Depot in the valley. The Americans are building a big supply base there."

Madam again spoke to Charles who translated. "Madam would like you to stay for dinner; my father will be disappointed if he may not greet you."

Rising from the table, Jimmy said, "Sorry, we must be on our way; official duties, youse know."

ONCE BACK IN THE JEEP the two had to wait for the column of POWs to pass. Suddenly Sally saw Jimmy once again, without explanation, leap from the jeep and run at breakneck speed to catch up to a little POW with a bandage wrapped around his left arm. When one of the MPs saw the American soldier jogging along the side of a POW and smiling at him, and the POW returning the smile, he hurried to Jimmy and jabbed a carbine into his side. But Jimmy's talk must have been good enough, thought Sally, because she saw the MP left Jimmy standing by the roadside as the column of prisoners trudged on.

Returning to the jeep and getting in behind the steering wheel, looking grim, Jimmy said, "That's him all right. That's Himmler's werewolf. The blond-haired, blue-eyed Hitler Youth who probably knocked out more Sherman tanks than any one 88 in the whole German army. And Peewee was right! He shot him in the arm."

"Did you tell that to the MP?"

"Of course not," said Jimmy. "I'm no squealer, and that kid can't do us any more harm now. At one point, I would have been happy to kill him.... Anyway, I know someone who'll be glad to learn of his whereabouts."

"Who?"

"Can't, honey. Army stuff."

SERGEANT KEVIN "SULLY" SULLIVAN was capable when he was sober and on the job. He knew railroading, and some thought he was just the man to have in the control-center of the Depot.

The control-center was located in a standard army tent with a raised wooden floor, and it was situated in the center of the Depot. Among its limited furnishings were a small coal-burning stove, an overhanging 150-watt light bulb, and some rough wooden benches. Operating from this makeshift control-center, Sergeant Sullivan had the responsibility of seeing that freight trains got loaded and unloaded and dispatched all over the ETO. However, he shared his knowhow between two supply depots: one in Liege and one at Charleroi. When Whip Johnson joined the 75th Greyhounds at Charleroi early in April, 1945, Sully was back in Charleroi.

Because of his dissolute eyes and yellow, oily looking skin, Sully looked slippery and evil to Whip Johnson. Claiming to have been once a taxicab driver in New Orleans and a personal friend of the "Kingfish," Huey P. Long, Sully hardly ever reported to his quarters but shacked up with an assortment of girl friends; nevertheless, once he stepped inside the control-center, he was all business. Under Sully's direction the Depot functioned like a precision instrument. For this reason, Major "Slick" Draisy looked the other way with respect to Sully's off-work interests.

AT FIRST ASSIGNED to the control-center, Whip Johnson was fascinated at having close contact with individuals wearing the grey-green uniform of the Wehrmacht, who months earlier he might have been trying to kill. "Cripes, they look and act just like I do," he said. Because many of the POWs spoke some degree of English, Whip questioned them at length: "Where did you fight? How were you captured? Do you hate Jews? What do you think of Hitler? Do you believe in Democracy?" Whip's questioning was endless.

It should not have surprised Whip that the POWs' answers varied. But it did. He had been conditioned to believe most Germans were Nazis and all Nazis thought as Hitler thought; accordingly, Hitler's Germans were supposed to be simplistic robots.

At first, Sully was amused by Whip's childish naiveté and enthusiasm. But after a while, Sully got annoyed with it, and took Whip aside. "Listen, Johnson, we got work to do here. The war's still on, ya know. You heard Major Draisy remind us there's to be no fraternization. For us, the POWs are here just as a means to an end—to get these damn trains unloaded and reloaded and shipped out of here. Our relationship with the Krauts has got to be strictly business. The MPs will take care of any of their personal problems at the stockade. If you don't cut this shit out, asking them all your stupid questions, I'm reporting you to Major Draisy."

Sully's remonstrance had its desired effect. Whip had no trouble imagining Major Draisy ordering him back into combat duty—maybe even the infantry. So for a time Whip put the wraps on his insatiable curiosity regarding the POWs, but they continued to intrigue him just the same. Maybe that was because of his own German ancestry.

WORKING IN THE CONTROL-CENTER proved to be boring. Whip never could fathom the significance of all the little, colored pins stuck into a large, rectangular strip of wood. Reminding Whip of a cribbage board, it was really a display panel representing the Depot and the progress of the work going on there. Taking up most of one side of the tent, Sully had positioned the panel behind his desk, though someone had to constantly monitor and change the pins in it. Whip could not figure out the paper work either—bills of lading and the like; and, unfortunately, he was always screwing up the panel when he wasn't dozing off to sleep.

In disgust, Sully finally gave Whip three crews to watch over. Two POW crews and one Belgian. Each crew was composed of a dozen or so workers with one man appointed foreman. It served the American's purposes to go with rank; so the German officers and noncoms got the gravy, supervisory jobs. Fortunately, by the time Whip became their overseer, the crews knew how to use the rollers and the conveyor belts. They also knew how to stack the cardboard boxes and how to load the boxcars as well as where to tack the bills of lading. They also were pretty good at covering each stack with a tarpaulin so the wind could not blow it off.

Soon Whip had made several interesting observations about working in the Depot. First, the GIs carried no firearms, nor did there appear to be any need to do so. The prisoners were extremely docile and cooperative. Second, the POWs were cheerful, intelligent hard workers; for the most part, they did the work satisfactorily without GI supervision. Third, they appeared to harbor no grudges against Americans, whom they claimed to like. Most said they had relatives in the states and swore to have no love for Hitler or the Nazi Party. To a man, fellow GIs said, "That's all bullshit from the POWs."

However, they had developed one skill to perfection—pilfering! That included the Belgian crews as well as the POWs. The Germans loved Vienna sausages, canned peaches and any carton containing cigarettes, World War II's medium of exchange in Europe. The Belgians had a relish for fresh fruit. After the crews had finished their foraging, either consuming or concealing their contraband, the immediate area looked like the aftermath of a Kansas twister. *"Irreverent waste to the American taxpayer,"* said Major Draisy.

The devastations usually occurred during a break. Because the POWs ate at the stockade in shifts, there were usually some idle crews within the Depot, noon being a high-priority time for pilferage. Sully viewed the depredations of the POWs as small potatoes and nothing to worry about. He said, "Shit, I'd do the same thing if I were in their shoes."

Of course, Major Draisy thought otherwise. He said the pilfering had to be stopped! He was expecting inspectors from Washington—maybe even Congressmen. Though he didn't say it, he figured his military career was on the line. By this time, however, Sully had identified Whip Johnson as an inveterate, lazy goldbrick; and to get him out of his hair, Sully assigned Whip along with some other GIs to patrolling the Depot at large.

Though the need for cannon-fodder had abated, throughout the year there remained a shortage of GIs in the Depot. But, here at last, Whip Johnson found his niche in the U.S. Army. From the first he liked his new job because it brought into play his love of sport.

Whip's playing field was now the huge Depot, three-quarters of a mile wide and a mile and a half long, His goal, if he could lay his hands on them, was to catch POWs or Belgians in the act of pilfering. With self-righteous indignation, Whip would then take an offending culprit to the exit gate where MPs meted out the punishment. What that punishment might be never concerned Whip, though he was told the Belgians were fired. Nevertheless, he noticed that the infringing POWs shortly returned to their work crews, and recidivism was a constant occurrence.

What made the sport fun for Whip was the "chase." The food stacks were laid out in straight rows about three feet apart. Each stack was equally dimensioned, twelve feet by twelve, and tapered toward the top at about thirteen feet. For hide and seek purposes, the Depot represented a maze with a few wide pathways indicating the locations of different types of food parcels.

Whip would fantasize that each Kraut he caught represented a hypothetical kill. Soon by his own count he was an ace, and it didn't take him long to surpass Eddie Rickenbacker's score (27 kills). Yet on the sly when no GIs were within sight, he continued to fraternize. During the POWs' break periods, he was always friendly and plying them with questions. One man claiming to be a poet attracted Whip's attention. After the man said he had no pencil or paper on which to write his poetry, Whip made up his mind to procure these necessities for him.

At battalion headquarters he sought the articles. But as Whip was collecting them from a supply cabinet, he suddenly noticed Arnd looking over his shoulder. He turned, facing the office boy and at the same time glancing to see if Warrant Officer Stone was watching.

With a look of amused-respect, Arnd said, "The POWs have a name for you down in the Depot."

Whip never had any doubt as to the true identity of Arnd, the once deadly snake to American tankers; but probably because he didn't want to be noticed, Whip had chosen to let the matter rest. The war was nearly over, and the kid was undoubtedly one of the greatest victims of child abuse in the history of the world.

"What is it?"

"My friend tells me the POWs call you 'Der Rote Bomber'—The Red Bomber. . . . But he told me to warn you; while most of the POWs enjoy your little game, some don't. There are those with long knives, and my friend might not always be there to protect you."

At that moment Whip saw Mr. Stone hurrying toward them; so he did a quick about-face and hurried back to the Depot and the poet who waited for him there. But Arnd had given Whip food for thought.

That evening lying on his cot and staring at the high ceiling in the ever lighted room, Whip pondered the significance of Arnd's message. The POWs called him "The Red Bomber" obviously because of his red hair. But who was this friend of Arnd's who was protecting him from those with "long knives"? Was that an idle threat or did danger really lurk? Whip locked his teeth as he thought, "If that damn Warrant Officer Stone wasn't so fucking militant about enforcing the non-fraternization rule, he could try and worm it out of the office boy. But, shit, that was out of the question. Stone might also send him back into combat. A long war with Japan loomed ahead."

Picturing himself riding his tank into battle against fanatical Japanese soldiers triggered Whip's recall of the Battle of Puffendorf. He remembered his buddies from Fort Knox: Dale Jenks and John C. Smith—Dale, the great lover and, John, the great philosopher. He remembered his company commander, mighty Captain Tom Appleby and Whip's likable, redheaded platoon leader, Second Lieutenant John Jordening; he thought about Sergeant "Polack" Witkowski and Nate Talbot. But again, thinking about the events at Puffendorf was a kind of torture. Almost more than anything in this world, he longed to know what had really happened there. Again Whip ground his teeth. "Shit, his tank wasn't shooting at anything when they were hit and he had been wounded! How could it have happened? He'd give anything to know—short of returning to that outfit and having more combat!"

AFTER V-E DAY was announced for May 8, 1945, Whip continued working in the Depot, but he toned down his enthusiasm for chasing pilferers. He did his job and got his share of offenders, but he remained on the lookout for danger. Some of the fun had vanished.

The POWs posted lookouts for Whip as the athletes among the Krauts enjoyed testing Whip's speed. As in nature, the advantage lay mostly with the prey, and the predator won only when matched against the very young, the sick and the old. Three times one old man in a long grey army coat was Whip's victim. The third time, after being tackled on a railroad track, the old man lay moaning and writhing on the ground. Suddenly Whip realized he was being surrounded by POWs. Their circle tightening around him, he was on the verge of panic.

Then Whip heard someone say, "Achtung!" The circle parted to admit an unkempt, disheveled figure. Looking like a ghost, the apparition appeared to limp toward Whip. With a scarred face and eyes the brightness of a welder's torch, the face appeared well proportioned and tanned.

Looking disdainfully at the man wailing on the ground, scarface said, "This is a sick man. Select a more worthy rabbit. I'll see he doesn't open any more of your precious boxes, but leave him alone."

Like snow striking pavement on a spring day, the gathered POWs evaporated before Whip's wide eyes, and scarface and the old man disappeared behind a food stack.

During the next few days Whip attempted in vain to learn the identity of the POW with the scar. Later he would wonder if scarface's appearance hadn't really been in one of his nightmares.

But one fact that could not have been in a dream was the disappearance of the wrist watch his parents had given him for his high school graduation. Whip figured he might have lost it when he tackled that old man on the railroad tracks.

Some days later when Whip was at battalion headquarters, Arnd approached him with a mischievous smile. "I have something in my hand that Der Rote Bomber lost in the Depot."

"Yes," answered Whip, looking to see if Warrant Officer Stone was watching.

Opening his hand, Arnd revealed Whip's gold, inscribed wrist watch. "Take it before Mr. Stone sees us. . . . And you'd better remember the advice I gave you."

"Can I give the finder a money reward?"

The office boy shook his head and returned to his desk.

IT WAS LATE in the afternoon a week later that two young, athletic-appearing POWs approached Whip. He could not recall having ever seen their faces. The taller of the two said, "We know you are a fast runner. Would you be willing to race us?"

Looking around Whip saw no other GIs or POWs in the area. Whip also knew in high school he had been a miler, not a sprinter, but as he had finished working and was now just leaving the Depot for his quarters, he figured, "What the hell." Pointing at a telephone pole about a hundred yards in the direction he was headed, he yelled, "Go."

As Whip had the jump on his competitors, he took the early lead, but out of the corner of his eye, he saw them rapidly gaining. He was still leading when he stopped abruptly. With consternation on their faces, the two Krauts returned to Whip, claiming the race was not supposed to end until the next telephone pole.

At that contentious moment Sergeant Sullivan suddenly appeared and the two Germans melted into the stacks.

"What in the hell do you think you're doing, Johnson?" roared a bleary-eyed Sullivan.

Whip could see Sully had been on a toot and was just now coming to work.

Derisively Sully continued, "Do you think this is the Boy Scouts, and you're playing capture the flag?" Turning, he wobbled toward the control-center. "I'm reporting you to 'Slick.'"

The next day a sober Sullivan gave no indication that he remembered the incident, and Whip was never called on the carpet before Major Draisy. But it again served as a reminder for Whip to pull in his horns.

Though he was continuously on the lookout for the German runners, Whip never saw their faces again either. The next day in the control-center, Whip chuckled. Those POWs probably thought his actions proved what Dr. Joseph Goebbels, the German Minister of Propaganda, had been telling the German people for years— *Americans are dirty liars and cannot to be trusted.* Suddenly Whip couldn't suppress his sense of humor and began laughing.

As he was the only GI in the control-center, Whip was startled when one of the clerks, who was probably still in his teens, correctly guessed the subject of Whip's outburst. The young POW said, "Ja, those men who raced you yesterday say you aren't so fast and that you cheat."

His confirmation made Whip laugh even louder.

Then with a sudden change in manner, the POW asked, "Is it true that you wish to learn what happened to your 15th Armored Division at Puffendorf?"

The question startled Whip. "Yes."

"I heard you talking with Sergeant Sullivan about it some time ago."

"Okay."

"Well, I was taken prisoner at Heerlen, Holland, and was rescued from a civilian who wanted to beat me. My Dutch rescuer visited me at the POW camp and gave me his address. He is Second Lieutenant Philip Vossmaar, and he was an interpreter for the 15th Armored Division. Heerlen is not very far from here, and he might be able to tell you something about your old division. I can give you his address."

On the way to his quarters that afternoon, another surprise unfolded before Whip's eyes. In front of the headquarters' building, he saw Arnd engaged in serious conversation with a tall American officer. Nearing the two, Whip saw the officer had single stars on his dark-gray trench coat. His bearing was military-straight and his face finely etched. Grey hair showed around the brim of his officer's parade hat. In front of the building stood a jeep with the standard of a brigadier general attached to its front bumper.

Whip thought, "Oh my God, why is an American general fraternizing with a Kraut POW? Especially Arnd!"

Whip's first impulse was to rush forward and warn the general about the little "werewolf." But he thought better of it. From a distance the conversation of the two appeared more like a father-son relationship than a conqueror with his prisoner. "So, what the hell? Who was he, Whip Johnson, to tell a general what to do?"

ONCE AGAIN STARING at the ceiling from his cot, Whip considered the POW's offer to give him the address of a Dutch officer in Heerlen, Holland. "Craps, Heerlen is only a few hours away by train."

Because he had a three-day pass coming, Whip decided to act on the POW's suggestion and go to Heerlen and see if he could locate this Dutch officer and learn from him what had happened to the 15th Armored Division and what, if anything, the Dutchman might know about the Battle of Puffendorf. The chance of obtaining answers to some nagging questions made going to Heerlen interesting. By coincidence, it was there that Whip had joined the 15th Armored Division at a Secondary Technical School just before he had seen action. His research, however, had to be played cool. Though the war in Europe was over, Whip still thought the 15th Armored would likely storm the beaches of Japan, and Whip was very happy remaining with the 75th Greyhounds for the duration of the war.

CHAPTER 17

ON THE 5TH OF MARCH, 1945, following the successful completion of the drive to the Rhine River, the 15th Armored Division was placed on XIX Corps reserve. For three weeks the famous fighting machine cooled its heels, though the interval was used for maintenance and training. As the officers considered a breakthrough likely on the other side of the Rhine, one part of the training included demonstrations on how to attack a town with a reinforced tank battalion. The demonstrations were highly successful, all spectators deriving much benefit from them—with the exception of a few German farmers who witnessed the land they had just completed plowing torn up again by tanks and half-tracks.

At last on the 27th of March, General Quinn gave the order sending two forward observers of the 92nd Armored Field Artillery to each battalion, a sure harbinger of impending operations, and the Division was again divided into two motorized striking forces: Combat Command "A" and Combat Command "B" with each receiving a quota of air tanks, armored artillery, tank destroyers, engineers and armored infantry.

On the morning of the 28th the Division moved north and east toward the Rhine River, coming to a halt near Wesel. Here the scene was bustling activity. Barrage balloons drifted lazily over a pontoon bridge site, convoys of troops and supplies rolled up in an unending procession. The scene was reminiscent of the beachhead days in Normandy.

Chapter Seventeen

Engineer bridging equipment lay everywhere. Another bridge was under construction downstream. However, it was not until after dark that the Division moved across this last great barrier protecting the heart of the German fortress. Although the engineers working on the crossing downstream had their area well illuminated and troops on the far side had bonfires blazing, the Division crossed the swiftly moving stream under complete blackout.

The thoughts of the command personnel as they passed over this vital barrier were many and varied. Some thought of the men who had made the original crossings and of those airborne troops who had won the bridgehead on the far side. Evidently they did their work well, not a round of enemy artillery could be heard. Others thought of the imminence of contact with the enemy once again, a prospect pleasing only inasmuch as it seemed to offer the opportunity of striking the final blow to end the conflict in Europe.

That the crossing was made without enemy hindrance was surprising to most. However, the men of the Division had long ago ceased being optimistic over first impressions. That the enemy would permit foreign armies to advance at will was unthinkable. The enemy no longer had the soil to trade for time. If the Luftwaffe had been saved for anything, surely this must be it. All expected a hard fight before the end of the struggle. But the members of the command did have the satisfaction of competence and confidence in themselves steeled in the hell of countless Puffendorfs.

This time, though, there was less joking about the last "five minutes" and "The Law of Averages" because everyone knew in his heart that the last five minutes had actually arrived; that for some, the "Law of Averages" would soon claim compensation.

As THE SPEARHEAD of Combat Command "B," Lieutenant Colonel Richard Burk's 1st Battalion moved from an assembly area at Spellen to the vicinity of Bricht on the evening of the 29th, and then proceeded to pass through elements of the 17th Airborne Division near Haltern during the hours of darkness. At 0100 hours on the 30th of March, initial contact was made. The infantry rapidly dismounted from the tanks and deployed, but after rounding up a few enemy stragglers, no fighting developed, and the Battalion continued on in column formation through the darkness. Near Seppenrade, on the Dortmund-Ems-Canal, the Battalion paused at 1000 to refuel and resupply while the infantry and engineers, covered by Sergeant Talbot's 1st Platoon of "D" Company (5 tanks), the assault guns and the Air Tank, wrested a crossing of the canal. In the interim, the kitchen served warm meals and coffee.

At 0130 on the 31st, forward progress continued. Along the main highway running between Kappelle and Nordkirchen numerous abandoned enemy vehicles cluttered the roadsides, but action was limited to brief exchanges of small arms fire. After leaving Benteler, the Battalion ran into its first violent opposition outside of Herbern.

In the morning, the Battalion deployed in the fields before the town and were met by stubborn resisting enemy infantrymen armed with rifles and panzerfaust. Heavy small-arms fire swept the field as the doughs of the 41st Armored Infantry advanced. The enemy infantry were dug in behind a series of hedgerows and trees, many of them defiladed from the direct fire of the infantry and tanks; but the mortar platoon placed a deadly barrage of mortar shells on them.

As the combined forces of the 1st Battalion (which included about 50 tanks) at last moved forward, over forty German dead and wounded were counted behind one hedgerow, but the desperate remnants fought on until they were driven into the open where the infantry quickly rounded them up. Over fifty had been killed and ninety now were taken prisoner. According to the prisoners, this represented almost every man in their group, an OCS (officers candidate school) detachment from the school at Detmold. They had been on their way to commissions, until the American mortars delivered their valedictory.

The Battalion continued toward the vital road junction of Ahlen. Sights reminiscent of the march through France and Belgium greeted the eyes of the men. Here in the heart of enemy territory the streets were jammed with thousands of civilians waving white flags, few of whom seemed displeased at the entry of the American soldiers. Perhaps they had been chilled by the winds from the east. German police undertook to guide the various column elements through the town with military efficiency.

After putting out the necessary blocks and outposts for security, the Battalion then coiled, setting up a command post in a mansion 1.5 miles east of Ahlen as twilight fell. Those who could, tried to snatch a few minutes of sleep while commanders spread maps on tables and awaited orders.

But both sleep and preparation were interrupted by the sound of 20mm flak guns firing long burst from the direction of the railroad yards. Three hundred yards to the west, an armored train was advancing eastward along the rails parallel to the Ahlen-Beckum road from the huge marshaling yard in Ahlen. The train was immediately taken under fire by all vehicular weapons. It was later discovered that the train, in addition to mounting numerous antiaircraft guns, carried a huge 16-inch railway gun and large quantities of military supplies.

In the meantime, plans for the continuation of the attack were held up pending negotiation by telephone for the surrender of Beckum. General Quinn was unable to secure an unequivocal answer from either the civil or military authorities; it was apparent, however, that both were reluctant to fight for the town and would surrender it if it were possible to do so with what they called "honor." General Quinn was adamant.

The Battalion with its attachments left the outskirts of Ahlen shortly after midnight, the column looking ghostly in the flaring light from the burning train. Their orders were not to shoot unless fired upon by the defenders of Beckum, as it was not definitely known whether or not the town would resist. Upon reaching the outskirts of Beckum, the column halted.

Attached to the 15th Armored Division from XIX Corps was the Psychological Warfare Tank. Equipped with a loud speaker and an officer speaking fluent German, this tank moved up to broadcast an appeal to the town—specifically, to the burgomeister or commandant to come forward and negotiate, before it became necessary for the Allied Armies to take the town apart. In his propaganda, the enthusiastic officer often confused one small tank battalion with the "Allied Armies" and the liaison planes with "demonstrations of America's aerial might."

After a short parley with the burgomeister, the latter agreed to go with the American officer and broadcast over the speaker an appeal to the citizens and soldiers to offer no resistance. After this was done the Battalion moved through the town without firing a shot.

Continuing east into the heart of Germany, meeting little opposition, elements of the Battalion entered the town of Lippstadt, a major road junction, the afternoon of April 1st. On the outskirts of this city, tanks of "D" Company and "A" Company encountered 3rd Armored Division vehicles, effecting the linkup of the First and Ninth Armies, sealing off the entire Ruhr industrial region, and with it 300,000 of the best remaining troops of Germany. Strong roadblocks were immediately set up to repulse any attempt of the encircled enemy to break out of the trap.

CHAPTER 18

Eyes white and face curled in a snarl, Sergeant Nate Talbot ran toward Lieutenant Red Jordening.

Company "D" had just completed setting up a roadblock on the main highway leading south from Lippstadt and Red was preparing to look for a place to locate his command post. He was sitting behind the steering wheel of his jeep as Nate approached.

"Joe and Morbid have gone rogue."

"What?"

"Lieutenant Nicholson and Private Morris, just the two of them, have taken their tank and headed for Warstein."

His brow wrinkled, Red demanded, "What's going on? Where's the rest of Joe's crew?"

"They were left behind on orders," said Nate. "The assholes.... You see, Red, Nicholson and Morris captured a German general, and they tied him to the front of their tank—spread eagle. They're now on the way to Warstein, the captured general as their shield."

"That's crazy."

"I know. . . . From some civilian they learned there's a cache of shotguns and other souvenirs to be had at a hunting lodge near Warstein. It was owned by some bigwig Nazi general. This civilian told them the general had stashed away stolen art work and other treasurers. The men then heard Lieutenant Nicholson say to Morbid, 'This is it, Morbid. Your big moment has come at last!' The men said the two of them pretty well roughed up the German general before they had him bound to the tank. Then with Morbid driving, they headed off for Warstein."

Hastily retrieving a map from the dashboard and spreading it on his lap, Red studied it a few minutes. "I see Warstein is located about 12 miles south of here in a National Forest. . . . It should now be occupied by units of the 3rd Armored. . . . Did anyone happen to hear the name of the German general?"

"Yeah. One of the men heard the general say he was Field Marshal Stein and wanted to surrender to General Quinn."

For a moment Nate thought his company commander was going to explode.

As if he were talking to himself, Red mumbled, "Oh my God! My God! If he's really Field Marshal Stein, he's the group commander of all the enemy forces in the Ruhr; if he wants to surrender, the war would probably be pretty much over for us. Sonofabitch! Get in the damn jeep, Nate. We gotta find Quinn!"

As General Quinn heard the news from Jordening's lips, he too blanched. Because there were reporters from the states at his CP, Quinn quickly grabbed Red by the shoulder and led him to a side room.

Uncharacteristically the general turned profane. "What the fuck's gone wrong with your men, Red?"

"It's just Nicholson and Morris, sir."

Nodding his head, his eyes burning, his voice lethal, General Quinn said, "Take whatever forces you need, Red. But get those bastards, Nicholson and Morris; kill them if you have to. But bring the Field Marshal to me as quickly as possible!"

As WEEKS PASSED after Nicoline's rescue, she grew more despondent by the day. Bep told her the situation behind German lines was too unsettled and dangerous for another return to Warstein. "It would be suicide," he said. Later he consoled her. "The Americans will soon reach the Rhine and shortly thereafter fight into the heart of Germany. I've made arrangements to travel with their army. I can be in Warstein shortly after the Americans reach that city."

However, Bep did not share Nicoline's passion to protect the children of an SS general. In fact, he had become distrustful and apprehensive about Nicoline's commitment, though he was surprised at the jealousy he seemingly felt toward the Nazi general's children;

maybe deep down he considered them a kind of threat to his possession of Nicoline. Yet Bep wanted to defer to Nicoline's wishes.

Bep's reasons for not attempting an immediate rescue barely satisfied Nicoline. Nearly every time she closed her eyes she could see a likeness of General Fritz Kraus fade and be replaced by images of Felicia and Max. Then a cavalcade of disconnected thoughts would follow: How quickly the children had shown their affection; their small gestures, as offering her a blanket or a chair; how sweet and remarkably intelligent they both were; Max, redheaded and freckled like his father, and Felicia, blond with clipped hair and sparkling round eyes; what a beauty Felicia could be someday with long, flowing hair; then Max tumbling into the pond, and she swimming to the rescue, but Hektor, the dog, beating her to his master; Felicia exclaiming at how beautiful she, Nicoline, had appeared with wet clothes clinging to her body, Felicia giggling about it; then Max shooting the hawk that was attempting to make a meal of Snow White, the pet pigeon; the children lying to protect her from the Gestapo agents—and Aunt Gertrud's intense dislike of her.

Melancholy and depression always followed these daydreams. Nicoline had always wanted children, but apparently could have none of her own. She recalled Fritz's premonition that something mortal might happen to himself, and, therefore, he had felt an urgent need to provide for his children's welfare. To be sure, he had clearly stated his trust in herself and his equal distrust of his sister-in-law.

As week followed upon week, Nicoline fretted more and more. She declined food and slowly her health ebbed as she took to her bed more and more.

Concerned for her well-being, Bep spoke roughly. "By making yourself sick you're never going to help the children. Please be patient, Nicoline, the American offensive is about to begin. We'll soon be in Warstein. But for God's sake eat something. Don't make yourself sick now, just when the children may need you most."

Bep's news that the American offensive was imminent encouraged Nicoline. Bep had promised they would be right behind the front line troops. He had General Quinn's word.

"You know I'm going with you, Bep!" reminded Nicoline. "Of course, my dear."

WHIP JOHNSON boarded the train at Charleroi, Belgium. Even with a border check and a change of trains at Maastricht, Holland, Whip figured he'd be in Heerlen in less than four hours. His first visit to Heerlen had been the past October. On that occasion he had ridden in an army truck as a "reinforcement" (replacement) for the 15th Armored Division. Now it was May 16, 1945. Hitler was dead. V-E Day had come and gone, and Whip still patrolled the big food Depot at Charleroi, attempting to prevent pilfering by the POWs.

For their part, the POWs were content to stay put. By May 1945 Germany had ceased to exist as a viable nation. Thanks to Adolf Hitler, their country's infrastructure lay in ruin and their land was overrun by invading armies. Food and fuel shortages and disturbances with DPs (Displaced People) occurred daily in the former Reich. Consequently, many of the POWs at Charleroi were in no hurry to return home and place a further burden on their struggling families. From time to time some did escape, and often with the connivance of their American guards; but the truth was, they had an easy job and plenty of food to eat. Usually they received adequate medical attention and were treated fairly. They all knew eventually they'd be shipped back to Germany and released—though many feared what the Russians might do in revenge, considering what the Nazis had done in Russia.

On the other hand, the war was not yet over for Whip Johnson. There was still the Pacific Theater of Operations; and from what Whip had been reading in "The Stars And Stripes," that war was heating up, getting more gruesome by the day with the Japanese turning to suicide "banzai" charges and "kamikazi" airplane raids. He read that few Japanese soldiers chose to surrender, most preferring to fight to the death. Whip wanted no part of that war in the Pacific if he could help it. Though his curiosity about the fate of his former outfit and some of his comrades-in-arms never lessened, it wasn't so important that he'd chance being sent back to rejoin them.

Nevertheless, it was curiosity to possibly learn about the Battle of Puffendorf and the fate of the 15th Armored Division that motivated Whip to take the train to Heerlen, Holland. Coincidentally, the young POW who had been rescued by Philip Vossmaar from a Dutch civilian, worked in the control-center. As the POW had overheard Whip talking with Sergeant Sullivan about Whip's interest in learning what had happened to his former outfit, the POW had offered Whip Philip Vossmaar's address in Heerlen, claiming the Dutchman had been an interpreter with the 15th Armored Division at the time of the Battle of Puffendorf. Solely on a chance and a hunch, Whip had decided to see if he could locate that Dutchman and learn something about the 15th Armored. If nothing came of it, he could pass his time away as a tourist. In grammar school the land of windmills and wooden shoes had always fascinated him.

THUS ON AN EARLY afternoon in spring, Whip knocked on the door of the address given him by the POW. The day was bright and warm with the fragrance of flowers in the air.

A tall, young man with rusty-blond hair, a high forehead and a beak-like nose, opened the door. He was dressed in a khaki uniform with an organizational patch representing a lion sewed to the front of his blouse.

"Hello. What can I do for you?" he asked with a faint smile and a friendly voice.

After several false starts, Whip at last explained to the Dutchman the nature of his visit and the source of the address given him.

"Ah so," said the Dutchman. "I remember the incident, and how sorry I felt at the time for the young German soldier who could hardly be responsible for the actions of his elders. . . . I guess I did establish a brief acquaintance with him, though I forgot I had given him my address." Offering his hand, he continued, "My name is Philip Vossmaar. Although I still work for the American army, I'm no longer with the 15th Armored Division.

I too have lost contact with that unit, and probably will not be able to help you much. But come inside and meet my parents. Then we may talk."

Whip was impressed by the young Dutch officer's American-English and the warm friendliness he expressed. He appeared to be about Whip's age. After meeting the parents, who did not speak English, Philip led Whip to a living room with comfortable, upholstered furniture and offered him coffee—"American instant." Philip also offered Whip a cigarette—"Dutch terrible," he joked.

"I don't smoke," replied Whip.

"I'll bet you're an athlete," said Philip.

"A little. But I like reading, too," answered Whip.

"What have you read?" responded Philip.

"For the past months I've been struggling with Will Durant's *The Story of Philosophy*. Ever hear of him?"

"As a matter of fact, I have; but I'm surprised you have an interest in philosophy. Since the liberation I've met quite a few Americans, and you are now one of the few to indicate a philosophical interest."

Not wishing to reveal his ignorance, Whip returned to the subject of his quest. "Who did you know in the 15th Armored?"

Philip rattled off a few names.

Whip had heard of some of them, but the one Whip wanted to hear most about—Captain Appleby—was not mentioned. "Where is the 15th Armored now?"

"I've heard they're in Berlin or soon will be. Do you want me to contact their officers for you?"

Whip's body pumped adrenaline. "No. Please don't. I'll get in touch with them in due time. . . . I was wounded in a German village not far from here—Puffendorf, Germany. Would it be possible to go there and look around?"

Stroking his chin with his hand, Philip said, "You would have to have a special pass. Your request would have to state your reasons for going there. But I believe I could arrange it for you."

"No. I was just thinking about it. Maybe sometime later. For now it would probably bring back bad memories."

"Yes, of course. I understand that."

"Anyway, I think I'm just going to be a tourist and walk around your nice city. I certainly like your country. It's so clean and nice."

Wrinkling his brow, Philip inquired, "When do you have to be back to your unit?"

"Monday morning. I'm on a weekend pass."

"Do you have a place to sleep?"

"I was thinking of staying at the USO (United Servicemen's Organization) in Maastricht."

Quick to respond, Philip said, "As with you, I'm also on a weekend pass, and I invite you to stay here. We have an extra bedroom. My older brother is in Dutch Indonesia. During the occupation I was in the Dutch underground, and we hid American pilots at our house; so you would not be the first American to sleep here. Besides, you say you're interested in philosophy. I have some friends who I believe you would enjoy meeting."

Always cautious, but sensing a golden opportunity to learn about a foreign country, Whip said, "Okay. I thank you very much."

AND PHILIP WAS NOT WRONG. His friends delighted Whip. At an evening session of the Gorgo, Philip's debating club, Whip met them. About Whip's age, they reminded him of foreign versions of John C. Smith and Dale Jenks.

Explaining the nature of the Gorgo, Philip said, "I selected the name Gorgo after the Greek goddesses who turned beholders to stone. I wanted to warn the very pious who might join us not to be petrified by our heresies. We argue and debate anything; but above all, we are a literary club. So a lot of our time is spent reading and reciting poetry and essays, some of which we ourselves write."

Such a direction excited Whip. This is what *The Story of Philosophy* was all about, he believed—a quest after the meaning of life.

ARTHUR DE HONDT was the first to arrive. His shoes, removed at the door, were caked with mud. His shirt was torn and his hair, rumpled. "Sorry, Philip. I rescued a wounded rabbit which some dogs had chewed on. May I wash?"

"Yes. In the kitchen, but first I'd like you to meet our guest, Whip Johnson of the United States army." Then like a congressional sergeant at arms, Philip intoned, "He comes from the great state of South Dakota in America."

Smiling good-naturedly, Arthur shook hands firmly. "I understand you have an interest in philosophy. You have come to the right place, and I'm happy to greet you."

Whip replied, "An interest, but not much of an understanding."

"By the way, Philip tells me you're a chess player, so I brought my self-made chess set, hoping we might lock horns."

Whip smiled, "Sure. I'll be glad to play."

Servaas Konijn entered the room extending a limp hand and sounding unctuous. "I didn't know American soldiers had any time for serious thinking."

Grasping the hand, Whip heard himself reply, "One must be careful with generalizations."

The Gorgo was punctual. Servass was followed by Theo van Zeeland. Overhearing Whip's remark to Servaas, Theo interposed, "Do you believe, Whip, that America will ever produce another Mark Twain?"

Shrugging his shoulders as he shook hands with the speaker, Whip replied, "My two favorite authors are Mark Twain and Jack London. They wrote about subjects that interest me."

"And what are those subjects?" inquired a burly young man who was introduced as Louke Hellenar.

"The exploits of boyhood and dog stories."

"I fear there are trends in America that will leave such stories popular only with kids, and then they'll have to be expurgated," said a voice as cutting as a sharpened hunting knife.

"This is my friend Karel Konijn," said Philip. "Karel was very active in the Resistance."

"I suppose you have in mind the likes of Hemingway and the other expatriates after the First World War," answered Whip, amazed at how these Dutchmen should know anything about American literature.

Next a voice as soft as cotton candy and just as sweet interjected, "Karel goes for gore. I personally think there is hope for introspective writers like Thomas Wolf. I enjoyed reading his *Look Homeward Angel.* His novel gave me insights into the American character; and I discovered there is more to America than just cowboys and Indians, and boys and dogs—or do you disagree, Whip Johnson?"

Whip gasped as he turned to Philip in surprise. Philip, who had not mentioned any female members of the Gorgo, now had the look of an imp. Whip's eyes returned to the speaker.

As darkness had not yet settled, Whip observed she was the last one standing on the landing. Whip thought he saw a smallish, lithe figure with brown hair cut short. It was too dark to determine the color of her eyes, but he guessed they would also be brownish. Even at dusk they sparkled. Her face was a white, smooth ellipse highlighted by a delicate nose and mouth, but one expressing openness, friendliness, warmth, cheerfulness and curiosity.

Breaking the silence Philip said, "Lucie Heerkens is the brightest one of the Gorgo. I had hoped to surprise you with Lucie."

Whip was grateful for the dim light, as he knew he must be blushing. Because English was not Philip's mother tongue, Philip's expression "the brightest one of the Gorgo" left Whip wondering if Philip meant Lucie was the most intelligent one?

"Not only am I surprised, but I am delightfully surprised," said Whip as he bowed and took a small hand. "In answer to your question, I most wholeheartedly agree with you; Americans are as different and complex as people anywhere; and I, too, liked *Look Homeward Angel.*"

QUICKLY THE GORGO retired to a large living room with modern furniture of couches and chairs.

Arthur de Hondt was already laying out his chess set on a coffee table as he motioned Whip to be seated on a couch while he drew up a chair on the opposite side of the chess board.

Obviously the small composition of the Gorgo ruled out the

necessity of formality. Spontaneity and naturalness seemed to be the style, and all but Whip were soon puffing on cigarettes. Philip was the bartender offering everyone shot glasses filled with cognac.

This presented a problem to Whip. Whip was a teetotaler. So far nothing had weakened his resolve. He even recalled Lieutenant Appleby's intervention when the army guys were pressuring him to drink. However, this was a new day, and these were interesting people. Besides, he thought it was about time for the experiment.

Lucie had seated herself next to Whip where she could follow the chess match. Playing white, Whip opened with the familiar Roy Lopez and then took a defensive stance. But his mind was soon wandering as he overheard voices rising in other parts of the room. He sipped on his cognac, feigning pleasure with the burning sensation in his throat and chest.

Karel was needling Louke in their on-going dispute about God and dogma. "I believe in a creator—and that's about it. We're on our own. All your religions are nothing but dollops of superstitions invented by priests. The trembling masses will believe anyone who promises them a nirvana or heaven. The dictums of the priests become dogmas. Promoted by charismatic individuals, cults flood the world, and a few become established religions. In the final analysis, people believe what they want, hear what they want and do what they want."

"Even if it is contrary to the teachings and commandments of their church?"

"Maybe not. Maybe the priests, ministers, mullahs, rabbis and their dogmas can scare them into modifying their lustful, animal behavior."

Arthur was listening. As he exchanged queens with Whip, he turned to Karel. "I'm glad to hear you're coming around to my position on the evolution of the human species, Karel. But I fear you are incorrectly equating animal survival with ethics and thus 'bad' behavior. Remember, nothing is right or wrong but thinking makes it so. Carnivores have to eat to live. That's the nature of things."

Philip interjected, "In that case, wouldn't the world be less gory and more idyllic if all the carnivores were eliminated from the face of the earth and all survivors had to be vegetarians?"

Theo, sitting on the piano stool, whirled the stool until he faced Philip. "There goes your democracy down the drain, Philip. It'll take a dictator like Hitler to create your utopian, vegetarian society among men."

Servas, from a corner lost in his thoughts, implored, "No! No! You're all wrong. We can't have a utopian world without absolutes. But it must be our version. Might does make right! With victory for our side looming in this world war, we now have the golden opportunity to establish a new world order based on democracy and Christianity."

Whip felt drawn in. "Haven't we rejected the thesis that might makes right? It certainly isn't Christian.... On the supreme court building in Washington, D.C. are the inscribed words 'Justice Under Law.' That's what I believe in."

At least for this session of the Gorgo, Whip noticed there was no effort to structure the discussions. No moderator or judge. No defining of terms or sticking to the subject. Ideas seemed random. Points and counterpoints were made almost without regard to direction. The discussions reminded him of the hometown coffee shop. Most opinions were spontaneous and often irrelevant. Most drifted further and further away from the point of origin—the speakers' purposes eventually becoming more one of socialization rather than seeking after truth.

Attempting to play chess and at the same time participate in the arguments became too much for Whip; so he lay his king prostrate and said, "I resign."

Arthur de Hondt appeared pleased. "You are a good player, Whip. I hope we may have more matches this summer."

When Theo van Zeeland began roaming over the piano keys, the theme song from the movie "Sun Valley Serenade" emerged and soon everyone had gathered around the piano singing:

Why do Robins sing in December
Long before the Spring time gets through?
And even when its snowing, violets are growing.
I know why and so do you.

Whip was aware of Lucie standing beside him. Repeated shots of cognac were having their effect. The singing was loud, rendered in English but accented in Dutch. Lucie put her arm around Whip and Whip reciprocated.

When you smile at me,
I hear gypsy violins.
When you dance with me,
I'm in heaven when the music begins.

The warmth of Lucie's body heated Whip. Perspiration dripped from his forehead as he looked at the beautiful young girl by his side. He must—must get to know her.

I can see the sun when its raining,
hiding every cloud to my view.
And why do I see rainbows with you in my arms?
I know why and so do you!

The train ride back to Charleroi was anticlimactic; besides, Whip was experiencing his first hangover. Head throbbing and oversized, he felt terrible. But thinking about Lucie Heerkens made his suffering tolerable. His real pain was the fact he could not get another pass for several weeks.

BACK AT WORK in the Depot, Sergeant Sullivan noted a change in Whip and asked, "If a three-day pass is what it takes to lighten your step, I'll see you get one on schedule. . . . Did you get your first piece of ass?"

Without answering Whip smiled enigmatically as he left the control-center and casually walked toward the headquarter's building.

Several things were on his mind. First, when he returned to Heerlen on his next pass, he'd take his cigarette rations with him. The Gorgo smoked like fiends from hell. Second, from *The Story of Philosophy* he'd now center his study on the reliability of reason for discovering truth and beauty—epistemology.

Even Philip had observed that the Gorgo's discussions had been too rambling and that a restriction was needed. He had suggested epistemology for the next session. All had agreed. Now the strange thought occurred to Whip that not only had Will Durant's precious book saved his life, but it might now be opening the door to a relationship with the girl of his dreams.

SEVERAL DAYS LATER when Whip was at the headquarters building, Arnd approached him with a tight smile. "I understand Der Rote Bomber got laid over the weekend."

"That's bullshit," said Whip, sorry to hear one so young as Arnd use such gutter language. "How can one who looks like a child have such dirty thoughts?"

Showing pleasure at having angered Whip, Arnd quickly replied, "I guess I just reflect my environment. Don't you?"

Whip had noticed a subtle change in Arnd's attitude since V-E Day. The office boy no longer seemed so arrogant. Whip wondered if Arnd might be undergoing some kind of de-programming. Whip now knew Arnd's special friend who came frequently to visit him was Brigadier General Harold Quinn. What the American general's relationship to Arnd might be intrigued Whip. Was this former Nazi werewolf going to be tried as a war criminal? He had certainly wreaked havoc with American tankers; and there was no doubt he'd been a spy and a commando who had at least once dressed in an American army uniform behind American lines.

Arnd apologized. "My bunkmate at the stockade works at the control-center. He told me what Sergeant Sullivan said to you. . . . I suppose I shouldn't have teased you."

Out of nowhere Warrant Officer Willard Stone appeared like the avenging angel swooping down on the two. "God dammit, Johnson. How many times do I have to tell you not to fraternize with Arnd?"

"For God's sake, Mr. Stone, haven't you heard about V-E Day?" implored Whip.

"It's my fault, not Corporal Johnson's. I asked him about details at the control-center." Before the warrant officer could reply, Arnd had turned and was walking toward Major Draisy's office.

Taking Arnd's abrupt departure as a cue, Whip hurried out the door heading toward his sleeping quarters about a mile away in one of Charleroi's suburbs.

GRADUALLY WHIP'S FEELING of odium toward Warrant Officer Stone was replaced by more pleasant thoughts as the attractive face of Lucie Heerkens formed in his imagination. He would count the days before his return to Heerlen, and this very evening he would resume his study of *The Story of Philosophy*.

Trudging along a narrow, cobblestone street, lost in the meanderings of his mind, Whip suddenly realized that a towheaded youngster was walking in lockstep by his side. Figuring the kid was another "Please-Joe" beggar, Whip stopped, confronted the kid, and said harshly, "No I don't have any gum or candy. Beat it."

"Your Corporal Whip Johnson, aren't you?"

Wrinkling his forehead, Whip replied, "What am I?—an open book! How do you know my name?"

"From one of your soldier friends who told us you wanted to know what happened to the 15th Armored Division."

Whip thought, "God, I am an open book." Then he said, "Well I've changed my mind. I don't want to know anything about that outfit."

But the kid had his own purposes. "Colonel Burk, your former commander, said the 15th Armored Division was in Berlin and will be an honor guard for President Truman's visit at Potsdam."

Who in the hell was this little scamp who appeared to know so much about his old outfit? "How do you know that?"

"He and his wife visited us before they returned to the states."

"Who are you?"

Taking a deep breath, the boy blurted out his memorized lines: "I am Charles DeRuck, the twin brother of George DeRuck. The American soldiers called my brother George by the nickname of 'Please-Joe' or 'Little Joe.' He was the mascot of the 15th Armored Division, and was accidentally shot and killed. An American sentry thought he was the Hitler youth, Arnd Hauptmann. That killer of American soldiers is now a POW and works in your Depot."

Whip suddenly guessed this kid might be a reservoir of knowledge about the 15th Armored Division. "Did Major Burk say anything about the Battle of Puffendorf?"

"No. Both Colonel Burk and Private Malloti just got married in Germany at XIX Corps Headquarters. Private Malloti is one of those who returned my brother's body to us."

Charles' obvious sincerity and powerful connections had its effect on Whip. Meekly he inquired, "Why are you telling me this?"

His face reflecting anger, Charles blurted out, "Colonel Burk apologized to my parents for considering George to be the Hitler Youth, Arnd Hauptmann. Now my folks wonder why that killer is being protected at the Depot. My parents, Monsieur and Madam DeRuck, would like to meet you. They know you work with this spy and war criminal."

Feeling he was standing on quicksand, Whip shook his head and spoke in short, jerky sentences. "I don't work with that POW. I don't hardly know anything you're talking about. I was only with the 15th Armored briefly. I barely ever heard of Major Burk. Please thank Monsieur and Madam for the invitation, but I'm studying for a test when I'm not working; so, you see, I can't possibly accept any invitations; but tell them—thanks a lot."

With a wry smile Charles said, "Susan and Sally both said Madam is a wonderful cook."

Not wishing to appear intimidated, but not having the slightest idea who this Susan and Sally might be, Whip said, "Maybe later on. See you sometime." Whip pivoted on his feet and began jogging toward his sleeping quarters, hoping to see this little Charles never again, or for that matter, any of the DeRucks.

Charles, however, brought Whip to a complete standstill. "How would you like to rejoin the 15th Armored Division before they're shipped to the Pacific?" he called.

Whip's unsteady words floated back to Charles. "When would it be convenient to meet with your parents?"

"Madam said for you to come for dinner tomorrow night."

"Okay. . . . Be seeing you."

STUDYING *The Story of Philosophy* that evening was difficult for Whip. He kept wondering what the DeRucks had in mind. Maybe they would ask him to assassinate or poison Arnd—or to bring charges against the war criminal. How in the hell did he ever get into this fix? Just because he asked some stupid questions about his old outfit at the control-center. He should remember to keep his big mouth shut. Oh well, he'd just have to wait and see what was up with these DeRucks. No use crying over spilt milk.

However, he soon lost himself in *The Story of Philosophy* and began taking notes on some of the philosophers and their ideas. Not only did he like the vagaries of "epistemology," but he thought this study might at last lead him to the "meaning of life"— his "Holy Grail." Of course, he wanted to make a good impression on Lucie Heerkens—and, obviously, Lucie was some kind of a girl philosopher.

Then the dinner at the DeRucks intruded upon his consciousness. One thing for sure, he was going to learn how in the hell the DeRucks knew so much about him and if they really had any influence in the American army.

CHAPTER 19

WHIP APPEARED PROMPTLY at 6 P.M. for his dinner date at the home of Monsieur and Madam DeRuck. As a gift Whip brought a large jar of grape jelly, courtesy of the Depot. After an exchange of formal pleasantries, Madam fed everyone a boiled dinner of potatoes, carrots, cabbage and a small portion of beef, all joyfully prepared by Madam. Whip felt the DeRucks were desperately trying to please him. He didn't know whether to be amused or alarmed, but he did begin wondering why he'd bothered to come in the first place.

The seating arrangement seemed foreboding. As if none of the DeRucks wanted to get too close to Whip, they all seated themselves facing him from one side of an old rectangular-shaped dining table, leaving Whip feeling as if he were in a court room dock. Staring suspiciously at him, they reminded Whip of three judges about to rule on a request for leniency. Papa DeRuck, small, bald and dressed in a white shirt with tan pants, repeatedly grinned, revealing smoke-stained teeth; Mamma DeRuck, rotund, wearing a faded print dress, scrutinized Whip like an owl with large luminous eyes; and young DeRuck, looking scrubbed for the occasion, clad in a white, outgrown T-shirt and blue shorts, drummed his fingers on the table like a spring-wound toy soldier.

The dining area was cramped and stuffy, furnishings antiquated.

After eating his meal in silence, Whip broke the ice. "So how do you know so much about me?"

Charles did all the interpreting as Monsieur spoke only a little English, and Madam, who seemed bighearted enough, comprehended no English. When Charles wasn't around, Whip frequently asked, "Comprenez-vous?" and Madam always replied, "Je ne comprends pas." Whip realized, of course, he was just as stupid as Madam. Other than a few dirty slang words, he knew no French to speak of.

Monsieur said, "Sergeant Sullivan is our friend. It was he who first befriended George when George ran away from home. After Private Malloti and Private Silverman returned George's body informing us of what had happened, we met and became friends with Sergeant Sullivan. It's Sergeant Sullivan who keeps us informed about the 'Red Bomber.'"

Swallowing his Adam's apple, Whip inquired, "How do you happen to know Major Burk?"

Speaking sonorously in French with pauses for Charles' hesitant translations, Monsieur said, "He is now Lieutenant Colonel Burk. He recently married his Red Cross sweetheart, Susan Montgomery. His aide, Private Malloti, also married a Red Cross girl, Sally Brown. They have both been reassigned stateside and are taking their new brides with them." Laughing pointedly, Monsieur observed, "I see even in the American army, rank has its privileges."

Biting his lip, Whip asked, "Why did Colonel Burk come to visit you folks?"

"Because he wanted to console us before returning to the states and to tell us the whole story about George—'Please-Joe.' . . . But he also had another reason, and this is why we invited you to our house. . . ."

Whip felt the sweat on his forehead.

"He wants to have war criminal charges brought against that spy and killer of American soldiers, Arnd Hauptmann, who lives in your POW camp."

Beginning to burn, Whip asked, "What's that got to do with me?"

"Colonel Burk believes Arnd Hauptmann indirectly killed our George. Oh, yes, an American sentry pulled the trigger, but George had been previously kidnapped and then released by German commandos. The American sentry mistook George for Arnd Hauptmann who, Colonel Burk said, was the mastermind behind that operation in Heerlen, Holland."

"How can a child be a mastermind? . . . And I still don't see how that's got anything to do with me."

"Maybe a child—but the Germans call him a 'wunderkind'—a child prodigy. Colonel Burk believes someone is protecting this Hitler Youth, vicious killer, from being investigated by the War Crimes Commission. . . . Sergeant Sullivan informs us you have established an acquaintance with Arnd Hauptmann. We would like for you to give us what information you can about who might be protecting this war criminal."

All the DeRucks beamed expectantly.

Again abashed, Whip considered getting up and running. For one thing, he thought there were too many gaps and inconsistencies in what he'd just heard. He was tempted to say, "bullshit," but that would probably make the DeRucks mad. So he shook his head and said, "Sorry, I really don't know this kid. Occasionally I pick up office supplies from him for the central-control. Truthfully, that's the extent of my knowing him."

Damn if he'd say anything about General Quinn to these people. What's more, it didn't make any sense to Whip that Colonel Burk would turn to Belgian civilians to gather his information for the War Crimes Commission. Something stunk here. Whip did recall, however, that Burk had been considered an asshole by most of the men in Company "D."

Appearing somewhat disappointed, Monsieur said, "In that case, I have one more request of you, Corporal Johnson. . . . Sergeant Sullivan also says you go on pass regularly to Heerlen. We would like for you to place a wreath of remembrance near the place where George was killed. We will go there ourselves one day. Would you be willing to do this for us?"

Sensing the uncomfortable phase of the evening might be coming to an end, and feeling much relieved about it, Whip said, "Of course. Of course. Though I never saw or heard of your son during my brief stay with the 15th Armored Division, I'll be glad to place your wreath."

In chorus, the DeRucks said, "Thank you."

WHEN WHIP FINALLY did return to Heerlen on his next three-day pass, he kept his promise to the DeRucks by taking their wreath.

When he informed Philip Vossmaar of the facts connected with the wreath, Philip elaborated: "I knew Little Joe pretty well. In fact, he lived in Karel Konijn's home next door. He was a cute kid, much loved by General Clay who intended to have him adopted by Master Sergeant Hap Hardesty. Unfortunately, during the Ardennes offensive, German commandos sent to Heerlen killed Master Sergeant Hardesty. The Hitler Youth, Arnd Hauptmann, who had Dutch connections in Heerlen, is thought to have been involved in the plot. After the commandos released Little Joe, an American sentry, thinking Joe was Hauptmann, shot and killed him on the steps of the Secondary Technical School. . . ." Philip halted his speech to observe Whip's reaction.

Whip had listened intently with open-mouthed wonderment as Philip's account pretty much jibed with what he'd heard from Monsieur DeRuck.

Philip said, "Though the Americans are gone, I know the Dutch authorities will allow you to place the wreath near the spot where Joe was killed."

"Did you ever see this Hitler Youth, this Arnd Hauptmann?"

"Yes. For one day and a night he also stayed at the home of Karel Konijn—and at the same time Little Joe was staying there. They very briefly knew one another. . . . Arnd Hauptmann is the nephew of a Dutch Resistance fighter who was killed by the Gestapo."

"Isn't Arnd a German?"

"Yes. His Dutch mother married a German. . . . I understand both of his parents were killed in an American bombing raid. Goebbles, Hitler's Minister of Propaganda, made Arnd famous by publicizing and glamorizing his exploits."

Blinking his eyes, Whip said, "I know this Arnd Hauptmann. He is now a POW and works at the Depot in Charleroi."

Then it was Philip's turn to look surprised, as quickly Whip related his experiences with Arnd and the DeRucks.

Philip said, "I'm not surprised the DeRucks would like to see Arnd prosecuted. But I wonder why Colonel Burk is so interested, or, for that matter, General Quinn? . . . And in what way?"

"It beats the shit out of me," said Whip, ready to turn his mind from that topic to the evening's sublimity. The Gorgo was due to assemble, and Whip had Lucie Heerkens to think of.

LUCIE ARRIVED FIRST. Though she didn't have the body of a Betty Grable or the face of a Vivian Leigh, Lucie's shiny brown hair and eyes and petite figure heated Whip Johnson's blood. Eighteen-years-old, a recent high school graduate with an interest in theater, Whip considered Lucie a knockout. Before his death, her father had been a plantation owner in Dutch Indonesia and had sent Lucie back to Holland for her education. During the Japanese occupation both parents had died in Indonesia. An older brother, now a trade consultant with the Dutch government, was her closest living relative.

During the first part of the evening Whip had eyes only for Lucie. He laughed at her every joke and hovered around her like a bear after honey until an exasperated Philip said, "Just when I thought I'd finally met an American soldier whose ego was stronger than his libido, I find I'm wrong again."

Momentarily flustered, Whip knew he hadn't been paying attention to the proceedings of the Gorgo. Observing that most of the guests were regarding him with amusement, Whip self-consciously rose and from his musette bag began tossing packages of American cigarettes to the group. "Gosh darn it, I nearly forgot; I've been saving all my rations for you guys. This will be my contribution for the evening."

As EVERYONE EXCEPT Whip was lighting up, Whip felt obliged to restore his credibility as an "honorary" Gorgo. "Okay. Let me consider the subject of epistemology. Since our last get together I've been reviewing Will Durant's *The Story of Philosophy.*"

Whip and the Gorgo held forth for hours.

Then abruptly, with an empty cognac glass in one hand, Whip stood looking as if in a trance.

Philip rose and said, "It's getting late. Let's have something to eat. My folks made us some sandwiches."

Lucie looked admiringly at Whip; putting her hand in his she made a request, "After we eat, will you walk me home, Whip?"

"Of course," said Whip, his heart thumping wildly.

THE NEXT DAY back at the Depot, Whip was listless and the subject of teasing for having spent a bacchanalian weekend, but the jeers fell on deaf ears. He still lingered in the bliss of having been with Lucie. Her vivacious face was constantly in his mind's eye. The only bleak thought he had was the fact that Lucie would be gone for the remainder of the summer. She had told him she must go with her brother on a trade mission, which included the United States. The exciting possibility that Whip's parents could meet Lucie possessed his thoughts. Whip had given Lucie instructions to assure his family his wounds were trivial and that he hoped soon to be back in the states.

Next to Lucie, Whip's mind was captivated by the Gorgo. They were his kind of people. Their interests were his kind of interests. Instinctively, a priori—he laughed to himself, he knew Philip's and the Gorgo's ideas were nothing more than the conceit of youth, maybe a kind of esoteric snobbishness. But it was fun to pretend the Gorgo was in the forefront of man's eternal quest after truth and beauty. The Gorgo, about seven youth, had brains and the highest purpose for existence in this materialistic world—the study of philosophy. Damn, he was glad he had survived Puffendorf.

As Whip walked toward headquarters, he recalled his evening at the DeRuck's before going on pass. They surely had lingering ties with his old combat outfit. That they thought the killer of their son, a German war criminal, was now being coddled by the Americans concerned him. That somehow they had linked him to Arnd Hauptmann also was disturbing; and Whip wasn't certain what the DeRucks expected from him. All they'd asked for was information about Arnd's protector. Whip knew, however, that Arnd also had a continuing link with the 15th Armored Division. What an extraordinary world!

SOMETHING HAD CHANGED! After Whip entered the building, he was immediately approached by the office boy, and in front of Warrant Officer Willard Stone. Though Stone looked grim, he made no effort to intervene.

Smiling, Arnd baited Whip, "Well, I hear Der Rote Bomber had another rough weekend."

Whip still couldn't get over the brazen, worldly, adult posture of Arnd. Yet the kid was likable and obviously very intelligent—and the chameleon was changing. But maybe that's what Arnd was—a chameleon. Maybe still in his heart the Hitler Youth remained a fanatical Nazi.

Without preliminaries, Whip laid his newly found information on the line. "Did you have anything to do with Little Joe being killed?"

The highly trained commando revealed only a flicker of surprise. "No. Truthfully, I was sorry to learn he'd been shot and killed by an American sentry. From the brief time I knew Joe, I liked him. Our commandos had been instructed to kill him, but I would not allow it."

"Does your information about Little Joe come from General Quinn?"

His cheek wrinkling, revealing smoke-stained teeth, Arnd said, "I plead the 5th Amendment."

Observing that Whip didn't understand what he'd just said, Arnd elaborated, "I just don't want to talk about that."

"Okay. Would you do a favor for me then?"

"What favor?"

"One of my best army buddies was in my tank at the Battle of

Puffendorf. His name was Dale Jenks. I have no idea if he survived or was killed when our tank was hit. Could you check that out for me with your friend?"

"He was killed."

Stunned by Arnd's nearly instantaneous reply, Whip asked, "How can you possibly know that, as if you had it at your finger tips?"

"I do. I reviewed your file and I asked questions from one who was at the Battle of Puffendorf. You, your tank driver and your bow gunner are the only survivors."

Suddenly Whip was sweating. This little POW who stood before him seemed to have more knowledge and influence concerning Whip than anyone at the Depot. Possibly, he too could get Whip transferred back to his old unit when they were sent to the Pacific.

For a while Whip stood mute. At last he said, "Can we just drop the whole subject, Arnd? I need to get back to the control-center."

"Don't worry. I'll leave you alone. Just tell Little Joe's parents, the DeRucks, I didn't hurt their boy, and I tried to protect him. They'll never believe it, but I mourn his death, too."

As far as Whip Johnson was concerned Arnd Hauptmann had become a pariah, and Whip wanted nothing more to do with this former Hitler Youth. Leaving headquarters, Whip assured himself that in the future he'd avoid all possible contact with Arnd. This little, fuckin' Kraut knew too God damn much for his own good.

CHAPTER 20

SCENTING THE AIR, the great stag rose from his bed of dry leaves near General Kraus' duck blind. It was April, and Bismarck was in his velvet. Spring had come to the forest, and the day was warm, sunshine filtering through the trees. But what got the big buck's attention was the fragrance of wood smoke, telling him someone was again living in the cabin. Then he saw pigeons swooping over the pond, General Kraus' "Crown Jewel." Though his wound had healed, Bismarck had become wary of humans since being shot by the Gestapo agent last November. But one bad experience had not overwhelmed Bismarck's confidence in the one man who had patiently gained his trust. The man who had found him as an injured fawn and nurtured him to maturity. The great stag sauntered to a rise overlooking the cabin and watched and waited for a sight of the general.

FRÄULEIN GERTRUD SCHULTZ had reluctantly decided to take the children, eleven-year-old Felicia and ten-year-old Max, back to Fritz's hunting lodge for safety. She could have remained in Warstein, but had thought the remote hideaway features of the hunting lodge would offer greater protection from the rampaging American armies. After arriving at the lodge, however, she was not so sure. Being isolated with the two youngsters in the woods suddenly frightened her.

Going back, though, was too late; elements of the American armies already were entering Warstein even as Gertrud drove the black Mercedes down a back road toward the lodge. But to her relief, Herr Lüdwig, armed with a pitchfork, appeared shortly after their arrival. A widower and living in a small cottage not far from the lodge, he too had seen and smelled the smoke.

A day passed without incident and Gertrud hoped the storm had passed. She, Herr Lüdwig, and the children had just sat down to breakfast and were eating bread and jam when they first heard the clanking and grating noise of the approaching iron monster. The thought flashed through Gertrud's mind, "Oh, my God, the American soldiers are coming after the children of Nazi General Fritz Kraus." Fear showing on her face, she just barely said, "Quick, children, take Hektor, go hide in the blind."

Max grabbed the 20-gauge from its gun rack by the fireplace and, accompanied by Hektor and Felicia, raced to the blind.

SECOND LIEUTENANT Joe Nicholson had little doubt that some aspects of his heredity were the result of a bad roll of the dice. Because he was intelligent and educated, he had identified his fatal flaw years ago. Though Joe's parents would never dream of hurting a soul, for as long as Joe could remember, he had found gratification from the physical pain of others. The war now afforded him opportunities for gratifying his psychotic urges that normal social restraints had stifled. In combat he shot the enemy with their hands in the air and felt pleasure in their pain and agony; when a prisoner begged for mercy, Joe would instruct the Kraut to run for the trees; then, after gunning him down, brag, "Jerry's feet were just too big."

For the most part, his fellow combat soldiers excused Joe's behavior as justifiable. Self-preservation and fallen comrades had stoked the fires of hate in most of them. Only a few recognized the deeper delights Joe Nicholson derived from torturing, and mostly they were helpless to stop him. Teamed with Private Michael "Morbid" Morris, the two represented the potential for ultimate evil.

Though Joe Nicholson and Morbid Morris came to the same

sadistic end, they arrived from different directions. Joe's genes found a million-in-one combination; society was mainly responsible for fashioning Morbid's monstrosity.

True, Morbid had never experienced love and affection. Abandoned as a child, no one knew when he was first called Morbid; and certainly, no one at the orphanage could remember calling him by any other name. It was just one of those nicknames that seemed to fit perfectly. However, even as he matured, Morbid, of his own will, not only retained the moniker, but clung to it in defiance, daring anyone to knock it from off of his shoulder. So he went through adolescence, a fighter and a bully. Embittered and hardened by rebuke after rebuke and defeat after defeat, he stumbled through his teens with a growing antipathy toward everything of this world.

Twice Morbid was taken for adoption. In both cases the adopting parents had perverse reasons for accepting such a hard-featured youngster. Though Morbid didn't have much intelligence or wit to begin with, he wasn't exactly dumb. He soon fled from his foster parents when their selfish motives became apparent. But Joe was a survivor, roaming and living off the land at the time of Pearl Harbor. Incredibly, Uncle Sam found and drafted him.

An important event in Morbid's life began occurring in his preadolescent dreams. Gradually the dreams fashioned and gave meaning to his life. To a modest extent they even steered Morbid away from the corruption of street life as he laid down for himself an almost monastic discipline. He never smoked and only rarely swore. In time he found menial work and mostly avoided the pleasures of the flesh. In spite of this, before he began having his recurring dreams, he had considered suicide as likely his only option for release from this rotten world.

The dreams were simple enough—but their constancy underscored Morbid's fevered brain. Most nights an angel would appear and caution: "Hold fast. Your day is coming, Morbid. Your life does hold purpose, and someday the people shall sing your praises." Then the angel would fade away. As the years passed Morbid would often go to sleep in a depression and awaken in a bliss. At first he couldn't understand the dreams, but then he began assigning significance to the regular appearance of the apparition.

Since the beginning of World War II, he had fantasized that his purpose in life might be to kill Hitler or some other big-shot Nazi. That would certainly win him the praise of his fellow soldiers. Nevertheless, he was beginning to doubt such an opportunity when he revealed the nature of his recurring dreams to his superior officer, Lieutenant Nicholson.

Private Morrison, now the gunner on Lieutenant Nicholson's tank, provided Nicholson with a henchman; for crumbs of acknowledgment, Morbid willingly became Nicholson's lackey. That the two shared aberrant delights was obvious when they cornered a Kraut house dog and took turns shooting it in the legs and tail, enthralled by the beast's howling agony.

Accosted by their Company Commander, Captain Appleby, Joe said, "We're just putting the God damn dog out of its misery, Tom."

"By shooting at its legs?" Then Captain Appleby had ministered a coup de grace to the dying and frenzied animal with his own .45.

Shortly before the Battle of Puffendorf, Nicholson and Morrison had formed their unholy alliance. Joe had confided to Morbid that Major Burk's hope was Sergeant Witkowski might fall in battle. Because Morbid's sworn enemy, Whip Johnson, was also a crew member on Witkowski's tank, the possibility of "two in one" had intrigued him. Then during the height of the battle that opportunity had appeared, and Morbid had been quick to let go a round from his 75 at the dozer. As the Battle of Puffendorf raged, only Lieutenant Nicholson saw the hit, though the loader, Corporal John C. Smith, had appeared suspicious. Afterward, Major Burk had Smith transferred back to the states.

Following that battle Lieutenant Nicholson had said, "You're off the hook, Morbid. Jerry also shot the hell out of the dozer with his 88s." From that time on Morbid became Lieutenant Nicholson's shadow while their evil affinity ripened.

After crossing the Rhine River, with German resistance collapsing, Joe said, "Shit, Morbid, we're supposed to fuck Fraüleins and kill Krauts. To the victor belongs the spoils of the enemy; it says so in the history books. Look what God damn Jerry has done to us. Now that he's breaking, its our turn to help ourselves."

"What do you mean?"

"Keep your eyes open, Morbid. We'll find some young stuff and we'll find us some spoils. That's what your dreams have been telling you. Shit, Alexander The Great and Julius Caesar both turned their men loose on the women of the enemy and divided up their loot. It's history repeating itself, Morbid."

CONSEQUENTLY, WHEN gold-braided Field Marshal Manfred Stein surrendered to Lieutenant Joe Nicholson's advance platoon at Lippstadt, Germany, on April 1, 1945, Joe winked at Morbid. Quickly the two bound the befuddled Field Marshal to the turret, alongside their 75mm cannon.

Speaking English, the Field Marshall entreated, "I wish to formally surrender my command to General Quinn."

A patriot among the civilian population whispered to Lieutenant Nicholson. "Free the Field Marshal and I'll tell you where you can find the stolen treasures of a Nazi General only 20 kilometers from here."

When Morbid had finished working over the German patriot, everyone in the First Platoon knew the location of General Fritz Kraus' hunting lodge near Warstein.

Quickly Lieutenant Nicholson set up a road block with his remaining four tanks and ordered the crew out of his own command tank. Then summoning all of his men said, "This is a sideshow, but this may be our only chance to profit from the God damn war. About time, considering all the hell we've all been through. Morbid will drive my tank. If need be, I'll steal some gas from the 3rd Armored in Warstein. We'll be back 'toot-sweet' with booty; and we'll share it with all you guys—I promise."

His men were nervous. They saw the craving look in the eyes of both Morbid and Joe, and they doubted Nicholson had radioed their Company Commander, First Lieutenant "Red" Jordening. Someone asked, "What about the Field Marshal?"

"Screw the Field Marshal. He'll be our shield."

With those words Second Lieutenant Joe Nicholson nodded at Morbid who gunned the Sherman tank down the highway toward Warstein; Field Marshal Stein slumped in his bounds, only half-conscious from a beating.

WHEN RED WAS INFORMED, he passed on the information to General Quinn who went berserk. Following orders to rescue Field Marshal Stein and bring back Joe and Morbid, dead or alive, Red found Sergeant Nate Talbot, and the two followed after the rogue Americans in Red's jeep.

NOT LONG AFTER Lieutenant Jordening and Sergeant Talbot had passed through the roadblock, the Dutch resistance leader Bep Rieksen and his girl friend Nicoline Lindemann arrived in Rieksen's grey Citröen. As his papers were in order, Rieksen also was waved on. Guessing the two to be journalists, a voice said, "You gotta give the press credit. They've got guts. Jerry's probably still down that road."

After they had passed through the roadblock, Nicoline said, "We must hurry, Bep; I have this awful feeling that the children are in horrible danger."

"I share your concern, my dear, and I know of a shortcut."

TO PUT THE FEAR OF HELL into any residents of the hunting lodge, Lieutenant Nicholson dropped into the gunner's seat and took aim at the barn with the 75. The shattering explosion ignited the straw and the building burst into flames. Joe climbed back to his tank commander's seat as Morbid wheeled the tank up the front door of the lodge and stopped, both men arming themselves with tommy-guns in addition to their sidearms.

Herr Lüdwig appeared waving a white flag.

Not only had Lieutenant Nicholson gassed his tank in Warstein, but he had bought a flask of Old Granddad from a

3rd Armored Division tanker. Taking a swig and handing the bottle to Morbid, he leaped from the tank and confronted the old caretaker who was staring in horror at the Field Marshal impaled on the tank. The Field Marshal was moaning and bleeding from the mouth.

Noticing the old man's gaze, Joe said, "That's what we do to fuckin' Krauts who don't do what we tell 'em to do. . . . Now who in the hell else is here?"

"No speak English," said the caretaker.

Joe flew into a rage and struck the old man with his fist, knocking him to the ground, kicking at the prostrate figure. Gertrud ran from the lodge and threw herself upon Herr Lüdwig. She pleaded, "He's an old man, have mercy."

"Come here, honey," said Joe, motioning Gertrud to arise and approach him. "You do speak English."

"Only a little," said Gertrud as she shuffled to within arm's reach of the American officer. Her timid eyes focused on Joe like that of a cornered cat.

"Honey, we came here for General Kraus' treasure. We know he raped and robbed in the Nazi occupied countries and brought his ill-begotten loot back here. . . . That's what we came for, honey. We want the paintings, the jewelry, the gold, the silver and everything else that that Nazi pig stole."

In a sweeping motion Joe ripped the blouse from Gertrud's body. Keeping the Tommy gun pointed at Gertrud's midsection, he said, "Boy, look at those boobs, Morbid." Then he continued, "My partner is a sex maniac. Either produce the treasure or you're going to get laid, Fräulein."

Herr Lüdwig kicked at Joe's legs.

It was almost mechanical. Joe stepped back and blew the old man away.

Gertrud dropped to the ground in hysterics.

"Cover me, Morbid. I'm gonna search the God damn cabin," said Joe in rising anger.

When he emerged his face was livid with rage. "Nothing—but there is a trail in back."

Gertrud looked up from the ground and held her arms and hands in supplication, "Please don't hurt the children."

Reaching down and ripping off more of her clothing, Joe ranted, "Come on an fuck this old hag, Morbid."

Morbid said, "I can't, Joe. I tried it with that Red Cross broad in Heerlen. I just can't do it."

Joe's wanton eyes narrowed. Again, it was almost mechanical. He stepped back and blew the old woman away, too.

Then he mounted the tank and said, "Follow that trail in back of the cabin, we may yet find the treasure we're after."

THE CHILDREN HAD HEARD the shots and smelled the smoke from the burning barn. They were terrified.

Felicia chanted, "Oh, Papa, save us. Oh, Papa, up in heaven, save us. Please save us, Papa."

Max said, "Look out the periscope. Snow White is circling. Remember, after Snow White came, Father flew in and rescued Nicoline from the Gestapo. Father will save us from the Americans, Felicia."

Max put a shell into the chamber of the shotgun and released its safety as Hektor bristled and growled low.

SOON THE IRON MONSTER clanked and stopped in front of the duck blind.

Joe said, "Cut the engine, Morbid. I think we've found the treasure trove."

After Joe and Morbid had dismounted, Max yelled, "Go away, my sister and I are just children."

Joe had noticed the movement of the periscope. "We are under observation, Morbid. . . . If you children will come out, we won't hurt you."

Hektor began to bark and growl fiercely, and both Americans jumped back in their tank.

From his commander's hatch Joe yelled, "If whoever is inside

The Battle of Puffendorf

the blind doesn't come out with their hands up in five minutes, I'm crushing it under the tracks of my tank."

Five minutes elapsed and no one ventured forth. Restarting the engine Morbid slowly churned the Sherman ominously toward the blind. Suddenly the shooting panel crashed to the ground on the far-side. Out came a blond youngster firing a shotgun and a red-eyed raging dog. The boy fired at Lieutenant Nicholson and the dog leaped toward the driver's hatch. Neither were successful.

Joe dropped the boy with a shot from his .45 and Morbid struck the dog down with a brief burst from his tommy-gun. The dog crawled yelping into the bush and the boy lay still on the ground. Moments later a young girl ran from the blind and threw herself sobbing upon the boy's body. "Wo sinds du, Papa?" she repeated again and again in her anguish.

Frustration and lust consumed Joe Nicholson. Jumping from the tank he grabbed the slender young girl and began tearing at her clothing as the girl went limp, going into shock, offering no resistance.

Morbid had again cut the motor and dismounted from the tank. He called, "Leave the kid alone, Joe. . . . God damn it, Joe! Get off that child."

Lieutenant Joe Nicholson never heard Morbid's warning. He was too preoccupied with his own lust. Nor did Lieutenant Joe Nicholson feel a thing when his head was blown off by a burst from Private Morbid Morrison's tommy-gun.

A circling white pigeon and a great stag saw what happened. With his head turned to the sky, Morbid cast away his tommy-gun and slowly drew his .45. Inserting the barrel into his mouth, he was barely conscious of the cold steel when he pulled the trigger, fulfilling his dreams and winning his consummate praise in eternity.

As BEP BRAKED THE Citröen to a stop, he and Nicoline jumped out and ran to the pond.

Embracing the children, Nicoline screamed, "We're too late. They've been violated and killed."

"No," said Bep. "They're both alive, but we must take them to the hospital in Warstein. I'll get the car."

But before Bep could leave, Lieutenant Jordening wheeled his jeep next to the tank. He immediately saw Field Marshal Stein tied to the turret. As Red at once recognized Bep and Nicoline, he directed his attentions to the bewildered and battered Field Marshal.

After cutting the German's bonds and helping him to the ground, Red identified himself. He apologized for the unlawful behavior of the rogue American soldiers and assured the Field Marshal that General Quinn had sent him specifically to rescue the Field Marshal.

It was a bloody scene, with one man's head blown off and another's with a gaping hole. To Red, Bep said, "The children appear to be recovering, but we must get them quickly to the hospital in Warstein. The boy is shot in the shoulder, but the girl appears to be physically uninjured."

As Bep and Nicoline carried the children to the Citröen. Red Jordening radioed General Quinn and called for medics and other support vehicles.

As THE VARIOUS reinforcements arrived on the scene, Nate Talbot heard sounds coming from a bush. Producing his carbine, he cautiously parted some branches. There he saw the wounded dog, panting for breath. Because Nate had a job as a game warden awaiting his return to the states, he had been looking for a German Shorthaired Pointer, a breed that was rare in America.

After careful inspection of Hektor, who responded to Nate's soft voice by licking his exploring hand, Nate said, "This dog's wounds appear superficial, Red. I'm taking him with us." They gently laid Hektor on a blanket in the back of Red's jeep. On the way back to Lippstadt, Nate sat in the back with Hektor's head on his lap, many times repeating, "You're gonna to be okay, boy."

Though Hektor recognized a different tongue, the dog instinctively knew it was in friendly hands. For a while Hektor wagged his stump of a tail, but at last he shut his hazel eyes and went to sleep. Continuing to caress the dog, Nate purred, "You're gonna to be okay, boy. Good dog."

From overhead Snow White continued circling the "Crown Jewel" and the hunting lodge. As the last embers of her home burned to the ground, the bird searched in vain for a surviving companion. Then, as Snow White made one last pass over the smoldering ruins, a flock of wild pigeons suddenly appeared, dipping their wings, swooping low, beckoning. Snow White saw them and arced up gracefully, joining the flight of the free, boundless ones.

IN LATE JUNE Whip Johnson received a latter from Philip Vossmaar informing him that there would be no more meetings of the Gorgo because both he and Karel Konijn were now serving full-time with the American Army of Occupation. As Lucie Heerkens was now traveling abroad with her brother, the news did not disappoint Whip too much.

One strange development at the Depot, however, was the sudden disappearance of the office boy, Arnd Hauptmann. Nor could Whip learn what had happened to him. Obviously, Warrant Officer Willard Stone took a special delight informing Whip that all information regarding POW, Arnd Hauptmann, was now classified and that Whip could get himself into deep trouble by getting too nosy.

Though Whip had been avoiding the DeRucks, the news of Arnd's disappearance, he guessed, would be passed on to them by Sergeant Sullivan; somehow, Whip expected to hear from them. However, their voices remained silent.

The balance of the summer of 1945 passed as routine until on August 6, the atomic bomb was dropped on Hiroshima and V-J Day was announced shortly after on September 2. World War II was over.

Now came the stampede to dissolve America's fighting machine. Most GIs wanted immediately out of the army to get on with their careers and lives. Back in Washington, Congressmen felt the pressure from their constituents. On behalf of a grateful nation they passed the GI Bill of Rights granting a free college or technical education to its service people. Also, a point system was invented for the rapid demobilization of the troops. At the Depot the hot topic of conversation among the GIs was their points and how soon they might expect to be shipped home and discharged. And it seemed like overnight everyone was sewing little yellow cloth bars on their sleeves which represented some of their accumulated points.

As the "cold war" with the Soviet Union was already in the making, the army was cautious to preserve at least a modicum of its fighting force in Europe. To that end, Whip Johnson was offered a chance at OCS in Paris if he would sign up for another four years. Whip was tempted, but decided he wanted more to get on with his college education. Consequently, he waited impatiently his turn to be shipped home; to display with pride the "ruptured duck"—the irreverent name given to the yellow pin with the eagle on it given to every honorably discharged soldier.

AS THE MONTHS PASSED another concern began to gnaw at Whip. His relationship with Lucie Heerkens! He thought she must still be in the states. As planned, both she and his parents had met at the airport in Sioux Falls, South Dakota, and they had hit it off big. His parents wrote glowing accounts of what they thought of Lucie, and Lucie had written how lucky he was to have such handsome parents. Then came a lull in her letter writing. This bothered Whip, as Lucie had been so faithful with her pen. He could hardly wait to hear that she was once again at home in Heerlen. If need be, he'd go AWOL just to hold Lucie in his arms again. Nevertheless, the silence lengthened, and by each passing day Whip grew more desperate and despondent. Finally, early in December at mail call Lucie's long-awaited letter arrived. But it would be 50 years later before Whip would ever read the letter in its entirety:

The Battle of Puffendorf

Dear Whip,

I better start telling of you everything that happened to me since I left the states as you must be wondering by now what is what. In the first place, however, I hope that this letter will find you and your parents in the very best of health. Thanks very much for the picture you send me before I left the states and the letter with it. And now my story.

On August 22 I arrived in Holland and three days later some cousin of my father happened to visit my home. The poor fellow! Because I fell head over heels in love with him and two weeks later I had him convinced that I was the ideal wife for him. On October 8 we announced our engagement to be married and on November 27 we got married....

AFTER READING THESE WORDS something in Whip Johnson died.

Shortly after receiving Lucie's letter, Whip was transferred from the Depot at Charleroi, Belgium, to the 91st General Hospital at Liege, Belgium. This was to be the outfit Whip would return to the states with, arriving in New York City on January 31 and being honorably discharged at Camp McCoy, Wisconsin, on February 6, 1946.

With one exception, Whip's whole experience from the moment he received Lucie's letter until he received his discharge was one of living in another world. He was barely cognizant of his existence or identity. Sadly, in his last days in the service, excessive smoking and drinking became a problem. But, throughout his life, the recalling of one unusual event always warmed his heart:

He was on the troop train heading from Liege to the embarkation port in France. He was standing in the crowded passage way of a passenger car with open windows. Suddenly he observed that the train was barely creeping through the Depot at Charleroi. POWs stood idly watching the slow moving train when Whip recognized some of them. Impulsively he thrust his head out the window and began waving to them. They instantly recognized Whip and took up the chant: "Der Rote Bomber—Der Rote Bomber—Der Rote Bomber" until in a rising cresendo their voices cascaded off the railway cars.

As the POWs waved wildly and cheered at Whip, the other GIs, none of whom knew Whip, began looking at him as if he might be a Nazi spy. For the remainder of the trip to the channel port, they kept their distance. For years Whip would recall this incident and laugh and laugh and laugh. Then he would cry.

EPILOGUE

AFTER PUTTING THEIR HEADS together via long distance telephone, John "Red" Jordening in California and Nathan "Nate" Talbot in Illinois, decided for the life of themselves they could not remember anything about this Leo "Scotty" Andrusyshen. Like a phoenix bird risen from the ashes of World War II, the obviously energetic and inspired man rang their telephones day and night and flooded them with literature about a coming reunion of the veterans of Company "D."

When World War II ended, Red was Company "D" commander and Nate was his First Sergeant. They had both fought together from the beaches of Normandy to the banks of the Elbe River in Germany. Now, between the two men, they racked their brains to recall any Leo "Scotty" Andrusyshen, but always they came up with a blank. In time, however, after more researching they discovered, sure enough, Scotty had been a tank commander in the First Platoon, and had joined the outfit in Belgium as a replacement during the Battle of the Bulge. Both Red and Nate figured this Scotty person must have been one heck of a quiet, unobtrusive individual back in those World War II days to escape their complete notice—but he obviously wasn't quiet or unobtrusive anymore!

On the other hand, Scotty had a good point. If the surviving veterans of Company "D" were to relive their great adventure together with their former comrades, they must act soon as time was running out on them for it was 1980; and in this "Scotty" person, it appeared, there lived a firebrand willing to bear the labor and expense necessary in organizing such a reunion. So Scotty, a retired school teacher, by exhorting and begging, pushing and shoving, got the deed done—and successfully so! Not once but twice—and he was now planning for a third and final reunion of the Company "D" veterans. In this case, Scotty informed the veterans he was preparing a unique surprise that had not been on the table at the other two reunions!

Unfortunately, it was not until this third reunion, scheduled for October 5–9, 1988, at Columbus, Ohio, that Whip Johnson, a Company "D" veteran, first heard of the reunions. By then, some who had attended the first two had either died, become disabled or were otherwise too preoccupied to attend the third.

For years Whip Johnson, now also a retired school teacher, had considered writing a book about his World War II experiences. In 1947 Whip had received a large hardbound copy of an illustrated and partly indexed book, titled, *History 67th Armored Regiment.* It had been compiled largely from the "After-Battle Reports" and reminiscences of those involved in the various campaigns of the regiment. The book was put together, printed and bound in Germany in 1945.

Whip had devoured it. Within its covers he had found answers to some of his most baffling questions about the Battle of Puffendorf and his being wounded. As Arnd Hauptmann, the young German commando, had told Whip at the Depot in Charleroi, Belgium, Dale Jenks and Sergeant Witkowski had both been killed when the bulldozer tank was hit "repeatedly by 88s." This had puzzled Whip because he had been a crew member of that tank and they had not been engaged in any duel with a German tank when they were hit, nor had he seen any bodies when he had made his own escape from the burning tank. In Whip's mind many troubling questions remained about the battle and the hit on their tank.

In any case, it was with shock and sadness that he had read the details about the death of Captain Tom Appleby during the Battle of the Bulge. Again and again he reread the account almost in disbelief. Without doubt Captain Appleby was the most forceful and striking person Whip had ever met.

With amazement Whip had also read that Red Jordening, his 1st Platoon leader, had not only survived the war without a scratch but was the Company "D" commander at its end; and topping that, the driver of their bulldozer tank, Nate Talbot, had made First Sergeant of the company. Who could have guessed such an outcome?

Now it was 1988 and when a fellow teacher informed Whip about the scheduled Company "D" reunion at Columbus, Ohio, Whip decided to attend. But it was with mixed emotions that he dialed the telephone number of the listed organizer of this event, a Leo "Scotty" Andrusyshen. For his projected book, Whip wanted to learn everything about Tom Appleby's life in the service, but he was apprehensive about how these old veterans would react to himself. Having joined them as a replacement, Whip was with them for only about three weeks before being wounded and evacuated.

However, when Scotty answered the phone and learned who was calling and why, he babbled: "God, I've been trying to locate you for six years. There are just too damn many of you Johnsons in the telephone books.... Yes, Nate Talbot, the driver of your bulldozer tank will be there; also, Francis Baker who was Sergeant Witkowski's best friend.... Maybe Red Jordening, but he's in doubt at this time, though I can give you his telephone number.... So you're writing a book and want to learn everything you can about Tom Appleby.... You must come!... You're worried because you were only with the outfit for a few weeks? Don't be! You were a casualty at Puffendorf, right! I understand Puffendorf was the biggest tank battle the company ever took part in.... I'm so damn excited I can hardly talk. I'll get a letter off to you right away."

UPON MAKING THE DECISION to attend the reunion and finally get around to writing his book, Whip placed a call to his Dutch friend, Philip Vossmaar, who now lived at The Hague in The Netherlands, asking if Philip could possibly accompany him back to Heerlen and the German village of Puffendorf. Whip did not want to make a special trip to Europe researching his book without going with someone familiar with the places and the languages. Unfortunately, Philip was busy and didn't know if he could get someone to stand in his place. But he did agree to call Whip at the hotel where Whip would be staying in Columbus.

AFTER ARRIVING AT THE REUNION Whip soon discovered that most of those in attendance had been at the other reunions and had rekindled old bonds or formed new ones, and most had brought their wives with them. But Whip had never married; for after all these years, he still carried the torch for Lucie Heerkens, his wartime Dutch sweetheart. The first day Whip spent most of his time moving from room to room introducing himself.

Nearly all of the thirty or so veterans brought their war memorabilia. And Scotty, true to his word, had accumulated mountains of the stuff, much of it about the legendary Tom Appleby. Whip soon discovered that Appleby was still revered almost as a god by these old Company "D" tankers, though some had never met the man personally, including Scotty himself. So on the first day of the reunion Whip busied himself listening to war stories, taking notes and duplicating some documents. Though everyone was friendly enough, Whip felt he wasn't quite accepted. But that was okay with Whip for he was getting the stuff he had come for.

When he wasn't chatting with the veterans, Whip moseyed about outside. The tops of Columbus' distant skyscrapers reaching their lofty heights seemed to summon him. Though at 65 Whip considered his marathoning days over, he wondered if he might be able to jog the distance to downtown and back. After making inquiries from a doorman, he was told it was about ten miles to the center of town. Whip then made up his mind if he got a chance he'd take a tour of Columbus under his own locomotion.

ON THE SECOND DAY Whip went to lunch with the Talbots. With Nate Talbot Whip came closest to bonding. Nate's face was brown and weather-beaten and his voice sounded raspy. He told how he'd been covered with blood and flesh, presumably that of Corporal Jenks and Sergeant Witkowski; how he'd helped the new bow gunner escape from the burning tank, probably at the same time Whip was getting out; how he'd jumped up on the turret to look inside and another 88 shell had struck the dozer; and later how he was surprised to discover Whip alive at the aid station. When Nate Talbot at last finished describing his participation in the Battle of Puffendorf, he was drawn and trembling.

Thinking to change the subject, Whip asked, "What did you do after the war?"

"I was a game warden." Suddenly Nate's face lit up like a marquee light. "By the way, I brought back from Europe a dog, a German Shorthaired Pointer. His name was Hektor, and he belonged to a rich Kraut kid who had become involved with the outfit."

ON THE THIRD DAY Whip listened to talk that appeared mostly inconsequential to him, but the program of the evening called for a banquet at the hotel, and Scotty asked all the tankers to stand and say a few words.

Scotty was about five foot eleven, thin, and wore glasses. He combed his dark hair in various directions attempting to hide bald spots. His voice was resonant and steady. Everything considered, the Company "D" veterans had only high praise for Scotty's efforts at bringing about this reunion.

When all the veterans and their wives had gathered for the banquet, they saw sitting next to Scotty at the head table a comely young man, probably in his early twenties. His long blond hair was neatly combed to his shoulders, and he displayed a small earring in his left ear lobe. Something about the young man stirred Whip's memory—something hauntingly familiar about his face though Whip could not make a connection—if, indeed, there was one.

After all the veterans had made their brief statements, Scotty rose again and simply said, "I'll let the young man to my left introduce himself."

With all the veterans and their wives focusing their eyes on the young man, he began, "My name is Arnd Hauptmann III. I am here . . ."

Audibly gulping and choking, Whip at once apologized, "I'm okay. Sorry." But now Whip knew why the face looked so familiar!

Arnd Hauptmann III laughed good-naturedly and continued: "I'm here, in a way, to apologize for the actions of my grandfather who died last year from lung cancer. He would want me to tell you men of Company 'D' that he was later very sorry for the things he did to your outfit and for the death of your mascot, Little Joe, even though my grandfather prevented the other German commandos from killing Joe, as they had been ordered to do.

"However, there is more to my grandfather's story that he would want me to tell you. As with millions of German youth, he was brainwashed into thinking of Hitler as almost a god; and it took the love of one man to transform my grandfather from a Hitler Youth fanatic, who would do anything for his Führer, into an open-minded grandfather who could even forgive his grandson's long hair and wearing an earring."

Some snickering, but the speaker continued to hold everyone's rapt attention.

"General Quinn who died last year, as you may know, befriended my grandfather at Heerlen, Holland, when my grandfather was a German commando. Both my grandfather and General Quinn came to be the closest of friends."

AT THAT POINT, Whip Johnson turned off his brain to the proceedings. Skipping the entertainment, he excused himself and went to bed rehashing the opening remarks of Arnd Hauptmann III.

The next day Whip figured he had what he had come for. As far as he was concerned the reunion was over; yet his return flight was not scheduled until the next day. How would he pass the time? Then he remembered the beckoning towers of downtown Columbus ten miles distant.

Nevertheless, it was not until the middle of the next morning before Whip jogged out of the hotel lobby and headed toward Columbus' business district. In his imaginative mind Whip likened the concrete and steel spires of downtown Columbus to the towers of a medieval castle summoning him to a new Shangri-La. But at about a ten-minute-a-mile pace he soon reached a neighborhood which definitely was not the Valley of the Blue Moon. Quickly he jogged back to a main roadway and not long after found the bustling heart of the city.

After stopping briefly at a water fountain, he was soon on his way back to the airport. The sun shone and colorful leaves dropped from maple trees. It was a wonderful morning for a long-distance jogger to be on the road. He even got a high from the gasoline fumes he inhaled.

Nearing his hotel at about the 19.5-mile mark, Whip was startled to see an all-white pigeon strangely circling and following him all the way to the entrance of the hotel. When Whip stopped before entering the building, the bird promptly perched on the roof of a parked automobile, cocking its head and making a cooing sound.

Just then, the doorman informed Whip that in his absence he had received a long-distance telephone call from Holland and the caller had left a number. Whip went straight to a telephone booth and soon had his Dutch friend, Philip Vossmaar, on the line.

Philip said, "Yes, Whip, I'm very happy to say that I can go with you to Puffendorf if you come. Let me say one other thing quickly. It might interest you to know this. Lucie Heerkens is back in Heerlen. She is now a widow woman. I called her yesterday and said you were thinking of coming back to Holland for the first time since World War II. She exploded in joy. She said she would rather see you than any other person in the whole wide world. Now what do you think of that, Whip Johnson?"

Speechless for a moment, Whip said, "I'm dumbfounded. I'm flabbergasted. . . . Get a bottle of the best champagne you can find for the three of us, Philip. I'll be seeing you soon!"

After Whip hung up the receiver, there was still one thing on his mind. He walked outside to see if the white pigeon was still perched on the roof of that car.

All at once Whip Johnson's brain was jolted, and he staggered. He was thinking he had indeed inhaled too many car fumes while jogging. He blinked and words appeared before his mind's eye: *From overhead Snow White continued circling the "Crown Jewel" and the hunting lodge. As the last embers of her home burned to the ground, the bird searched in vain for a surviving companion. Then, as Snow White made a last pass over the smoldering ruins, a flock of wild pigeons suddenly appeared, dipping their wings, swooping low, beckoning. Snow White saw them and arced up gracefully, joining the flight of the free, boundless ones.*

Whip shook his head twice to be sure he really was seeing the white pigeon still perched on the roof of the car when suddenly it spread its wings and lifted upward. Looking overhead, Whip saw a flight of wild pigeons just as the white pigeon disappeared into the flock.

DENOUEMENT

WHIP JOHNSON became a high school basketball coach and history teacher, but never married as he always carried the torch for his wartime Dutch sweetheart, LUCIE HEERKENS.

After the war GENERAL QUINN established a prosperous publishing business. In time he brought ARND HAUPTMANN to the United States and provided for his education. Eventually Arnd became a citizen and an executive in General Quinn's business. After the death of the general, Arnd inherited the business. Arnd died of lung cancer in 1987.

BEP RIEKSEN and NICOLINE LINDEMANN married and adopted the German children MAX and FELICIA KRAUS taking them to Holland. After the children matured they returned to Warstein, Germany. Having had the considerable wealth of their father bequeathed to them, they both prospered and eventually had children.

NATE TALBOT was able to restore to health the German Shorthaired Pointer, HEKTOR, which he brought back to the states. He married his high school girl frind and became a gamewarden in Illinois. Long after the death of Hektor, an adult Max Kraus discovered the name of the man who had saved the life of his first dog. In time Max visited Nate in the United States, and Nate gave Max a puppy with Hektor's bloodlines for Max's children back in Germany.

JOHN JORDENING, married and found a gold mine in the insurance business in California.

PHILIP VOSSMAAR became a leading educator in The Netherlands.

SUSAN MONTGOMERY and COLONEL BURK became bigwigs in the Republican party.

SALLY BROWN and JIMMY MALLOTI were both killed in a car bomb explosion in New York City.

GENERAL CLAY lived out his years in retirement in California following a distinguished military career.

GENERAL HAN OTTO DIETRICH died in 1986 following a successful business career in Bonn, Germany.

FIELD MARSHAL STEIN died in Berlin in 1985.

GENERAL BARTHOLOMAUS died shortly after the end of World War II.

CHARACTERS

AMERICANS
WHIP "VD" JOHNSON—protagonist
Members of Whip's tank
SGT. BRIAN "POLACK" WITKOWSKI—tank commander
CPL. DALE JENKS—75mm gunner
T/5 NATHAN "NATE" TALBOT—tank driver
PVT. HANK HENRY—bow gunner
Soldiers
1ST LT. and then CAPT. TOM APPLEBY—Company "D" commander
CPL. JOHN C. SMITH—loader on Lieutenant Nicholson's tank
2ND LT. JOHN "RED" JORDENING—Appleby's executive officer and 1st platoon leader
MAJOR and then LT. COL. RICHARD C. BURK III—1st Battalion commander
2ND LT. JOE NICHOLSON—tank commander and 2nd platoon leader
BRIG. and then MAJ. GEN. BRIGHTON D. CLAY—commander of the "Fighting" 15th Armored Division
MAJ. JACK COLLINS—Clay's operations officer
PVT. MICHAEL "MORBID" MORRIS—gunner on Nicholson's tank
PVT. MILTON "PEEWEE" SILVERMAN—orderly for Lieutenant Appleby
CPL. WESLEY "WES" WILLOW—personnel clerk at Company "D"
T/5 JOSH HIGGINS—driver of the "clubmobile" for the Red Cross girls
PVT. JIMMY MALLOTI—jeep driver for General Clay
SGT. KEVIN "SULLY" SULLIVAN—runs "Control-Center" in the Depot
COL. and then BRIG. GEN. HAROLD QUINN—commander of the 67th Armored Regiment and then the 15th Armored Division
STAFF SGT. and then MASTER SGT. "HAP" HARDESTY—1st Battalion cook
SGT. BECK JONES—infantry platoon leader
MAJ. "SLICK" DRAISY—officer in command of the Depot
WARRANT OFFICER WILLARD STONE—in charge of the office staff at the Depot
Red Cross girls
SUSAN LAVET MONTGOMERY—"doughnut dolly"
SALLY BROWN—"doughnut dolly"

GERMANS

Prussians
BRIG. GEN. GERD VON BARTHOLOMAUS—commander of the "Hammer" Panzer Division
FIELD MARSHAL MANFRED STEIN—commander of Army Group "C."

SS
BRIG. GEN. FRITZ KRAUS—commander of the "Lightning" Panzer Division
MAJ. KRUGGER—adjutant to Kraus
CAPT. SNODGRASS—adjutant to Kraus
LT. GEN. FRANZ RHEINHARDT—commander of the III Panzer Corps
MAJ. and then BRIG. GEN. HANS OTTO DIETRICH—battle-group commander
CAPT. ALFONS RIGOR—adjutant to Dietrich

Gestapo
COUNT SIEGFRIED VON DER SCHULENBURG—Gestapo leader in Holland
CAPT. SPAULDING—aide to Count Siegfried

Hitler Youth
ARND HAUPTMANN—14-year-old commando

Residents of Brig. Gen. Fritz Kraus' hunting lodge
FELICIA—Kraus' 11-year-old daughter
MAX—Kraus' 10-year-old son
FRAULEIN GERTRUD SCHULTZ—Kraus' sister-in-law
HERR LUDWIG—caretaker of General Kraus' property
SNOW WHITE—the homing pigeon tamed by General Kraus
HEKTOR—Max Kraus' German Shorthaired Pointer
BISMARCK—the great stag of the Arnsberger hunting preserve

DUTCH

Resistance
PHILIP VOSSMAAR—Whip Johnson's friend, Dutch liaison officer with General Clay, and founder of the Gorgo
BEP RIEKSEN—Resistance leader
KAREL KONIJN—aide to Rieksen and member of the Gorgo
HANS SPOOR (alias THE GREAT SAMSON)—double-agent

Civilian
MR. LINTENS—Dutch Nazi sympathizer
NICOLINE LINDEMANN—Rieksen's girl friend
LUCIE HEERKENS—member of the Gorgo
SERVAAS KONIJN—brother of Karel and member of the Gorgo
LOUKE HELLENAR—member of the Gorgo
THEO VAN ZEELAND—member of the Gorgo
ARTHUR DE HONDT—member of the Gorgo
GEORGE DERUCK (aliases Please-Joe, Little Joe)—the 12-year-old son of MONSIEUR and MADAM DERUCK and twin-brother of CHARLES DERUCK

ABOUT THE AUTHOR

OTHER THAN THE TIME spent growing up in Mitchell, South Dakota, followed by nearly three years of service in the army during World War II, Verne Hull was either in school working on a college degree of some kind or teaching high school. Then after twenty years of teaching government and history classes at Lexington Senior High School at Lexington, Nebraska, he retired in 1987. During the first few years of his retirement, he continued to train bird dogs at his Platte River Kennels at Lexington. And he also wrote and published his first novel, *Pinky's Dog*. In the fall of 2003 he moved to Yankton, South Dakota, where he resides today.

To this day, the author judges his war time experiences as the ascendant events in his life: first, his assignment to the cadre as an instructor at Fort Knox; second, his joining the 2nd Armored Division as a replacement in Holland just prior to The Battle of Puffendorf; third, the two days he witnessed combat in Germany; fourth, the wounds he suffered as a result thereof (for which he was awarded the Purple Heart); fifth, his evacuation back to Belgium and then to England for medical treatment; sixth, his subsequent assignment to the big supply depot at Charleroi, Belgium; and, lastly, his passes to Heerlen, Holland, and his interactions there with members of the Gorgo. All of these war time episodes in the young life of the author he weaves into *The Battle of Puffendorf*.

ACKNOWLEDGMENTS

As I planned writing a novel based on my World War II experiences I deemed it essential to revisit the sites where the action would take place. Making this possible was my Dutch friend W. H. Mannesse, who acted both as my chauffeur and English translator in the summer of 1989. Then as I began writing the book, Marion and Bart Kline encouraged and helped me most of all. Marion, the English teacher, proofread what I scribbled and Bart, as a soldier, shared his wartime experiences. Later, Tom Kruger offered his knowledge of tanks; and both Bruce Whitehead and Gary Druckemiller scanned the produced pages for their readability. Furthermore, whenever it appeared I was faltering in my efforts my stepbrother, Roy Wilcox, would cajole me with the need to finish the book. In the final steps, Kitty Herrin guided and copy edited the work to its completion. To all of the above mentioned people, I offer my thanks for making this segment of my legacy possible.